PRAISE FOR
⸎ MAGRUDER'S CURIOSITY CABINET ⸎

"It's a rare novel that manages to combine humor, tragedy, powerful friendships, outcasts, insiders, detached satire, and deeply felt emotion all in one, but H. P. Wood's *Magruder's Curiosity Cabinet* manages to pull off the trick—just don't ask how it's performed! Fascinating and deeply compelling...compulsively readable."

—Lauren Willig, *New York Times* bestselling author
of *The Other Daughter*

"A death-defying feat of creativity and imagination, *Magruder's Curiosity Cabinet* is gloriously original, colorful, and alive. Wood's magnificent riot of unique turn-of-the-century characters—fools and sages, snakes and saviors—charmed me completely. Pick it up, and it'll run away with your weekend and your heart."

—Greer Macallister, bestselling author of *The Magician's Lie*

"I inhaled *Magruder's Curiosity Cabinet* in a single sitting. Wood has written a cracking Coney Island roller coaster of an adventure, full of marvelous, colorful, and unapologetically authentic characters. A bright, breathless debut."

—Jessica Brockmole, author of *Letters from Skye*

"Oh, how I adored this marvelous, magnificent, magical book! There aren't many books I'll lose sleep over, but this was one of them. This is a story that won't let you go, stuffed with gloriously quirky characters and brimming over with sumptuous sentences—a startlingly original debut novel."

—Menna van Praag, author of *The Dress Shop of Dreams*
and *The Witches of Cambridge*

"*Magruder's Curiosity Cabinet* is an enchanting, darkly wondrous adventure. Beautiful and tragic, this stunning debut novel transports the reader to the heart of New York's Coney Island in the 1900s and the sideshow Unusuals who live there. Open *Magruder's Curiosity Cabinet* and prepare to be dazzled!"

—Jennifer Kincheloe,
author of *The Secret Life of Anna Blanc*

"This wonderful, wacky, moving tale is a curiosity cabinet in and of itself, stuffed with a makeshift family of lovable freaks and misfits, pompous rich Victorians, outrageous plot turns, and all manner of old-timey gadgets, con games, elixirs, and ooh-and-aah-inspiring spectacles—all in the irresistibly strange and enchanted carny setting of 1904 Coney Island. It calls to mind old-fashioned gonzo classics like *A Confederacy of Dunces* or *Around the World in 80 Days*, as well as newer titles about the period like *The Alienist* and *The Devil in the White City*. It's a steampunk roller-coaster ride that draws from true, turn-of-the-century developments and sentiments while creating a uniquely colorful universe of its own, one that you won't soon forget."

—Tim Murphy, author of *Christodora*

MAGRUDER'S CURIOSITY CABINET

a novel

H. P. WOOD

sourcebooks
landmark

For Maia, who if
you deem "strange" will say "thank you"
and truly mean it.

Sourcebooks and the colophon are registered trademarks of Sourcebooks, Inc.

Quotations taken from *The Souls of Black Folk: Essays and Sketches* by W. E. B.
Du Bois (Chicago: A.C. McClurg & Co., 1903); *The Wonderful Wizard of Oz* by
L. Frank Baum (Chicago: George M. Hill Co., 1900); "Wade in the Water"
(Negro spiritual, author unknown); "Oh Didn't He Ramble," words and music
by Will Handy, 1902; "My Little Coney Isle," words by Andrew B. Stirling,
music by Harry Von Tilzer, 1903.

Published by Sourcebooks Landmark, an imprint of Sourcebooks, Inc.
P.O. Box 4410, Naperville, Illinois 60567–4410
(630) 961–3900
Fax: (630) 961–2168
www.sourcebooks.com

Library of Congress Cataloging-in-Publication data is on file with the publisher.

Printed and bound in the United States of America.
VP 10 9 8 7 6 5 4 3 2 1

A T LAST, THE GIANT REACHES HELL GATE. HIS SHREDDED TUXEDO IS WET with blood. His own? Someone else's? He's no longer sure… Maybe both?

Probably both.

The giant's skin is dotted with bruise-colored lumps. The tips of his fingers are black and decayed. So are his toes, crushed into his vast patent-leather shoes. His rotting feet force him to limp and shuffle, determined and yet aimless, pushing forward on some vital errand he can no longer remember.

He coughs—not politely as a tuxedoed giant should, but violently. Bloody projectiles splatter on the boardwalk.

Above, a massive, winged demon crouches atop the gate of Hell. In between coughs, the giant peers up at the red-eyed monster. "Help?" he suggests, knowing better. The demon makes no move. "Just kidding," the giant says.

"There he is!" Shouts and footsteps. "Get him!"

Oh yes, the giant thinks. *That's what I was doing. I was running.*

His only escape is through Hell Gate, and he stumbles toward it. Just beyond, a seething whirlpool drags the damned into the very center of the earth.

"Don't lose him! Take the shot, Crawford! Take the damn shot!"

A bullet to the back. The giant goes sprawling. His pursuers approach—slowly, fearfully. It strikes the giant as very funny that *they* should fear *him* when they have all the guns. But his laughter just gurgles and splutters.

The men gather in a circle around the fallen colossus.

"He dead?"

"'Course he ain't dead, dummy. Still coughin', ain't he?"

"Dead soon, though."

"Not soon enough."

Another shot, and a blinding white light rips across the giant's vision. As the light fades, he sees the demon—witnessing everything, feeling nothing.

"Help..." the giant whispers again, and then he's gone.

1

THE CYCLONE

ZEPH UNLOCKS THE HEAVY OAK DOOR OF THEOPHILUS P. MAGRUDER'S Curiosity Cabinet. As he does every morning, he considers propping the door open to give the museum a more welcoming "come on in" sort of feeling. But as he does every morning, he decides against it. Opening the door only increases the likelihood some fool might actually come on in.

Fortunately, not many fools do. Why would they? The Cabinet is on the wrong end of Coney Island.

The other end of the beach, the "proper" end, braves the weight of thousands upon thousands of tourists every day. Now that Dreamland has thrown open its sparkly gates, the 1904 season will bring the biggest crowds ever. And the eye of the storm is Surf Avenue, with its chic restaurants and bustling music halls. Live shows re-create the flooding of Galveston, Texas, and the volcanic demise of the city of Pompeii. Amusement rides terrify and delight with the mysterious power of electricity. A town populated solely by midgets makes visitors feel tall, and a genuine replica of a headhunters' village makes them feel civilized. Strange young men guess the weights of passersby, while strange old women tell their fortunes and mechanical calliopes play strange little tunes.

That's there. Here, on the wrong end of Coney? Theophilus P. Magruder's Curiosity Cabinet is just a homely old building with blacked-out windows and a faded sign. Thousands of souls may visit

Coney Island, but few of those souls are hearty enough to peer inside Magruder's heavy oak door.

Which is exactly the way Zeph likes it.

He climbs onto his stool behind the counter at the front entrance, removing his worn, fingerless work gloves. On the counter, Doc Timur has left him a present: a book. Typical.

The old man hides in the museum's attic for days, emerging periodically to shout a few half-sane commands. Last night, he'd come downstairs barking that he needed more copper, which was sensible enough, but then he muttered something about a salt bridge. Salt has to be the stupidest idea for building material Zeph has ever heard, and he said as much. Which is when the insults started flying, mostly in Timur's native language and thus incomprehensible. But Zeph doesn't need to speak Uzbek to know when his intelligence is being questioned.

But the storm passed, and Zeph has arrived this morning to find this little apology waiting. Usually the apologies take the form of some gadget that Timur, in his guilt, assembled the night before. One time, he left Zeph a pocket watch—or, rather, it looked like a pocket watch until Zeph wound it. The casing of the watch split open like a beetle's shell to reveal little brass wings. Then the watch took to the air, flying a circle around Zeph's head before coming to rest on the counter again. "Nice trick, you crazy old man," Zeph had muttered, "except I did actually want to know what time it is."

Today, this book instead: *The Souls of Black Folk* by W. E. B. Du Bois. Zeph has wanted a copy since it came out last year. But an Unusual like Zeph can't just go shopping anytime he pleases. Had he mentioned the book to Timur? Zeph flips through the pages, trying to remember. Maybe Timur was just too busy to build an apology from scratch, so he'd gone rooting through his library—giving the book with "black folk" in the title to the black fellow at the front counter. But you never know with Doc. Maybe it's something else.

Zeph pulls his hair back and ties it into a knot so he can lean over the book without his locks obscuring the pages. It had been the Doc's idea that Zeph should let his hair grow into locks. One day, he'd reached into one of the museum's cabinets and pulled out a photograph of some Maasai hunters holding up a dead hyena. "You should look like this," he'd said.

"Aww, hell no," Zeph had replied. "I'm done with that Wild Man of Borneo freak-show crap. I'll work for you, but no chance I'll put on some moth-eaten costume and pretend to—"

"No, stupid. Hair. You look the hair like this."

Zeph had studied the photo. The hunters grinned out at him from behind long black ropes they grew themselves. "Yeah? You think I'd look good?"

Timur had rolled his eyes. "You look terrible, obviously. But you spend less time fixing the hair and more time doing the work. This, I like."

Zeph smiles at the memory and starts to read. Before long comes that familiar, unwelcome pounding on the front door.

"Zeph! I need to speak with you!"

He recognizes the voice. "That's all right, Joe. Y'all start the revolution without me."

"Come on! I have something of yours!"

"Ain't nothing you got that I want, mister."

"Zeph!" Joe thumps again, even harder.

Zeph frowns. The pounding and shouting risks drawing Timur out of his lab in a rage. "For God's sake, come in if you're gonna!"

The door cracks open, and sunlight floods the dim museum. Joe pokes his head around the door conspiratorially. "You alone?"

Zeph folds over a page in his book. "You're the only man I know so desperate for a scrap he'll try to break down an open door. Yes, I'm alone, what's it look like? What do you want?"

"Like I said, I have something of yours." He opens the door a bit wider, and a young boy skulks in. Eight years old with skin the color of Coney beaches, he wears a newsboy cap, a checkered shirt, and short pants with no shoes. He looks up guiltily.

"P-Ray," Zeph says. "What are you doing with this guy?" He glares at Joe. "Why are you messing with him?"

"My comrades and I liberated your boy from the *politzya*. You're welcome." Joe comes inside. The left sleeve of his white shirt, where his arm used to be, is folded up and pinned at the shoulder. The pin has a tiny black flag on it.

"Comrades…what, you mean your gaggle of anarcho–circus freaks or whatever you're calling yourselves?"

Joe smiles indulgently. "Anarcho-syndicalists. It means we're concerned with the exploitation of labor by the—"

"Circus freaks."

"Your boy here was fooling around with the police horses at the precinct, and it's just luck that we came along and—"

Zeph ignores him and turns to P-Ray. "You catch some good ones?"

P-Ray grins and holds up a small jar.

"Good job, little man," Zeph says. "Go put them with the others. Must be feeding time by now anyway."

P-Ray scampers behind a black velvet curtain that hides the rest of the museum from view.

Joe looks confused. "What was it in that jar? Bugs?"

"Fleas."

"Off the horses? That's disgusting. Why'd you let him bring fleas in here?"

"Don't fret yourself about it. Okay, well, thanks, Joe. Sorry you can't stay, but—"

"Now wait a minute." Joe leans over the counter, and Zeph gets a look at the jagged, poorly healed scar running down his cheek. "I brought your boy back to you, brother. It seems like I deserve something in return?"

"It *seems like* P-Ray was doing fine on his own."

"The *politzya* would have pinched him if I hadn't—"

Zeph shakes his head. "Cops around here all know P-Ray. He ain't no trouble. So why don't you go back to your anarcho-cymbals, and I'll—"

"I want to talk to your boss."

Zeph frowns. "Trust me, you don't. And the Doc don't want to talk to you."

"I've got business."

"Nope."

Joe drops the cheerful tone. "I must talk to him, brother."

"Listen, *brother*. Timur don't talk to nobody. If you truly have business with him, then you tell me. That's what he pays me for."

Joe chuckles. "Is that so? Looks like he pays you to sit here like a chump, taking tickets at a crummy museum with no customers."

"You ain't exactly helping your case, you realize. Just tell me what you want, and in the unlikely event it ain't completely stupid, I'll pass it on."

Joe straightens up contemplatively. He drums on the counter with his five remaining fingers, gazing at the tapestry hung behind Zeph. It shows a large, golden wheel with spokes dividing the image into sections. In one, a rooster bites a pig, who in turn bites a snake. In another, men battle against strange beings—gods or monsters or both. There's a man in a boat, another with an arrow through his eye, another carrying a corpse. The entire wheel sits in the lap of a red-faced demon, who grasps it with needlelike fingers and bites it with sharp fangs.

Joe grimaces. "What in the Sam Hill is that picture anyway?"

"*Sipa Khorlo*, the Tibetan wheel of life."

"Yeah, so why's that monster trying to eat it?"

Zeph sighs. "Private tours of the museum cost extra, Joe. How 'bout you run along and—"

"All right, all right. I'll tell you. Very soon, on this fine Coney of ours, a Decoration Day event will be attended by no other than His Highness, President Theodore Roosevelt. Parade, speech, and a party at the Oriental Hotel. All the hogs will be at the trough, every swell in New York, pouring claret down their gullets and congratulating one another on—"

Zeph rolls his eyes. "Yeah, I get it. And y'all gonna what? Pull some anarcho-cinder-block nonsense on them, is that it?"

Joe gives a vague "why not" one-shouldered shrug. "We intend to spoil their party, yes. Just like we spoiled McKinley's trip to the World's Fair."

"Come on—it was that one guy did that. You and your dimwit battalion had nothing to do with killing President McKinley."

"Didn't we?" Joe says smugly. "Well, obviously *you* know everything, Zeph..."

"So let me understand. All y'all gonna attack the president on *Decoration Day*. Decoration Day, the one day of the year when everybody—black, white, rich, poor, North, South—everybody sets all their shit aside to say thank-you to our boys in uniform. And on *that day*, y'all gonna try to kill the commander in chief?"

Joe nods, his eyes glimmering. "Quite the irony, don't you think?"

"Oh, it's quite something," Zeph says, eyebrow arched. "That's sure to gather folks around your cause..."

"That's exactly what I've been saying."

"Gather 'em to watch your cracker ass swing from a rope."

"Shows how little you know. This country is ripe for revolution. Like the prophets say, it's time for the bourgeoisie to reap the whirlwind. And when I spotted your boy on the street today, I got to thinking about Timur. What contraptions does that madman have in his attic?"

"I have no idea what you're talking about," Zeph says, only somewhat believably.

"Sure, sure, the picture of innocence, ain'tcha. Everybody knows there's something ain't right up there in that lab of his. What *couldn't* we accomplish with a man like that on our side?"

"Timur ain't on nobody's side but Timur's."

"Come on," Joe scoffs. "Are you going to look me in the eye and say that man doesn't build bombs?"

"I'm saying that Timur don't build bombs *for you*. Now hustle off before *I* call the *politzya*."

✦ ★ ✦

When Joe's gone, Zeph turns around and addresses the dark museum. "I know you're there, little man…"

Sheepishly, P-Ray pulls back the velvet curtain and steps forward. "You hear all that?"

The boy nods, his eyes wide.

"Don't be afraid, little man. Ain't nobody killing nobody. That Joe…I swear, he's so full of it, place was starting to smell like my daddy's farm. Nothing bad gonna happen. Zeph won't let it, you hear?"

The boy nods again but can only force a half smile.

"Okay, how can I make you feel better? You want me to read to you?"

Before Zeph can even finish the offer, P-Ray races to the shelf next to Zeph's stool and pulls out a book. He hands it to Zeph and arranges himself on the counter, his bare feet dangling over the edge.

Zeph looks at the cover. "Not *this* again?"

P-Ray nods solemnly.

Zeph makes a big show of sighing in misery as he opens the book for the hundredth time. But he winks at P-Ray and begins to read.

> Chapter One: The Cyclone. Dorothy lived in the midst of the great Kansas prairies, with Uncle Henry, who was a farmer, and Aunt Em, who was the farmer's wife…

THANKS, BUT NO

K ITTY PREFERS THE LITTLE BIRDS. SHE SITS ON HER PARK BENCH AND watches them work as the sun rises over the ocean. Fat seagulls swoop effortlessly overhead, riding the sky like kites set free from their strings. Meanwhile, tiny birds flap furiously just to stay a few feet above the waves. For the little birds, nothing is effortless. One little bird spots something in the water and drops into the sea like a stone, only to force its way back up a moment later with a fish in its mouth. The others follow, one at a time—*flap-flap-flap-drop, flap-flap-flap-drop*. Exhausting.

The gulls seem amused by their tiny, hardworking cousins. They remind Kitty of her older brother, Nathan. How he'd laughed at her as she'd struggled ungracefully across their grandparents' frozen pond last winter, all flopping limbs and tearing petticoats. Meanwhile, he glided past as though he'd been born with skates on his feet. "Go ahead and laugh," she'd called to him from the ice where she'd fallen yet again. "You don't have to skate in this foolish dress."

But it had never been about the dress—not really. Nathan was a gull, always had been. He was handsome and graceful and fine, and life seemed to open itself to greet him, as if the world had waited thousands of years for his arrival. Kitty was one of those tiny birds—*flap-flap-flap-dropping* with all her might against forces far beyond her control.

"So, Nate," she says aloud. "How is it I'm here and you're not? Why'd you fly off without me?"

She shivers. It's so cold here by the water. *Leave it to me,* she thinks, *to get myself stuck someplace with worse weather than home in London.* And it's even colder this morning, somehow, than it had been at night. Or perhaps Kitty just hadn't noticed. She'd been too busy gawping at the Coney Island skyline, which was unlike anything she'd ever seen. Towers and spires and minarets assaulted the clouds, lighting up the sky with electric bulbs uncountable in number. Thousands upon thousands of fireflies caught in tiny glass jars. There is electric light back in London too, of course, but nothing as lavish as this, nothing so theatrically unnecessary. Nothing so American.

How Nate would have loved this, she'd thought. How unfair that I should be here and not him.

Now daylight has come, and the firefly army has marched on. There's not much to distract Kitty from her predicament or from an early-morning wind rolling off the sea. The moistness cuts through Kitty's overcoat, the bodice of her dress, her corset, all of it. All her armor, nothing but a soggy cage now.

Not that it matters.

But truly, how can it be so cold? Isn't this May? And isn't this meant to be a resort? How can one do any manner of resorting in this weather?

She smiles a bit at the thought, despite her circumstances. Kitty sits alone on a bench at the edge of the world. She's been here for two days. She knows no one in this city. She has no luggage, passport, or money. No family or friends. No one waiting for her. No one to care if she remains on this bench for another two days, or two weeks, or two years.

If ever there was a last resort, this is surely it.

Against her will, Kitty's gaze travels toward the west, in the direction of the majestic hotel she'd called home for all of ten hours and thirty-six minutes. She knows she shouldn't keep looking, shouldn't give that blasted hotel the satisfaction. But she can't stop hoping Mother will suddenly appear, robust and smiling, and turn the past two days of misery into a joke. She can practically hear her mother's voice. "Bless us," she'd say. "You simply will not believe what nonsense our Kitty got up to in New York!"

Imagining her mother causes Kitty's eyes to sting, and she forces herself to stop.

Instead, looking out at the tide, she imagines herself lying facedown, rocking lifelessly with the current, her petticoats blossoming on the surface of the sea. The gulls would squawk in confusion, but the little birds would understand. It takes a lot of energy to keep flap-flap-flap-dropping. Sometimes energy runs out.

Kitty stands with the indignant air of someone who's waited too long for a tardy friend and has decided to give up and go home. She takes a few steps closer to the shore. *And why not?* she thinks. *Why shouldn't I chuck myself into the sea? What do I have to live for? Father long dead, Nate gone, and Mother…Mother apparently lost as well. I'm only seventeen,* Kitty reminds herself. *I've no skills, no way to get by, no way to get home. Anything, even drowning, has got to be better than just sitting here, day after day, waiting and waiting for exactly no one to come and precisely nothing to happen. No one back home is fretting over me anyway. No one here knows me, and no one there wants me. Wouldn't it be more convenient if I floated away?*

She takes another step closer to the water.

But Kitty has never been convenient. Not from her first breath— the infamous moment when her mother took to her bed, expecting to deliver another baby Nathan. She hadn't even bought any new baby clothes, so certain was she that she'd produce a second agreeable, easygoing son. But she'd ended up with baby Katherine instead. A colicky daughter, red-faced and squalling.

Convenient? No, Kitty thinks, *I've never been convenient to anyone.*

Coney Island would be a right silly place to start.

✦ ★ ✦

Morning turns to afternoon, and the sun saunters indifferently across the sky. Bathers come and go; children laugh and cry and laugh again; couples hold hands and fight and make up and hold hands some more. Kitty sees it all, but no one sees her.

Although she sits quietly, there's a squelching, sickening fear inside, turning her limbs to water. What will she do? Where will she go? Will she die on this bench, unseen and unmourned?

Battling with her fear is fury. At the hotel, for tossing her out on the street. At her mother, for somehow allowing it to happen. At the children, for frolicking in the waves without a care. How dare they? She knows the thought is irrational, but it comes anyway. How dare they be so happy?

As intense as her fear and anger is her hunger. It's been two days since she's eaten. There had been a splendid breakfast on the steamship delivering her family into New York Harbor. But she'd been sullen, pushing the eggs around on her plate and rejecting the fruit course. *Lesson learned*, she thinks to herself now. *Never, ever refuse breakfast.*

There's a screeching sound just behind her bench. She turns to see two squirrels tumbling over one another like playful children. Even the rodents, it seems, are having a better day than she. But suddenly things turn serious. The squirrels square off like a couple of boxers, both up and dancing on their hind legs, chittering at each other, mad-eyed and desperate. One lunges for the other and sinks in its teeth. The other squirrel shrieks, wrenching itself back and forth, but the first squirrel just digs in, tearing his enemy's throat. They are a tangle of limbs and tails and blood, wailing and screeching. Then it ends as suddenly as it started—the dominant squirrel stands triumphant over his lifeless foe. He glares up at Kitty, daring her judgment.

Kitty shudders and turns back to the sea. *I don't think I care for New York.*

★ ★ ★

The afternoon slips away, as summer afternoons are inclined to do. Tired and sunburned, the bathers pack up and depart for dinner at home, hotel, wherever they belong. Even the little birds have somewhere to go. Not Kitty.

From the street behind, a strange sound. A conversation—no, multiple conversations—in mysterious, clicking tongues. Five women approach, with young children orbiting like hyperactive satellites. Four appear to be Africans, with dark skin and ample, rounded bodies swathed in colorful, patterned materials. The upper lip of each woman is stretched outward four or five inches by a ceramic plate inserted in the skin. The plates look painful, and how the women can speak at all is a mystery to Kitty. But they do, and they seem perfectly happy. Their children run down the beach and splash into the water, while the mothers laugh and chitchat, always with one eye on their young ones in the waves.

The fifth woman hangs back from the group. She is lighter skinned and very tall. Her stretched-out neck is decorated with dozens of brass rings. The other women give her friendly glances but do not speak to her; she is with them but not of them. The tall woman has two young children with her—a girl and a boy—and they stay close to their mother, clinging to her long, embroidered skirt. She leans down and urges them, in yet another language Kitty doesn't understand, to go play with the others. Before long, the children forget their shyness and race down to the water's edge.

Satisfied, the tall woman approaches Kitty and smiles. She points questioningly at the empty space on the bench.

"Oh yes, please," Kitty says. "Please, sit."

The woman nods. She reaches into her yellow bag and removes a leather canteen. Noticing Kitty's naked envy at the sight of fresh water, she holds out the canteen.

"No, I couldn't," Kitty says out of ritual politeness. The woman offers the canteen again, and this time, Kitty can't resist. She seizes it like a life raft and takes a long drink of the fresh, miraculously still-cool water. Although she knows she shouldn't, she takes another drink. And a third.

She wipes her mouth, embarrassed. "Thank you." Kitty tries to return the canteen, but the woman refuses it. She puts up her hand. *Thank you, but no.*

"Thank you, ma'am. That's so…" Kitty takes another sip, blinking back a few grateful tears.

The woman's daughter runs to the bench, her brother close behind. The girl cries and points at her brother, babbling a list of offenses. The woman puts her arms around her daughter, kisses her on the forehead, and smacks her playfully on the bottom, sending her back toward the beach. She addresses her son, firmly but kindly. He nods begrudgingly and follows his sister to the water. The woman smiles at Kitty and shakes her head.

"Oh, I know," Kitty says. "I have an older brother too." She bites her lip. "Had. I had an older brother."

The woman tilts her head thoughtfully. She pats Kitty on the knee and says something incomprehensible yet comforting. She reaches into her bag, and as she does, a handful of postcards spill out.

Kneeling to pick them up, Kitty sees that the cards are not true postcards at all. They are multiple copies of the same photograph, a portrait of the woman sitting beside her on the bench. Garish text sits at the top of each photo: CONGRESS OF CURIOUS PEOPLE PRESENTS... And at the bottom: OOWANA SUMBA, SAVAGE HEADHUNTRESS OF BORNEO! In the photos, the woman is topless, wearing only a tangled grass skirt. She wields a machete in one hand, and with the other, she grasps a still-dripping severed head by its long, black hair. Startled, Kitty can only laugh at the contrast between the courtly lady before her and the primitive person in the photograph—from her hair (wild in the picture but neat in real life) to her clothing (minimal in the picture, modest in person) to her expression (crazed in the portrait, kind in reality).

The woman snatches the cards from Kitty, embarrassed.

"That's you?"

The woman nods, then shakes her head no, then reconsiders and nods again. Finally, she gives up and shrugs, her neck rings tinkling a friendly little song. From her bag, she retrieves an oblong package in silver foil and hands it to Kitty.

Kitty gasps. Nate had told her about these—invented in Coney Island not long ago, they have become world famous in a few short years.

Hot dogs.

"I couldn't!" Kitty exclaims. She hands the treasure back. "No, really… It's your dinner!"

They debate the frankfurter in informal sign language. Finally, the woman snatches the package, unwraps the hot dog, and tears it in half. She holds out Kitty's half and glares at her, unblinking. This is a woman skilled in making children eat.

Kitty eats.

It's wonderful.

✶ ★ ✶

Too soon, the sun sets, and the African women fold up their blanket. Amid the children's howls of protest, the women begin the trek back up to the street.

The woman with the neck rings stands up and studies Kitty. She points at the bench, then up the street. She shrugs and says something apologetic.

"I'm all right," Kitty says. "Thank you for the food. Really, I'm fine."

The woman's children approach the bench. Their mother speaks to them, and they curtsy to Kitty, politely whispering something that sounds like good-bye.

Kitty waves to them as they walk away. The little boy drops to one knee, and his sister climbs onto his back. She rests her head on his shoulder. Although he is only a few inches taller than his sister, the boy manages to stand back up. He takes his mother's hand and carries his exhausted sister toward home.

Big brother, Kitty thinks. *What a lovely big brother he is.*

Kitty makes a decision. "This is silly," she says aloud. "All this sitting about, moping. I should go find Nate."

✶ ★ ✶

Kitty walks along Surf Avenue, the street lit so brightly it looks like noon rather than night. The street is dotted with private bathhouses, restaurants, and the entrances to the three major amusement parks—Steeplechase, Luna Park, and the newly opened Dreamland. Roller coasters whoosh by overhead, and steam-powered calliopes toot in the distance, while barkers call out for suckers to take their chances on unwinnable carnival games. Kitty barely registers any of it. Her mind has only one focus—finding the magic words that will get her on board the ferry to Manhattan, back to her steamship to find her brother…all without so much as a penny for a ticket.

The ferry terminal is crowded with cranky, sunburned Manhattanites. Children whine, and couples snipe at each other, and Kitty wonders if this was a good idea.

After a twenty-minute wait in a long, confusing line, she takes her turn at the ticket counter.

"Where to?" drones the bored man behind the counter.

"Ah, one passenger, to Manhattan, but—"

"Fifteen cents."

"Yes, the thing is…"

The man sighs the sigh of someone in hour eleven of a twelve-hour shift. "I said, fifteen cents."

"You see, sir…quite an amusing story, actually…"

He rolls his eyes. "Price of the ticket is fifteen cents."

"Right. But you see, I'm separated from my family, and I need to—"

"See that man behind you? He's got fifteen cents. Lady behind him? She's got fifteen cents too. You don't got fifteen cents? You don't gotta be in this line."

"But, sir—"

"Miss, get outta this line before I have somebody take you out."

"But—"

"Next!"

✦ ★ ✦

Kitty tells the same story to the other clerks, always with the same result. Disinterest followed by annoyance followed by "Next!"

A police officer offers to arrange a ride back to…where is she staying exactly? Kitty admits she isn't staying anywhere *exactly*; she's trying to get back to the steamship *Arundale*, because her brother is still on it.

The cop chuckles. "The good news is, the *Arundale* ain't going nowhere, so you for sure don't have to worry about missing it. The bad news is, it's under quarantine."

"Quarantine? Is that normal?"

"What do I look like, a harbor master? Point is, if your brother's on it, he ain't getting off, and if you ain't on it already, you ain't getting on now. So how's about we find you some place to sleep tonight? We got a settlement house over on Henry Street that—"

Kitty's stomach turns over. "A what? Oh, no, I—"

"Nothing to be afraid of. Nice bunch of do-gooding gals."

Kitty knows all about settlement houses—upper-class ladies reading *Peter Rabbit* to grimy children covered with scabs and lice. "I don't think you understand! My mother and I volunteer at a settlement house in London. My family doesn't *use* their services; we *provide* their services."

The cop frowns. "Don't take this the wrong way, but you know what they say about beggars being choosy, right?"

"No, no, I couldn't…" She backs away. "Thank you, but… No, I'll find some other way." She hurries out of the terminal.

"Hey, miss! Come back! It ain't a garden party on the streets at night, you know! Miss!"

✦ ★ ✦

Kitty hurries back down Surf Avenue toward the park. It's very late, and the businesses are closing up. She races across stretches of darkness from one pool of light to the next, praying that she will be able to find her way back to her park bench. It's not that the bench is a particularly endearing spot; it's just the only spot she knows.

She passes the entrance to Steeplechase Park, closed now but still lit brightly. On a huge sign, the words "Steeplechase…A Funny

Place!" encircle a leering face with a creepy smile baring far too
many teeth. On the ground, a dead rat lies on the boardwalk, its four
stiff legs pointed up at the sky. Kitty shivers and moves on.

She takes a few more steps down Surf Avenue when a man
appears out of the shadows and blocks her path. "Evenin', pretty
lady," he sneers.

Kitty's breath catches in her throat. The young man is not wearing
a shirt—startling to a proper girl who never saw her own brother
undressed, much less a stranger. But he has nothing but suspenders
on his bare, sinewy shoulders. Instead of a shirt, the man's entire
upper body is decorated with a massive, intricate tattoo of a castle.
A long stone wall crosses his abdomen, and turrets and flags reach
up to his neck. Below the castle wall, the beginnings of a moat peek
out above his belt buckle. He smirks. "I got an alligator in my moat.
You wanna see?"

"What? No, I…I'm sorry. I'm very late…" She tries to leave, but
he grabs her wrist, hard, and yanks her close. The tallest tower of the
castle is tattooed up his neck and across the entire left side of his face,
disappearing into the bowler hat on top of his head. His bright-green
eye peers out one of the castle windows. Stones from the castle wall
are tattooed across his forehead and nose. They fly across his face
and fall into a pile of debris running along his jawbone. The tattoo
has captured the precise moment when the barbarians arrived to lay
waste to the kingdom.

Kitty tries to wrench herself away. "I insist you release me!"

"Aha!" His grip on her wrist gets tighter. "You sound English.
You English?"

"My friends are waiting for me, and they'll be terribly upset if—"

"Fancy English, sounds like. You a princess or something?"

Kitty jerks her arm again but can't get free. She looks around—
there is no one else on the street. The man pulls her so close she can
smell his whiskey breath.

"Whaddya say, princess? You wanna have some fun?"

"My friends will be along any moment!"

He laughs and puts his other arm around Kitty's waist, pulling her into an awkward waltz. "You know what? I don't think you've got any friends, do you? Don't lie to Crumbly Pete, now. That's what my friends call me. Crumbly Pete. You wanna be Crumbly Pete's friend?"

"Stop it right now! You let me go this instant!"

"Come on, now, princess…" He pulls her closer, and Kitty spits directly into one of his gleaming green eyes. Caught by surprise, Pete lets go, and Kitty takes off down Surf Avenue as fast as she can.

Crumbly Pete's laughter echoes. "Princess! Was it something I said?"

3

SITTING WITH
SHAKESPEARE

❦

IN THE MORNING, ZEPH ASSUMES HIS USUAL POSITION AT MAGRUDER'S entrance, hoping to greet as few customers as possible. He is about halfway through his new book and dreads the thought of being interrupted. Du Bois's words rip through Zeph's mind like bolts of lightning.

> America is not another word for Opportunity to
> all her sons.

Zeph underlines this sentence. Twice.

But it's Saturday, the busiest day of Coney Island's week. The chance of a full day of undisturbed reading is slim. And sure enough, it isn't long before Zeph hears a youthful quartet loitering on the other side of Magruder's oak door.

First, a young man's snide voice: "An 'abinet? Would someone please explain to me what an 'abinet is? And why I should want to see one?"

Zeph whispers a quiet prayer. "Don't come in, don't come in, go away, go away, go away…"

Then an irritated female voice speaks up. "It clearly says 'Cabinet,' Mr. Tilden. The sign's just a bit faded."

"Theophilus P. Magruder's Curiosity Cabinet and Theatron Prodigium." The first voice, Tilden, spits the words out like they taste bad. "And about this other sign, over here? 'The Race to Death. The Racers Are Small, but the Mayhem Enormous. No Dogs Allowed.' Sounds like a bunch of hooey. Tell me, Miss Celik, how'd you hear about this ridiculous place anyway?"

The irritated lady answers, "I *read*, Mr. Tilden. You might try it sometime."

"Ha. Ha. Ha."

"Now, now," says another male voice, more assured than his friend and painfully genteel. "We promised Miss Celik we'd visit this… museum, cabinet, whatnot, and we shall." The door cracks open.

Zeph groans. He unties the knot in his hair, and his locks descend over his face like a curtain. He stares down at his book and hopes it will be over soon.

Four people enter—two young ladies on the arms of two young men. From behind his hair, Zeph watches them peer into the museum like a pack of moles, their eyes adjusting to the gloom. They look to be about Zeph's age, early twenties roughly. The one called Tilden is easy to spot. The only thing about Tilden more pompous than his voice is his everything else: the sideburns and waxed mustache, which would be more appropriate on a man three times his age; the short, baggy pants pinned at the knee, which would be more appropriate for foxhunting than beach-going; the stiff felt hat known as a homburg, which hasn't been appropriate on anyone since 1880. Attached to his arm like a barnacle is a boringly pretty white girl, her nose in a permanent scrunch of distaste.

The second couple is more interesting. The young man is clearly their leader; he has that gilded air about him. The ease of his attire—slicked-back hair, clean-shaven white face, his shirt and trousers very simple but pointedly, breathtakingly expensive—only makes Tilden more clownish by comparison. This young man was born at the front of the line. He knows it, and he knows you know it too.

But his date. She can only be Miss Celik, with the irritated voice. Unlike Tilden's pallid blond barnacle, she is raven-haired and olive-skinned. And not wispy and underfed like the other girl—she's curvy and sturdy like a woman ought to be. She's neatly dressed, but her long skirt has been mended more than once. And she apparently declined to wear a proper ladies' hat, practically a revolutionary act. What, Zeph longs to know, is a fine gal like her doing with a trio of braying asses like these?

"Ten cents a head," he mutters without looking up.

The leader of the pack reaches into his billfold, while Tilden the clown leans over the counter. "What's that Race to Death you're advertising?" he demands. "Whose death?"

"Special show, once a day only, 2:00 p.m.," Zeph says. "For connoisseurs."

Tilden whistles. "*Connoisseurs*... That's quite a fancy word for a boy like you."

Boy. There's no chance Zeph is a minute younger than any of them. He looks up, his brown eyes gamely meeting Tilden's blue ones. "The Race to Death is ten cents extra...but I doubt a *boy* like you would appreciate it."

"Don't you *dare* speak to me that way, you little—"

"All right, now, Gibson." Tilden's friend claps him on the back. "Don't get all steamed up."

"Spencer, you heard what he—"

"Yeah, and *you* heard what I said: don't get all steamed up." Spencer smiles beneficently at Zeph and tosses a dollar on the counter. "We're busy at 2:00, so this'll just be the regular admission. We'll have to Race to Death some other time."

Zeph looks at the dollar and sighs. Regretfully, he turns over a corner page of his book and pulls a cigar box from underneath the counter. He roots around in the box, removes some coins, and frowns. "Y'all don't have no change?"

"Sorry," the young prince says. "No change."

"Trouble is I only got fifty cents here." Zeph makes a vague "oh well" gesture. "I don't know what to tell ya..."

Tilden growls. "Mr. Reynolds gave you a dollar. Ten cents

apiece means you owe him sixty cents, not fifty. So get to it—we don't have all day, boy."

That word again. Zeph stares at Tilden with murder in his eyes.

Miss Celik glances from Zeph to Tilden and back again. To Zeph, she mouths, "Sorry." And then, turning to her companion, she says, "Mr. Reynolds, it's just ten cents."

"You know what they say, Miss Celik: look after the cents, and the dollars take care of themselves."

Zeph sighs. He really, really did not want it to come to this. *Here goes nothing.* He pulls on his leather gloves, reaches up with both arms, and grabs the shelf ledge. The visitors boggle as he clambers up the shelves, revealing a perfectly normal torso with no legs underneath. His trousers, having nothing to cover, have been cut short and pinned underneath his backside. Zeph scales the shelves toward the ceiling.

Miss Celik watches, dazzled. Then she glances at her companions, who also stare at the half man scrambling up the wall. But they look less dazzled than revolted.

Zeph's abbreviated body swings beneath him and then angles outward as he dives deep into one of the shelves. He gropes around, searching for something. Victoriously, he pulls out a dusty piggy bank. "There you are!" He holds up the bank with one arm, keeping himself balanced against the shelf with the other. Then his arm arches back, and suddenly piggy is airborne, sailing just inches past Tilden's head and crashing into pieces on the floor.

"Good God!" Tilden cries. "What do you think you're doing?"

From his perch, Zeph shrugs with his whole body. "Sorry," he says, not sounding especially so. "Lost control of it, I guess." He climbs back down and settles on his stool. "Anyhow, there's your change. Go on and look after it." He returns to his book.

Spencer glowers but gets down on one knee to retrieve his sixty cents from the coins rolling around on the floor. Miss Celik looks away, ashamed for him.

Tilden glares at Zeph. "That must be one funny book," he says dangerously, "because you sure do look like you're grinning under all that hair."

Zeph holds up the thin volume. "W. E. B. Du Bois," he says. "It's about how the most talented tenth of my people are gonna rise up and kick y'all's backsides. It's *hilarious*."

"Are you laughing at me, boy?"

"Good book," Miss Celik says, swiftly placing herself between the young men. "Although it's a little short on backside kicking."

Zeph stares at her. "You telling me you read this?"

"Yes." She smiles. "I'm telling you I read that. Not the chapter where his son dies, though. That was too sad for me."

Spencer stands, pockets his change, and kicks the rest of the coins away with his boot. "This has been fascinating," he says, "but we have a lunch reservation at the Palmetto at 1:00 and big plans this afternoon." He pulls back the velvet curtain. "Who can tell what wonders await us inside Magruder's Curiosity 'abinet?"

As they disappear into the museum, Zeph sighs. Keeping one finger on the page he's reading, he flips to the table of contents.

Chapter Eleven. On the Passing of the First Born.

He looks at the space where Miss Celik just stood. "Well now…I'll be damned."

★ ★ ★

The white alligator glistens in the half-light, its mouth stretched wide, its razor teeth dripping with blood.

Or wait. Nazan Celik looks more closely. Red paint actually. Nice effect, though.

She and her companion, Spencer Reynolds; Spencer's friend Gibson Tilden; and Gibson's date, Chastity Poole, all stand in a large, rectangular room. The room has been divided and subdivided and subdivided again by giant, glass-fronted cabinets that scrape the ceiling. The floor plan of Magruder's is like a hedge maze, forcing

visitors to turn right, then left, then left again, then right, around and
around in a dizzying spiral of mismatched furniture.

But although they vary greatly in style, Nazan notices that the
cabinets all do have one feature in common: lines of iron handles
bolted to the side of each cabinet, starting at about waist height and
continuing to the top. She thinks of the young man up front, swinging his shortened body along the bookshelf. This is not just a room
of cabinets, she realizes—it's a room of ladders, all of it jerry-rigged
for a caretaker with no legs.

Trinkets and gewgaws are all stuffed in together with no apparent
logic. The jawbone of a saber-toothed tiger partly obscures a tiny
oil painting of Buckingham Palace, which sits beside an anatomical
model of the human heart. A large jar of glass eyes sits on top of
a thick book titled *Ought I Be Baptized?* One large cabinet by the
front houses several terrariums full of insects, some alive and some
not, with tags like *Orchid Mantis* and *Madagascar Spitting Cockroach.*
Over here are sets of shackles that once bound the witches of Salem,
Massachusetts. Over there, a sign assures its reader that yes, it really is
Abe Lincoln painted on that grain of rice.

A larger cabinet is home to the skeletons of conjoined twin
girls, Daisy and Maisy. A smaller cabinet next to the twins houses a
narwhal horn, a collection of thimbles, a pair of ladies' boots made
from peacock feathers, and a family of fruit bats carved out of wax.
Beside the grasshoppers, a baby pig with two faces floats in a jar of
murky, yellow liquid, right behind a human thighbone on a gold-
leafed stand. *Kangling,* the sign says. *Thigh Trumpet from Deepest Tibet.*

Everything about the Cabinet is grimy and fusty and strange.

Nazan smiles. It's everything she'd hoped it would be. It's perfect.

But then Chastity cries, "Eww," and Nazan sighs. The *Cabinet* is
perfect. The company leaves much to be desired.

Nazan knows she shouldn't be so petty about the company. In
fact, she should consider herself lucky to even be here. Men like
Spencer usually pass their time with the beautiful ladies, the ones
with wasp-thin waists and peaches-and-cream complexions, with

pale blue eyes and straight, blond tresses. Nazan is darker and curlier and curvier, and to make matters more challenging still, she has a mole hovering over her left eyebrow. Her mother insists on calling it a beauty mark, but as far as young men are concerned, it may as well be a tattooed stop sign.

So when the wealthy Spencer Reynolds showed a glimmer of interest, Nazan's family practically turned cartwheels across the living room floor. "Son of a senator!" her mother had said breathlessly.

Nazan shook her head. "Son of a *state* senator. Very different from a *senator* senator."

"You're twenty-one years old! In the old country, you would have three children by now! It's time to get your head out of those books and find a—"

"But isn't that why we left Constantinople for a *new* place, so that your daughter could—"

"Meet a senator's son! Exactly! What does it matter whether his father is state senator or *senator* senator? Perhaps we will not be so picky? Perhaps we—" Her mother stopped, suddenly alarmed. "You aren't going out dressed like *that*, are you?"

In his defense, Spencer had been kind enough to include this trip to the museum on the day's agenda. He certainly didn't need to—Magruder's was Nazan's interest and hers alone. She thinks, *Things could be worse.* Then she hears Chastity's shrill carping.

Not much worse.

✶ ✶ ✶

Back at the museum entrance, Zeph hears and tries to enjoy the squeals of the terrified blond. Tries but fails. After all, moments ago, she'd squealed the same way at the sight of him.

Sure, sometimes it's fun, torturing the pretty ones. The more privileged Magruder's customers are—the stronger the hand that life has dealt them—the more appalling the dark relics of the Cabinet tend to be. It's been Zeph's experience that Normals have no idea how much most Unusuals like him enjoy the discomfort of spectators. Normals, even the well-meaning ones, think things like: *How sad to be so strange; it must be terrible. How tragic they are, who can never be like us.*

Not necessarily. Unease, disquiet, fear? Heebie-jeebies? This is the daily bread of the Unusual. This, Unusuals understand, is power. However fleeting, however meaningless, this is the only power Unusuals will ever know, and most of them drink it down in big, thirsty gulps.

But Zeph tends to choke on it. Maybe it's because he wasn't born an Unusual; he had been, in fact, utterly average until bad luck intervened. Maybe it's just not in his nature to take pleasure in the displeasure of others. Or maybe, as his mama would have said, he just reads too damn much.

Because when he looks down at his book, there is W. E. B. Du Bois, speaking Zeph's heart in black and white.

> I sit with Shakespeare, and he winces not. Across the color line, I move arm in arm with Balzac and Dumas... Is this the life you grudge us, O knightly America?

Zeph frowns. *Brother, Shakespeare never got a look at me.*

✦ ✦ ✦

Among the cabinets, a shaft of daylight cuts through the shadows—someone has pulled aside the velvet curtain and stepped inside. Nazan hears very light footsteps, like the approach of a timid cat. She turns a corner around one of the cabinets and sees that a small boy, nine or ten at the oldest, has entered the museum. Startled, he looks up at Nazan and freezes in place. The newsboy cap on his head makes him look very young, but the eyes peering out from underneath look very old indeed.

"Hello there," Nazan says gently. She smiles, hoping not to startle him further.

The boy just stares.

"Are you visiting? Or do you work here?"

He still doesn't move. Or blink.

Nazan's frozen smile starts to feel a little awkward. "Can I... help you?"

Slowly, the boy approaches a cabinet. Inside is a small, stripy circus tent. But the boy pays no attention to the little big top. Instead, he opens a drawer underneath and pulls out a pickle jar. From his back pocket, he removes a dirty handkerchief, which he puts on top of the jar. He slides his hand underneath the cloth, unscrews the lid, and sticks his hand into the jar. Then he looks up at Nazan.

"Do you... Are you trying to show me something?" The boy doesn't respond, so Nazan approaches, the way one might approach a stray animal. "What have you got there?" Inside the pickle jar are a dozen or so fleas, bouncing around inside the jar and biting the boy's hand. He lets them. "Are these...pets?"

Spencer appears around the corner. "Hey, I just found the neatest thing..."

The boy jumps at the sound of Spencer's voice. He gives his hand a quick shake, shuts the jar, shoves it back in the cabinet, and slams the drawer. He takes off at a run and disappears.

Spencer looks at Nazan and grins awkwardly. "Did I say something?"

She shrugs. "I don't think it was you. He seems very shy."

Spencer inspects the cabinet. "Toy circus? What's it for?"

"Not sure. He was feeding some—oh, of course. Fleas. It's a flea circus."

"Oh, very clever."

"Mr. Reynolds..." Nazan takes a step closer to him and lowers her voice. "I hope this isn't inappropriate of me. But Mr. Tilden was terribly rude to the young man out front."

"Miss Celik, the young man was rude to Gibson first. He threw a piggy at him," Spencer says, and Nazan chuckles. "Now, don't laugh—an inch or two different, and he would have hit Gibson square in the face."

"What a shame *that* would have been."

Spencer grins. "Shh, you. He's lurking around here somewhere."
She whispers. "Really, though. Very rude."

"Gib's not so bad," Spencer whispers back. But Nazan lowers her
face slightly and looks up at Spencer from beneath skeptical eyebrows.
"Look, his father, Gibson Tilden Sr., taught at my prep school. That's
where we met—Master Tilden failed me in geometry."

"But you went to Princeton, didn't you? No offense, but how
does somebody who can't do basic geometry get into Princeton?"

Spencer laughs. "My father bought the school a new library, and
you wouldn't believe how fast I got good at geometry. Anyway,
Gibson's just a teacher's kid, but he has, you know…*aspirations*. My
father wants me to take him under my wing, as they say."

"I don't care for him."

"Oh, don't you? All right then, Miss Celik. I promise that next
time, it will be just the two of us. What do you say to that?"

"*Next* time, Mr. Reynolds?"

Spencer swallows a smile and rocks back and forth on his fine
leather shoes. "Well, let's see what the rest of the afternoon holds."

✦ ★ ✦

In her quest to find a place to stand within Magruder's where her eyes
aren't assailed by morbidity, Chastity thinks she has found a haven.
One unloved cabinet in a dimly lit corner is home to a collection of
glass bottles filled with colorful liquids. A blown-glass wine bottle in
the shape of a fish is filled with lovely blue water. A painted perfume
bottle with pink water. A pickling jar with cheerful yellow liquid and
an index finger…*a finger*? Chastity squeaks and backs away, only to
bump into another cabinet. She turns and finds herself nose to nose
with a human head the size of a grapefruit. She screams.

Gibson comes running first, with Spencer at his heels. Nazan
arrives more slowly, having had enough of Chastity's helpless girl
routine. She peers into the cabinet. "It's a shrunken head. From the
Amazon, or so the tag claims." She turns to Chastity. "So it's a head.
What's the problem? Did it wink at you or something?"

"No! What? No, it...it's just..."

She is interrupted by a whirring sound—a small, grumpy engine being roused from its slumber. The whirring is followed by the sound of grinding wheels, as though they're being pursued by a set of wheelchair-bound grandmothers. The sounds are strange enough to distract them all from Chastity's distress. They stare at the corridor of cabinets as some mechanical monster wheezes its way closer. Around the corner of the wall of cabinets comes Zeph, seated atop a tall, three-wheeled metal cart. He gazes distastefully at the stunned group.

"Did I hear screaming? Y'all didn't break nothin', did ya?"

MR. DESCHAMPS

ॐ

KITTY'S STOMACH GROWLS AGAIN. ANGRIER THIS TIME THAN THE LAST— the half a hot dog yesterday somehow made the hunger worse, not better. Or perhaps it's the encounter with Crumbly Pete that's making her stomach churn. Her mind keeps returning to his green eye, peering out the tattooed castle window. Kitty looks around the park uncomfortably. Did he follow her to the park? Is that eye watching her still?

As her hunger pains are joined by a vague dizziness, Kitty knows she has to do...*something*. But without so much as a penny, she can't think what that something might be. The very act of thinking is becoming difficult.

A seagull limps along by the waterline, dragging its wings in the wet sand and making an odd coughing sound. Kitty stares at the sick gull and tries to force her mind into focus. *What do I do, what do I do...whatever do I do now?*

"Good morning, miss!" says a jolly voice. "Would it trouble you if I rested a moment on your bench?"

Kitty turns to see an older gentleman smiling at her. He wears a knee-length, cream-colored frock coat, twenty years out of style at minimum, but clean and well cared for. There is a white carnation in the buttonhole of his coat, and he has a brightly colored scarf wrapped several times around his neck and tucked into his vest—a cravat, Kitty believes it's called. A few white curls peek out from under his narrow-brimmed straw hat. His face is deeply lined and tanned, as though he spends every day piloting a yacht somewhere. He seems jovial and serene, but Kitty notices something deliberate in his approach, as though he's already weighed and measured her, already tallied precisely how much she's worth.

The man gestures at the bench. "Do y'all mind?" He has a fine heirloom of a Southern accent, and he's not afraid to use it.

"Ah, no...no," she says. "Of course not. It's a public bench, after all."

He chuckles and settles himself beside her. "Not for long, I don't suppose. Not if the capitalists get their way. I don't know if you've noticed, but all the beach access is private now—*owned*, or so they claim, by the bathhouses and hotels. Pah! As though one can own a beach!" He brushes his lap with dainty hands and crosses one leg over the other. "Before you know it, the Manhattan Beach Hotel will pressure the moon for a more convenient timing of the tides!" He turns to face Kitty directly. "I'm sorry, I must sound like one of those anarchists. I'm not, I assure you. I'm just a passionate beach-goer. Archibald Deschamps, at your service."

When he puts out his hand, Kitty is startled to see the letters *SS* branded into his palm. She stares at the brand for a moment, then looks up, embarrassed. "My name is Kitty," she offers by way of apology. "Kitty Hayward."

"Miss Hayward. Delighted to make your acquaintance. From your accent, I gather you are of English extraction, yes?"

She nods.

"Ah, merry old England," he says nostalgically. "Never been there. I hear it's lovely, just lovely."

She shrugs.

"And how long is your intended sojourn on our fair Coney Island? Not really an island, by the way."

"I'm—it's not?"

"Not for long. Coney Island Creek separates us from the town of Gravesend and the rest of Brooklyn. Barely more than a stream.

Rumor has it there are plans to dredge the creek and make it passable by ship, but don't you believe it. That will never happen. Look at all the—I'm sorry, have you visited Manhattan yet?"

Kitty shrugs again, remembering her ill-fated trip into the city days earlier. "Briefly."

"That's the best way to visit. But the next time you do—and you will; it's inevitable—look around. Look at all the building they're doing. All the constructing and moving and reshaping. Rabid bands of capitalists, bending the tiny isle of Manhattan to their will. It's a lot of dirt to move around, Miss Hayward. And when they're done? Where will they put the leftovers? Coney Island Creek, of course. You mark my words. Before long, nothing at all will separate us from the swindlers in Brooklyn. Oh, there I go again. Rambling away. But what can I tell you? I'm passionate about my beach."

He reaches into his coat and removes a small, wooden pipe. He puts the pipe in his mouth and fumbles around in his pocket for a box of matches. "In any case, Miss Hayward… Ah, here we go…" He lights his pipe and puffs on it contemplatively. "In any case, it does occur to me that you, yourself, are rather passionate about this beach."

"I'm sorry? What do you mean?"

"My dear, I promenade this end of Surf Avenue with some regularity. It is, if you like, my very own ground for stomping. And I couldn't help but notice you were here on this bench yesterday and the day before. And, dare I say, even the day before that?"

Kitty looks away. It never occurred to her anyone would notice. She can't decide whether attracting Mr. Deschamps's attention is a blessing or a curse. Her stomach growls again.

"Three days, then? I agree this is a most delightful bench and a most felicitous view, but still I wonder…why has a charming, young English lady such as yourself taken up residence here? If I might ask."

Kitty turns to him. She can see that he is studying her closely, perhaps too closely. His tone is friendly, but his eyes hold something else.

"Well, I…I'm not sure…"

"It's perfectly all right, Miss Hayward. Please, don't hesitate to share. Don't you worry: Archie Croydon is here now. He'll help get you sorted out."

"I'm sorry. Didn't you say your name was Deschamps?"

"Did I?" he asks mildly. "Hmm. Let's just stick with Archie. So tell me, Miss Hayward, what demon ties you to this pew? Surely Mummy and Daddy must be terribly fretful by now."

She shrugs. "My father died years ago and…well, my mother isn't in a position to be concerned about much of anything at the moment."

"Ah," Archie says. "I see."

"With apologies, I am quite sure you don't." Kitty sighs and looks at the tide coming in. The little birds continue their frenzied flapping and diving. "What kind of birds are those?"

"Hmm…diving terns? I think? I'm not much for ornithology."

"Terns. I like them."

Archie smiles. "Odd little beasts, aren't they? Doesn't make a lick of sense, fishing that way. Too much energy expended. I'd like to see Mr. Darwin explain terns, eh?" Archie takes another puff on his pipe. "So. We have before us a damsel in distress. Daddy has passed to the other side, and Mummy is…otherwise occupied. Whatever can Archie do to aid the poor damsel?"

Kitty studies the strange old man. *Does he really want to help me? Or will he drag me beneath those waves?* Then she pictures Crumbly Pete, remembers his firm grip on her wrist and his whiskey breath on her face.

"I'm hungry," she says finally. "Terribly hungry. And thirsty. And a bit wet. I haven't any money, or clothes, or…anything." She gestures with her hands, palms up. "I haven't anything."

"My dear child! And here I thought you were going to confront me with something difficult! Miss Hayward, these so-called problems are no problems at all!"

"They're rather substantial problems to me!"

"Nonsense. Let me buy you a meal. How about Feltman's, down the way? Caterers to the millions, or so they claim. Seven differ-ent kitchens serving up the most appalling things—frankfurters and bratwurst and such—but in one of those kitchens, the good one? I'm led to understand the entire staff is *French*. They put foie gras in the dinner rolls."

The kitchen staff could be a tribe of Hottentots for all Kitty cares. A meal? She tries to hide her delight at the prospect of any rolls whatsoever, foie gras or no.

"But I couldn't. I've no way to repay you."

"I won't hear it! If it is lunch Miss Hayward requires, it is lunch she shall have." Archie removes the carnation from his coat and hands it to her flirtatiously. "I just need a tiny favor first."

Kitty takes the flower but frowns. "Sorry? A what?"

5

PORTRAIT OF
A LADY

❧

ZEPH'S CART IS POWERED BY A STRANGE DOUBLE-BOILER CONTRAPTION with a mass of tubes and wires connecting to the wheels and to the underside of the carriage. He is kept steady on the cart by a fence of brass bars encircling his torso. Sitting on the bars at about belly height is a brass lever, which he pushes forward to go and pulls back to reverse.

Spencer points at the cart in amazement. "What is that thing?"

"So you're all good?" Zeph asks, ignoring him. "All right." He pulls back on the lever; the cart sighs and begins his retreat.

"No, no, wait," Spencer says. He kneels down and studies the rolling cart. "How do you power this thing?"

"Naphtha."

Gibson grimaces. "What the h—what precisely is *naphtha*?"

"Kinda like tar. Your basic boiling oil sort of situation. Light it up and…vroom."

Spencer looks up from his crouched position. "Isn't naphtha flammable, though?"

Zeph smiles. "I don't smoke. Let's put it that way."

Spencer stands up. "What's your name?"

"Zeph Andrews."

"Mr. Andrews, did you build this chariot of yours?"

"Nah, this here is the Doc's doing."

"Doc… You mean Dr. Theophilus Magruder?"

Zeph laughs. "No, never met any Theophilus Magruder. Pretty sure there ain't one. Doc's name is Timur."

Spencer reaches into his jacket pocket and removes a calling card. "Whatever his name is, I want you to make sure he gets this, okay? I have a business proposition for him. I want you to make sure he calls me."

Zeph shrugs and takes the card. "Yeah, whatever you say."

Nazan is surprised by Spencer's enthusiasm for Zeph's cart, but she has more pressing interests. "Mr. Andrews, how does one shrink a head?"

"Ah, fascinating question." He powers over to the cabinet beside her. "The interesting thing about shrunken heads? The hardest step is the first. Gotta remove the bones of the skull without damaging the skin. You smack the head around to break the bones, then…"

"Mr. Tilden," Chastity says, "I'm about ready for some fresh air. Would you join me?"

"…exit's around the back," Zeph says. "Oh, for an extra nickel, you can see the Fiji mermaid. One hundred percent authentic. Interested?"

Chastity wrinkles her nose. "I'll pass, thank you." She takes Gibson's arm and sweeps out of the room.

"Y'all have a nice afternoon, now," Zeph calls.

"Right," Spencer says. "Miss Celik, we should get going too, if we want to make our—say, what's this?" On the wall is a poster of a kangaroo in boxing gloves; beside the poster sits a machine with a viewfinder in the center.

"For a nickel, you can watch a kangaroo knock the stuffing out of a grown man."

"No, really?"

"Sure. Go see for yourself."

While Spencer reaches in his pocket for a coin, Zeph turns to Nazan. "So once you got them bones removed, you fill up the head with hot sand. Real hot, right? The sand boils the water in the skin and"—Zeph makes a sucking sound—"shrunken head."

Nazan frowns. "But doesn't the sand fall out the mouth?"

"Yeah! I forgot that part. You gotta sew up the mouth. The eyes, the nose. Look close. You see the stitching? You sew it up tight, and it shrinks down."

At the kinetoscope, Spencer guffaws. "Miss Celik, you have to see this! You look into this viewer, the pictures flip by, the kangaroo bounces around for a while, and then pow! He takes this fellow down! Knocks him flat! Come see!"

"No, I'm fine. You go ahead."

"All right, your loss." He retrieves another nickel and drops it into the coin slot.

"You know, Miss Celik—" Zeph says.

"Please. I'm Nazan."

He grins. "Miss Nazan. Seems you appreciate the finer things. Could I show you something special? It's around back."

"Yes, I'd like that. Mr. Reynolds, if it's all right, Mr. Andrews is going to—"

"Good Lord, look at that kangaroo go!"

Nazan smiles at Zeph. "Please, lead the way."

"Sure," he says, smiling back. "But only if you call me Zeph."

She follows Zeph's cart around one corner, and another, and another, to a small storeroom. The space is dominated by a large platform that looks like a bed with a painted headboard. Nazan assumes this must be the something special she'd been promised, but Zeph directs her to the opposite corner. "Miss Nazan, you stand right there. See that X on the floor?"

Nazan stands in front of yet another cabinet, but instead of a collection of artifacts, this one houses the life-sized torso and head of a boy made entirely of clockwork. He has a delicate porcelain face and wears a suit and tie. His skeleton hands are made of brass, and the right one holds a pen. An artist's sketchpad sits in front of him. An elaborately painted sign above the cabinet reads *Robonocchio, the Automatic Boy!*

Zeph bangs on the cabinet. "Okay, Chio, we got ourselves a customer!" Zeph fumbles about at the back of the cabinet, and a small light comes on at the top, illuminating the sketchpad. "You do a nice job, now," Zeph says to the machine. He moves back and grins at Nazan. "Watch this."

Slowly, the hand holding the pen begins to move. The automatic boy tilts his head slowly down toward the pad, up at Nazan, back down again. The pen moves faster.

"What's this?" Spencer has tired of the kangaroo and followed them into the storeroom.

"Shh, now," Zeph says. "Wait."

The mechanical boy looks up at Nazan and then back at the paper, again and again. He abruptly stops. The sketchpad tilts, and a piece of paper slides off the pad and drops down, appearing in a slot at the bottom of the cabinet, which goes *ding*.

"Voilà," Zeph says. He yanks the paper out of the machine and presents it to Nazan. "There you go. Portrait of a lady."

Nazan takes the paper—a rough pen sketch of a girl with long, dark hair. She stares at it and then at Zeph. "Oh my! That's incredible! That's… Mr. Reynolds, look! Mr. Andrews, how did you do that?"

Zeph shrugs. "Me? I didn't do a thing. That's Chio, doing what Chio does."

"Well, Chio is amazing."

Spencer grins knowingly. "Punch cards, am I right?"

"Sorry?" Zeph asks.

"Punch cards. Normally they're used for accounting—nothing so theatrical as this. But still."

Nazan frowns and yanks the portrait back.

"It's… I'm sorry. But what you do is, you take a set of cards and punch holes in them. Maybe one set of holes tells the machine to move the arm a little bit to the left. The next card tells the machine to move a little bit to the right. Next card, a little to the left, and so on. It would take a fair number of cards, I admit. But if you had enough…you'd have a picture."

"Whatever you say," Zeph replies. He looks at Nazan. "Sure does resemble you, though."

"That's rubbish," Spencer says. "Gaslight like this? A monkey could draw Queen Victoria and claim it looked like Nazan. How would we even tell? Please, don't misunderstand. It's a great little machine. I just—"

Nazan turns to Zeph. "Is any of this true? Is it just a pile of cards?"

Zeph tilts his head. "Far be it from me to tell a white boy he don't know what he's talking about."

Ignoring him, Spencer moves to the side of the cabinet to study the clockwork from behind. "Where do you wind it?" he asks.

"Don't." Zeph shrugs.

"It's electric? I don't see a cord anywhere."

"No cord."

"What's the power source?"

"There ain't one."

Spencer scoffs. "What are you talking about? Of course there's a power source. There's always a—"

"You see that glass chamber in there? That's a barometer. It registers changes in air pressure, which condense or expand the springs in the clockwork. I been here more than four years, and Chio never stopped, not one day."

Nazan smiles appreciatively, but Spencer rolls his eyes. "A perpetual motion machine violates the laws of thermodynamics." He winks at Nazan. "Bad at geometry, but not so bad at science. But, Mr. Andrews, I do wonder why you don't have a clever machine like this on more prominent display."

"Well," Zeph says wryly, "it's a bit surly of you to keep referring to Chio as a *machine*. And I don't show him to just anybody, because it ain't polite to put friends on display."

Spencer laughs. "You consider this contraption a *friend*, do you? Now, isn't that—" An annoyed-sounding cuckoo clock suddenly bleats the hour. Spencer turns to see the carved figure of a woodsman appear from a door in the center of the clock; the woodsman chases a young maiden with his ax and disappears as the cuckoo chirps five o'clock. Spencer checks his pocket watch: it's twenty minutes to one. He glances at Zeph. "Not even close."

Zeph shrugs. "What can I say? We got a lot of clocks at Magruder's. They do what they want, like the rest of us."

"Your *clocks* do what they... Oh good Lord. Miss Celik, it's late. If we don't leave now, we'll lose our table at the Palmetto."

She smiles at Zeph. "However it works, it's wonderful. Tell Chio I said thank you."

"Tell him yourself, Miss Nazan. He's right here."

"Thank you, Chio," she says self-consciously.

Spencer rolls his eyes. "Next she'll be thanking the streetcar for taking us uptown." He gently takes her elbow. "Come along, Miss Celik."

"Mr. Zeph," she says. "The Fiji mermaid! May we see it?"

"Nah, don't bother," Zeph replies. "I'd have to charge you extra, and it's a lousy gaff."

"A what?"

He laughs. "Sorry. Carnies got our own talk. A gaff is something fake, rigged up to fool folks like you. Like our mermaid—just an ol' monkey head glued onto a dead fish." He looks at Spencer. "I suppose a fellow like you wants to save his money. Gotta look after them nickels, am I right?"

Spencer nods. "Make sure your Doc calls me. I mean it."

As the back door shuts behind them, Zeph laughs bitterly. "*Make sure your Doc calls me.* Fella thinks everybody in the world got their own phone." He hollers at the door. "This ain't no Waldorf, son!"

✦ ✦ ✦

Nazan and Spencer blink as their eyes adjust to the bright sunshine. They join Gibson and Chastity, and Spencer delights them with his impression of a boxing kangaroo.

Nazan looks at the portrait again, now able to truly see it. It's a young woman with long hair, but she has to admit, it could be nearly any woman. She sighs. It's a portrait of a lady, all right—any lady.

She begins to fold the paper and put it away when something

catches her eye. Just a speck, probably a stray ink spot. Right above the left eyebrow.

A mole.

Spencer touches her elbow. "Let's get going, yes?"

"But wait," Nazan says. "Look at the—"

"Come along, Miss Celik. We'll admire your *portrait* another time."

Nazan looks up at Magruder's shabby building. "Yes," she says resolutely. "Another time for sure."

✦ ✦ ✦

Back at his post, Zeph tries to return his mind to Du Bois, but he can't concentrate. Did he really tell Miss Nazan that their Fiji mermaid is a fake? It's one thing to explain how shrunken heads are made—that only increases interest. But warning *against* paying to see a gaff?

He sighs, yanking off his gloves in defeat. "I gotta stop talking to pretty girls."

THE TINY FAVOR

⌘

"T HAT'S ALL?"

Kitty and Archie stand in the public area of the Manhattan Beach
Hotel. The wide corridor is dotted with shops—a ladies' hair salon,
a barber shop, a florist. Kitty's stomach is aflutter at being in this hotel
again. "I should tell you I was tossed out of this hotel a few days ago."

Archie laughs. "I'm impressed! But don't worry, you'll be fine.
It's not the hotel that concerns us; it's that establishment there." He
points at one shop in particular: Pearson's Fine Art and Collectibles.

Kitty looks at Archie again. "That's all you want?"

He smiles. "That's all I want. Go in, do as I told you, say what I
told you, and then? We'll enjoy a fine meal."

Kitty's stomach roars at the thought. She is about to open
Pearson's door when a young man passes by. Kitty recognizes him
immediately. He's dressed in street clothes, not the bellhop uniform
in which she'd met him earlier, but his freckles and wayward red hair
are unmistakable. "Excuse me," she says. "Seamus? Seamus?"

The young man turns, and his face somersaults from recognition to disbelief to something much like horror. "Err…I'm sorry,
miss," he stammers, backing away. "You must have mistaken me for
someone else?"

Kitty grabs his arm. "You're Seamus… You had a name tag.
I remember. You brought our bags up to our room. You must
remember! It was just a few days ago. Surely you—"

"I'm sorry, miss," he says, backing away. "I don't know you? We've never met?" His Belfast accent turns even the simplest statements into questions.

"But—"

"No! No, I don't know you." He looks at her sadly. "I'm sorry? I can't help you?" He flees.

Kitty calls after him. "But, Seamus, please! I've nowhere else to turn! Seamus!"

"That's enough," Archie says sharply. "Don't make a scene. Go do as you're told." He nudges her roughly toward the door of the art gallery.

Kitty watches Seamus disappear into the crowd. She sighs. "All right, I'm going." She takes a deep breath and reaches for the door. But as she opens it, she catches a glimpse of her reflection in the glass. *Good Lord.*

She's sunburned, for starters. And not a lovely, holiday-in-Sardinia sort of sunburned. Her skin is splotchy and red, and the skin on her nose is starting to peel. Her eyes are bloodshot, her lips are chapped, and her long, blond locks are "braided" only in the most charitable sense. She'd hide the whole catastrophe with her hat, but she seems to have lost it somewhere. She's trying to remember where she left it—did she have it at the ferry?—when Archie hisses "Go on!" and shoves her across the threshold.

The walls of the narrow art gallery are crowded with dreamy visions of seaside holidays: delicate young ladies in bathing costumes, hearty young men piloting sailboats, suntanned children building sand castles.

A polished gentleman in a fine suit approaches, sizing her up. Kitty freezes, and her stomach flips over. He knows. She can see it written on his face: she looks less like an art collector and more like a Bedlam escapee, and *he knows.* Next, he'll toss her out, and Archie will abandon her, and she'll either starve to death or be eaten alive by the tattooed wolves that hunt Surf Avenue. Or he'll call the police, and next will be jail and then deportation, shipped back to London in a steerage container full of rats...

But then she thinks, *Dinner rolls*. Might as well give Archie's plan a go. In seventeen years, she's never had so little to lose.

"I'm terribly sorry to trouble you," she says pitifully. "I've no wish at all to—"

The man tilts his head curiously. "You're English?"

"Yes. My name is Katherine Hayward." Archie had advised that she use her real name; he said it would add authenticity to her voice. But her voice still catches a bit as she stands on the precipice of reciting Archie's first lie. "Of the…Cornwall…Haywards? My father is in railroads. I assume you've heard of him?"

The man's eyes widen, his suspicion morphing into obsequiousness. "Of course, of course, the great Hayward family. Jewel in the crown of Britain's transit system. Who hasn't heard of them? I am Edward Pearson, at your service."

Relief washes over her, and Kitty struggles not to laugh. *Is it really going to be this easy?* "My parents have taken a house out in Sea Gate."

Pearson smiles. "How delightful! I do hope you enjoy our modest accommodations. Would you care for some tea?"

"I couldn't…"

"I insist." He smiles even wider.

Kitty is gobsmacked. "Tea? Well…all right. Why not?"

Pearson guides Kitty to a seating area in the back of the gallery. He arranges her in an overstuffed chair, calls to an assistant for some tea with lemon, and settles down beside her. "So tell me, Miss Hayward, how might Pearson's Fine Art and Antiques be of assistance?"

"You see, Mr. Pearson—oh, thank you!" A young shop assistant has appeared with a cup of tea and a few cookies. "You see, this home we've let for the summer is lovely. A bit smaller than I'm used to, of course."

Mr. Pearson brays his understanding. "Of course. American architecture cannot possibly hope to offer the sophistication of what you are accustomed to back home. Still, the weather is lovely by the seaside, and one must make do, mustn't one?"

"Exactly, Mr. Pearson. And truly, it is a charming home, absolutely charming. Unfortunately, the decor of the place…"

"Mmm-hmm?"

"Well, it's not quite up to our standards. No offense intended, of course." She nibbles on a cookie, forbidding herself to swallow it in one bite.

"My dear, none taken! Indeed, that is precisely why Pearson's Fine Art exists! We understand that our visitors have much more sophisticated tastes than the average American."

"My mother is of a rather sensitive disposition, you see, and some of the artwork in this home we've rented is…a bit…"

"Of course!" he says. "Here at Pearson's, we specialize in providing soothing, relaxing images for refined customers. Here, let me show you. I have a portfolio of all our best work right in the—"

"But you see, Mr. Pearson," Kitty says, "I'm afraid my parents have rather unique tastes."

"How so?"

"They'll only be truly comfortable with art that resembles their own collection back home."

"*Of course*, I understand completely. Whatever their tastes, Pearson's can—"

"Dutch Masters."

Pearson nearly spits out his Darjeeling. "What?"

"Rembrandt, Vermeer…" Kitty struggles to remember the other names Archie had told her to say. "Umm, Hall, is it?"

"Frans Hals," Pearson says miserably.

"Right, Frans Hals. Busty washerwomen, men in large hats… everything lit via that same window on the left. That sort of thing." The first sugar to hit Kitty's system in days makes her giddy. "By the way, why are the windows on the left?"

"I'm sure I don't know, Miss Hayward."

"So," she says, starting in on her second cookie. "Got anything like that?"

Pearson glances at his gallery walls—a cacophony of tasteful seascapes with nary a washerwoman in sight. But then he remembers a large painting covered in newspaper, tucked at the back of the shop. "In fact, I may have just the thing…"

✶ ✶ ✶

Ten minutes later, Kitty has finished her tea and several additional cookies. She shakes Pearson's hand and assures him that her father will visit the shop at closing time in order to purchase a Dutch Master for a healthy sum.

Kitty meets Archie as planned in the lobby of the hotel.

"Well?" he asks eagerly. "How did it go?"

"Fine, I think? He can't wait to sell some horrible painting to my nonexistent father."

Archie smiles. "Excellent. Wait here while I pay Mr. Pearson a visit."

"I don't understand," she says. "How does this earn me lunch?"

He leans over and whispers, "As luck would have it, a few days ago, I brought Pearson a painting of men in large hats, lit from the left. He assured me it was utterly out of fashion, that there was no market for it. I told him to keep it for a while and think it over, and if he still felt he couldn't sell it, I would be more than happy to take the painting away and never trouble him again." Archie straightens his tie. "Something tells me Mr. Pearson may have altered his thinking on the subject." He takes three steps toward the gallery but turns back. "Once I am paid and you are fed and everything is in its right place, you and I are going to have a chat about that young fellow Seamus."

CHAPTER

★ ★

7

MISSGEBURTEN

❦

THE RACE TO DEATH IS ABOUT TO BEGIN. SPECTATORS LINE UP OUTSIDE Magruder's, and Zeph stands by the door in his cart, taking their dimes and directing them to the back room. He collects admission from respectable ladies in summer bonnets with their escorts in straw hats. He makes change for a trio of shopgirls and a gaggle of sunburned teenagers. He exchanges gossip with some Moon Maidens from Steeplechase Park; they've found themselves with a free afternoon after the Trip to the Moon ride was unexpectedly shuttered for the day. And he greets an elderly couple, unmistakably foreign in their heavy wool coats. The husband struggles to understand American money, while his wife sweats aggressively into her striped scarf.

Zeph smiles. "You might take your scarf off, ma'am. No cooler inside, that's for sure."

"*Was ist los?*" the husband demands suspiciously.

"The…uh…" Zeph starts to point at the scarf but thinks better of it. "Never mind. Enjoy the show. Follow the others around to the back."

Finally, lurking like a vulture waiting for the lions to finish their dinner, a scarred and scowling fellow with only one arm arrives. "What in hell are you doing here?" Zeph demands.

Joe holds out a dime. "Here to see the show, just like anybody."

"I told you, Timur ain't helping with your—"

"I want to see the show. I swear, the Race to Death is all I'm interested in."

"Yeah, that's what worries me." But he sighs and takes Joe's dime. "All right, go on back. Don't blow nothing up while you're back there."

Zeph is about to close Magruder's heavy door when he hears a familiar voice.

"Hey, wait for us!"

Zeph smiles to see a small old friend with a tall, young companion. "Hey, Chief! Come on in, brother!"

Whitey Lovett is the fire chief of Lilliputia, the little people's village at Dreamland. He stands four feet, two inches in lifts, which he wears in direct defiance of Dreamland's policy that little people remain as little as they can possibly be. With piercing blue eyes and a fashionable walrus mustache, Whitey has a richly earned reputation as the biggest ladies' man in Coney Island. This afternoon, he's accompanied by a willowy blond who Zeph vaguely recognizes as a fortune-teller from Luna Park. He can't remember her name, and he knows better than to ask Whitey, as there's little chance he remembers it either.

They all exchange pleasantries, but Whitey's expression quickly turns serious. "Was that who I think it was?"

"Who? You mean Joe? You recognized him from all the way over—"

Whitey nods. "He's Black Hand, you know."

"Yeah, and?"

"Is he recruiting?"

Zeph laughs. "Me? Nah."

"Good. Unusuals can't afford to be anarchists, Zeph. Look at me—I'm a dwarf and a Jew. You're a Negro and legless. Add 'anarchist' and you've got the Trifecta of Fucked. Don't do it."

"Don't worry."

"All right. See you inside, my friend."

✳ ★ ✳

The stage, such as it is, is an elevated platform made from an old bed frame. The frame is set at about waist height, and it sits atop complex machinery—gears and levers and pulleys—like the honeymoon bed of a mad watchmaker. Ringing the edges of the bed are handheld magnifying glasses, attached to the structure by long chains. What used to be the headboard is painted with a large—and not half bad, if Zeph does say so himself—mural of the Palace of Versailles in France, with its thousands of windows. At the foot, a second mural faces the first—the comparatively modest Royal Palace of Madrid. A red velvet curtain is laid out across the bed, obscuring everything else from view. P-Ray scuttles around and underneath the platform, finalizing his preparations.

Zeph motors into the room in his cart and parks by the headboard. "All right, little man? We ready?"

P-Ray's head pops up at the foot of the bed, and he nods.

"Everyone!" Zeph calls the audience to attention. "Please, gather round. Come in close, and grab yourself one of them magnifying glasses. You don't want to miss nothing. C'mere, Chief. You can watch from up here by me, if you like."

Whitey pulls himself up onto Zeph's cart, his beautiful fortune-teller standing beside him. The rest of the crowd assembles in a circle around the platform, each holding a magnifying glass up to one eye. "You are about to witness a reenactment in miniature of the infamous road race from France to Spain. Twentieth-century gladiators facing off in the modern arena of the open road. More than two hundred took part in that doomed race last year. Who survived? Who perished? Ladies and gentlemen, Theophilus P. Magruder's Theatron Prodigium presents the Paris–Madrid Race of 1903. Or, as the papers called it, the *Race to Death*." He winks at P-Ray. "Okay, kid. Do your stuff."

P-Ray runs to the headboard and turns a crank, which eases the red curtain off the bed to reveal the landscape separating Versailles and Madrid—seven-hundred-plus miles of countryside rendered in miniature. Green felt for grass, blue for water, brown for sand and dirt.

Rolling hills dotted with little wire trees and shrubs, with a line of tiny flags marking the border between the countries. A winding gray road connects the two palaces. It stretches up hills and down valleys, twists sharply right and left, through towns, over bridges, across borders. Scattered along the route are collections of tiny black specks. The crowd leans in, squinting through their magnifying glasses.

Fleas. Dozens of fleas.

Each flea is in costume. There's a French pastry chef flea, with a white apron and puffy hat. A pair of flamenco dancer fleas in dramatic black-and-red outfits. A soldier flea, a priest flea, a little old lady flea, a mother flea pushing a baby carriage. A flea dressed as Émile Loubet, the president of France, and one dressed as Alfonso XIII, king of Spain. Photographer fleas with tiny cameras at the ready, and firemen fleas on little red trucks. One sad old flea costumed as a town drunk.

They are arranged in clumps at various points along the gray road—witnesses to the coming horror. The human audience stares down at the insect one. The fleas waggle their little legs in the air.

"Wait a minute," one of the teenagers says. "They're alive?"

Whitey's date casts him a worried glance. "They won't come after us, will they?"

"No," Whitey assures her. "Of course not. They…" He pauses, feeling the sudden need to scratch. He turns to Zeph. "They won't…right?"

"Don't worry," Zeph replies with a smile. "The costumes are attached to the board…keeps 'em pretty well tethered."

One of the respectable gentlemen huffs and itches. "Pretty well, eh?"

"More or less," Zeph says with a wink.

Joe the anarchist chortles into his single sleeve. "I love this place."

P-Ray scuttles underneath the bed, and soon a small motor whirs to life. Then he runs back to the headboard and pulls another lever. A panel in the headboard slides open, and four cars smaller than matchboxes roll forward. Each has a tiny flea driver and a tiny flea engineer, all wearing tiny hats and goggles.

Zeph claps. "Here come the starting cars. There are several French drivers in our opening lineup today. On the far left, Marcel Renault in a car his brother designed, and beside him, a second French driver, Charles Jarrott. Next to Jarrott is Camille du Gast, one of the first ladies to earn a driver's license—"

"The beginning of the end," Whitey intones, and his date smacks him playfully.

"—and that fourth car is driven by none other than William Vanderbilt, of the illustrious Vanderbilt family."

Joe spits on the floor. "May they rot in hell."

"P-Ray, a little racing music, if you please."

P-Ray hustles to the corner. Beside Robonocchio's cabinet sits Timur's homemade orchestrion, a silver player piano rigged with a kettle drum, two flutes, cymbals, and a triangle. The boy pulls a lever, and the machine shudders. The kettle drum pounds, and the cymbals crash as the orchestrion floods the room with a sarcastically happy tune—surely the most chipper version of Chopin's Funeral March ever played. Timur programmed it himself; it's the only evidence Zeph has ever seen that the Doc might possess a sense of humor. *Dum, dum, da dum, dum da dum, da dum, da dum* (*ting!* goes the triangle).

Zeph reaches into a small drawer in his cart and removes a starter pistol. He holds it up. "Ready, set...and as they say in Versailles, *allons-y!*"

Bang! Zeph fires the pistol, and the audience jumps. He gazes at them happily. *Startled and itchy*, he thinks. *Just how we like 'em at Magruder's*.

The cars toddle down the road, little puffs of smoke rising from their engines. And no sooner have those four cars begun their journey than four more appear at the headboard and start down the track as well, followed by four more and four more.

Zeph continues his narration as the cars chug along the track. "Ah, Monsieur Renault has taken an early lead. You know, the Renault car is capable of reaching an astonishing ninety miles per hour."

A Moon Maiden gasps. "Isn't that dangerous?"

"Well," Zeph says with a smile, "we don't call it Race to Tea and Crumpets, now, do we?"

He gives P-Ray a tiny nod, and the boy pushes another lever. Suddenly, one of the cars in the middle of the pack skids out. It flips over twice, sparks shoot out of the engine courtesy of a small firecracker in the back, and the car bursts into flames. Oncoming cars swerve to avoid the crash. One miscalculates and hits a tree.

"No!" Zeph cries. "Our first incident! I'm so sorry, that's a German driver down." He addresses the last to the old couple. The husband smiles politely, but the woman doesn't respond. She daubs at her wet face with her scarf, looking as though she'd rather be anywhere else.

Zeph gives P-Ray a subtle wink, and this time, a small panel in the road flips over, revealing a flea dressed as a small child, holding a tiny red balloon. "Look!" Zeph shouts. "An innocent child has wandered into the road! Whatever shall we do?"

P-Ray pulls a string, which drags the brave soldier flea into the road to rescue the child, just as a car veers around the bend. The child flea goes flying into the shrubbery, but the soldier can't escape in time. Car and soldier tumble down a tiny hillside in a puff of smoke.

"Oh dear," Zeph says. "The ultimate sacrifice."

Joe bangs his sole hand against the bed frame by way of applause. The German lady starts murmuring, and her body starts to quiver. Zeph watches carefully—occasionally, you get a bad reaction to killing a soldier, even a six-legged one.

"Tragic but historically accurate," he says quickly. "Look now! Camille du Gast has stopped her car to provide first aid! Isn't that the most noble—"

The German lady cries out, her body stiffens, and she falls face-first onto the track. The audience backs away from the bed fearfully—*is this part of the show?*—except for Joe, who leans in, fascinated.

As her husband tries to peel her off the bed, the German lady moans and convulses. She smashes the platform with her face, her hands, her heaving body. Trees are crushed, cars sent flying. P-Ray screams and starts to cry. He tries to rescue his pets, but Zeph pulls him back, afraid the boy will end up on the wrong end of the woman's flailing sausage fists. She foams at the mouth, and white spittle sloshes over the little gray road.

Then, as quickly as it began, the seizure ends. The woman lies in the middle of the miniature landscape, panting and sobbing. The audience stands in shocked silence while the orchestrion sings away heedlessly. *Dum, dum, da dum, dum da dum, da dum, da dum. Ting!*

"My word," Whitey says. "I do believe the German has flattened Barcelona! International incident, for sure."

"You're not funny," his date mutters.

The spell broken, the rest of the audience retreats: from the back room, from the Cabinet, as far from this lousy part of town as possible. As they file out, P-Ray rushes around the bed, trying to collect his fleas. But like the humans, most of them have fled.

Whitey offers to fetch an ambulance for the sick woman. The husband says, "*Nein, nein.*" Zeph and Whitey object, but the old German is stubborn and angry—as though Magruder's were somehow to blame for his wife's episode.

"*Ich sagte nein!* We go to hotel!" He takes off his coat and puts it around his wife as he drags her off the bed and into a standing position. "*Wir brauchen keine Hilfe aus einer Gruppe von gottverdammten Missgeburten!*"

"What was that now?" Working for Timur has provided Zeph with a wide variety of experiences—being insulted in foreign tongues is one of his least favorite.

Whitey turns to his date. "You're vaguely Prussian, aren't you? Did you get any of that?"

"Ah…" She hesitates. "*Gottverdammten* is, ah, *goddamned*. And *Missgeburten* is…*freaks*."

"Right!" Whitey says brusquely. "No ambulance for you!" He pulls his fortune-teller to the door. "Enjoy your doom, *mein herr*. Zeph, I'll stop by later."

Zeph goes to P-Ray and rubs his back as the little boy sobs. "Shh, it's okay, little man. Machines get fixed. Fleas get found. Don't worry… It's okay."

Joe looms over them. He's holding one of the smashed-up cars in his hand, and an eerie expression plays across his face. "Quite a show," he says. "You should charge more."

8

CANTILEVER

R EAL RAT ORCHESTRA! REALLY REAL RATS!"
Kitty and Archie pick their way along Surf Avenue, past
the many independent operators plying their trade in the
nooks and crannies between the major parks. Shooting galleries
and catchpenny games and crayon portraitists. Hot pretzels, cold
beer, three chances at a prize for one thin dime. In the distance, a
brass band plays.

Kitty pauses at the painted banner. Beneath the lettering is a
picture of a chamber orchestra comprised of eerily chipper rats with
big, black eyes. She turns to Archie. "Really real rats?"

"They're really real, all right. Really dead. Taxidermied rodents
with violas and sousaphones, with Schubert playing on a Victrola in
the background. Care to see?"

"The image you've painted is plenty."

They continue. Kitty stops at a booth with an elaborate display
of china settings—a perfectly Victorian sitting room crowded with
dinner and salad plates, cups and saucers, sugar bowls and creamers,
all painted in demure blue and white. She reads the sign. "Can't
Smash Up Your House? Smash Up Ours! Four balls for five cents!"

A man in a white suit and straw hat pops his head around the
booth. "Afternoon, miss! Care to have a go? Release your frustra-
tions with the modern age!"

"But…it seems such a waste."

"Don't be coy, child." Archie hands the man a nickel. "Aim for the teapot with Queen Victoria on the front. It'll do you good."

Kitty's first ball goes low, not even worrying the dishes.

Archie scoffs. "Surely you've more spirit than—"

She fires her second ball into a serving platter with a picture of Buckingham Palace, which shatters delightfully. The shards take out teacups as they fall, which in turn knock down some dessert plates—a waterfall of destruction.

Kitty laughs. "What a wonderful sound!"

✱ ★ ✱

Twenty cents later, Kitty's had her fill of smashing china, so they continue past the Bowery. A crowd has gathered on one corner. "Well, well," Archie says. "Look who's here. Come—this you must see." He elbows his way through the crowd, maneuvering himself and Kitty to the front. "Feast your eyes, Miss Hayward."

She looks, then blinks a few times, then looks again. No. Yes. Can't be. Really?

In front of Kitty is a young woman of Asian descent in a voluminous black robe, embroidered in gold, with long, wide sleeves. She wears a cylindrical hat wrapped in multicolored ribbons and edged with ivory beads that dangle down her face. Her eyes are closed, her expression one of purest relaxation. Her right hand holds an intricately carved walking stick with a dragon's head at the top, while her left hand rests serenely in her lap. She sits cross-legged...hovering about three feet off the ground.

Kitty turns to Archie. "Is she...?"

"I certainly don't know. Do *you* think she is?"

New York audiences are a voluble bunch, but this crowd stands silent, a mixture of awe and disbelief playing across their faces. Finally one brave—or just obnoxious—soul steps forward to run his hand along the space between the girl's robes and the ground.

He reports his findings with a shrug. "Ain't nothin' under her."

People shake their heads and whisper.

"Of course there isn't," says a young man. Kitty was so taken with the girl, she hadn't even noticed she had an assistant nearby. "Ladies and gentlemen," he says, "in this city of hucksters and frauds, you are the fortunate witnesses of a true act of spiritual majesty. May I present Yeshi Rinpoche, holy priestess of Tibet."

"Ha!" Archie snorts. "Rinpoche, my eye!"

"Rinpoche?" Kitty asks.

"A Rinpoche, my dear, is a highly respected teacher of Buddhism." He takes a step forward. "If this scalawag is a Rinpoche, I'm a llama. The four-legged kind."

The levitating girl tilts her head, causing the beads along her face to rattle slightly. Her assistant nods. "I'm sorry," he says to the crowd, "but we must end our demonstration. Yeshi Rinpoche cannot possibly continue in such a *hostile* environment. We hope our demonstration has intrigued you and that we will see you soon at West Eighth Street, where Her Holiness is available for spiritual consultations."

Archie chuckles. "Ahh, so that's her game. I was wondering."

The disappointed crowd disperses, and the assistant opens up a trifold screen, placing it in front of the girl so she can leave her trance in privacy.

A moment later, she bursts through the canvas and storms up to Archie. "What in *hell* is your problem?"

He bows low. "Your Holiness…"

"Oh, shut up. I've got a right to make a living, you know."

"You were making a perfectly fine living with me, as I recall."

"No, Archibald, I was making a perfectly fine living *for* you. Very different." She notices Kitty. "Who is this, then? Found a new pigeon, have you?"

"This is Miss Kitty Hayward, recently of London. Miss Hayward, may I present the most celestial Yeshi Rinpoche, formerly known as Yeshi Lowenstein."

Kitty coughs. "I'm sorry? Lowenstein?"

"Archie here loves to imply that I'm a fraud, but I am actually from Tibet. But we Tibetans don't have surnames. So when I arrived in America, I borrowed the surname of the people in line ahead of me."

Archie smiles. "My practical girl."

She frowns. "I'm not *your girl*, Archibald. Not anymore. My brother and I make our own way." She points to her assistant, chatting up the crowd and passing out business cards. "That's him. Tenzin."

Kitty raises an eyebrow. "Tenzin…Lowenstein."

Archie laughs. "I love America! Miss Lowenstein, if you please, Miss Hayward and I had a rather profitable morning. Would you and Mr. Lowenstein care to join us for lunch?"

"We're too busy, no thanks to you." Yeshi glances at Kitty disdainfully. "Mind yourself around the old man here. If he tells you how many fingers you have, count them anyway." She stalks off toward her brother, but Kitty stops her.

"Please, wait. The levitation. How is it done? I must know."

Yeshi smiles. She stretches her out her arms, and her long sleeves brush the sidewalk. "I am Her Holiness Yeshi Lowenstein, the first American Rinpoche. I can do anything."

✦ ★ ✦

The trout stares vacantly up at Kitty. *You don't scare me*, she thinks. *I'm so hungry, if you sat up and begged for your life, I'd eat you anyway.*

The unlikely companions attack their platters. Archie and Kitty are seated in one of Feltman's numerous outdoor dining areas. The court-yard is bordered by high trellises on three sides, with lanterns strung along the top. The trellises create the illusion that diners are gathered in an intimate environment where they were terribly lucky to get a table—rather than in the three-acre behemoth that is Feltman's, serving thousands of patrons every night from its many kitchens.

Feltman's menu is itself a marvel of mixed signals, with French cuisine competing for attention with sausages and hot dogs for fifteen cents each. "Bratwurst versus meunière," Archie muses. "It's the Franco-Prussian War on a plate. Of course, we'd be eating even higher off the hog if Pearson had done right by us. You should have heard the greedy little muskrat. 'Boohoo, this painting will sit in my warehouse for months, la la la,' all the while licking his chops over the image of your father's big, fat wallet. I had to take the painting halfway out the door before he raised the offer to a hundred bucks. Meanwhile, Pearson stands to collect *ten times* that amount."

Kitty raises an eyebrow. "But he won't collect one thousand dollars. In fact, he just *lost* one hundred dollars."

"Pearson, as far as he knew, was about to earn the easiest grand of his entire pointless life."

"As far as he knew."

"Yes, as far as he knew."

"You're angry because you *only* stole one hundred dollars? That's a great deal of money!"

"Aren't we Miss Morality all of a sudden? You're welcome to send back the fish, you know, if you're troubled by this terrible stealing."

Kitty grins and takes another bite. "Fair enough."

Archie removes his napkin from his lap and tosses it on the table. Leaning back in his chair, he removes the pipe from his jacket and lights it. "So, now that we've dined, tell me about Seamus. Why is he so important?"

Kitty glances at Archie; he's got that look again—that weighing, measuring look. She puts down her fork. "I don't expect you'll believe it."

"Try me."

Rather than answer, she looks around the courtyard. A few tables over, two young parents struggle to get a few bites of hot dog into their rambunctious, ketchup-smeared children. Next to them, an older man sits alone, coughing violently into his handkerchief— nearby diners give the old man the stink eye, but he ignores them and keeps on coughing. Immediately to Kitty's right, a pair of young lovers make eyes at each other over their beers, while to her left, an elderly couple consumes bratwurst in stony silence. Not a soul on Feltman's three acres has the slightest interest in Kitty's problems. Except Archie.

All right, she thinks. *Nothing to lose.* "I arrived in New York three days ago, on a steamer from Cape Town."

"South Africa? That's exotic. Why ever were you there?"

"My mother and I sailed there to see my brother. He served in the conflict with the Boers and—"

"Oh, he's joining the Boer War show, of course! *That's* what brought you here. I might have guessed."

Kitty frowns. "I don't understand."

"Out at New Brighton Beach! There are a thousand veterans involved. They reenact the war every afternoon—ten cents a person, not a bad seat in the house. Thrill to the exploits of General Cronjé, Buffalo Bill of the Transvaal! Yes?" Kitty's appalled expression tells Archie he's turned down a blind conversational alley. "Boer War show…very popular…no?"

"I'm afraid not," she says coolly. "I must confess, I find the notion of a Boer War *show* to be in poor taste."

"Welcome to New York, kid. All right, carry on with your yarn."

She takes a deep breath and another bite of trout to collect herself. "His service had ended, and we went to fetch him. Nate was determined we move to America, you see. Father died years ago, so it was just the three of us. I wanted to start university, but the fees were atrocious. Nate didn't get the placement he wanted at an architecture firm, and… Anyway, it's not important. The point is, things all started to fall apart. As they do."

Archie sings, "*Ol-i-gar-chy ain't what she used to be, ain't what she used to be…*"

Kitty grimaces. "In any case, Nate resolved we should make a go of it in America. What a lovely new life we would start, the streets paved with gold and so forth. But you see…" She pauses to peel off the trout's cheek with her fork—the most flavorful part of the fish, Kitty had been saving the cheek for last, for when she really needed it. "There are these Boer men—bitter-enders, they're called—who wouldn't accept that they'd lost the war. They disappeared into the…I don't know, the *veldt*, I suppose. Periodically, they'd blow something up or shoot someone. And…a few days before my mother and I arrived, the bitter-enders staged an attack."

"Uh-oh."

"We arrived from England only to learn that Nate… They attacked in the middle of the night, and he…well…he was…"

The words stop.

"Child," Archie says quietly. "I'm sorry. Teasing aside. Is this how you came to be on the bench? Because of what happened to your brother?"

Kitty blinks hard and looks at her plate. The trout bones swim again before her wet eyes. "I wish it were that simple. After they told us…my only thought was to get back to London. Have a funeral. It's what one does, isn't it?" She looks up at Archie. "Isn't that what one does?"

"People do all kinds of things, I suppose."

"That's well said. Because what Mum wanted to do—what she insisted we do—is to follow through with Nate's plan. *It was his last wish to go to New York*, she kept saying. So we sailed here anyway. Here," Kitty says distastefully. "Some American resort, of all ridiculous places."

"So here you are in this admittedly ridiculous place, with… Oh! Not with your brother in tow, I don't suppose?"

"The army intended to bury Nate right there in Cape Town! Sink him in the same ground where his killers still walk. Does that make any sense at all?"

He shrugs. "It might, if I was paying for the shipping."

"Mum wasn't having it. She said, 'Nathan wanted to be buried in New York, and we shall see to it.' Of course, Nate wanted to *see* New York before he was buried here! Instead, his body is just sitting on the *Arundale*, out in the harbor!"

"Meanwhile, you've taken up residence on a public bench, and your mother is where?"

"My mother is…" Kitty's voice cracks. It's one thing to think a thought but quite another to speak it, to make it real. "I can't… I'm sorry… I just…" She holds her napkin in front of her face, struggling not to make a scene.

"Miss Hayward, tell me what happened. Even if it hurts, do it anyway. Where is your mother? Does that kid Seamus know where she is? He knows something, doesn't he? Be a brave girl, now. Take a deep breath and tell me."

She breathes as best she can. And she tells him.

CHAPTER

★ ★

9

FLAMINGOS
DON'T LIE

∝❦∝

T O THE LEFT OF THE BIG OAK ENTRANCE TO MAGRUDER'S, THERE IS A SECOND
door, this one unmarked. Through that door and down some
stairs lies a part of the Cabinet that few Normals ever see. There,
in the basement of Magruder's Curiosity Cabinet, is Zeph's true
home: Magruder's Unusual Tavern.

From behind the bar, Zeph looks up at the sound of footsteps
on the stairs. "Ah! Afternoon, Maestro! How'd it go last night?
Everything explode okay?"

"Meh," the man says. "*Così così.*" Enzo Morrone has a body like
a barrel and looks far older than his thirty-two years. The left side of
his face is purpled and leathery, scarred over from some ancient, fiery
accident. A bushy mustache stretches across his bicolored face like a
train track running from a good neighborhood to a bad one.

"Enzo, switch the plugs on that old beast, would ya? There's an
afternoon show at the Oriental I want to hear."

Enzo nods, crossing to a squat wooden cabinet in the far corner
of the room. Once an icebox, it now accommodates something very
different. It's a box of sound.

Enzo flips the latch to open the box's front door. Inside, a disor-
ganized tangle of cords, keys, and jacks is a mad-scientist version of
the telephone switchboards being installed all over town.

"Which channel you want?"

"Oriental Hotel ballroom…I think it's channel six?"

The icebox speakers spit and burp as Enzo manipulates the cords and keys. After a few moments, a man's disembodied voice dances its way through the receiver.

"Come, listen all you gals and boys.
Ise just from Tuckyhoe;
I'm goin' to sing a little song.
My name's Jim Crow."

"Wrong!" Zeph shouts. "That's the whorehouse on West Eighth. Try channel seven."

Enzo nods again and yanks the cords out, silencing the minstrel show. "Should I ask," he says as he works, "why you give to some whorehouse a channel?"

Zeph laughs. "They got a fella there plays ragtime who's pretty good, but only on the weeknights. Weekends, they got that other shit."

When Enzo has finally adjusted the receiver to the new channel, the room fills with angels singing in close harmony.

"If I get there before you do
Coming for to carry me home
I'll cut a hole and pull you through
Coming for to carry me home."

"*That's* what I meant." Zeph is smiling now. "That's my Fisk Jubilee Singers—hometown boys and girls from back in Tennessee. *Grazie*, Enzo."

"*Di niente.*" He saunters to the bar and hefts himself onto a stool. "*Ciao*, Signorina Rosalind."

Perched two stools down, Rosalind smiles for Enzo but does not turn his way. "*Ciao*, Maestro."

Enzo removes his bowler and hands it to Zeph, who hangs it on the corner of the large, gilt mirror behind the bar. Without needing to be asked, Zeph fills a small glass with green-tinted liquid from the faucet of an enormous samovar. He sends the glass skating down the bar to Enzo, who reaches out and snatches the glass just before it topples over the edge. Enzo downs the drink in one swallow and slides it back to Zeph, who grins and fills it again. This time, he rolls himself down the bar to deliver the drink in person. Zeph sits atop a platform that's attached to the bar and has casters at the bottom, enabling him to practically fly from one end of the bar to the other.

"Zeph, when do you make the proper music on that icebox? Caruso! Caruso, he would class this place."

Zeph grins at his friend. "First of all, ain't nothing *not* proper about my Jubilee Singers, so you just watch yourself. Second, you wanna hear Caruso, you get on over to the Metropolitan Opera House and buy a ticket just like everybody else. Doc's receiver only picks up sound within a couple-mile radius."

"Well, make bigger the signal!"

"I'll just magically make *bigger* the signal for you, shall I?"

"*Sì*! Give one of the…uh, *come si dice*, the little boxes…"

"Transmitters."

"*Sì*, transmitter. Give transmitter to one of your friends who moves the scenery at the Met—"

Zeph shakes his head, laughing. "My *friends* at the opera? You overestimate me…"

"—and he hang transmitter right above Caruso's head. *Perfetto!*"

"How about Caruso comes out here to Coney, what do you say to that? He deigns to bless us with his presence, and I swear to God, I'll put a transmitter in his hat, just for you."

"Or," Rosalind interjects, "Enzo and I might venture into Manhattan one evening…"

Enzo grunts. "People like us, we no go to Metropolitan Opera House."

"Oh, I don't know." Rosalind takes Enzo's hand. "I think we clean up fairly well."

The unburned half of Enzo's face blushes, and he pulls his hand away. Stung, Rosalind says, "*Really?* Tell me, signore, just how many times do I have to shake your sheets before you'll hold my hand in an *empty* tavern?"

"Ach, is not so simple, Rosalind. You know this—"

"I know *you* think it isn't!"

Zeph leaps in to change the subject. "Hey, ah…how'd the new fireworks come off, Maestro? You were planning, what was it… chrysanthemums? Did they work?"

"Bah. I plan, I plan, but when rockets take the air, they do as they like. All over Steeplechase Park, they say *ooh, ah, oh*. They happy. But to me? Rockets look less like chrysanthemum in bloom, more like chrysanthemum squashed under horse."

"Sorry to hear it, brother. Guess it's rough all over these days."

Enzo looks up from his drink. "What does this mean?"

"We lost the Race to Death today. By which I mean, we actually lost it. Some ol' hausfrau had a fit, destroyed the entire topside. Gonna take weeks to rebuild."

"The people, they no deserve us, Zeph."

"Poor man," Rosalind says, more than a hint of sarcasm around the edges. "So cranky this afternoon."

"And you, what is this you wear?" Enzo points grouchily at Rosalind's dress—a roiling sea of iridescent green fabric with ivory-colored roses sewn into the bodice. "You look like peacock at Bostock's animal show."

"So I am, darling. Exotic bird, that's me."

Enzo grunts, and Rosalind arches an eyebrow.

"Maestro, if this face displeases you, would you prefer my other?"

"No, no. You should not look so loud, I am saying. Is no safe."

Rosalind's eyes narrow. "I don't recall giving you authority over how I—"

The tavern door opens, and Whitey Lovett stumbles down the stairs. He wears a fireman's uniform and holds a sopping handkerchief to his head. His face is covered with blood.

Rosalind gasps. "Whitey! You poor thing!"

The little man heads straight for the bar and climbs on a stool.

Rosalind moves to the one beside him. "Here, let me have a look. Zeph, is there a first aid kit?"

"Sure, it's in the office at the back. Enzo, would you mind—"

He is already standing. "*Sì*, on my way…"

Zeph hands Whitey a glass of green liquid. "I told you to stay away from Princess Rajah. Her manager don't like men coming around and—"

Whitey shakes his wounded head and winces. "No, no… It was Crumbly Pete."

Rosalind gasps anew. "For heaven's sake. What's he done now?"

Zeph looks at Rosalind. "You need to speak to that boy. He's out of control."

"Me? Why me?"

"You and Pete work together. You got history—"

"That doesn't mean he listens to me, Zeph! Pete doesn't listen to anyone."

Enzo returns with Magruder's excuse for a first aid kit—a crumpled shoe box with brass tweezers, a few lengths of dusty bandage, an empty aspirin bottle, and a tincture of iodine. "This, she is all I could find."

"It'll do, thank you." Rosalind takes the tweezers to Whitey's busted head. "This wound is full of glass! What did he hit you with?"

"*Che cazzo*!" Enzo says. "Who beat the midget?"

"Crumbly Pete," Zeph answers, and Enzo harrumphs his lack of surprise.

"Well." Whitey sighs. "It's like this. I'm on my way to work this morning. It's early—sun's just coming up."

"Is that so?" Zeph asks. "Whose bed were you sneaking out of?"

Whitey grins. "Nosy Parker. Anyway, the garbage men are cleaning up Surf Avenue. But it's strange, because there are dead rats everywhere. City must have done some kind of poison control, I guess? I'm tripping over the things, there's *that* many. I pass Steeplechase, and Pete jumps out. He's loitering by the entrance like he does. So yeah, crazy bastard startles me. But I don't want to look like a chump, so I says, 'Hey, Pete. How's about these rats, huh?' Guy just *glares* at me. He says, 'What about the rats?'

Now, I don't know what's going on with this lunatic. I'm just trying to get to work! So I made a joke. Not even a very good one. 'Well,' I says, 'I guess we know what today's special at Feltman's is gonna be.'"

Enzo chuckles. "Is not bad."

"Right? Thanks, Enzo. So I keep walking, and Pete calls after me. 'I'm gonna remember you said that, Whitey. I'm gonna remember.' What does that even mean?"

"It *means*, Whitey"—Rosalind picks some more glass out of his head—"that our Pete likes rats better than people."

"Well, the feeling is mutual."

"Stay still. I need to put on some antiseptic and a bandage."

"Sure," Whitey says, and then, "Ow! Dammit, that stings!"

"Sorry."

"Gah…anyway. So I go to work, put the rats out of my mind. Had a good day, lunch date with…um…a lovely lady…"

Zeph hoots. "I *knew* it! I knew you didn't know her name."

Whitey shrugs. "Hardly matters. I won't get another chance with her after that scene at the Race to Death today. Christ, Zeph, what was that? Anyway, after lunch, I go back to work, but they closed the park early. Something about disinfection—no idea why. So I'm walking back down Surf Avenue, past Steeplechase? Pete leaps out at me again! 'You think that's funny, do ya? All them poor rats poisoned, murdered in cold blood like that. It's just a big joke to you, huh? Well, this'll teach you to laugh at the dead!' And wham! Smacks a bottle of whiskey over my head. Then he's gone, and I'm standing there bleeding like an idiot."

"So," Rosalind says, "you came to the tavern? Not, oh, the first aid station at Steeplechase? Or Reception Hospital?"

Whitey sips his green elixir and grins. "Your point?"

Rosalind sighs and finishes the bandage.

"Say," Whitey says. "You folks hear about Count Orloff?"

"No," Zeph says. "What about him?"

"Dead."

Everyone gasps. "What?" Zeph asks. "No, I just saw him the other day!"

Whitey lifts his glass. "The Transparent Man is dead. Long live the Transparent Man. That was a hell of a show he put on. Miss Rosalind, did you see the new bit he added?"

Rosalind stiffens. "I *perform* in the sideshow. I do not attend it."

Whitey chuckles. "Well, you sure missed out this time. All right, so, you know his skin, right? All see-through? In his new show, they'd shine a *spotlight* on him. And you could watch the blood pumping through his veins—*bum bump, bum bump, bum bump*. From the heart, through the veins, all the way around. Incredible. You saw it, right, Zeph?"

Zeph smiles. "No, but I heard tell. Good and creepy, sounds like."

"Add that to the wasting disease...Orloff's limbs all withered and bendy? Poor son of a bitch. Me and Zeph here might be small, but at least they don't carry us around in a handbag."

"Stop being crude," Rosalind says, "and tell us what happened to him."

"I don't think they rightly know," Whitey says. "Apparently he woke up with a cough this morning. This afternoon? Dies screaming with these black lumps on his neck."

Rosalind grimaces. "He got sick and died in *one day*? Where did you hear this?"

"That cutie Susannah told me. You know her? The Flamingo Girl at Steeplechase, the one with her knees on backward?"

"I don't believe you."

"Hey, flamingos don't lie."

"I don't like it," Zeph mutters. "We got dead rats in the street, hausfraus having fits, now Orloff's gone? What's going on in this town?"

The drinkers and their bartender fall silent, and Zeph's hometown singers drift across the room like ghosts.

"Wade in the water
Wade in the water, children,
Wade in the water
God's gonna trouble the water."

10

ONLY IN
NEW YORK

∞

KITTY SITS IN A FLAT-BOTTOMED BOAT IN THE SKY.

Back in England, Nate the budding architect had bored her senseless with his stories about the size and scope of Manhattan: five-story buildings giving way to seven-story, to ten, fifteen, twenty. And the engineers weren't finished, Nate declared, not by a long shot.

"Only in New York!" he'd cried. "That's what they say! Only in New York do they sort out how to charge you for a piece of the sky."

Sitting at the top of Dreamland's Shoot the Chute ride, she feels her brother's enthusiasm tickle her spine. *Oh, Nate, if only you could see this.* But Archie, seated beside her, just looks irritated.

Their boat will sail down a track at a forty-five-degree angle, travel underneath a footbridge, and splash into a rectangular lake at the center of the park. Dreamland is arranged in a U-shape around the lake, and from her perch, Kitty can see crowds milling about the many attractions along the promenade. All the buildings are painted white, and the most remarkable one glares across at her from the far end of the lake—Beacon Tower, stretching almost four hundred feet into the sky.

Archie scowls down at the track. "They'd best not dampen my suit. This is bespoke, straight from Saville Row."

Kitty looks away, the better to hide her skepticism of that particular boast. After the ordeal at the restaurant, when Archie practically forced her to relate every excruciating detail of her last few days, he'd offered to take her to Dreamland. This was meant as a kindness, to take her mind off her troubles. But this much time spent with an older man she barely knows strains the limits of propriety, and Kitty is becoming concerned about what he's really after.

She told herself as they mingled with the crowds on the promenade that the strangers glancing their way saw nothing more than a pleasant father-and-daughter outing. But the occasional twinkle in their eyes, the odd hat tipped subtly in Archie's direction, made Kitty suspect that father and daughter was not precisely the relationship other people were picturing.

Still, she is hardly in a position to complain. What else can she do, go back to that bench?

She smiles at Archie cautiously, and then suddenly they're off, gliding straight down with wind whipping their hair and buildings flying by, all blending into one expanse of white with candy-pink sky overhead, and there's the footbridge right ahead of them, and it seems for a moment like it's all gone horribly wrong and they are about to crash, but then the boat dips a bit lower, and they sail under the bridge, plunged into total darkness for half a second before coming to a dramatic, splashy stop in the middle of the lake.

Archie is, indeed, rather wet. Cranky, he mutters that it's time to visit one of the beer sellers at the far end of the park. On their quest for refreshment, they pass the entrance to Lilliputia. Archie explains that inside the gate is a true-to-life version of the German city of Nuremberg but rendered in half size to suit its three hundred small residents. Lilliputia has its own "royal family," who travel in an elaborate carriage pulled by ponies, as well as its own police force and fire brigade. It has a beach with midget lifeguards, its own theater, its own farm—even its own laundry. "A Chinese midget doing French cuffs." Archie chuckles. "Have you ever heard the like, Miss Hayward?"

A giant strides past them in a natty pin-striped suit and beret. Archie calls to him. "Master Coyne!"

The giant squints down and smiles. "Archibald, how are you?"

He has an odd, echoing voice that seems to emanate from deep beneath his massive black shoes.

"I'm very well, aside from my damp suit! Allow me to introduce my companion, Miss Kitty Hayward. Miss Hayward, this is Bernard Coyne, tallest man in the known universe."

Kitty takes Bernard's badminton racket of a hand with both of hers. "Pleasure to meet you, Mr. Coyne."

"Pleasure is mine, miss. Although, I'm not the tallest man in the universe. Don't tell my boss, though." He winks down at her with one of his giant turtle eyes.

"On your way to Lilliputia?" Archie asks.

"Just leaving. I've got a date with a table girl from Koster's."

"You sly dog!" Archie goes to clap him on the back, but given Bernard's height, the gesture winds up as more of a slap on the rear.

"Mr. Coyne," Kitty says. "I'm terribly curious. What's *your* role in a place called Lilliputia?"

He laughs. "I loiter around and magnify the effect of the place."

"Bernard Coyne," Archie says, "making the small look smaller since 1897." He pumps Bernard's hand. "I wish you good fortune tonight, sir."

Bernard glances at Kitty one more time. "And *you*, sir. Pleasure to meet you, miss." The giant saunters off into the crowd.

"Doesn't have a chance in Hades with a table girl, the poor bastard," Archie muses. "Still. Good man, our Coyne." He steers Kitty back into the flow of traffic on the Dreamland concourse.

She stops abruptly. "Oh my," she says. "What on earth is *that*?"

Archie follows her gaze toward an open-fronted building with a white, brick facade. Perched on the roof is a demon, his massive wings stretching from one end of the building to the other. The demon leans over the roof, his sharp claws digging into the facade. His expression suggests he'd happily devour every human on the promenade and spit out their bones, if only he could be bothered to get up.

"That's Hell Gate. Silly, but the rubes seem to enjoy it. You pay your nickel and board a boat that runs along a track that's laid beneath a pool of water. Why so many rides in this blasted park involve getting wet is beyond me."

"You aren't wearing a corset," Kitty points out. "I confess, I welcome a little moisture now that it's warmed up so."

Archie nods. "Fair enough. Anyway, when the ride begins, the boats travel in circles, faster and faster, as though you're caught in a whirlpool. And you travel around and around, closer and closer to the abyss, and eventually the boats are sucked down into the very pit of hell!"

"That sounds terrifying!"

"Hardly. Just a chintzy stage set. Sad fact is, it doesn't take much to amuse most people. But this is what you need to understand: any good confidence game is built on two pillars—what people want and what they fear. At the gallery today, Pearson wanted money, and he wanted the satisfaction of knowing that snobby Brits patronize his establishment. And he feared looking like a fool who missed a big sales opportunity. People who plunk down for the Hell Gate ride—what do they want? A thrill? A good scare? Perhaps that's all it is. Or perhaps they fear, deep down, that there's nothing more to their existence than the fifty or sixty years they'll spend scrabbling around this benighted planet. Maybe they'll plunk down their hard-earned cash at Hell Gate just to feel, if only for a few minutes, that there's more to human experience. Once you understand what people yearn for as well as what terrifies them, you'll have them wrapped around those pretty fingers of yours."

Kitty shakes her head. "I'm sorry? Why would I want that?"

"You did well today," he says with a shrug. "At Pearson's. You did well. With a little education, you could do even better."

A loud siren pierces the air. Kitty covers her ears, but Archie claps delightedly. "Young Miss Hayward!" he says. "*This* you must see."

✦ ✦ ✦

The siren continues to blare, and Archie hustles Kitty down the sidewalk to yet another attraction. They dart through the entrance and are confronted with a five-story building of the sort common in New York's less desirable neighborhoods. Flames shoot out from the lower floors, and panicked residents lean out every open window, calling for help. A rapt audience crowds together on bleachers, but Archie urges Kitty up toward the front.

A sudden explosion ignites the third floor. People dangle out windows and cling to fire escapes, waving fruitlessly at the audience for assistance. A hook-and-ladder truck arrives; its telescoping ladder is leaned against the building, and a firefighter scrambles up to pull people from the higher floors. Meanwhile, other firefighters spread out a large net. One by one, the panicked residents leap from the building into the air. The audience tenses. "Jump!" they cry. "Jump! Jump!" They cheer at every successful rescue. A pump wagon pulls up in front of the building, and the fireman's hose springs to life, spraying a cascade of water that does exactly nothing to tamp the flames. Victims appear on the tenement roof, while the fourth floor also catches fire. A young woman leans out her fifth-floor window, clutching a baby swaddled in a blue blanket. "*Il mio bambino,*" she sobs at the sky. "*Si prega di Dio, salva il mio bambino!*"

Kitty can't help but get caught up in the drama. "Is she quite all right?"

"Pah," Archie says. "They do this a dozen times a day."

"How's it work?" Kitty whispers.

"Gas jets. Pipes installed inside each window send out those flames. Since it's gas, it doesn't respond to water, which makes for a good show. But it's completely controlled. Glorious, no? Hold on, here comes the best bit."

A second fire truck pulls up to the building, and an enormous ladder extends upward, leaning against the side of the tenement. A fireman clambers up the ladder as the young mother waves to him frantically. "*Mio Dio,*" she cries. "*Salva il mio bambino!*"

"Oh, *mio Dio,*" Archie mutters. "*Mio Italiano es horrible-o!*"

Even at the top of the ladder, the fireman is still slightly below and to the side of the woman in the window. He braces his body against the ladder and reaches up to her, while she reaches down toward him, their hands inches apart. "Pass me the baby," he shouts. "*Bambino!* Give me the baby!"

"*Non posso! Non riesco a raggiungere!*" She stretches her arm out farther, starting to lose her balance on the window ledge.

"Come on, lady! Pass me the darn kid!"

An explosion rips through the fifth floor, sending the woman tumbling out the window and knocking the fireman off the ladder into the net below. The woman clings to the window ledge with one arm, still holding her infant.

The audience is riled, and people stand up. "Jump into the net!" "It's your only hope!" "Save yourself!" "Save your baby!"

The woman sobs hysterically and clutches the window ledge. "*Oh Dio! Mio bambino!*"

The roof moans and collapses on itself. People trapped on the roof leap from the building, some landing in the net, others crumpling into broken heaps on the street.

Kitty looks to Archie, wide-eyed.

"It's a padded floor," he whispers. "Painted to look like sidewalk. It's completely choreographed. *Il genius-o*, no?"

The young mother clinging on to the building appears to be losing strength in her arm. Her body swings as she struggles to grip on the ledge without dropping the baby. She screams, an inhuman shriek that rattles Kitty's bones. A firefighter climbs toward her, while others gather by the net, imploring her to hold on. But she loses her grip and drops, curling her body around her infant like a comma.

The crowd cheers and celebrates as the firemen send one last blast of water at the burning tenement—somehow extinguishing the flames, while previous efforts had failed—and the building too, is saved. Then one miracle more: the bodies on the street spring to life again, bowing and waving.

Archie joins the crowd in applauding and whistling. "Now *that* is a show!"

Kitty claps along but shakes her head. "No, *that* is bizarre!"

"How do you mean?"

"Well, it's a 'show' about something tragic that happens all the time, to real people! And real people who are forced to choose between burning and jumping? They don't take bows afterward."

"Precisely my point! Child, look around you." He gestures at the happy crowd, now gathering their belongings and streaming out in search of the next miracle. "These sheep live the most dreary lives imaginable. Lives that will, for the most part, end very badly indeed. What was it the poet said? 'Eat, drink, and be merry'?"

"For tomorrow we die in a tenement fire?"

"Quite so. *Tomorrow*, we die in a tenement fire. But *not today*, you see. Today is our lucky day. Today, we cheat death once again."

Kitty smiles sadly, thinking of Nate. How his lucky day had come and gone. "Only in New York," she says quietly.

"Come! I've a mighty thirst, Miss Hayward. But not that watered-down swill they sell in the park. I have a better idea."

11

UNFLAPPABLE
GIRLS

⟨∞⟩

A S NIGHT FALLS ON MAGRUDER'S, ROSALIND SENDS WHITEY HOME WITH A fresh bandage and strict instructions to get some rest and avoid entanglements with princesses and tattooed men alike.

At the bar, Zeph, Rosalind, and Enzo nurse their drinks and mull over the strange events of the day. The door opens, and a young woman soon appears at the bottom of the steps. She wears a modest, ankle-length skirt in a warm-brown color with a white, high-necked shirtwaist top. Enzo nudges Rosalind and jerks his thumb at the girl. "See, peacock?" he says. "This is how proper ladies dress."

"Humph," Rosalind mutters. "Dress like a mud pie with a face to match."

The young woman's escort carefully ducks in the doorway. With his hat removed, he can just barely stand upright without bumping the ceiling. "Afternoon, folks," he says, and his deep voice makes the glasses vibrate.

Zeph smiles. "Bernard! How's every little thing?"

Bernard nudges the young woman toward the bar. Beside her towering companion, she looks like a midpriced china doll. They each take a stool—Bernard sits sideways to stretch out his massive legs. "This is my new friend Miss Maggie."

"Welcome to Magruder's, Miss Maggie. Any new friend of Bernard's and so forth. So, a glass of the good stuff for Bernard, and for you, miss? Can I get you something? I can make you a Belle

Epoque; it's a cocktail I invented for Rosalind. You'll think you're at the Manhattan Beach Hotel."

"I'll try it, thank you."

As Zeph gets the drinks, Bernard says, "Maggie's a table girl at Koster's Music Hall."

"Table girl, huh? So you sit on their laps and talk 'em into order-ing more beer than they should?"

"And I sing!" Maggie says indignantly. "Sometimes I sing."

"She sings something beautiful," Bernard says proudly.

"Wasn't criticizing." Zeph rolls back with the cocktails. "We all gotta make a living."

"I'm confused," Maggie says, looking around. "You said Magruder's, but I thought Magruder's was the dime museum? I guess I had it wrong?"

"No, miss, you have it just about right. We prefer 'curiosity cabinet,' but dime museum is close enough. That's upstairs. Couple years back, Doc Timur built this big ol' boiler contraption, kinda by accident, and he said"—here Zeph affects a thick accent—"'Vell, Zeph, too-day aye make zis! But aye doo not know vat zis is!' And I says to him, 'Well, I do—zis is a still!' So I went to work on it. We had nothing going on down here, so I thought, why not? Now, late afternoon rolls around; I close the Cabinet and open the tavern. Excuse me, be right back." And whoosh, he's off, flying down the bar to minister to Enzo's empty glass.

Maggie's eyes follow Zeph but come to rest on a young man several stools down. He's well turned-out in a fine waistcoat and pin-striped trousers; his Roman profile is accentuated by short, slicked-back hair. Maggie sits up a little straighter on her stool. Bernard is nice enough, but she can't imagine a future with a man so towering that he has to stoop several feet to kiss her. This fellow at the bar, on the other hand, has potential…

But then the fellow speaks to Zeph. "I'd adore another drink, darling."

Maggie frowns. *Darling?*

The fellow continues. "I've always meant to ask you about that story, Zeph. Who *accidentally* builds a still?"

Zeph shrugs and fixes another cocktail. "Who knows what the Doc gets up to in the lab? He could be up there turning crab shells into gold, for all I know." He sees Maggie staring. "Ah, sorry, Miss Maggie. This here is Rosalind. Ros, meet Bernard's girl, Maggie."

The Roman prince turns, and Maggie squeaks. On the right side is a fashionable young man. But the waistcoat that had so captured Maggie's attention only covers half of Rosalind's body; it is stitched into a fussy gown covering the other half. On the left, Rosalind is a fashionable young woman, with half a face of makeup and half a head of long, black hair pinned behind the ear. Rosalind's female hand is adorned with rings and handmade porcelain fingernails, each painted like a peacock feather.

Rosalind smiles at Maggie indulgently. "Charmed, I'm sure."

"*Oh my goodness*," Maggie says before she can stop herself. "But… I mean… Why, you're so strange! Have you always been this way?"

"Darling, I was born precisely this way."

Pale and spluttering, Maggie turns to her date. "Bernard, have you… What is he—she… I mean…"

"Good evening, Rosalind," Bernard says.

Rosalind smiles coquettishly. "Evening, you big lug."

"Maggie," Bernard explains, "Ros here is what's called a half-and-half."

"I prefer *double-sexed*," Rosalind says decorously. "But *half-and-half* does seem to be the preferred term among the Dozens."

"Dozens?" Maggie asks.

"That's what we call you…normal people. You call us Unusuals, freaks, monsters… Did you never think we'd have our own name for you? Dozens. As in, dime a." Rosalind shrugs. "Offense intended, I suppose."

"So, Zeph," Bernard says, "Miss Maggie had herself one hell of a day."

Zeph fills Bernard's glass. "Do tell, Miss Maggie."

She pivots awkwardly on her stool, trying to keep Rosalind out of view. "I had this big table today—eight. One of them was coughing a lot, which was a little…off-putting, I guess. They seemed nice enough, though. But when I came back to check on them? They were gone. Entire table, vanished."

Zeph tuts. "Koster's took the bill out of your pay, didn't they? Sons of bitches."

"No, that's what's so strange. I went to the manager, tears in my eyes. I thought for sure he'd fire me. But he said, 'Forget it, kiddo; it happens.' And he gave me five dollars! He said, 'Take this as your tip and forget this happened.'"

Zeph exchanges glances with Enzo and Rosalind. "*It happens*, he says? And then he gives you five whole dollars? That don't sound like no Koster's manager I ever met."

Bernard nods. "Seen dozens of Dozens tossed out over the years—for stealing, scrapping, screwing… But coughing?"

"I'm telling you," Zeph says. "Something ain't right."

Magruder's door opens again, and a couple descend the stairs—an older gentleman, on his arm a young woman, her clothes rumpled but expensive. This is a young lady in the wrong part of town, and she hovers uncertainly by the entrance. Meanwhile, her companion strides in like he owns the place.

When he sees them, Zeph raises his arm like an umpire ejecting a player. "Turn around right now," he says. "I told you, I don't want you in here."

The old man removes his hat. "Master Zephaniah—"

"Nah, none of that, Archie. You've had your chance—*plenty* of chances. Then you sneak out of Magruder's with one of *our paintings* under your arm? What were you gonna do with that ol' Vermeer, anyway—it wasn't even real, you know!"

"Well," Archie says, "it doesn't *need* to be real if—"

"Get out. Bernard, do you mind?"

Bernard rears up to his full height and advances on Archie.

"I have money," Archie says quickly. "A lot of money."

Zeph rolls his eyes. "Yeah, I heard all about it yesterday when I fell offa that turnip truck."

Archie holds up a ten-dollar bill. "I'm on the level this time, look. To show my good faith, next round's on me."

Bernard snatches the money and walks it over to Zeph, who inspects the bill carefully. "Nice chunk of boodle here, Archibald. Looks legit enough." He sighs. "Okay, I s'pose if—now, hold on one minute. This ain't one of them things where you ask me for change and I give you change and then you say, 'Not so many ones, please,' and before I know it, I'm down ten bucks? 'Cause I ain't falling for that again."

Archie laughs. "I would never run a grift like that on you, Zephaniah. Not more than once, anyway." He gestures at an open stool with his hat. "So? Might we stay?"

Zeph shrugs.

Archie leads his companion to the bar. "Drinks for us, please, and one each for the assembled. Good evening, everyone. May I introduce Miss Kitty Hayward? That's Zeph Andrews behind the bar here, the lug down the end is Enzo Morrone, and this eerie creature is either Miss or Mr. Rosalind Butler, depending on where you sit."

Zeph nods, pouring the green liquor from the samovar. "Miss Hayward, welcome to Magruder's."

Kitty smiles. "Thank you. But I don't care for absinthe."

"This ain't that. I mean, I hear ya—green liquor, looks like absinthe." He hands Archie his drink. "But I make this myself, and it's the usual corn mash. Let me fix you a Belle Epoque, you'll see."

"But how is it—"

"Secret ingredient. I add a little something to the mash, to make it more...beach-like, I suppose." Zeph puts some lemon juice into a cocktail shaker, along with brandy and the green whiskey. He pours the drink and places the glass in front of Kitty, who eyes it suspiciously.

"Give it a try, darling." Rosalind approaches Kitty, giving her the full-on, double-sexed experience. "I absolutely swear by them."

Kitty stares at the extraordinary creature before her—fully male on one side, fully female on the other. Suddenly, London has never felt so far away. But Kitty grew up with a mischievous older brother. She knows when she's being teased, and she knows when she's being tested. "Lovely costume, Miss Butler," she says with a deliberate mildness. "I must meet your seamstress."

"It's just Rosalind, please—no 'Miss' or 'Mister.' And I am my own seamstress."

Kitty raises her glass. "Charmed, I'm sure."

Rosalind laughs. "I do love unflappable girls."

Inspired, Kitty takes an unflappable swig on the strange concoction. The green liquid warms her lips, her gums, her mouth, ambling down her throat like an unexpected visit from a friend. She turns to Zeph. "What's the secret ingredient?"

Zeph raises his hands. "I don't tell nobody that."

Kitty shrugs. "Fine. Don't, then."

"Oh, all right, I'll tell you." Zeph leans over the bar, so close that his locks brush against her porcelain skin. "Tomalley," he whispers.

"I'll take another down here," Maggie calls.

Zeph winks and rolls away. So Kitty turns to Rosalind. "Tomalley?"

"Lobster liver, darling. The liver of a lobster is green. It's called tomalley. Once a month, we all sit here at Magruder's eating lobsters for hours so that Zeph can collect the tomalley for his mash."

Kitty grimaces. "That's…interesting. At least it explains the smell in here."

Rosalind laughs again and raises a glass to her. "To new friends. And, of course, to Archibald, our old enemy but new benefactor."

"Why, thank you," Archie says. "But we ought to toast Kitty. Thanks to her, I had a very good day today. And when you hear Miss Hayward's story, you'll see she's a potential source of many good days to come."

Rosalind turns to Kitty. "Is that so? Let's hear it—I love a story told by an unflappable girl."

CHAPTER

★ ★

12

A PRACTICAL
MATTER

◇◇◇

THE SUNLIGHT PIERCES KITTY'S EYES LIKE A RAILROAD SPIKE. SHE GROANS
and turns over. But terrible as she feels, sleep has gone and won't
return, so she sits up and looks around. She's in a large bed in
a small room, oil paintings hung haphazardly on the walls and racks
of clothing in each corner. A large mirror dominates the far wall,
and below the mirror is a long table, laid out with enough personal
items to furnish a store. The right half of the table is home to straight
razors, aftershave lotions, pomades—the tools of the male world.
The left half hosts makeup, false eyelashes, wigs—the weapons of
women. Slowly, it dawns on her. Kitty is in Rosalind Butler's room.

She sees Rosalind stretched out on a daybed by the window.
"Good morning, my dear. How are you feeling?"

Kitty starts to shake her head when the sharp pain behind her eyes
stops her. "I feel terrible. I'm sure I've never felt so terrible."

"Mmm, the Belle Epoque is a cruel mistress."

Kitty rubs her eyes. "How did I end up here? And where is here?"

"Here, my sweet, is my bedroom on the third floor of Theophilus
P. Magruder's Curiosity Cabinet."

"Is Magruder the owner?"

"Don't think so. I've certainly never met him, if he exists at all.
This place has been Timur's domain long as I know of. He lives here,
as does Zeph, of course."

"And you."

"And me," Rosalind agrees with a smile. "You aren't the first bit of sea glass to wash up on Magruder's beach, you know."

As her eyes painfully begin to focus, Kitty gets a better look at Rosalind. Without the makeup, without the wig and the gown, it's clear that Rosalind is male. Midtwenties, with delicate cheekbones and soft eyes framed by long lashes. But his cropped hair, which is slicked back in the manner fashionable for young men, only serves to highlight his teardrop-shaped pearl earrings. He wears a button-down shirt that *might* have been designed for a man, except that it's pale yellow with lace accents at the sleeves. His pin-striped trousers lead the eye down to lace-up boots with a distinctly feminine heel.

"You're a man," Kitty says in surprise. "I mean…you're a man?"

Rosalind grins. "As a matter of biology, I am most tediously male. Lots of people assume my male half is the act—that I'm a woman dressing as a man. I suppose it obliterates their peace of mind to contemplate the alternative. But there's no denying."

"Do you wish you were female?"

"My, we get right to the point, don't we?" He considers the question. "You know, I don't think anyone ever asked me what *I* want before. And the answer…is no. No, I don't. Which is not to say I'm particularly attached to being male. My parents named me *Edward* Butler." He pronounces the name like it's a synonym for *vomit*. "I took the name Rosalind because I like it better. Some days, I wear dresses because I like them; sometimes, I wear trousers because I like those too. Frankly, I don't know why it all has to be so complicated. Actually, that's not true. Of course I know *why*; I've just chosen not to care very much. Isn't our little earth grim enough without denying ourselves the perfect lipstick? It's not so much that I wish to be female—what I wish is that they'd stop insisting I choose! Why can't—" He stops himself, smiling shyly. "Sorry, I'm speech-ifying now. But does that make *any* sense?"

"Once, I wore bloomers to school," Kitty offers, "and the headmistress sent me home to change. Is it like that?"

Rosalind laughs. "A *bit* like that. Although with me, it goes deeper than bloomers. But as far as trousers are concerned—your day will come, my pet. Don't you worry. I'll loan you a pair, if I have to."

Kitty blushes at the very idea. "Maybe *one* day."

"Now, trousers may not be fetching, but you'll find they can be very practical."

"You have the best of both worlds, then."

Rosalind gazes out the window thoughtfully. He has a sad, unreadable smile. "I suppose, in a sense. Also the worst." He stands, shaking off the melancholy. "That's enough philosophy for now. The boys are waiting to speak with you."

"With me? About what?"

"Why, about your mysterious past. You started telling us last night, but you weren't making the greatest amount of sense at that stage. Something to do with the Manhattan Beach Hotel? Or was it a trip to Manhattan? That wasn't clear."

Kitty looks down at her hands. "It was both. Both of those."

"I see. Well, let's go downstairs and sort it out, shall we?"

As Kitty gets out of bed, standing causes her head to pound anew. She groans.

"You poor thing." Rosalind chuckles. "Don't worry, we'll get you fixed up." He pilots Kitty to the full-length mirror and stands behind her, doing his best to tidy her messy braid. It's the first time anyone has touched her with gentleness in what feels like infinity, and Kitty can feel her insides melt a bit. "After we have our chat, I'll run you a hot bath. And I must have a clean corset and dress somewhere that can be made to fit you while we launder your clothes. How does that sound?"

"Like heaven."

"Excellent!" Rosalind puts out his arm. "Come with me, then, mysterious girl."

As they walk down the stairs, Kitty says, "Rosalind, what about Mr. Morrone?"

"Enzo? What about him?"

"Last night, you two seemed…" She shrugs. "I apologize. I'm

being rude, and I'm probably wrong anyway. I thought I noticed something between—"

"Oh, you aren't wrong. May God help me, but you aren't wrong. So, go on. What's your question?"

"I just…I was just curious. Does Mr. Morrone wish you were a lady?"

Rosalind smiles sadly. "With all his heart, I'm certain. But here in Coney Island, we learn to take each other as we are."

✷ ★ ✷

"*Buongiorno*, Signorina Hayward, Signorina Rosalind." As Enzo stands, his eyes flick across Rosalind's creative mix of male and female attire. Rosalind looks him squarely in the eye, daring him to comment. But Enzo keeps his own counsel, pulling out chairs for both Rosalind and Kitty and sitting back down.

Zeph and Archie remain seated at the table; Zeph can't stand up, while Archie can't be bothered—he's too busy studying the day's form from the Gravesend Race Track.

"*Buongiorno*, everyone," Rosalind says. He gestures at the green drinks on the table. "We'll take two of those, if you please."

"Done," Zeph says, and he hands Rosalind a glass.

"Good morning, everyone," Kitty says. "But please, no alcohol for me. Ever. Again."

"Hair of the dog, Miss Hayward," Archie sings without looking up from his form.

She collapses into a chair. "I'll pass."

Zeph laughs. "Ros thought you might say that, so he had me make you this." He nudges a china teacup over to her.

Kitty takes a sip of the hot, strong tea. "May the Lord bless you, Rosalind," she says.

"My pet," Rosalind says. "One can only hope."

"So!" Archie folds the racing form and slides it into the inside pocket of his coat. "Now that the guest of honor has arrived… Kitty, perhaps you can tell them what you told me."

Kitty sighs and takes another sip of tea. "Yes. So Mum and I left England for Cape Town to fetch my brother, Nathan, who was about to be discharged from the army. But…" She pauses and looks at Archie.

"It's all right. We'll help you."

Enzo grunts. "We'll see about that, Archie."

"Just listen. Honestly. Go ahead, my dear."

Kitty stares into her teacup. "When we arrived, we learned Nate had been killed several days earlier. There was no telegraph on the ship, I suppose, or if there was, they didn't bother sending word."

Rosalind takes Kitty's hand. "So your expected reunion was…"

"Not what I expected."

"My sweet, I'm so sorry."

Zeph nods. "Sorry for your loss, Miss Hayward."

"*Le mie condoglianze*, signorina."

"Thank you." She takes a deep breath. "A few days ago, we docked at the seaport in Manhattan, and Mother and I took a ferry here. We checked in at the Manhattan Beach Hotel, and the bellboy—Seamus, his name was—helped us with the trunks. A lovely suite, number 218. Overstuffed velvet furniture and the sweetest wallpaper, with little roses on it. But, you see, Mother had been looking rather wan for the past day or so. Just a bit off."

"Who can blame her?" Rosalind says. "Her son gone and all."

"By the time we reached the hotel, she was feeling poorly. Her forehead was hot, but she was shivering. She kept saying never mind, it's nothing, but she had a coughing fit, and I saw blood on her handkerchief. So I rang for the hotel doctor. He came up to our room and examined her. He said…he said she had the flu, that it was very common on these big ships to pick up something. He told me that there was medicine that would make her more comfortable, but someone would have to go into Manhattan to pick it up."

At this, the men exchange glances.

"Manhattan?" Rosalind asks. "Why so far? Was every chemist in Brooklyn closed?"

Archie nods. "I told you this was going to get interesting."

"I realize it sounds odd now," Kitty says. "But I'm not from here! How would I know?"

"My dear," Rosalind says. "We're just surprised is all. No one blames you."

"You're wrong. I blame me rather a lot." She bites her lip. "But I didn't know what else to do. I made the trip. Ferry to streetcar to second streetcar to chemist, and then the whole thing in reverse. It took all day. It was far—somewhere north of Central Park, even."

"This don't make a lick of sense," Zeph says quietly.

"Yes, I kept thinking that too." Kitty isn't sure whether having her suspicions confirmed makes her feel better or worse. "But the doctor said to go, and I thought…"

"You wanted to protect your mother," Rosalind says. "We understand, I promise."

Enzo nods. "For the mamas…"

Kitty blinks back tears. "Yes. But when I returned… When I returned, I went to collect my key, and the man at the desk refused to give it to me. He said that he'd never seen me, that I had the wrong hotel. The *very same man* who checked us in. He said someone else was checked into 218 and had been for days. I protested and protested, but some men came and tossed me out—no money, no baggage, nothing! How *sorry* the man claimed to be, terribly sorry! I loitered outside the hotel for several hours, and I finally spotted the doctor on his way home. I followed him down the street, calling out, but he wouldn't even look me in the eye! Later, I saw Seamus, the bellhop? Archie was with me—you saw, Archie, how he pretended not to know."

"Trust me," Archie mutters. "The little mick is full of crap."

"I don't know where Mum is, or if she's alive, and I don't know anyone in this whole country except you all, and I don't know how to get home, and…I don't know anything." She sniffles, biting her lip to stop it from trembling.

Rosalind reaches into his pocket and hands Kitty a handkerchief.

"My pet, is there anyone in London we can contact? We could send a telegram, or…"

Kitty shakes her head. "No one close, no one who would…no."

Helpless, Rosalind rounds on Archie. "You!"

"What the devil did *I* do?"

"You bring this poor girl to us, bragging about your latest acquisition like you won her on the midway? Spouting garbage about how she's going to bring us good days? What about *her* days, Archie? What about what she's going through? What is the matter with you?"

"Listen," he hisses. "I don't know what fantasy world you live in, but here in the real world, it's every man—or should I say man-girl—for him-herself. If we can reunite the Dozen child with her Dozen mother—in whatever shape Mummy may be at this point—there certainly will be good days for us all. Look at her! She practically sweats money."

Kitty pushes away from the table and runs back up to Rosalind's room so they don't see her cry.

Rosalind stands. "You are foul. You are a foul, pathetic excuse for a man, and you will die alone and unmourned." He turns on his heel and follows Kitty out.

"Maybe so, you little fruit," Archie calls, "but I'll die rich." He polishes off his drink and wipes his lips with the back of his hand. "So, gentlemen, now that the lasses have departed, let's talk business. How do we begin to untangle this mystery in the most beneficial manner?"

Enzo eyes Archie dangerously. "We begin by *you* being very quiet now."

"Enzo, my man, I didn't—"

"Shh! *Sta' zitto.*" Enzo turns to Zeph. "What say you? *Questa bambina*, lose her brother, her mother… Mama swallowed by Manhattan Beach Hotel? What you think?"

Zeph shrugs. "They bent over backward to get Kitty out of the way, that much is for sure. Mama must have had something management didn't want nobody to know about. What that might be, who knows? As far as actually finding her…"

Enzo scratches his chin. "Maybe we bring her to *il Dottore*."

"Doc Timur?" Zeph shakes his head. "No way. Trust me, he does not wanna hear we got some bourgie British baby socked away upstairs. You didn't see how he got when I let Ros move in—I thought he was gonna blow up the place. And he *likes* Ros."

"*Sì, sì*, you know best. Still, the child…she has right to know. She has right to her things, her clothes and so on. She has right to bury her brother, maybe bury Mama too."

"Yeah, but what can we do? You got friends in high places I don't know about?"

"*Nulla*. Don't know nobody nowhere."

"Right, you and me both."

"Boys," Archie interjects, "I'm sure there's someone who owes me a favor at the—"

"Shut up," Zeph and Enzo say as one.

"You don't know nobody neither," Enzo adds.

Zeph agrees. "Don't kid a kidder."

"All right, fine. Perhaps I don't. I do have a plan, though."

"Do tell," Zeph says, eyebrow raised.

"Well…" He looks down at his palm, idly tracing the line of his scar. "It seems to me that it all starts at that hotel—in suite 218, with the rose wallpaper. That's where this began. So that's where we search first."

"Come on," Zeph says. "How are we going to get into a room like that? I mean, look at us."

Enzo nods. "He has a point, Archie."

Archie smiles. "As it happens, I have a thought on that subject. Of course"—he glances at Zeph—"you won't like it."

13

MIASMA

❧

ARCHIE AND ROSALIND PROMENADE INTO THE LOBBY OF THE MANHATTAN Beach Hotel like visiting royalty. Archie wears a natty pin-striped suit and bowler, while Rosalind is decked out in full Gibson Girl—a flowing dress of canary-yellow chiffon with a breathtakingly tight corset and ample bustle at the back. His wide-brimmed hat is piled high with colorful fabric and feathers, and a long strand of pearls is wrapped multiple times around his neck.

"Tell me," Archie says, "how did you acquire such a valuable necklace?"

Rosalind smiles and nods at the doorman as they pass, but his voice is cold. "You keep your mind off my jewels, old man."

A bellhop struggles with Rosalind's oversize trunk while the glamorous couple takes their place in line at the front desk. Rosalind looks around, soaking up the luxurious atmosphere of the lobby. But his eyes settle upon the pile of newspapers stacked on a nearby table. "Archie, look at the headline."

"Where? Oh, I see." He picks up a paper. "'Dreamland's Deceased Dromedary Disaster!' Dear, dear, dauntingly dramatic! Let's see… 'A heartbreaking moment for Coney Island's newest park…' Blah blah blah… 'Mr. Frank Bostock announced today his animal show would be closed after all thirty of Dreamland's camels succumbed to a mysterious illness.' Blah blah blah… 'A grim Bostock announced a day of mourning…' Don't be fooled. I promise you Frank's delighted—he hated those camels. They smelled like the devil, and they were so foul tempered you couldn't even train them to—"

"You're missing the point," Rosalind says, irritated. "First all the rats die, now camels? What is going on?"

"That's an error in logic, my dear. *Post hoc, ergo propter hoc*, as the scholars say. Dead camels following on dead rats has no connection other than a lot of unfortunate smells."

"You see only coincidence here?"

"That corset must be cutting off the oxygen to your brain. Rats and camels can't get the same diseases. They're barely in the same class of—"

"Don't you *dare* address me in that—"

The man ahead of them finishes his transaction, and the clerk motions Archie forward. "Good afternoon," he says.

Consummate performers, Archie and Rosalind instantly switch their masks from tragedy to comedy. "Hello, my good man," Archie says jovially. "The wife and I are here to see about a room."

The clerk is nonplussed. "Do you have a reservation?"

"I'm afraid not. But surely we can work something out, can't we?"

"I don't have much available. It's our busy season, you see."

Rosalind leans over the desk and flutters his long eyelashes. "As it happens," he says, "only one room truly interests us—number 218?"

The clerk drops his pen. "What do you want that room for?"

Rosalind squeezes Archie's hand. "It's the room where this gentleman proposed to me, one year ago tonight. So you see how terribly important that suite is to us." Flutter, flutter, flutter go the eyelashes.

"That's…ah…sweet? But if it was so important, you should have made a reservation."

Rosalind tosses his head and laughs. "Oh, what a funny man you are. Please, sir. Check and see."

"Ma'am, I'm telling you—"

"Let me handle this, dearest." Archie slides a quartet of dollar bills across the desk. "My good man, humor me. Check your reservation book, and see how full you truly are."

"I can't promise anything," the clerk says. He slides the dollars into his pocket and opens the reservation book in a single, well-practiced gesture.

"Of course we understand," Rosalind says. "But something tells me we might get lucky."

The clerk makes a show of looking through the list of rooms, but it's clear he already knows the answer. "Let's see…well, look at that. Suite 218 is unoccupied."

Rosalind gasps and claps his hands. "Really? What luck." He turns to Archie. "What do you think, my darling? I'm just your lucky rabbit's foot, aren't I?"

Archie rolls his eyes. "Yes, *darling*. Later, I'll take you to the dead camel races."

✦ ★ ✦

A red-headed bellhop opens the door to 218, now wallpapered in a sickly pale green. "Oh," Rosalind says, disappointed. "Have you redecorated? I seem to remember there used to be…what was it?"

The bellhop smiles. "Roses?"

"Roses." Rosalind waggles an eyebrow at Archie. "Of course, roses."

"What's that smell?" Archie demands.

"I don't smell anything?" the bellhop says too quickly.

"Better get your nose checked, because it reeks in here."

Hoping to change the subject, the bellhop goes to the door. "Is over here all right for your trunk, ma'am?"

"Yes, of course. Darling," Rosalind says to Archie, "do you have anything for the young man?"

"What, you mean…a *tip*?" Archie shrugs. "Okay. The house always wins."

Rosalind sighs. He removes a quarter from his clutch. "Here you go."

"Thank you, ma'am." He turns to leave.

"Oh, Seamus," Rosalind says casually.

The red-headed boy turns around, surprised.

"You are Seamus, aren't you."

"Yes?"

"Seamus, I do believe you and I have a friend in common."

Seamus shakes his head politely. "I'm sorry, ma'am? I can't imagine that's true."

"Oh, but it is. A young lady, British. Lovely girl. Checked in a few days ago, then checked out under somewhat, ah, odd circumstances?"

Seamus blinks repeatedly, as though Rosalind is an apparition that might vanish if he could only wake himself up. "Sorry?"

"Miss Kitty Hayward. Surely you remember her."

"I can't say I do?"

Archie laughs. "Oh, we know you can't *say* you do."

"I don't remember." Seamus stares at his shoes. "I don't."

"Young man," Rosalind says, "our poor young friend is in quite a state. Mother missing, no money, no way to get home. Terrible, don't you think, Seamus?"

"Yes, ma'am," he tells his shoes. "Sounds terrible."

"Young man, here is your real tip." Rosalind reaches into his clutch again and retrieves a visitor's card from Magruder's Curiosity Cabinet. "This is where you can find us, should you decide to help Miss Hayward."

Rosalind holds out the card, but Seamus makes no move to take it. "I'm sorry, I…I'm just a bellhop? I can't do anything?"

"My sweet boy." Rosalind tucks the card into the vest of Seamus's uniform. "Not one of us knows what we can do, until one fine day, we stand up and do it."

★ ★ ★

"Let me out of this goddamned trunk, or I swear to Christ, I'll kill you both in your sleep."

Rosalind laughs. "Poor man, let me help." He unlocks the trunk and lifts its heavy lid.

Zeph's head pops up, gasping for air. "I thought I was gonna suffocate for sure."

"Someone your size has no business being claustrophobic," Archie says. "Limits your opportunities."

"I'm the same damn size as you, old man—just misplaced my lower half along the way." Zeph grabs the edge of the trunk with both gloved hands and hoists himself out. He travels across the floor on his hands, his torso swaying back and forth behind him. "I can't believe I let you freaks talk me into this."

"Given your special abilities vis-à-vis confined spaces, I thought you might spot some things that Mr. Butler here and I cannot."

Rosalind's eyes narrow. "I'll thank you to *never* call me that again."

"All right, *Lady* Butler. Better?" A decanter of whiskey is displayed on a side table; Archie is drawn to it as if magnetized. "Have a drink with me?"

Rosalind accepts the drink but sighs. "No, *lady* isn't better. I'm Rosalind, period."

"Then let's toast, Rosalind Period," Archie says. "We're not here five minutes, and we've already confirmed Kitty's story. Room 218 used to have rose wallpaper."

"Oh," Zeph says, heading for the second bedroom. "Somebody call the papers—they changed the wallpaper!"

"We did meet Seamus," Rosalind offers. "That's interesting."

"Yeah, for all the good he'll do us," Zeph calls.

Archie nods. "But, Zeph, what do you make of the smell in here?"

Zeph returns from the second bedroom and ambles to the bathroom, sniffing as he goes. "Ah, let's see…perfume? A fairly nasty perfume?"

"No doubt," Archie says. "Something else too. Fetid, a sort of… Blast it. It'll come to me."

"You and your fussy nose," Rosalind says. "Anyway, I found that boy Seamus charming. Lovely accent. He senses he's on the cusp of something important, but he doesn't know which way to turn. Perhaps we've shown him the way."

"Don't you have a boyfriend already, Ros?"

"Do shut up, Archie."

Zeph emerges from the bathroom. "Y'all, those hotel boys scrubbed this place *clean*. I don't think—wait, what is that?" He points under the bed.

Rosalind goes to him and bends down. "I don't see anything."

"A little glimmer, over there, see? Right there!"

"Not from this angle, no."

Zeph sighs. "Does the phrase *useless as a Dozen* mean anything to you?"

"Now, don't be that way. I got you in here, didn't I?"

Zeph flattens his body against the rug and pulls himself under the bed. Moments later, he emerges from the other side, clasping something in his teeth. He holds it up—a long, silver chain.

Rosalind gasps. "How did they miss that?"

Zeph shrugs. "You missed it, didn't you? It was all the way in the back, stuck behind the headboard." He inspects the necklace. "Looks nice. 'Course, it could be anybody's."

"Come now," Rosalind says. "What are the odds? It must be Mummy's!"

"Zeph is right," Archie says. "Proves nothing. Still, we could sell it—earn back the bribe I had to pay at the desk. Reminds me of this one time, when I was a boy, I found a pearl necklace lying on the street outside Lafayette Cemetery. Can you imagine? Some widower dropped it when—oh my gods. That's it, isn't it?" He stalks around the room, sniffing like a bloodhound—the walls, the curtains, the overstuffed chairs, the bed. He even sniffs the rug. "God help us. That's it." He flops down on the floor, defeated.

"Archie, what on earth has gotten into you?"

He looks up at Rosalind. "When I was a boy. Every summer, Yellow Jack would arrive in New Orleans. That's what we called yellow fever. First, one person in the neighborhood would get sick, then another, then five more, then ten. Fevers, coughing. Blood everywhere—thick, like wet coffee grounds. Bleeding out their eyes, inside their bellies. People coughing up half-digested pieces of themselves. And seizures—people went insane from the fever.

Hurting themselves, hurting each other. Doctors didn't know what to do. They'd strap patients to their beds and watch them die.

"At the cemeteries, carts and carriages lined up for miles. Gravediggers couldn't keep up—they buried piles of strangers together in shallow graves. Of course, being New Orleans, the bodies washed up with the first good rain. Floated down the street, some of them. Terrible sight. And the city swarmed with green bottle flies. Big fat ones, gorging themselves sick off the corpses."

Rosalind sits on the edge of the bed as Zeph ambles over on his hands. "Archie," Rosalind says, "why are you telling us these awful things?"

He stares at the rug, remembering. "No one knew what brought Yellow Jack. People blamed the Irish, the Italians. They blamed the Negroes, of course—especially the free ones. Anyone new, anyone weak. Anyone strange.

"They tried everything to keep Yellow Jack away. They'd put leeches on each other, drink acid, lock up anyone suspicious. Nothing helped. Lot of folks thought it was something in the air. *Miasma* they called it. They set off bombs—the idea was that the smoke from the bombs would drive out the miasma. Mostly they just used gunpowder. But one time…one time, I'll never forget, somebody got clever. Tried something different: sulfur. Yellow powder, not black. Fumigate the city, chase the miasma away. It coated the buildings a mustard color, filled the air with this…this stench of a thousand eggs all rotting at once. I'll never forget it—there's no question why sulfur is what they say hell smells like. And that's what I smell now. Underneath the rosewater, underneath the jasmine and lilac perfume and whatever else they sprayed to cover it up. They fumigated with sulfur."

Rosalind takes a deep breath through his nose and exhales. "Yes, yes, I think I might smell it now. But assuming you're right, what's the point? Why would they use sulfur, of all things?"

Archie smiles sadly. "My blushing bride. Sulfur is the devil's aftershave—it's eleventh-hour stuff. Sulfur is the last thing you try before you burn the goddamn thing down."

14

TRY ON MY
STARRY CROWN

ᴄᴏ҉ᴏ

KITTY STALKS THE DIMLY LIT CABINET LIKE A CRANKY LEOPARD. ROSALIND, Zeph, and Archie are off on their little adventure at the Manhattan Beach Hotel. Kitty isn't entirely sure how she feels about this. Not good. Of course, she *should* be grateful to have a team on her side at last. But considering the team—a con man, a half man, and a half woman half man—she isn't brimming with confidence.

Anyway, what can they possibly expect to find? A hastily written note?

Dear Kitty: The bad men have taken me to such-and-such an address. Please send a clowder of carnies straightaway.

Absurd.

It's not as though Kitty doesn't know what they're all thinking. Archie made his expectations perfectly clear: help the rich damsel, collect the cash. *I'm not a person to them*, she thinks bitterly. *I'm a payday. But the joke is on them: my fairy castle was put up for auction long ago.*

While pacing the floor, she almost collides with a knight in shining armor leaning against a display cabinet, lazily guarding its contents. But his armor is not so much shining as it is tarnished and dented. His breastplate and chain mail look to be roughly fourteenth century in origin, but Kitty knows perfectly well that his flat-top helmet is of a style at least two hundred years older, and his sword is a Japanese katana for certain.

"Some museum this is," she mutters. "They certainly don't let historical accuracy get in the way."

Among the gewgaws in the knight's cabinet is a dusty old lobster carcass with a squirrel's head glued onto the front. She frowns at the squobster in dismay. "My question," she says aloud, "is simply *why*? Why ever would someone…" She sighs. "Never mind."

Beside the squobster is a dried-out snake skin, coiled on a small velvet pillow. The label reads:

SKIN SHED FROM THE VERY SAME ASP THAT
KILLED POOR OLD CLEOPATRA BACK IN 30 BC!

"ALL STRANGE AND TERRIBLE EVENTS ARE
WELCOME, BUT COMFORTS WE DESPISE."
—SHAKESPEARE, *ANTONY AND CLEOPATRA*

Kitty rolls her eyes. "Oh yes, the very same asp, I've no doubt!"

Somewhere in the museum, a cuckoo clock bongs three, easily five hours off the correct time. And Kitty has had just about enough.

"This is ridiculous!" She rounds on the defenseless knight. "Just look at you! Foolish old thing. *You* are ridiculous, and *this place* is ridiculous. It's absolutely filthy, absolutely everywhere, and everything is fake. The squobster's a fake, and you're a fake, the tenement fires are fakes, even the bloody…what was it…*Rinpoches* are fakes, and I've no idea why I'm even here!" Tears prick her eyes.

The silence answers her question. Where else could she go?

She turns away from the knight and rubs her eyes with her fists, forcing the tears back in. Then, in the distance, a chipper, mechanical sort of sound.

Ding!

Kitty looks around. Every blasted clock at Magruder's is set to a different time, so perhaps one of them just—

Ding!

But it doesn't sound like any cuckoo clock she's ever heard.

Ding!

A timer. Must be some sort of timer. She sighs again. Best see to it—what if a kettle's been left on or some such? *Typical*, she imagines Nate teasing. *Our Kitty finds herself a refuge at last, and she lets it burn to the ground.*

Ding! Ding!

"My, you're insistent, aren't you?" Kitty follows the sound through the maze of cabinets. *Ding! Ding! Ding!* "Yes, I'm coming! Honestly!"

In a musty back room, wooden shelves are packed with more "treasures" of Theophilus P. Magruder. An old bed frame lies in pieces on the floor. And then, against the far wall, a brightly lit cabinet topped with a sign: *Robonocchio, the Automatic Boy!*

Kitty approaches, peering at the clockwork boy with a porcelain mask for a face. A gentle smile plays across his lips, but his green, painted-on eyes look sad. She looks all around the cabinet, trying to sort out what exactly is causing the chipper little alarm.

Ding!

"All right!" Kitty says, frustrated. "I'm here! What do you want?" She rubs her temples, embarrassed. "Look at me. I'll be talking to the icebox next."

Ding! Ding! Ding!

"I don't see—oh." At the bottom of the cabinet, a piece of paper sits in a slot. Kitty removes the paper, and her eyes widen. It's a picture of a young woman with a long, messy braid. She sits on a bench with her back to the viewer, looking out at the sea.

"But that's…" She looks up at the machine's shiny white face. "How could you… That's exactly how I…"

Oh. Ohhh. Kitty recovers herself and chuckles. "Clever! *Clever.* Everyone who visits a beach town gazes at the ocean eventually. As it happens, I recently visited a breathtakingly terrible art gallery, and they had pictures just like this covering every surface. Any portrait-drawing automaton worth its salt has *got* to have 'Girl Stares at Sea' in its repertoire." She raps the cabinet appreciatively. "Well done! Truly. Mr. Zeph must have set this up to entertain me while he was gone. I suppose he—"

Inside the cabinet, the clockwork starts to move.

The metal hand holding the pen rises slightly, swings right, and dips into a bottle of ink. The arm swings back, and the machine begins to draw.

"Another one, eh?" She shrugs. "All right. Let's see what you've got."

The automaton's head looks up, staring sightlessly into the darkness of the storeroom, then back down at the paper. Up, then back down. Pen to ink, pen to paper, pen to ink, pen to paper. This goes on for a long time.

Kitty paces silently as the machine works. *Silly old parlor trick, really. Wasn't there some Ancient Greek chap who made a mechanical dove fly about? Or was it an owl? Any case, if they could do it that long ago, then surely…*

Ding! At last, the picture is finished. The "writing desk" tilts forward, and the paper slides down inside the machine and out the slot.

This new picture has the same setting as the first: seaside, bench, girl gazing out. But this time, a nattily dressed older gentleman stands beside her, also looking at the sea. A dark-skinned young man sits beside the girl on the bench, his long, black ropes of hair tumbling down his back. And on the other side of the bench is a barrel-chested chap with no interest in the view at all. He only has eyes for the person beside him, who is dressed in a most extraordinary way—half as a woman and half as a man.

Kitty stares at the image, then at the automaton. She opens her mouth, then closes it. On the street outside, a brass band marches past the Cabinet. "Down by the Riverside" creeps into the store-room, fills the space, and then sneaks away as quickly as it arrived. As the music fades, Kitty suddenly realizes she's forgotten to breathe.

She reaches out to Robonocchio's cabinet and strokes it with her fingertips. Standing there, she hears Magruder's big front door creak open. She carefully folds both drawings and tucks them in the waistband of her skirt. "I should go," she says quietly. "My detectives have returned. But…" She takes a step forward and comes nose to nose with the automaton, their faces separated only by glass.

"Thank you. I don't know what you are, but you're very kind."

✦ ★ ✦

Out in the main part of the museum, Kitty finds it's not her detectives returned at all. It's a barefooted boy with a mop of black hair. "Hello there," she says. "Do you work here? Zeph said it was all right if I stayed and waited for him. I hope you don't mind?"

He stares at her.

"I'm Kitty. I'm…I'm a friend of Zeph's. And Rosalind's. What's your name?"

The boy walks to a table with a toy circus on it, opens the drawer underneath, and removes what appears to be a pickle jar. He turns to Kitty and stares at her some more.

"What is it?"

From his trouser pocket, he removes a pair of tweezers. He places the jar on the table and opens it, captures a flea with the tweezers, and shuts the jar. He picks up a very thin thread, one end tied in a tiny noose. With the ease that most boys put leashes on their dogs, this boy deftly slides the thread around the flea. From inside the circus tent, he removes a two-wheeled carriage not much bigger than a thumbnail. It has a tiny blue flag attached to the back. He puts the carriage on the table and ties the flea to the front. Then he repeats the process with a new flea and a new tiny carriage, this time with a red flag.

"Chariot races! Outstanding!" Kitty grins. "I'll put a penny on red, if you please."

✦ ★ ✦

Rosalind, Zeph, and Archie return to Magruder's, arguing the entire way about whether they were justified in sneaking out of the hotel without paying. "We didn't stay the night," Archie says. "Why should we pay?"

"Tacky," Rosalind mutters.

"Feh."

"Y'all can stop acting like a married couple now," Zeph says. "You're giving me a headache."

"Kitty, darling," Rosalind calls to the darkened museum. "We're home."

Rosalind, Archie, and Zeph round the corner to find Kitty engrossed in a fairly ahistorical reenactment of the Battle of Bull Run.

Zeph ambles over to the circus table on his hands. "Hey, P-Ray, you keeping Miss Kitty company?"

The boy nods without taking his eyes off the battling fleas.

"Hmm," Zeph says. "Things look bad for the Union."

"P-Ray?" Kitty asks. "Is that his name? He wouldn't tell me."

"Don't know if it is or ain't," Zeph says. "That's just the only word we ever get out of him."

"So, did you find anything at the hotel?"

Zeph exchanges glances with the others.

Rosalind says, "P-Ray, you should be in bed, darling. The South will rise again some other day."

P-Ray sighs and gathers up his pets.

"Should I even ask what happened?"

Zeph shrugs. "We either found out a lot or not much, depending."

"Lovely," Kitty says glumly.

Rosalind rests a gentle hand on Kitty's shoulder. "I wish we could say we learned where your mother was taken, but we didn't. We did find one small thing. I'm not sure whether it will mean anything to you." From his clutch, Rosalind removes the necklace.

Kitty's eyes go wide. "That's hers! Mother was wearing that when we arrived! Oh, Rosalind…" Kitty takes the necklace with both hands. Her eyes well up. "It's… She…" She looks at Rosalind helplessly.

"My sweet girl…"

"I'm sorry I'm crying. I don't know why this necklace would…

I knew you wouldn't find her, but somehow... Oh, this *stupid* old necklace..."

Rosalind puts his arms around Kitty, who sobs into his neck.

"Look, Miss Hayward," Archie interjects. "If you could pull yourself together, we need to ask you some questions about your mother's illness."

"Don't scare her with your Yellow Jack claptrap. We'll discuss it tomorrow," Rosalind says.

"Rosalind, it's important that we—"

"Not now, Archie."

"But—"

"*Not now!*" Rosalind drops his voice a bit lower, reminding Archie that a vigorous twenty-nine-year-old male lurks underneath the corset. "Don't make me say it again, old man."

Archie shrugs. "As you wish, your ladyship. By all means, wait until breakfast. Leave it till teatime, what do I care? It's just a plague, after all."

Rosalind strokes Kitty's hair. "Don't you worry about him—he's terrible. You go ahead and cry if you need to."

She does.

✦ ✦

15

EXACTLY LIKE THIS

◈

WHEN KITTY WAKES THE NEXT MORNING, ROSALIND HAS ALREADY LEFT for work, wherever that might be—Kitty isn't sure. But before departing, he'd thoughtfully laid out a clean outfit: an aubergine-colored walking skirt and matching shirtwaist that almost fits. Kitty dresses, fixes up her hair as best she can, and puts on her mother's necklace. She glances at herself in Rosalind's big mirror and sighs. *Mum wore it better.* She heads downstairs.

Kitty finds Zeph perched on his stool at the front entrance of Magruder's, so engrossed in his book, she hesitates to interrupt him. "Good morning," she says. "Sorry to disturb you."

"Oh! Hello, Miss Hayward. How are you keeping this morning?"

"I'm…I'm fine. Thank you for allowing me to stay here."

"Aw, you're no trouble. You fit in better here than most Normals would."

She blushes at the compliment. "What are you reading, if you don't mind?"

He shrugs. "Aw, nothing you'd know. It's just—" He holds up the Du Bois.

"I see. 'I sit with Shakespeare and he winces not.'"

Zeph boggles. "Has everybody in the damn world read this book 'cept me?"

"I doubt that very much," Kitty says with a laugh. "But Mum was always one for causes. Suffrage, of course, and settlement houses, and

Negro rights. She took me to hear Du Bois speak at the Pan-African Congress in London a few years ago. I was only about twelve, I think? Thirteen? Hadn't a clue what he was on about at the time, but he was a fine speaker."

Zeph whistles. "That's quite a life you got, Miss Hayward."

"Well, that was Mum's doing—*we must make ourselves useful*, she'd say. She saw the world the way a housekeeper sees a dirty kitchen, do you know what I mean? *Look at the state of this place!* Not much time for, you know, playing and whatnot. *We must make ourselves useful!*" Kitty smiles sadly. "Mum could be rather annoying."

"Now, don't be so quick with the past tense. We found her necklace, didn't we? Don't give up hope yet."

Kitty runs her fingers along the chain. "Did you find anything else?"

"Nothing specific. Oh, but Ros and Archie did see that Seamus you told us about. Looking all shifty. That boy knows something, that's for certain."

"Right, but how do we—"

The front door creaks open, and Spencer's head appears. "Hello?"

Zeph rolls his eyes. "Look who's back. Hope you brought exact change this time."

Spencer nods. "That I did." He pulls the door open farther, and both he and Nazan enter.

"Well, hello there!" Zeph brightens considerably, and Kitty arches an eyebrow at his sudden change in tone. "I mean…good morning, Miss Nazan."

"Good morning, Mr. Zeph," Nazan says with a smile. She sees Kitty. "Hello."

"Hello there. I'm Kitty Hayward."

"Yeah, uh, this is Kitty. Kitty, this is Nazan Celik, and this fellow is some cheapskate she runs around with."

Spencer rolls his eyes and tips his hat. "Name's Spencer Reynolds, Miss Hayward. A pleasure. Are you touring the Cabinet today?"

"Ah, not exactly. I'm sort of—"

"She's one of us, Reynolds. Don't you fret on it." He turns to Nazan. "So, Miss Celik, you're back for more?"

Nazan smiles. "I was hoping I could see the Automatic Boy again."

Kitty gasps and takes Nazan's hand. "Isn't he just extraordinary? The most remarkable thing happened last—"

"Right," Spencer interrupts. "All the ladies are smitten with your *magical punch-card machine*, whereas I want to speak with you about that cart of yours. Is the doctor you mentioned in this morning? Perhaps I could—"

"Doc don't talk to nobody. You want a cart, go buy yourself your own inventor."

"This is important."

Zeph shrugs. "Not to me it ain't."

"*Please.* It's…it's for my brother."

Nazan now turns to Spencer, confused. "You have a brother?"

He nods. "I have a brother. You aren't meant to know I have a brother. No one, actually, is meant to know."

Zeph and Kitty exchange looks. She says, "You have a secret brother, Mr. Reynolds?"

"Yes, I—"

Zeph leans forward with an intensely serious expression. "Now, sir, lemme ask you. Can other folks *see* your secret brother? Or is this one of those *very special* sort of brothers, just for you?"

Kitty covers her mouth with her hand to stifle her laugh.

"Ha-ha, yes, very funny. You'll be ashamed of your joke when I tell you that I do, indeed, have a brother, named Charlie. He contracted polio five years ago and lost the use of his legs. My father was in a tough campaign at the time, so he informed the newspapers that Charlie *died* so he could collect the sympathy rather than bear the shame of an incapacitated son. Proud of yourself?"

"Well…" Zeph scratches his chin. "I ain't proud of your daddy, that's for sure."

"Spencer, that's terrible!" Nazan says.

"The problem now is the only person in my family more

stubborn than my father is Charlie. And Charlie's pride won't permit him to be pushed around in a wheelchair, which means he's barely left his bedroom this century. But I saw your self-powered cart, and I just thought—"

The door flies open, and Archie hustles in, all business. "Zeph, we need to talk about the—Good Lord, it's like Grand Central in here!" He looks around. "Two whole customers? Why that's more than the Cabinet's seen in—wait a minute." He peers at Spencer. "You're that Reynolds boy, aren't you?"

"I am he," Spencer says stiffly. "May I help you?"

Archie laughs. "Not likely! But you might help *her*." He points at Kitty. "Doesn't anyone know who this is?"

Zeph shrugs. "White boys all look alike to me."

"This is none other than the son of Senator William Reynolds!"

Zeph stares at Archie blankly.

"William Reynolds, who built Dreamland! Owns the whole damn park! We have the very *dauphin* of Coney Island in our midst." Archie glares at him. "So since you've deigned to bless us with your royal presence, why don't you tell us what the devil is going on in this town?"

"Sir, I have no idea what you—"

"Don't try that with me, son. All the dead camels? Exotic fumigations? Well-bred British ladies disappearing from hotels?"

Spencer looks away. "Ah, sir, it's true my family owns the one park, but I certainly don't have anything to do with hotels or—"

"Oh please!" Archie scoffs. "Nothing happens in this town without the Reynolds family hearing about it!"

"Spencer?" Nazan says carefully. "Is something wrong?"

"Mr. Reynolds, sir," Kitty says, her voice trembling ever so slightly. "A few days ago, my mother went missing from the Manhattan Beach Hotel. If there is *any* chance you might know something, I must beg of you—"

He shakes his head. "I'm sorry, I can't help you."

"Now," Zeph mutters, "*that* particular line is gettin' old."

Archie takes an impudent step toward Spencer. "You listen

to me, you spoiled little lickfinger. A British citizen's life is at stake, and if you think for one second that you are getting out of here without—"

Archie's tirade is cut short by an inhuman howl just outside the door.

"What in hell is that?" Zeph asks.

They rush out, Zeph and Kitty first, followed by Spencer and Nazan, with Archie following reluctantly behind.

A woman stands screaming in the middle of the street. Oddly dressed for a warm May morning, she wears a full-length cloak with a hood obscuring her face.

"Hey, ah…hey, miss?" Zeph approaches carefully.

She stops screaming and glares down at him.

"Miss Maggie? Is that you?"

"You!" Maggie lunges for Zeph, fingers outstretched like she means to pluck out his eyes. "You did this to me!"

Protectively, Spencer places himself in front of Nazan and Kitty, but Kitty pushes past him. "Maggie, please calm down. You remember me from the other night, don't you? I'm Kitty…"

Maggie's hood drops onto her shoulders, revealing a face covered in oozing black sores.

"My God," Zeph says. "Miss Maggie, what happened to you?"

Maggie's bloodshot eyes roll back, and she shrieks. "You freaks happened is what! I came to your freak tavern with your freak drinks and all your freak friends, and now look at me!"

There's a sudden squeak behind Archie. Zeph turns and sees P-Ray peeking out the door, his eyes wide.

"P-Ray! That's the last thing we—somebody get him *out* of here," Zeph says urgently.

Nazan nods. "I can." She kneels beside P-Ray. "Hello there. We met the other day. Do you remember me? Come along. Don't you worry about this—Mr. Zeph can handle it. Why don't you show me your flea circus again?" She takes P-Ray's hand and drags him back into the Cabinet.

"Miss Maggie," Zeph says, "you need to calm down, and we'll talk about—"

"I'm dead, can't you see? I'm dead already. Let go of me!" She wiggles one arm free, reaches into her cloak, and produces a boning knife with a long, narrow blade.

✳ ✳ ✳

Inside, Nazan and P-Ray stand beside the flea circus. He has pulled the jar of fleas out of the drawer for Nazan to see, but his interest lies elsewhere. He listens nervously to the struggle going on outside.

"So, these are wonderful beasts you have here. However do you train them?"

No answer.

Nazan studies the boy for a moment. "Zeph called you P-Ray. That's a funny sort of… Wait a minute." She says the name again, but with the emphasis on the second syllable, and a little roll of the R. "*Pire?*"

"*Pire,*" he agrees.

"*Merhaba, küçük adam,*" she says. *Hello, little man.*

The boy nods excitedly. "*Merhaba!*"

"Why, you're Turkish like me!" Nazan exclaims. "P-Ray isn't your name at all, is it? *Pire* means *flea!* What is your name, really?"

The boy shakes his head no.

"Come now," Nazan said. "*Adın ne?*"

"P-Ray," he asserts.

Nazan laughs. "You are a stubborn little flea, aren't you?"

✳ ✳ ✳

"Please now, Miss Maggie," Zeph says, "you don't want to do this. Think, just think now… You don't want to do this."

"Oh, but I do." She laughs and cries simultaneously. "I very much do. You freaks killed me, and I'm returning the favor."

"That's enough!" Spencer steps forward and reaches for Maggie's arm, but she scuttles away, howling like a wounded animal.

"Look at this!" She slashes at a black spot on her cheek, and dark red fluid sprays from the wound. "Look at this!" She slashes at an inflamed lump on her neck. "And there's more here." She slices across her waist, ripping her corset open. "And here." She hacks at the top of her thighs, jabbing the knife through her skirts.

Spencer reaches out again. "Miss, please stop—"

Maggie screams again. "Don't touch me! Don't you goddamned freaks touch me!" She looks around, wild-eyed and delirious. "You all want to see a Dozen die? Huh? Is that what you want? Step right up! Step right up and watch a Dozen die, and why not? You got a dime? If you got a dime, we got a Dozen."

They all watch, horrified, as she suddenly draws the knife across her throat, cutting a deep red line from one black lump to the other. Maggie tries to speak as the blood pumps out. Retching, she collapses on the sidewalk.

"We need an ambulance! Do you have a telephone?" Spencer asks Zeph.

"Here we go again with the phones. Does this seem like the kind of neighborhood that got telephones?"

Spencer looks around the street helplessly. He realizes that Maggie hadn't been entirely unhinged—she did, in fact, have an audience. Old gray heads peek out of windows, small children perch on fire escapes, and grown men lean over roofs. Front doors crack open, and curious eyes peek out.

"Does anyone on this street have a telephone?" Spencer yells to the onlookers. "Anyone? Can anyone fetch an ambulance? Please! This lady needs help!"

Every spying eye vanishes, disappearing behind doors and curtains.

"I see you all, you know," he shouts. "I see every damned one of you!"

Silence.

"My God, what's happening to this city? It didn't used to be like this."

Archie shakes his head. "I'm much older than you, son," he says.

"And I assure you the city has always been and will always be *exactly* like this."

"Miss Maggie?" Kitty creeps toward her gingerly. "Are you still with us?"

Maggie shudders and then goes still.

✦ ✦

16

YE WHO ARE
CURSED

〰

A SMALL SPOTLIGHT SNAPS ON. DUST MITES TANGO ALONG THE BEAM OF LIGHT that cuts across the dark tent, illuminating the tattooed body of the sideshow talker. He stands silent for a moment, allowing the audience to get an eyeful of the decimated castle splashed across him. His pet rat sits obediently on his shoulder and nuzzles his neck. Crumbly Pete's lips curl into a wide, alligator smile.

"Ladies and gentlemen, you know me. And I know you. I know you didn't trek all the way out here to Coney Island to see some overfed princess riding a tricycle in a tutu. You are a discerning audience, and you want the best. You want to see the *true* freaks, the ones that chill the heart of the Almighty himself. And that's what we're going to give you. Ladies and gentlemen, the Captivating Congress of Unusuals presents 'Robert or Roberta?: Half Man, Half Woman, All Freak!'"

The audience applauds, and Rosalind enters in complete darkness. He sits sideways on a stool for a moment, letting the anticipation build. A man in the audience coughs.

Rosalind takes a handheld lighter, made for him by Timur, and lights a long sparkler, made for him by Enzo. The sparkler hisses, shooting tiny stars in every direction.

Seated sideways, only his male half is exposed to the audience. Rosalind pushes his voice into a lower register and slathers on a thick Southern accent. "My name is Robert Percy," he intones. "I am the seventh son of Colonel Kintzing Percy, who was himself the seventh son of Ephraim Percy. Before I was born, my father served under Robert E. Lee in the War for Southern Independence. His finest moment came during the Spotsylvania campaign. When the battle was over, thirty thousand boys lay sprawled across those Virginia fields." Rosalind arches his male brow. "Far more of *your* boys, of course, than ours."

The sparkler slowly burns down, and the audience leans forward to study Rosalind's deviant profile. Another cough rings out, followed by a sharp "Shh!"

"When the war ended, my family, which then numbered six boys plus my mother, headed west to begin a new life in San Francisco."

"Good riddance!" someone calls out.

Rosalind smiles—he has them right where he wants them. He glances quickly at the sparkler to gauge the timing of his spiel. "One day, my mother discovered that she was again with child. A surprise, given her age. She knew this was her last opportunity to obtain what she had always wanted…a daughter. She had already produced six children—all of them boys. Her body, it seemed, had been designed by God to produce ever more sons of the South. What was she to do? How could she ensure the birth of the daughter she desired so desperately? She searched everywhere for answers."

The sparkler burns low, and the stage grows dimmer. Rosalind feels the audience's attention on him like a caress.

"In Chinatown, she purchased a lotion made from sea horse oil. You see, the sea horse male raises its young and is thus believed to contain mystical feminine properties. For months, my mother rubbed the sea horse oil on her expanding belly. And she waited."

With a final hiss, the sparkler goes out. The audience holds its breath, waiting to see what monster emerged from the traitorous mother's womb. Rosalind lets them wonder.

The tense silence is broken by the coughing man, followed by a woman's voice: "Will you please stop that!"

"Sorry, ma'am, can't help it," the cougher whispers.

"At the very least," the woman snarls, "you might cover your mouth!"

Rosalind groans inwardly. All that effort expended on building tension for his big reveal, and it's being ruined by squabbling. Nothing to be done, of course—just keep going. He pivots on his stool to face the audience and whispers to the darkness. "Ladies and gentlemen, it is said that we must be careful what we wish for, because we may get it. But what is not said, what my mother learned, is that we must be careful what we wish for, because we may only get…*half*."

He claps twice, and Pete turns on the spotlight. The crowd gasps at the full Rosalind—left side Southern belle, right side Southern gentleman. On the left, half an ample bosom slopes outward and then down to half an hourglass waist. On the right, half a male chest is barely contained by a too-tight tuxedo jacket. Rosalind wears half a fake mustache on one side of his face. On the other, theatrical women's makeup emphasizes his features, creating the illusion that the female half of his face is slightly larger than the male.

"It was the will of God that my mother raise seven sons," he intones. "*This* is what happens when we deny God's will."

Rosalind cools his feminine side with an elaborate lady's fan. He offers to entertain questions from the thunderstruck audience.

Leaning on the spotlight, Pete grins. Most of the Captivating Congress is merely strange or vulgar. Rosalind manages to be both strange *and* vulgar—also beautiful and somehow terrifying, all at once.

Milo the Goat Boy taps Pete on the shoulder. "Cops outside," he whispers.

"Goddamn it. Really?" Pete sighs. "All right." Pete sneaks behind the audience to a hidden area of the tent where the performers change and await their turns onstage. He pokes his head through the curtain.

Amelia the Fat Lady sits at the mirror, combing her hair.

"Hey," Pete says. "We're gettin' raided."

She groans, annoyed. As Coney Island becomes increasingly respectable, scandalous shows like the Captivating Congress are getting pushed out. But Pete has always been able to talk the right people—or, more likely, frighten them—into allowing the Congress to continue. "Pete," Amelia complains, "I thought you worked out a deal with—"

"Apparently it's off." Pete heads for the tent's main entrance, trying to remember if he has enough cash in the till to make this problem go away.

Lifting the tent's flap, he expects to see a few beat cops on the take. Instead, he's confronted with four men in nondescript tan uniforms with what look like potato sacks over their heads, goggles sewn into the front.

"Gotta interrupt your little show," says their leader, his voice muffled from inside his hood.

Pete won't be intimidated by a few masked men. "Listen, I'm paid up with George Tilyou. If there's a problem, you gotta speak to—"

The man shakes his head. "This ain't that. We're from the Committee on Public Safety."

"The hell is that, now?"

"Committee on Public Safety. You got a health problem."

"Well, wait a few goddamn minutes for the show to be over."

"Now."

"Listen," Pete growls, "we got rights. You can't just barrel in here and—"

The four men elbow Pete aside and enter the tent. The leader announces, "Ladies and gentlemen! We represent the Committee on Public Safety. We're looking for James Warren. He's on the passenger list of the SS *Arundale*. James Warren, stand up, please."

The crowd murmurs, looking from Rosalind onstage to the men in the back. *Is this part of the show?*

Rosalind squints into the darkness. *Committee on Public Safety? What is that?*

The masked men circle the audience, which remains seated, unsure what to do. "James Warren? Where is James Warren?"

The coughing man stands up. "My name is James Warren. Is there some sort of—"

The men are on him, wrenching his arms behind his back and dragging him to the exit. "You're coming with us."

Warren protests and struggles, but they are four and he is one, and out of the tent he goes, shouting all the way.

"What are you *doing*?" Rosalind shouts from the stage. "You can't do that! He's a customer. He has a right to… You in the audience, stop them! They can't do that!"

But the crowd is confused and reluctant, some still thinking this is part of the act, others unwilling to tangle with uniformed men with bags over their heads. *Whoever he is, he must have done something.*

The men depart with their prey, and the audience turns its attention back to Rosalind. A man in the front row stands. "Uh, so, I have a question. Do you shave your—"

"Go screw yourself," Rosalind snaps, fake accent gone. "Did you see what just happened? Were you here a moment ago? Or were you all asleep?"

The man shrugs. "I'm sure they had a reason."

"I hope that's a comfort when your turn comes." Rosalind spits on the floor and stalks offstage.

"What—that's it?" asks the man. "If that's it, I want my money back!"

Others in the crowd murmur agreement.

Crumbly Pete dashes up to Rosalind and grabs him. "Where do you think you're going? We got a full house!"

"You know what you can do with your full house."

"Hey." Pete's grip gets tighter. "Don't think you can—"

"You can't bully me, Pete. Let me go, or I'll knock you all the way down the Bowery."

The two carnies stare each other down. Out in the audience, the calls for refunds grow louder. When Pete's eyes dart toward the empty stage, Rosalind wrenches himself away. "Go on, Pete. Your *marks* need some attention." Rosalind strides out, leaving Pete and the angry Dozens to fend for themselves.

Outside, Rosalind scans the crowds milling around the Bowery.

Garish yellow banners flutter in the summer breeze, each advertising a different Unusual on display—all of them, as the signs say, Live on the Inside. There's the *Robert or Roberta?* banner, of course. Another for *Milo the Goat Boy*, for *Amelia, Fattest Lady in the Known World*, for the *Last Living Dragon*. There's even a banner for the no-longer-live-anywhere Count Orloff, which, Rosalind notes with dismay, no one has had the respect to take down.

At the far end of the street, Rosalind finally spots the masked men, dragging James Warren to a waiting Black Maria. Horrified, Rosalind can only watch as the men toss him roughly into the back. The vehicle pulls into traffic and drives away.

"Satan's minion stands before you!"

Rosalind whirls around to see a dour undertaker of a man in a dark suit, pointing at him with a gray, bony hand. A flock of overdressed churchy types cower by the undertaker like frightened chickens around a rooster. They nod eagerly, sneering at Rosalind as they look him up and down.

"Here in Sodom by the Sea," the undertaker man shouts, "the devil and his minions dwell! This plague is God's judgment upon us!" He turns his accusing finger to the banners, one by one. "Judgment upon the satyr, upon the gluttonous eaters of meat, and upon the dragon that is Satan himself! And *you*!" The undertaker man rounds on Rosalind again. "The degenerate she-male. It is *you* who have inspired God's most righteous wrath!"

Rosalind rolls his eyes. "Oh, do tell."

"Depart from me, ye who are cursed!" The undertaker man is screaming now, his finger shaking and his gray skin turning purple. "Depart into the eternal fire crafted for the devil!"

"*For I was hungry and you gave me nothing to eat,*" Rosalind recites. "*I was a stranger, and you did not invite me in. I was sick, and you did not look after me.*"

The church ladies stare at Rosalind. Even the undertaker looks shocked.

"How do ya like that—I can quote Matthew too, you dried-up

old witches," Rosalind says. And then he raises a finger of his own, turns away, head high, and stomps back up the Bowery like he owns the pavement itself. But on the inside, nausea floods through him.

"Archie was right," he mutters. "They'll come for us first."

17

TOURIST SEASON

◦⟨⟩◦

O N THE STREET IN FRONT OF MAGRUDER'S, KITTY AND ZEPH DUMP BUCKETS
of water onto the sidewalk. Maggie's blood turns a watery pink as
it flows into the gutter. Spencer's longed-for ambulance eventually clip-clops up to the Cabinet, long past the point of usefulness.

"Busy day," says the driver by way of apology. "It's madness out
there. Horses are exhausted."

Spencer grimaces. "What are automobiles *for* if not you boys?"

"Tell it to the mayor." The driver shrugs. He takes Maggie's body
anyway, checks a box marked *suicide*, and makes Zeph sign the form.

Rosalind returns from the sideshow, still in his double-sex
costume, to find that he has walked out of one nightmare and into
another. "What happened?" he asks, not certain he wants to know.

"That gal Maggie, the one with Bernard the other night? She was
here." Zeph sighs. "And now she's gone." He hooks the handle of
the bucket over his shoulder and heads inside for more water.

"She was ill," Kitty explains. "And a bit mad, I think? And...at
least she isn't suffering anymore."

"Poor thing. What a terrible day. I saw a man arrested for coughing."

Kitty turns her bucket upside down and watches as the water
carries a bit more of Maggie away. "My mother had a cough too."

"My dear..." Rosalind pats her shoulder. "You came to
Magruder's looking for a safe place. I'm sorry it isn't working out
that way."

They go inside, where Zeph has climbed up to a small sink behind the bar, and Archie helps him refill his bucket. "Zeph, Archie," Rosalind says, "we need to talk about what happened at my—who's this?"

"Afternoon, Rosalind," Archie says. "The chap at the table is Spencer Reynolds. You recognize him from the society pages of course."

"Charmed, Mr. Reynolds," Rosalind says, offering his gloved hand.

Spencer nods uncertainly. He had started to stand when Rosalind first walked in, but then started to sit when he saw the male half. Now he hovers uncomfortably somewhere in between. Finally, he shrugs and shakes Rosalind's hand. "This is my friend, Miss Nazan Celik."

Rosalind joins them at their table. "Miss Celik, pleasure to meet you."

"Ahh…" Nazan's eyes go wide at Rosalind's costume, but she smiles. "Pleasure to meet you too."

"You're just in time, Ros," Archie says. "Archduke Reynolds here was just about to tell us what in the blazes is going on in this town. Not that we don't have a fair idea at this point."

"I'll say it again, sir," Spencer protests. "I have no idea what—"

"Please don't," says Rosalind. "Some hooded thugs just pulled a customer out of my audience and drove off with him."

Spencer looks down at his hands. "I see."

Archie pulls out a chair and joins them at the table. "So, martial law it is, then. But why?"

"Spencer, do you know something about this?" Nazan asks.

"I'm not… It's not for public…" Spencer sighs. "Oh, to the devil with it. There's this…informal sort of…I don't know, consortium, I guess. Hotel owners, restauranteurs—"

"And daddies," Archie adds.

Spencer rolls his eyes. "And *yes*, my father. They all look out for one another, you know. Common interests. Those men in the hoods were hired a couple of days ago. Apparently, they specialize in solving certain…ah, problems. So." Spencer glances around the room, hoping everyone will let him leave it at that. But he gets only blank stares. "All right, fine. It's plague."

"There's clearly a plague," Archie says, irritated. "We've spent an hour washing it off the sidewalk! What we're—"

"No, you old fool. It's *the* plague."

"But, Spencer," Nazan says. "Plague as in...what, the Black Death?"

Kitty thinks of her mother and gasps. She leans on the bar as the floor seems to shift under her feet.

But Rosalind shakes his head. "That's absurd."

"No, sir—uh, ma'am. It's true."

Archie frowns. "You're telling us the *bubonic plague* is in Coney Island. You realize how ridiculous you—"

"Not bubonic," Spencer says. "That's the bad news."

At the bar, Zeph glances at Kitty, who is pale and getting paler. "Well, *not bubonic* sounds like good news?"

"No, it isn't. My father is in communication with the public health department. Apparently, the illness begins like bubonic plague, with these black lumps on the skin. They're called buboes. That's why it's called bubonic—"

"Yes, yes," Archie interrupts impatiently. "We just saw that too clearly."

"But it doesn't stay that way. This form spreads very quickly in the body. The doctors call it *pneumonic* plague, 'of the lungs.' All it takes to spread is a cough."

"A cough..." repeats Kitty very quietly.

"Correct. There were only a few cases the first day, but it multiplied by a factor of ten the very next day, and again the next."

"I don't understand," Rosalind says. "Plague is from the Middle Ages."

"I'm afraid not. They had it in San Francisco just a few years ago. It's been in Honolulu, in Europe—Lisbon, I believe. Now—"

"Forget Europe," Archie interrupts. "Let's address the real issue: Do I have it or not?"

Rosalind rolls his eyes in disgust. "Archie, *really!*"

"What? We *all* drank with that girl the other night. We had a front-row seat to her attempted murder-suicide. It's a reasonable question!"

"Archie, it's a terrible, selfish—" Rosalind stops. "Okay. Yes." He looks at Spencer. "So?"

Spencer shrugs. "I'm not a physician. Did she cough on you?"

"Ah…" Rosalind looks around. No one is certain. "Not sure. I don't think so?"

"Then you're probably fine. Or"—he turns pointedly to Archie—"I'm wrong, and you'll be dead by Wednesday."

Zeph sees Kitty start to wilt. He'd like to take her hand, but the gesture seems too forward.

"How does it travel?" Nazan asks. "Just by coughing?"

Spencer shakes his head. "The going theory is that plague is spread by rats."

"Rats," Zeph says. "Well now. Remember what Whitey told us about the street cleaning the other day?"

"But it may not be rats at all," Spencer says. "There's another theory. Not proven, mind you. But it could be the fleas *on* the rats."

"Fleas," Zeph repeats. He and Rosalind exchange worried looks. *Uh-oh.*

"So how did these little bastards get here?" Archie asks. "By ship? From Lisbon, I suppose?"

Kitty looks up. "It wasn't Lisbon, was it, Mr. Reynolds?"

Spencer turns to her, surprised. "No, it wasn't, as a matter of fact. The prime suspect is a ship from—"

"South Africa."

"Oh, Kitty…" Rosalind goes to her. "Sweet girl…"

As he doesn't understand Rosalind's words, Spencer opts to ignore them. "The ship had been in Calcutta first. They think that's where the illness came from."

"But, Spencer," Nazan says, "don't they screen passengers for this sort of thing?"

"Only steerage. But there could have been rats in the hold, or there—"

Zeph interrupts him. "Wait, what was that, now?"

"Yeah, back up there, Viceroy," Archie agrees. "What was that about steerage?"

Spencer gazes at them. *Do they really not know?* "Only steerage passengers receive intensive health screenings, obviously." He glances around the room, and it's clear this information is far from obvious. "But surely… I mean… It's been that way since…I don't even know, really. That's how it's done."

Nazan turns to Kitty. "Miss Hayward, when you arrived, were you given a medical screening?"

"Certainly not."

"No one asked… I don't know… 'Have you been exposed to yellow fever?' Or…"

Zeph jumps in. "'Did you vacation in a leper colony?'"

"'What's that seeping boil on your neck?'" Archie volunteers.

Kitty has had enough. "I don't see why you're all picking on me. It's not my fault no one asked!"

"Shh, pet," Rosalind says. "No one's picking on you."

But Nazan, Zeph, and Archie glance at each other with matching raised eyebrows. "What about you, missy?" Archie asks Nazan.

"I was born here," she replies. "But when my father and uncles came over, the authorities practically took their organs out and washed them. Of course, that was *steerage*." She turns to Spencer in amazement. "They don't screen rich people."

"Why would they?" Zeph asks. "Rich folks don't get *plague*." A lifetime of acid is packed into those five words.

Archie snorts. "The leisure class is in for quite a surprise."

Kitty rears up in self-defense, but her voice is shaky. "That is *my mum* you're talking about! We didn't make your policy, you know! I wish they *had* screened her. Maybe I wouldn't be here listening to your rubbish now!"

"Pardon me, Miss Hayward," Spencer says. "What does your mother have to do with—"

"The missing *mummy*," Archie snarls. "The one we asked you for help with earlier. Which you refused, by the way!"

Spencer sits forward. "I've had about enough of your tone, sir. I'm trying to help—I'm helping you right now, in fact! I'm not supposed to be telling you any of this!"

"Spencer," Nazan says soothingly. "We're just trying to understand. Why the secrecy? Shouldn't we tell everyone, so people can take precautions?"

Spencer takes a deep breath and exhales. "We can't. It's…it's complicated."

But Archie laughs. "*Why the secrecy?* Why the strange disappearances? Why keep millions of New Yorkers in ignorance, at the risk of their lives? Hmm, I wonder." He eyes Spencer coolly. "Do you care to explain reality to your friend here? Or shall I?"

Spencer just glares.

"I'll take that as a no. Miss, I can answer your questions with two words: *tourist season*."

"No, it can't be that." She turns to Spencer. "Surely, there must be more to it."

But he deflates, rubbing his forehead with his hands.

"Oh, Spencer. No."

"Oh, Spencer, yes," Archie says. "We must keep those hotels filled, miss! Keep those dance halls crowded, keep that Shoot the Chute flying down the track. And if you develop a slight cough, if your complexion goes a bit lumpy? The men in masks will scoop you up and take you—say, where are they taking them all, anyway?"

Spencer shakes his head no. "I'm done helping you."

"My poor *dauphin*. Look at your lady friend's face—she looks positively stricken. Something tells me you aren't done by a far sight." He stands and goes to the bar. "Anyone else thirsty? What do you say, Zeph?"

"May as well. Oh, speaking of which…" Zeph dives into a cabinet beneath the bar and reemerges with an armful of lemons. He tosses one to everyone in the room except Spencer. "For you, Ros, and you, Miss Nazan…Miss Kitty…Archie…"

Archie catches his lemon. "What, are we making our own cocktails now?"

"No, sir," Zeph laughs. "I'm your eternal bartender, I promise. Lemon juice makes a good flea repellent."

"Really?" Nazan asks. "How'd you learn that?"

"You live with a flea circus, Miss Nazan, you figure that stuff out, quick as ya can. And even if it don't work, think how pretty we'll all smell. Use it carefully, though. I don't have many more. So cocktails, eh? First round's on the house. Reynolds?"

Spencer ignores him, reaching across the table for Nazan's hand. "Please understand, my father really does have the best of—"

"Don't speak to me." She goes to the bar to sit beside Archie. "I'll join you."

"Most excellent. Rosalind? Miss Kitty?"

Kitty wipes her eyes. "I'm going to go lie down for a bit."

"All right, dove," Rosalind says. "You go rest."

Kitty leaves without a word.

"Poor lamb… And, *Archie*. How can you drink at a time like this?"

"Jesus, Ros, how can you *not* drink at a time like this?"

Rosalind sighs. "I see your point. One for me too, Zeph. Let's have a toast to the leisure class."

Archie raises his whiskey. "Long may they cough."

✦ ✦ ✦

Upstairs, Kitty sits at Rosalind's dressing table and tries to collect herself. But when she looks down, a carved ivory hair clip of Rosalind's makes her cry anyway.

The biggest fight her parents ever had took place on the occasion of their twelfth wedding anniversary: Father presented Mother with an elaborate hair clip carved from ivory; Mother refused the gift due to her objections to big-game hunting; Father did not take the news especially well. Kitty and Nate had hidden themselves in an upstairs wardrobe, the better to listen in on the battle.

"I've accepted your views on abolition, Jemma!" their father ranted. "And on suffrage and child labor and immigrants and even, Lord help me, on teetotaling! But *elephants*, now? By God, that's enough!"

Things were rather chilly in the Hayward house for a time. But after a week of sleeping in the guest room, Father admitted defeat and returned the hair clip to the shop.

"Don't you two look so smug," he muttered to his bemused children over dinner. "You watch. She'll be declaring herself vegetarian next, and then we'll all be made to suffer."

"Don't test me, David," Jemma Hayward replied. But she'd winked at her children mischievously.

Oh, Mum, Kitty thinks as the tears spill down. *I miss you.*

✶ ★ ✶

Back in the tavern, Archie raises his glass. "Another toast! To living in Dreamland."

"Dreamland..." Zeph says thoughtfully. "Oh. Oh no. We've got another problem."

"I'll pass," Archie says.

"I agree." Rosalind nods. "No more problems, thank you."

"This is serious. Bernard. He was real cozy with Miss Maggie the other night. You think she might have...shared anything with him?"

"*Shared?*" Archie snorts. "If *share* is the going euphemism these days, that little quim would give Saint Nick a run for his money."

Nazan blushes, and Rosalind smacks Archie's arm. "Rude! Zeph's right, though. He could be ill. We should find him before—"

"Before Reynolds and the Huns do."

Spencer stands. "Now, that's not fair—"

"You know what they say." Zeph shrugs. "If the hood fits."

"Zeph's right," Rosalind says. "Of course, I've no idea what we'll *do* with him when we find him, but still. I hate the thought of that sweet, old giant tossed in a Black Maria to who knows where."

"Hang on," Spencer says. "You're talking about Bernard Coyne? This Maggie person was Coyne's girl? Look, Bernard is an employee of Dreamland. I can help him."

Archie grunts. "So *him* you'll help. Well, guess what? He sees you, he'll run the other way so fast he'll trip over a midget."

"Nonsense."

Zeph says, "No, Archie's got a point. How is Bernard to know— hell, how are any of us to know—that you won't turn him over to those hooded fellas?"

"I would never!" Spencer flushes. "How could you—"

"Send *her*." Archie points at Nazan. "Bernard has never once said no to a pretty face."

Zeph considers this. "What do you say, Miss Celik?"

"Of course I want to help, but…how will I know when I see him?"

"Easy," Archie says. "You see somebody looking *down* at a lamppost, you found him."

"Where do I look?"

"The two of us," Rosalind says. "I know Coney as well as anyone. We'll look together."

18

A PIECE OF PAPER

Bernard the Giant peers in the mirror and sighs. But not for the usual reason.

Given that he is—in the words of his own banner—*eight feet of strange*, mirrors have given Bernard plenty of reason to sigh over the years. But almost overnight, Bernard got even stranger. His neck sprouts giant lumps, and his face is crawling with black, slug-like sores. He looks like he's been attacked by a demonic tattoo artist.

He'd awoken in his too-small bed at Mrs. Golodryga's boarding-house, a few blocks off Surf Avenue. He had the proverbial song in his heart, due to an evening of drinking and flirting with beautiful Miss Maggie down at Magruder's, and a thundering in his head, which also had something to do with the drinking and flirting. Or so he thought. He rolled over and went back to sleep.

Hours later, he awoke throbbing with fever. It took him a minute to remember *who* he was, much less where. His throat felt like there was a nest of scorpions trapped inside, stabbing their way out. There were other strange miseries too: egg-like lumps in his armpits hurt so intensely he could barely lower his arms below his head; meanwhile, other lumps where his massive legs met his torso felt like they were on fire. In his distress, he cursed Miss Maggie for giving him some sort of intimate disease—a horrible thought he immediately wished he could take back.

Miss Maggie is an angel. How could I think such a thing?

Then fever overtook him, and he collapsed into sleep.

Bernard awoke the next morning to Mrs. Golodryga banging on the door and hollering in her personal combination of Russian and English. The upshot was that if the *Урод* (freak) wants breakfast, he needs to get his *жопа* (ass) downstairs, or he won't get *хуй* (shit).

Bernard opened his mouth to reply, but only a croaking sound came out. He pulled a pillow over his face and wept.

✶ ★ ✶

It's now early evening, and Bernard stands by the mirror in his custom-made tuxedo. It took almost an hour to get dressed—he had to keep stopping to catch his breath. The slightest brush of fabric against the angry sores sent pain like bolts of lightning across his body. But he'd done it. Done it for her.

The voice of Bernard's sanity insists that he not go out. *I should be in bed, a hospital bed probably. This is madness.* But he'd invited Miss Maggie to go dancing at the fine new ballroom at Dreamland. She'd smiled at him and said yes—*she'd said yes!*—and no sore in the world would keep him from her. Surely her face was all the medicine he needed anyway.

On his dresser, he locates the finishing touch for his outfit: a pair of diamond cuff links won in a craps game. He smiles, thinking how Miss Maggie will admire the diamonds. Then he frowns, discovering how difficult it is to get them on. His hands are even clumsier than normal, as though they belong to someone else.

He holds up his fingertips to examine them. They are dried out and black, like stubby chunks of coal.

The sane voice in Bernard's head pitches a fit, demanding to know why his fingers are rotting. But the only voice Bernard hears is the one in his heart. And it has a more pressing concern.

Will she still hold hands with me?

✶ ★ ✶

Nazan and Rosalind spend the next few hours politely nudging their way through the crowds, searching for their giant. Rosalind has changed into his male garb to make it easier for them to pass among the crowds unremarked upon.

He sticks out his elbow, offering it to Nazan with a laugh. "Just a regular John and his regular Jane," he chuckles in a lower-than-usual register. "Ain't nothin' interestin' here at all, no, sirree."

Together, they stroll around Dreamland, Luna Park, Steeplechase Park, up to the racetracks, and back down Surf Avenue. Everywhere they go, they stop anyone Rosalind knows—which, to Nazan, looks to be about 80 percent of everyone. *Have you seen Bernard? Have you seen our giant?* No one has.

"So, Miss Nazan," Rosalind says as they go. "I expect this was not the afternoon you envisioned? Wandering the streets in search of a giant?"

Nazan smiles. "No, not exactly. I was hoping to see the Automatic Boy again. Do you know of it?"

"Chio? Of course I know Chio. I've never had a finer portrait than the one Chio did of me."

"Yes, exactly! That's why I'm so curious. But is it just a trick?"

Rosalind shakes his head, confused. "A trick? What do you mean?"

"Spencer says it's all done with punch cards or some such."

"That boy can take the fun out of just about anything, can't he?" Rosalind laughs and takes Nazan's arm. "I'm afraid your Spencer doesn't know half as much as he thinks he does. Oh, I know! Let's try Feltman's. Maybe someone on the waitstaff has seen Bernard. I could use a knish anyway—I'm famished."

"What's a knish?"

"My dear! So very much to learn."

✳ ★ ✳

Kitty sits at the window in Rosalind's bedroom, looking out at the city. The street in front of Magruder's is dark and quiet, but just down the way, the party remains in full swing. Coney Island at dusk is pandemonium, even on a weeknight. Stark electric lights assault the eyes, while sideshow talkers and souvenir vendors compete for the ears, shouting over calliope music that's as inescapable in Coney as oxygen. But all the hurly-burly outside just makes Kitty feel more alone.

Her visit to Coney was supposed to be so different. Nate had it all planned: "I'll take you on the Ferris wheel… I'll take you to the racetrack… I'll swim circles around you at the shore."

Mum, of course, had her own ideas: "I understand that the Association for Improving the Condition of the Poor does wonderful work with destitute children. Perhaps we can assist."

At which Nate would groan theatrically. "Mum, can't we have a bit of fun for once?"

"Nathan, 'Unto whom much was given—'"

"*Please*, not this again…"

"'—of him (or *her*) shall much be required.'"

Meanwhile, Kitty stared at the ceiling, begging for a lightning strike to silence them both.

Now, she's all alone, gazing out the window at a skyline flecked with tiny electric stars. What a fool she'd been.

A soft knock at the door.

"Rosalind, is that you?"

The door opens, but it isn't Rosalind: it's Spencer, carrying a tray. "Sorry to disturb you, Miss Hayward. Zeph thought you might be hungry."

"That's lovely. Thank you."

Spencer puts the tray down on Rosalind's dressing table. "Rosalind is out with Miss Nazan, looking for Bernard Coyne, the giant. Do you know him?"

"I do, actually. " She looks at him curiously. "You didn't go with them to look?"

"I was specifically *not* invited to join the giant hunt."

"She blames you."

"So it seems."

Kitty looks Spencer up and down. "She'll forgive you."

"Hmm." He shakes his head. "I hope so."

"So you're just waiting here, then?"

"I'll go back just as soon as I've seen Nazan home safely."

"Such a gentleman." Kitty fingers her mother's necklace. "Mr. Reynolds, I do understand you are in a difficult situation."

He smiles. "Really? You're the only one, then."

"Miss Celik will come around. But if there *is* anything else you know that might help…"

"I… It's… Well, we're calling it the Calcutta Cough."

"I'm sorry? I don't—"

"Instead of the plague. Can't say *plague*; it's too frightening. Calcutta Cough makes it sound more…"

"Foreign. Naturally."

"None of this was my idea, you know. I'm just the *son*, Miss Hayward. It's not as powerful a position as everyone seems to believe. But I do want to help you, and I will try. I promise." He looks down at the tray. "You should eat before it gets cold. Circuit hash."

Kitty makes a face. "Excuse me?"

"*Good ol' home cookin'*, Zeph says. It's, ah, let's see: tomatoes, corn, pork? Some type of bean. I had some—it's good." Putting the tray down on the table, he gives Kitty a wink. "Nothing as sophisticated as *British* cuisine, of course."

"Oh ho ho," she says, smiling. "The dauphin *does* have a sense of humor after all."

✦ ★ ✦

It's dark by the time Rosalind and Nazan return to Steeplechase Park. Bernard doesn't work there and would have no reason to go, but Rosalind has run out of better ideas, so they resolve to give it one more look. Neither wants to face Magruder's empty-handed.

Along the way, they pass the High Striker, a test-your-strength game in which customers hoist a sledgehammer and attempt to ring a bell sitting atop a tall pole.

"Hang on," Rosalind says. "I know this blackguard." He waves to the fellow running the game. The man is outlandishly tall and nearly as thin as the pole itself, and he's decked out in a red-and-white-striped suit and straw hat. "Mr. Fitz!"

Fitz ambles over to them, grinning. "Hello there! Rosalind, you are a vision as always. Although I prefer you in a gown, if I may be so bold."

"You are not alone, my friend. Fitz, I'd like to introduce my friend Nazan Celik."

He tips his hat. "Evening, miss." Fitz gestures at his game. "Care to have a go?"

Nazan smiles. "That sledgehammer looks a bit heavy for me."

Fitz and Rosalind laugh. "Anyone can win this game," Rosalind explains, "*if* Fitz likes you enough to push the button that makes the bell ring. But I'm afraid Miss Celik and I are on a rather urgent mission. You're friends with Bernard Coyne, aren't you, Fitz? You wouldn't know where he is?"

"Hmm…I reckon today is Coyne's day off."

"Any thoughts as to where he might be? It's urgent."

"Ah, well. You know, he's quite taken with some girl…"

Rosalind nods vaguely, trying not to betray too much. "Miss Maggie, yes."

"Right, Maggie. He bragged to me he was going to take her dancing with all the swells at the Dreamland ballroom."

"The ballroom." Rosalind nods. "Oh boy."

✦ ★ ✦

Dreamland's ballroom is lit by hundreds of individual lightbulbs overhead, with a luminous oak dance floor under foot. One long wall is exposed to the sea, and a cool breeze wafts through the windows, balancing the sizzling heat drifting down from the lights. An orchestra plays a waltz, and a large crowd of well-dressed couples glide to the music.

Bernard stumbles around the ballroom like a vaudeville character who's blundered into the wrong play. Gentlemen give him a wide, worried berth, and their companions turn up their noses in disgust. But Bernard has been eight feet of strange for a long time—he isn't going to be put off by that kind of reaction now. He doesn't even see it anymore.

Where is she?

His balance is off somehow, as though the ballroom is a storm-tossed ship, but he's the only one who notices. He stumbles, colliding with an older man in a monocle three feet shorter than himself. The man shoves Bernard away as his wife squeaks.

"Sorry," Bernard mutters. "Very sorry."

He steadies himself and scans the room. It's so bright, and the music is so loud, so much movement, so many colors sweeping around on the dance floor and people sitting at tables drinking wine, chatting, chatting, chatting, so much babble, pretty girls laughing, but none of them are Maggie, and his eyes start to water.

"Maggie…"

★ ★ ★

Spencer leaves Kitty to her meal and wanders downstairs to the tavern. Zeph and Archie are at the bar, and there's an orchestra playing…somewhere? It's a waltz, Spencer is sure, but where is it coming from? He stares at the icebox in confusion. "Orchestra?"

"Mr. Reynolds," Archie says, "have a seat. Actually, take mine. I think I'll prowl around a bit, see if I can pick up any Surf Avenue scuttlebutt about this trendy Black Death all the kids are wild for. Zeph, we'll speak soon." With a quick doff of his hat, he heads up the stairs.

Before approaching the bar, Spencer eyes Zeph to see if Archie's invitation is acceptable.

Zeph nods, and he fixes Spencer a drink. "Go on, white boy. Have a seat. And the orchestra ain't in the icebox. It's across town in your ballroom at Dreamland. The sound is picked up by a transmitter that an electrician buddy of mine hid in the ceiling lights. The icebox is the receiver."

"No kidding," Spencer says. "I've read about Marconi's wireless, but this is another level of… This is Doctor Timur's doing, is it?"

"Nah, Doc's all about the *making* of things," Zeph explains, "but he don't ever know what to do with the things he makes. *Doing with* is my department."

"So why listen in on our ballroom?"

"Ain't just yours, son! I got a bunch of transmitters out and about. I like music, and that orchestra you got is damn good. That's Tchaikovsky they're playing now—a waltz from...ah...dammit, I forget now. Some opera—Enzo told me. He says the opera's no good, but of course, he only likes the Italians. I don't know. I think he's all right, that Tchaikovsky. Nice waltz. I ain't much of a *dancer*, of course. Beautiful to hear, though."

"Why not just go listen, if you feel that way? Wouldn't it be better in person?"

"Well, *gosh*, that ain't never occurred to me. Too bad I have more chance of flapping my arms and flying to the moon than I do goin' to hear music live down the Dreamland ballroom."

Spencer sips his drink to hide his embarrassment. "Sure, because of your leg...uh...situation. Yes, I can see how that might—"

"Not my leg situation, it's my *skin* situation. Your ballroom is whites only."

Spencer opens his mouth, then closes it again. "That's...that's not our policy. Not...ah...officially."

"Oh, not *officially*. Okay. Hows about next Saturday, I get together the prettiest group of Negroes I can find and we'll all go waltzing in your ballroom? Maybe we'll eat there too. Hey, how about we use the lavatories? How do ya reckon *that* will go?"

Spencer doesn't answer.

"Don't need some *official* policy, Reynolds. Everybody knows. So do you."

They listen to the waltz in silence. Spencer lays his hands on the bar and stares down at them. They look soft. Pink and soft and useless. His hands have never known the *making of*, much less the *doing with*. What are they even for?

"It's wrong," he says finally. "You're right. It's wrong. But I don't know what to do about it. I suppose…I pretend that I can't see the things that I know I can't fix."

"Good thing you're rich and pretty, Reynolds, because you ain't all that smart, are ya?"

Looking up, Spencer is surprised to see Zeph smiling at him. For the first time since they met, he's smiling. Experimentally, Spencer smiles back.

"So." Zeph pours himself a glass of his famous lobster whiskey. "Why's the Reynolds family so interested in Coney anyway? Daddy can't resist a clam shack or what?"

Spencer scoffs. "My *father*? No, Dreamland's just an investment to him. For my brother and me, though, some of our best memories are out here."

"Your brother—the one who needs my cart?"

"Yes, exactly. We used to swim here all the time. Before he… you know. Before polio. Charlie would come tearing out of the bathhouse, turn cartwheels down the beach, and then—*bang!*—into the water. He'd be a fish for the rest of the day."

"The Reynolds boys are swimmers, huh?"

"*He* was, not me! I was terrified." He chuckles. "I liked Surf Avenue better. One time, my father let me bet a dime on one of those Find the Lady games. I can still see the fellow's fingers, making these cards dance on the box, you know? Then he looks at me and says pick, so I pick, and there she is! Red queen, looking right up at me."

Zeph laughs. "Ha! You *won* Find the Lady. Now, that is a miracle."

"*Allowed* to win, more like. After all, Senator Reynolds was standing right behind me! Fellow wasn't stupid. Still, I'll never forget that feeling when the card flipped over. You know, the life of a politician's son is a little…ah…limited, I guess? Circumscribed?" Zeph arches an eyebrow, and Spencer quickly says, "I'm not asking you to feel sorry for me. I'm just saying that's how it is. But when I saw that red queen, I felt… I don't know. Like maybe anything *could* happen to me after all."

"Sure." Zeph nods. "Finding this place here was like that for me. I was touring with this sideshow, and Steeplechase Park hired us for—"

A bloodcurdling scream comes from the icebox.

Zeph and Spencer stare at the receiver. Shouts, crashes, plates smashing. The orchestra gives up on Tchaikovsky. More screams. Then the howl of a wounded animal.

Spencer looks at Zeph. "What kind of trick is this?"

"No trick. I don't—"

"It's not funny, Zeph!"

"I swear, it's not… That's coming from the ballroom."

"Nazan could be there." Spencer goes pale. "She and Rosalind both. They were looking for Bernard. What if they're—"

"No, no. They could be anywhere on Surf Avenue by now. You don't know if—"

Another feminine scream. Men shouting, "Stop him!"

Spencer stands up. "I have to find her."

"Now, think this through. Rosalind's plenty capable; he'll take care of her. And didn't you promise her you'd be here when they—"

"I won't just sit and listen to your magic box while she's out there, maybe frightened, injured, or maybe—no, I won't do it." He runs out.

"Reynolds!"

★ ★ ★

"Maggie…" Bernard says, or wants to, but his voice strangles in his throat, and only a choking sound emerges. The black lumps are so bad, he can no longer speak.

How will I tell her? How will I say everything I have to say?

He needs paper, a piece of paper and something to write with, and then he can explain. It won't matter that he can't speak; he'll write—he'll compose a love letter to Maggie while she sits beside him. He'll write about how sorry he is to be sick but how joyful he is to see her. He'll tell her about all the thoughts he's had, all these daydreams, holding hands and sharing secrets and apple picking—*you know, Maggie, apple picking is something giants are extremely good at*—and she'll laugh at this and throw her head back, and her lovely hair will glimmer in the lights just so.

He turns to a woman nearby, reaches down, grabs her shoulders. "Please, ma'am, I need paper! It's very important! Do you have a piece of paper?"

That's what he tries to say. What comes out is "Aahhhgggghahhrrrrrr…"

The woman shrieks, and her husband pushes Bernard away, sending the giant tumbling onto a table of champagne-sipping lords and ladies, and they leap up screaming as the table collapses and he crashes to the floor, glasses shattering and utensils flying. Somewhere, a woman shrieks and crashes into another table in a faint. Bernard stands up, and everywhere there is pointing and shouting and running. Even the band stops playing, and the entire ballroom focuses on the bleeding, rotting, retching giant as he sobs and tries to explain that he really just needs a goddamned piece of paper.

Suddenly, there are arms, policemen's arms, and they're all around—in front, behind, on him, under him, everywhere. With a roar, Bernard wrenches himself away, sending grown men flying like dolls. He stumbles forward on rotting feet, trying to get out, run, praying Maggie will understand why he had to leave. Maggie would never abide Bernard being treated this way, he knows it. "Maggie, where are you?" he cries out. "I love you. Where are you?" But a bleating "mahhhaarrrrrooooo" is all he can manage.

He stumbles into the night, struggling to put one foot in front of the other and one thought in front of the next.

The promenade. That's where she'll be. She's waiting there.

He runs on, ignoring the teenagers who point and stare, the God-fearing folk who turn hastily away, the young mothers who cover the eyes of their children. That's the life of a freak. It's nothing new.

He barrels through the gates, throwing himself down the wide boulevard. A fit of coughing lays siege to his whole body and forces him to stop. He covers his mouth as he coughs, but he can't stop the blood, can't force it back in. He just keeps coughing, and the blood keeps coming, and when he looks up, he sees the enormous winged demon of Hell Gate staring down pitilessly, and suddenly, he can't recall what he's doing at Dreamland in the first place.

Isn't Monday my day off?

He hears shouting and looks up to see policemen approaching, guns drawn.

Oh yes, that's what I was doing. I was running.

✦ ✦ ✦

Just outside Dreamland's main entrance, a small crowd is handing over their money to a sharp-dressed man who makes playing cards dance across a green-felt box. Rosalind and Nazan pass by on their way to the ballroom.

Rosalind gestures at the box. "Here's a tip, darling—*that* is a trick. Rest assured."

Nazan hears someone calling her name, and she turns. "Spencer!"

Out of breath, Spencer skirts through the gamblers and grasps Nazan's hands. "I'm so glad I found you both. Something terrible is happening at the—"

A sharp bang comes from inside Dreamland, followed by several more.

Nazan frowns. "Seems a bit early for fireworks, no?"

"No." Rosalind goes pale. "Those aren't fireworks."

TO WHOM MUCH
WAS GIVEN...

E VEN THE WORST NIGHTS END.

News of Bernard's murder spread like a fever through the Unusual community. First Orloff gone in a blink, now one of their own gunned down in the street. Unusuals live their lives with a nagging sense that the Dozens are set against them somehow. But *feeling* that way is one thing. Seeing a friend carted away in a bag is another.

The next morning, they gather. The very tall and very small, the very fat and very thin, the bearded and the shorn and the webbed fingered and the rubber boned—they all drift toward Magruder's Tavern without knowing precisely why. Like birds heading south, they are drawn to the zone of safety their friend Zeph has built. *The tourists can have the beer gardens and ice cream parlors and faux Parisian cafés. Magruder's belongs to us.*

From Rosalind's window, Kitty sees Unusuals drifting down the street in small groups. Holding hands, leaning on one another, heads low. It's oddly comforting. With her entire family dead or presumed so, being a castaway in the "people's playground" is a bit like being a widow at a wedding. *Now*, she thinks, *we can all be sad together.* She dresses quickly and goes downstairs to join her fellow mourners.

But when she walks in, she realizes there is no *we*—there is *she*, and there is *everybody else.*

In the tavern: painted faces, tattooed faces, faces with bones through the nose. And every face casts unwelcoming eyes at the blond British teenager. Their pain is their own, not to be shared with someone as perfect as she.

Who's that?

Some Dozen.

She's just a tourist.

What the devil is she doing here anyway?

Bernard ain't her people.

Just like a Dozen, thinking every damn place is hers.

Uncomfortably, Kitty makes her way over to Zeph. The bar is covered with platters of sandwiches and bagels and spreads of various hues. "Good morning, Zeph," she says as brightly as she can. "Lovely buffet here…"

"Morning, Miss Kitty. Yeah, ordered in from Feltman's. Reynolds took Miss Nazan back to Manhattan, but before he left, he shoved a fistful of cash in my hand and told me to do right by Bernard's people. Which, I reckon, is us." He shrugs. "Somebody dies, people gotta eat. Don't know why, but it's a fact."

A willowy lady in a floor-length coat and peacock-feathered hat elbows her way in front of Kitty. "*Bonjour*, Monsieur Zeph."

"Mornin', Vivi. How are ya? Can I introduce Miss Kitty Hayward? Kitty, this is Mademoiselle Vivi Leveque, leopard trainer extraordinaire. Miss Vivi, Miss Kitty here is from London. Y'all should talk. You both got that Europe thing going on."

Kitty smiles, pleased to try out her French. "*Mademoiselle, je suis enchantée—*"

"*Non.*" Vivi has nothing to offer Kitty but her back. "Monsieur Zeph, we must speak. With all this illness, I am concerned for the welfare of my leopards. Did you know all the rats are dead?"

"Leopards don't eat rats, do they?"

Kitty moves away, yielding to Vivi's greater force.

In need of something to do, she studies the buffet like a scholar, reminding herself of that hard-earned lesson on the beach: *never skip breakfast.* But she's far too self-conscious to seriously consider eating.

What if I pick the wrong thing? Or too much of it? What do I do with those fishy bits, anyway? There's no hope.

Spotting Rosalind in the corner, she moves toward him. But he's engaged in a serious conversation—argument?—with Enzo. So Kitty stops halfway and finds herself marooned in a glacial sea.

What do I do now?

Mum answers. *Make yourself useful!*

She scans the room. People are fed, talking. Nothing needs cleaning. Nothing needs fetching, arranging, or picking up. Nothing needs doing here.

Katherine Emmeline Hayward! Something always needs doing somewhere.

That gives her an idea—an idea that, if nothing else, will get her away from all these angry stares. But she'll need Zeph's help. She takes a deep breath and reinserts herself beside Vivi. "*Pardonnez-moi, mademoiselle.* I just need to ask Zeph something."

Vivi turns to her, affronted. "Monsieur Zeph and I are speaking!"

"*Je suis désolée…* One moment, I promise. Zeph, could you tell me where—"

"*Pas maintenant,* little church mouse. We are speaking!"

Kitty raises up on tiptoe, the better to look Vivi in the eye. "*Avec tout mon respect, est-ce que tu peux fermer ta gueule pendant dix secondes?*"

"How dare you! I won't be spoken to this way! I am a lady!" But this time, it's Vivi who yields, turning on her heel and huffing away.

Zeph eyes Kitty mischievously. "I don't know French, but did you just tell my girl Vivi to scram?"

"Well," she says, "my people didn't win the Battle of Agincourt so some overdressed *baguette* could push me around."

He laughs. "Fair enough. So what's up, English?"

"Is there a hospital nearby?"

"Yep, Reception Hospital. Of course, it's more like a snobby first aid station than a real hospital. But," he says, suddenly concerned, "why d'ya ask? You feeling okay?"

"Yes, I'm fine."

He peers at her. "You sure? Your mom got sick, and we did all of us get kinda close to Maggie. You sure you ain't, you know…" He fake coughs dramatically.

"No, no, I'm perfectly all right. It's just…yesterday, the ambulance man said they were terribly busy. I'm wondering if I might be able to assist."

"That's neighborly of you. Sure, it's on Sea Breeze Avenue, few blocks west of here. You want maybe somebody goes with you?"

"No, no, I don't want to put anyone out."

"Come on, English, it ain't a problem. Let me—"

All Kitty can think of is getting out of that room, away from all those eyes. "*I'm fine.* Sea Breeze Avenue, west. Thank you. I'll be off."

"Are you sure you don't—"

But she's gone.

✦ ✦ ✦

Out on the street, however, Kitty's confidence ebbs. "West…which way is west?"

At random, she turns right. But after passing nothing but run-down tenements for several blocks, she convinces herself she's made a mistake. Her attempts to ask passersby for directions are met with dead-eyed stares. Soon, all the buildings begin to look alike, and she has a vision of herself losing track of Magruder's too—wandering for eternity in a maze of cold-water flats and belli-cose Russian housewives.

She skulks back to the Cabinet. She's standing outside the door, trying to sort out how to brazenly walk back in and ask for directions a second time, when—rescue! The door opens, and Rosalind steps out, blinking back tears.

"Rosalind! I'm so happy to—oh dear. What's happened?"

He shakes his head violently. "Nothing. It's nothing. I don't want to talk about it. Don't ask me. What are you doing?"

"I was just on my way to the hospital. Thought I'd see if they need any assistance. Would you perhaps accompany me?" *Assuming you know where it is*, she thinks but doesn't say.

Rosalind frowns, then smiles. "Yes! Yes, I'll walk you there. No sense sitting around."

They go down one block and then turn left. "Of course," Kitty mutters. "That's west."

"What?"

"Nothing. You look lovely, Rosalind."

Naturally, Rosalind pulled out every possible stop in honor of Bernard—black top hat perched atop a flowing blond wig, tuxedo-style jacket in black brocade, and full skirt with a long, black train.

"I adore that skirt. Is it chiffon?"

"Mousseline de soie, actually, and thank you. I'm glad *someone* around here appreciates it."

"Is that…is that what you and Enzo were discussing?"

"I said I don't want to talk about it. Afternoon, Morty!" Rosalind waves at a man walking along the other side of the street. He's on stilts.

"Afternoon, Rosalind," he shouts down. "You're a pretty sight on a sad day."

"You have excellent taste, darling. Everyone's at the tavern, and there's food waiting. We'll chat later."

Morty waves appreciatively and continues on.

They walk awhile in silence.

"I'm rude, he says. Not feminine *enough*, he says. Insulting to Bernard, to '*play this game*,' as he puts it, this '*ragazza/ragazzo game*.' A game! How dare he?"

"Well, perhaps he—"

"'Would you rather I wear my dark gray suit?' I asked him. 'You won't even make eye contact with me dressed as a boy, and you know it.' And he says *I'm* rude."

"I suppose—"

"In public, it's 'Oh, *cara mia*.' But do you hear that? That little insult, tucked in with the romance language? *Cara mia*. Feminine. Because we're supposed to pretend, you see, like we're children. We're supposed to pretend I'm just some Dozen girl. That's just in public, of course. In private, he can't get my gown off fast enough."

Kitty flushes.

"Who is he kidding? Strutting around, Mr. Manly Fireworks Expert! Mr. Hypocrite. He only gets away with it because nobody can understand what he's saying half the time. If you get him talking about *opera*? Suddenly he's got more camp than Yellowstone!" Rosalind takes a deep breath and exhales. "It's over. I told him so. We're finished."

"Surely you don't mean that?"

"What do *you* know, little girl?"

Kitty shakes her head. "Nothing. About this? Less than nothing."

Rosalind softens. "I'm sorry, dove. It's been such a terrible day. I shouldn't take it out on—good Lord, look at that."

They've arrived at Coney's hospital, such as it is—a narrow, two-story building with a mansard roof and a small front porch. A giant sign over the porch spans the entire front of the building, declaring RECEPTION HOSPITAL. But that bold claim aside, it doesn't look prepared to receive anything more serious than sunstroke and jellyfish stings.

The hospital's wide lawn is ringed by a wrought iron gate. A large tent has been set up, where patients are laid out on cots, folding tables, even steamer trunks. Doctors in long coats and nurses in pinafores float among the patients, doing what they can. But as their hands are empty and their manner unhurried, Kitty surmises it isn't very much. Men in business suits hover around the perimeter, the uncomfortable representatives of somebody powerful.

Rosalind eyes the scene nervously. "All right if I leave you to it? My people and doctors…it's not what you'd call a love story. I'll be at Magruder's if you need me."

Kitty squeezes Rosalind's arm and smiles. "I'll be fine. Thank you for the company." She opens the gate but turns back. "Maybe don't give up on Enzo just yet."

Rosalind shakes his head. "I told you. I don't want to talk about it."

...OF HIM (OR HER) SHALL
MUCH BE REQUIRED

◦◦◦

KITTY LETS THE GATE CLOSE BEHIND HER AND CLIMBS THE STEPS OF Reception's porch. As she reaches for the door, a doctor rushes over from the tent. "Miss! Miss, what are you doing? If you're ill, you need to be checked in over here."

Kitty gazes down at him from the porch. "I'm sorry, no. I'm not ill. I'm just here to help."

He laughs ruefully. "There's nothing you can do in there, that's for sure. Check in at the tent, please. That's the procedure."

She nods, and the doctor returns to the business of trying to look busy.

The front door bursts open, and a figure in a pinafore tumbles out. She wears a cloth hood with goggles sewn into the front, which she yanks off just before projectile vomiting all over Kitty's shoes. Kitty leaps back, too late, and nearly tumbles off the porch.

The young woman looks up, horrified. "Miss, I'm so sorry. I didn't realize you'd be there."

"Please don't apologize. These things happen." Kitty looks down at her splattered shoes. Her stomach lurches, and it strikes her that sometimes it is, in fact, okay to skip breakfast.

"I'm Marisol." The young nurse wipes her mouth with the back of her hand and thoughtlessly offers it to Kitty to shake.

Kitty smiles but declines the hand. "I'm Kitty Hayward. You're new at this nursing business, aren't you?"

"I'm a student," Marisol whispers. She glances to make sure none of the doctors are nearby. "I'm just a student. And I can't do it—it's too terrible. No one should have to do this." Tears gather in her eyes.

"Of course you're right." Kitty adopts the tone her mother used with the urchins of the settlement houses. "*No one* should have to. None of this *should* be happening at all. But here you are." She takes a handkerchief from her pocket and wipes Marisol's face. "And here I am. And we'll make the best of it, won't we?"

Marisol stares at this strange arrival. "Who are you again?"

"Kitty Hayward. Now, which patients are inside?"

"Nurse Marisol!" One of the nurses has noticed the two girls on the porch. "I told you to get some water and bring it in. Don't take all day. I need you out here."

Marisol waves. "Yes, ma'am. I'll be right there." She rolls her eyes. "She's such a witch," she tells Kitty. "The coughers are inside. The bad ones. People come here, and if they've got a cold or a sprained ankle, they stay outside in the tents. The coughers go in. And it's…" She shudders. "I can't."

"I know, it's frightening. I saw someone with the cough pass the other day. It was horrible. But they're just people. And," Kitty says, perhaps a bit more smugly than intended, "it *is* your job, you know."

Marisol shoves the hood into Kitty's arms. "Not anymore."

✷ ★ ✷

Kitty pulls Marisol's pinafore over her head and tucks the hood under her arm. She walks around to the back of the hospital, where Marisol said there was a water pump and a supply of pitchers. She walks right past the doctor who'd stopped her minutes earlier.

"I'm just getting the patients some water," she says, and he nods disinterestedly. The pinafore seems to have rendered Kitty invisible.

But she is noticed by a male attendant in the yard. The young man stands beside a collection of sticks, each one poking straight up out of the ground, each one with a glove on the end of it. He's pouring a strong-smelling bleach across his little glove garden. "Hey there. You new?"

Kitty nods. "I'm meant to get water?"

Without looking up, he points at a pump just to the left of the building. Several pitchers stand at the ready.

"Thank you," Kitty says. She looks at the gloves. "Scarecrows rising from the grave?"

He shakes his head, confused, then chuckles. "Oh. Right. Nah, we reuse the gloves, so I figured, better clean 'em somehow. You're going inside, you'll want to get yourself a pair."

Kitty comes over and selects the smallest ones she can find. But she grimaces at the bleach. "Rather a pungent smell, isn't it?"

"You must be *really* new. Death has a smell, you know. Once you get a whiff of that? This bleach here's like fine perfume. Bleach smells like maybe I don't die today."

"Hmm." Kitty's brow furrows as she pulls on the gloves. "All right, then. Off I go."

"Maybe don't," he says.

"I'm sorry?"

He looks at her for the first time. "I don't know, it's just...you look like a nice enough person. And you're, what, giving those folks water? What's the point? They're gone already; they just don't know it yet. Won't change nothing."

"I do believe this is the *worst* hospital I've ever seen. When I'm breathing my last, I do hope someone can see far enough past their own noses to bring me a bloody drink of water."

The attendant returns to his cleaning. "Fair enough. Don't die today."

✷ ✷ ✷

Kitty pulls on the hood and steps inside. As the attendant promised, the first thing she notices is the smell. Vomit, certainly, although her own shoes are as much to blame as anything. Urine, sweat, feces. Something metallic—is that what blood smells like? And something else. Something musty and sweet, like a steak left out in the sun. *No, she thinks, not steak.*

Even on this fair-weather day, the light is dim in Reception Hospital. And no lights are turned on. *Could the staff just not be bothered?* Kitty wonders. *Or is it better this way?*

In the darkened foyer, she listens. Moaning, low and constant, like the tide, like a lonely wind. Heaving coughs. Sudden cries, begging for God or Mother or death itself. Someone snores loudly, and someone else shrieks for him to shut up already. A third voice offers to murder them both. Underneath it all, the unceasing complaints of ancient bedsprings.

There are two long rooms, one on either side of the main hall. Kitty peeks in and counts ten beds in each. She stumbles over someone's feet. So, twenty in beds, and untold numbers on the floor. She whispers an apology to whomever she stepped on, but no one answers.

Picking her way among the beds, Kitty tries to picture the human beings underneath the writhing piles of hospital linens. Between the darkness and the goggled hood, it's difficult to see much. Some of the patients look like Unusuals. She thinks, but can't be sure, that she recognizes one of the Lilliputians she'd met that first night at Magruder's. But most are of average size and shape. As she walks among them, Kitty wonders who they used to be. They could have been line cooks or showgirls, gamblers or chambermaids, ticket takers or pretzel vendors, or whoever it is who changes the myriad lightbulbs along Surf Avenue. They look young, most of them. They will not get much older.

Her pitcher of water is getting heavy. She thinks, *What am I going to do with this?* None of the beds have cups beside them. Certainly none of the poor wretches on the floor has a goblet handy. She might mop a brow or two, but her handkerchief is covered with vomit, and even if there were washcloths stashed away somewhere, there's little hope of her finding them in the dark. *What am I going to do?*

A hand reaches out and grabs her skirt. Caught off balance, she spills the pitcher on the floor. Another hand grabs her waist and pulls her down. She tumbles down onto the bed, suddenly lying nose-to-hood with someone—male or female, she can't even tell. Through her goggles, she can see a face, pock-marked and oozing, with blood seeping from its eyes.

"Take off your mask and let me see you," the face croaks. The voice is begging and threatening at once. Kitty tries to wriggle away, but the hands grip her strongly. "Take off your mask and let me see you!"

With all her strength, she wrenches herself away, her borrowed shirt ripping as she goes.

"Take off your mask and let me see you!"

The cry is picked up by other patients. "Take off your mask and let me see you!" The ones with strength left start pushing themselves up, reaching out blindly in the dimness. "Take off your mask and let me see you!"

Kitty stumbles backward, falling on yet another patient lying on the floor. She bangs her forehead on an iron bed frame as she falls. She tastes blood in her mouth. She hopes it's her own.

"*Take off your mask and let me see you!*"

She scrambles to the door, apologizing as she goes. "I'm sorry. I'm so sorry… Please let me go, please…"

Heaving herself out the front door, she rips off the hood and the pinafore and tosses them on the porch. She runs down the steps and out the gate.

"Nurse Marisol—or, er, whoever you are! Where do you think you're going?"

✦ ★ ✦

Kitty runs all the way back to Magruder's without stopping. She comes reeling into the tavern, weeping and afraid, paying no mind to the rolling eyes of the Unusuals or Zeph's greeting or Vivi Leveque's icy stare. She heads straight for Rosalind, who is holding court with Archie at a table by the window, and she throws herself into his arms.

"Jesus!" Archie says. "What happened?"

Rosalind strokes Kitty's hair as she sobs. "Our brave Miss Hayward went to Reception to help out."

"Reception? I heard they're stacking bodies like cordwood over there. There are easier ways to commit suicide, kiddo."

"Shut up, Archie. Poor dove…"

"I couldn't do it," Kitty cries into Ros's chest. "I can't help. I'm not Mum. I can't help anyone."

IN THE CITY OF
SIGHS AND TEARS

TINY LIGHTS FLICKER ALONG THE STREET AS BERNARD COYNE'S FUNERAL
march approaches Magruder's.

It's a few days after the shooting. The funeral procession was
planned for 1:00 a.m., when all the Dozens have finally trundled
home to their beds and the Unusuals have Coney to themselves at
last. Acrobats and opera singers, bellhops and belly dancers, clowns
and chefs walk shoulder to shoulder, each holding a single lit candle
in honor of their fallen friend. A black, bearded lady leads the parade
with Archie by her side. She sings, and Archie harmonizes with
uncharacteristic sweetness.

Oh, didn't he ramble, didn't he ramble.
Rambled all around, In and out of town,
Didn't he ramble, didn't he ramble.
Ramble till the butcher cut him down.

★ ★ ★

After the procession, Magruder's Unusual Tavern is packed once
again. Lazaro the Lion-Faced Boy circulates with a coffee can, collecting donations for Bernard's grave marker. At another table, Rosalind
consoles Bernard's best friend, Digby the Strongman. Digby weeps
openly. Zeph chats with Enzo, who is propping up the bar in his

usual spot. He glances over in Rosalind's direction occasionally but quickly looks away.

Zeph's singing icebox is of no use at this hour, as all the singers are either in bed or here drinking. Instead, people gather around a gramophone set up on the bar, and they tilt their heads toward its enormous bell-shaped speaker. Magruder's collection only numbers in the dozens of songs, but no one seems to mind. Unusuals call out requests, argue over the selections, and try to stop imagining pieces of Bernard being hosed off the Dreamland promenade.

Nearby, Kitty sits at a table with Archie, while P-Ray snoozes in her lap. Kitty hasn't slept much since Reception Hospital—every dream features her mother's face with blood dripping from her eyes. But if British reserve is good for anything, it's for getting through a funeral with grace. Whitey stands beside Kitty, flirting with her, and she flirts right back. *This is what we do,* Mum whispers. *We go on.*

The song on the gramophone ends, leaving the entire tavern in an awkward silence until the crowd restarts the argument over the next selection. "Play 'In the City of Sighs and Tears.'" "Ach, that's too sad—do you have 'Give My Regards to Broadway'?" "No, no, play the new one about Coney again." "Bernard preferred 'Give My Regards.' He told me so himself."

A lone voice rises above the others. "Shut up, all of you!"

Startled, the crowd looks toward the end of the bar, where a heavily tattooed man is hunched over a glass of green whiskey. The man glowers at the crowd. "Yeah, freaks. You heard me. Shut the hell up."

Zeph nods to the group and says, "Put the Coney one on," and then he rolls his cart down to the tattooed man. "Pete," he says quietly. "I think that's enough, don't you?"

Crumbly Pete scowls at Zeph and defiantly drains his glass. The gramophone starts to play, and the crowd sways along to the tinkling waltz.

There's one place on earth I call my land
not far away.

And that is a dear little island
just down the bay.
It's there you'll meet people so jolly
And just your style.
So jump on a steamer or trolley
For my little Coney Isle.

"You better turn that shit off, or somebody's gonna get hurt," Crumbly Pete growls.

Zeph shakes his head. "Don't make me toss you out of here, Pete."

"Aww, come off it. Don't tell me you *like* this crap."

"What I like ain't the point. It's disrespectful to Bernard, acting how you are."

Pete laughs insanely. "You're insects! You're all insects, and none of it matters, and you know why? You're dead, that's why! You're all dead already!"

"Enough." Zeph waves to Digby. "Hey, Digs, would you do the honors?"

Digby walks over and slaps two meaty hands on Crumbly Pete's shoulders. "Okay, Pete, let's go."

Digby hauls him out, with Pete hollering, "You're all dead, you insects are all dead," as they go.

From their table, Archie and Kitty watch Pete depart. Then she raps the table, hoping to change the mood. "So, Archibald, I helped Zeph fetch the groceries today, and I had a fascinating chat with that older lady at the vegetable stand. Did you know that there's talk of shutting down the schools? She also said her neighbor was taken to some island? Hoffman, I think she said? That sick people in Manhattan get sent to a tuberculosis hospital in Queens, but they're keeping all the sick people from Coney *imprisoned*. Do you think it could be true? I have to say, after what I saw at Reception Hospital, nothing would surprise me. What if Mother is there now, waiting for me?"

"The usual fishwife gossip, Miss Hayward."

"You're probably right." She sighs. "She also said the whole epidemic was started intentionally by the German empire."

He snorts. "Dozens will believe anything."

A figure steps out of the crowd and taps Kitty on the shoulder. "Excuse me, are you Miss Hayward?"

"Shove off, lad," Archie says. "The lady and I are—"

Kitty turns and sees the young man, his mop of unkempt red hair and his worried look. "Good Lord. You're Seamus. Yes, I'm Kitty Hayward."

"Yeah," he says. "I'm Seamus Nolan? From the Manhattan Beach Hotel?" His accent and his awkwardness render declarative statements impossible. "Your friends said I could find you here?"

"Yes, of course! Archie, would you pull that chair over for him?"

Archie mutters to himself but yanks over a chair.

"Uh, actually, I just wanted to talk to Miss Hayward?"

"Lovely." Archie leans back, folds his arms behind his head, and stretches out his legs. "Let's talk, then."

"Uh…" Seamus looks at Kitty.

"It's all right," Kitty says. "Actually, I'd like to have Archie's opinion on whatever you have to say."

Seamus looks uncomfortable but nods. In whispered fits and starts, he confirms what they suspected: when the hotel doctor discovered Mrs. Hayward's illness, the management resolved to handle the situation by making Mrs. Hayward disappear. Seamus, along with the rest of the hotel employees, was instructed on threat of termination not to acknowledge Kitty's existence.

"But people kept on getting sick? Dying? I went 'round to the kitchens on an errand and…I saw the freezer. There's bodies in there, Miss Hayward. A lot of bodies. Where the steaks used to be. And I can't sleep, and I can't eat nothing? And your ma's a proper sweet lady, and…I don't know, I'm just so sorry…" It's clear there's something else he wants to say, but he can't make it come out.

"What good are you?" Archie demands. "You come here to…

what? Confess? Make yourself feel better? And then insult Miss Hayward by telling her what she already knows?"

"I'm sorry. I…"

"Tell her something useful! Tell her one useful thing to redeem your otherwise pointless existence!"

"I don't—"

Archie stands up, threateningly. "By God, boy, if you—"

"There's an island!" Seamus cowers.

Archie sits back down. "An island."

"Yeah, where the sick people are. And maybe that's where the cure is? I mean—"

Kitty looks at Archie, wide-eyed. "It's just like the vegetable woman said! It's true. Archie, they're keeping her on the island!"

"No, no. Wait," Seamus says. "*That* ain't what I said. I didn't mean *her*. I meant there's medicine on the—"

At that moment, a group of men burst into Magruder's, dressed in hoods and goggles. "Ladies and gentlemen," shouts their leader. "This gathering has been deemed illegal by the Committee on Public Safety. You must all depart the premises immediately."

"Hey!" Zeph shouts. "What do you think you're doing?"

A scream comes from the back and everyone scatters, snatching up coats and overturning chairs, a river of carnies flowing toward the exit.

P-Ray wakes up and starts to cry, and Kitty hugs him. One of the exterminators points. "There!"

The men descend on Kitty and P-Ray, and Enzo leaps at them. "*Bastardi*, what you doing?"

Two hooded Committeemen shrug off Enzo, and they hold Kitty back while a third man wrenches P-Ray from her arms. The boy shrieks and thrashes like an animal in a trap as the man tosses him over a shoulder and makes for the door.

Rosalind screams. "P-Ray!"

Enzo roars and lunges at them again. He waves his muscled arms and knocks a pair of Committeemen aside like bowling pins.

Rosalind leaps in, throwing punches and scratching eyes, and the officers toss Kitty aside to defend themselves. One Committeeman gets his truncheon around Rosalind's throat and yanks him back. Enzo lands a couple of solid blows before the Committeemen subdue him by their sheer number. The leader says, "Put him in the truck too." The men wrestle Enzo down as he struggles and curses in Italian. Rosalind screams and reaches for Enzo, but a Committee officer kicks Rosalind in the groin and then laughs as Rosalind collapses in agony. "Guess he'll be even less than half a man tomorrow, eh, boys?"

Kitty goes to comfort Rosalind on the floor, and they watch helplessly as the men drag Enzo and P-Ray to an uncertain fate.

But no, Kitty realizes—no, their fate isn't uncertain. She knows precisely where the men are taking them.

"Listen," Zeph says to the leader, "I don't know what y'all are after, but that's just a little boy. He's not sick, and you've no cause to—"

"He keeps fleas," the leader says, "as you know damn well. Why, you wanna join him?"

The leader addresses his men. "Our tipster says the fleas are kept in a drawer upstairs."

"What are you talking about, 'tipster'? What 'tipster'?" Zeph demands.

"Should I go find them?" a Committeeman asks the leader.

"No, the whole place is contaminated. Boss says take the building down."

"Take it down?" Zeph cries. "It's just a handful of fleas, for God's sake. Look, I'll show you where they are! You can have the damn things! There's no cause to—"

"Stop!" Kitty bounds over. "I'm sick. I'm sick too. And…I'm a flea keeper. I keep the fleas, not the boy. Me. You're looking for me."

"English," Zeph protests, "don't you get in the middle of this, now."

"I'm a flea keeper," she repeats.

He stares at her. "What in *hell* are you doing?"

Kitty gazes calmly at the Committee leader. "I'm a carrier. And a flea keeper. And…a cougher. Forget the boy, and take me to the island or…or I'll cough all over the lot of you."

Rosalind gasps. "No, Kitty, don't…"

"Kitty," Zeph says, "stop and think here."

The leader shrugs at her. "Whatever you say, lady. But if it's all the same to you, we'll take all three of ya." He nods, and another hooded man takes Kitty roughly by the arm and escorts her out.

Zeph bounds after them, shouting, "Wait! Just wait, goddamn it!"

The bar, packed to the rafters not five minutes earlier, is empty except for Archie, Rosalind, and a terrified Seamus, who bursts into tears. "This is all wrong," he blubbers. "You have to stop her. She didn't understand—she didn't understand what I meant!"

Archie rounds on him. "What in the Sam Hill are you—"

"It's what I was trying to say! Miss Hayward's mother is *at the hotel*. Me and my mates, we have her hidden at the hotel! She ain't well, poor Mrs. H., and I just thought maybe they had medicine on the island, so—"

Archie rears up to his full height and roars down at the boy. "What in *hell* is Mrs. Hayward doing at your *goddamn* hotel?"

"I was trying to tell it before," Seamus cries. "Mrs. H. had the sickness, but she seemed so nice like, and our manager, he's so mean, and he was going to—I don't know, who knows—so me and the other bellhops, we took her! We told the manager she died? But she didn't never die; she's in the basement! I got no family, and my mate Fergal got nobody neither, and Mickey, his da' just beats him all the day long…but Mrs. H., she's sweet to us. I stole a book from one of the rooms, and she reads it to us, over and over and over; she don't never mind it. She's got the sickness something terrible, though—and *that's* why I come here! I thought at the island, maybe they could help—"

The leader of the Committee leans in the door. "Better clear out if you know what's good for you. There won't be much left of this place when we're through."

✳ ✳ ✳

Kitty is shoved into the Committee's armored vehicle with Enzo and P-Ray. "Don't be afraid, sweetie," Kitty says to the boy. "We're with you. Don't be scared."

The Committeemen climb into other cars. "Pierce, McKenzie," the leader says. "You two stay and do the cleanup. We'll meet you back at the pier."

Zeph and the rest exit the bar in time to see the armored truck peel away down the street. Rosalind cries, and Zeph squeezes his leg. "It's all right, Ros. We'll fix it. We'll get them back somehow, I pro—"

"Don't you tell me it's all right!" Rosalind shrieks. "They've taken my boys away!"

The two remaining exterminators lift heavy gasoline cans and storm Magruder's Curiosity Cabinet.

"No!" Zeph screams and chases them inside the Cabinet. He flings himself at them, howling.

One of the men seizes Zeph by the torso, lifts him up, and hurls him at the closest wall. "Go screw, you little freak!"

"Okay, you douse the near wall, and I'll go over by the—"

"What in name of the Carpenter is it that you are doing?"

The Committeemen look up, surprised. "Who is this, now?"

A few feet away, standing beside Cleopatra's asp and a historically confused knight, is a compact old man in a lab coat. He has a shock of white hair pointing in every direction, complicated goggles on his face, and a sawed-off, double-barreled shotgun braced against his shoulder. He aims the gun at the Committeemen. "I ask you again. What is it you do?"

"Committee on Public Safety. This building has been condemned, and you best get out if you know what's—"

"This my home," the old man says calmly. "Is best *you* get hell out."

"Put the gun down, old-timer. We work for the city, and we—"

"No, I think you don't."

The exterminators blink at the old man and then at one another. Chuckling, one says, "Ah, you think we don't work for the city? Because I assure you—"

"No. No, I think you don't, period. I think you don't anything, ever again."

"Who the devil do you think you—"

The old man squeezes the first trigger, sending an explosion of buckshot into the chest of one Committeeman, who tumbles backward into a cabinet crowded with insects in glass jars. He dies screaming in a cloud of shattered glass and Madagascar spitting cockroaches. His partner swings his truncheon as the old man fires the second trigger, and his hooded head evaporates in a spray of blood and bone.

The old man lowers the shotgun and massages his shoulder. "This will hurt later," he notes. He sees Zeph on the floor. "You good?"

Zeph nods, speechless, and Timur nods back.

"Is all right. You clean up tomorrow."

The mad old doctor pivots on one heel and retreats into the shadows of the Cabinet.

✶ ✶ ✶

The armored vehicle makes its way north. In the back, P-Ray's crying is the only sound. Kitty puts her arm around him, and she nudges Enzo's foot with her own. "Are you all right, Mr. Enzo?"

Enzo holds his face in his hands and does not answer.

Between two slats in the side of the vehicle, Kitty can just make out the lights of the Brooklyn Bridge. They're headed for the pier. And then…what? Kitty is just another prisoner. Even assuming she can find her mother, how on earth can she help? *Why have I done this mad thing? What was I thinking?*

P-Ray weeps, barely able to catch his breath between sobs. "Shh, love," Kitty says. "It will be all right. I promise it will." She tries to think of some way to make the boy feel a little better. "Shall I sing to you? Would you like that?"

P-Ray nods and sniffles.

But instead of a childhood lullaby, the first melody that pops into her head is one that played endlessly at Magruder's.

"There's no room for sorrow in my land,
It's always gay.
And light is as bright on the Island
As bright as day.
Sweethearts from all over creation
Just see them smile.
Come down, you need no invitation
To my little Coney Isle."

TWO DOLLARS

❧

I N THE CABINET, ZEPH SCRUBS THE FLOOR, A BUCKET OF SOAPY PINK WATER beside him. The two dead men are lumped in the corner.

He hears but ignores the knock at Magruder's front door. "We're closed," he mutters.

The knock comes again. "We're closed!" Zeph says, loudly this time.

But the door eases open regardless. A head peeks around the black curtain. Reynolds.

Zeph groans. "For cryin' out loud. What, you just lettin' your own self in now? You reckon you own this place too?"

"No, I just stopped in to see how—" Spencer takes in the bloody floor, the smashed cabinets, the bodies in the corner. "Holy jumping Christ! What happened here?"

Zeph tosses his rag down angrily and glares up at him. "What happened? Hmm, where do I start? We got ourselves a little visit from the Committee on Public Safety. Can't you tell? Don't we look perfectly damn *safe* right now?"

"But why? Why would they come here?"

Zeph nearly screams in frustration. "Why, oh why would they come here? Oh, who can say? Life is just one big *fucking* mystery to you, ain't it?"

"What? You think *I* sent them? Why would I do that, Zeph?"

"Then who was the *tipster*?"

"The what?"

"The tipster! Who was the damn tipster who told them all about P-Ray's fleas and *precisely* where those fleas were kept? Who else but you has connections enough to make this happen? Which lousy Dozen has even been inside this Cabinet long enough to—"

Zeph stops. He stares up at Spencer, and Spencer stares down at him.

"Gibson," Spencer says. "Goddamn it."

Zeph takes a deep breath and rubs his eyes. "Your little weasel friend from the other day."

"Gibson's not my friend—he's my father's errand boy." Spencer's voice has an unexpected edge.

"No-o-o, he's a big hero now, ain't he? Turning in the danger-ous flea boy, that terrifying forty-eight-inch threat to civilization."

Spencer scowls. "Gib Tilden wouldn't know a hero if one came up and clobbered him. Gib's sole interest in life is Gib. And sooner or later, there's going to be a reckoning. Sooner, if it's up to me."

Zeph looks up at Spencer. "Well now, white boy. That's the first thing I ever heard you say made any damn sense."

"Just the way I see it."

There's a silence. Zeph goes back to scrubbing.

"You need some help?" Spencer asks. No answer. "Zeph? I said, can I help?"

"I got it."

"Are you sure…"

Zeph sighs. "They took P-Ray."

"What? No."

"Yeah. And they took Enzo, 'cause Enzo tried to stop 'em taking P-Ray. And—you'll love this—they took Kitty too, because Kitty *volunteered*."

"Why on earth would she—"

"Apparently, she was under the impression that sick folks are being taken to some island somewhere, and she got the bright idea to go look for her mama there. But you wouldn't know anything about any island, now, would you?"

"Hoffman. Dammit." Spencer pauses. "Look, I… They wouldn't have taken her mother there. They—" He sees Zeph glaring at him. "Okay. *We* didn't have the island set up that quickly. Kitty's mother would have been one of the first cases, and *we* weren't using Hoffman Island yet."

"Gosh, too bad *we* didn't know that when Kitty got herself sent there on purpose."

"I…" Spencer kneels down beside Zeph. "Look, if Kitty's mother was on that South African ship, she never would have made it to Hoffman. I didn't tell her because I didn't want to give her false hope, that's all. Zeph, I'm sorry. I'm going to help, I swear. I'm going to fix this somehow."

Zeph takes a deep breath, exhales. "If you really want to help, drag them Committee fellas to the backyard. Still ain't figured what we're going to do with them, but we can't leave 'em in the middle of the Cabinet, that's for sure."

"Um." Spencer blanches. "You know, Zeph, I'm…um… It's just—"

"You wanna help or not? You too good for this job?"

"Yes—I mean, no. *Yes*, I want to help; *no* to the other." He takes a deep breath, removes his jacket, and rolls up his sleeves. Spencer tries to look nonplussed, but his stomach turns over when he gets close. Shotgun blasts at close range don't leave much pretty behind. One man's chest cavity is split open, and flies are already gathering for the banquet. Meanwhile, the other corpse retains only a vague suggestion of a head. Spencer stares at each corpse, unsure which nightmare to tackle first. After some consideration, he opts for the beheaded body. He takes a deep breath and, hoping Zeph hasn't noticed his hesitation, kneels down and eases his arms underneath the dead man's arms. The remains of the man's skull lull forward, sending viscera flowing down the front of Spencer's shirt. He stumbles back and retches but tries to mask it with a cough.

Zeph stays focused on his scrubbing, but he smiles. *Look at the prince of the city now.* But despite everything, Zeph can't help but feel for Spencer just a little bit. Ain't like he'd been eager to touch those bodies either. "Reynolds, it's okay if you need to—"

There's a pounding on the front door. "Open up! Committee on Public Safety!"

"Oh God," Zeph says. "They come back for their boys!" He and Spencer look around at the Cabinet, still sprayed with blood and showered with broken glass; at the corpses, decomposing on the floor; and at each other, not looking much better. "What do we do?"

"Okay, don't panic. Let me think."

"*Think?* We got to get out of here. Come on, we'll go out the back. You can hoist me over the wall, and we'll—"

Bang bang bang. "Committee on Public Safety! Open this door right now!"

"All right," Zeph whispers. "You gotta…I don't know, hold 'em off somehow, while I get Ros and the Doc, and we'll—"

"No," Spencer says. "No, we can't run. It'll never work. They'll still find the bodies. They'll still—"

Bang bang bang. "Open this door right now!"

Zeph grabs Spencer's pant leg. "Reynolds! Have you heard about Edison's electric chair? They're gonna put me in it. Maybe Timur too, but definitely me!"

"Zeph, let me think for one—"

Bang bang bang. "This is your final warning. I am authorized by the city of New York to break down this door!"

"Jesus!"

"I got it." Spencer kneels down, nose to nose with Zeph. He reaches into his pocket and pulls out two dollar bills. "Take my money."

"What? Brother, we can't bribe these guys! Certainly not with—"

"Zeph, you want me to help you? Take the damned money. Now."

Bang bang bang. "By the orders of the Committee on Public Safety, we are breaking down this door!"

Zeph takes the money.

"Now shake my hand."

"Spencer, what are you—"

"Fucking hell, Zeph, shake my hand!" He does. "Thank you." Spencer stands, wipes the brains off his shirt as best he can, and runs bloody fingers through his hair. He yanks his jacket back on, misbuttoning it as he marches to the black curtains. Before he steps through, he turns to Zeph. "Wish me luck."

The Committeemen have set about forcing the door when it suddenly pops open. Spencer stands before them, smiling broadly. "Gentlemen! How are you this morning? You know," he says with a wink, "we leave this door unlocked—there was no need for all the histrionics. Anyway, come in, boys. Please, come in."

Four Committee officers step into the dim entryway of Magruder's. Three wear the usual hood-and-goggles gear, while the fourth is dressed more officiously in the uniform of Dreamland security. Spencer peers at his uncovered face. "My goodness, you're McGrath, aren't you? Chief of security! I'm Spencer Reynolds. I'm sure you remember—we met at the opening ceremonies last month. Gentlemen, welcome to the latest acquisition of the Dreamland Consortium."

The men eyeball one another, not sure what to make of their young prince, disheveled and bloodstained. *Aren't we supposed to burn down this place?*

"Mr. Reynolds," McGrath says carefully, "I'm not sure I understand what—"

"This building has been purchased by the Reynolds family. We just now made the deal, didn't we, Mr. Andrews?"

Spencer turns back to the velvet curtains. Zeph peeks his head around, trying to figure out whether to run for his life. "Um," he says. "Yeah...we did?"

Spencer grins. "Of course we did! Just now. So, gentlemen, whatever concerns you might have about these buildings are completely—"

"Now, wait," McGrath says. "First of all, we're here looking for Pete McKenzie and John Pierce. They were here last night, but they never—"

"Well now," Spencer says, his mind racing. *Where would they go? Where would those boys have gone after their mission, if not home?* The answer is almost too easy. "Chief McGrath, we all know that Coney Island has more than her share of…distractions, shall we say? Some smelling of whiskey, some of perfume? I'm sure your men were diverted from their appointed rounds, as they say. But that's no reason to—"

"And second, why would Dreamland buy this shit hole? Dreamland is all the way on the other end of the island!"

Spencer laughs, a bit harder than necessary. "Chief McGrath. You're a man of the law. The ways of business must seem mysterious to you, so allow me to explain." He pauses to clear his throat. "Gentlemen, this current crisis—by which, of course, I mean the Cough—is very dire indeed. But like all crises, this too shall pass. And when it does? The number of visitors to Coney Island will expand tenfold, and it is visionary capitalists like the Dreamland Consortium who stand to reap the rewards."

"What are you talking about, Mr. Reynolds?"

"Here at Coney Island, we scour the history books for traumatic events to re-create. Pompeii. The flooding of Galveston, Texas. The apocalyptic crisis is our bread and butter. Now, thanks to the Cough, we have our own! And you think the Reynolds family would let such an opportunity go unexploited?" Spencer shakes his head. "I'm a bit insulted, frankly."

McGrath frowns. He can feel his men's allegiance shifting, and he doesn't like it. "Look, Mr. Reynolds. This building was scheduled for burning last night, but it's still standing. We're here to remedy that oversight. So by order of the Committee on Public Safety, I insist that—"

"The Dreamland Consortium is turning Magruder's into a Calcutta Cough History Museum. Nobody is interested in whether you think it's a good idea. Are we clear?"

McGrath studies Spencer's blood-splattered clothes. "If that's all this is—a business transaction—then why do you look like somebody chewed you up and spat you out? Look at yourself."

Shit. "Ah, you see, I—"

"I don't like him," Zeph pipes up from beside the curtain. "I don't like him, and I don't like his plans for *my* museum, and the two of us mighta got into it a little bit."

The men gaze down at Zeph and laugh. "Sorry," McGrath says. "But you're telling me—what are ya, three feet tall? *You* did that to Reynolds?"

Zeph shrugs. "What can I tell ya? That is one soft college boy, and I am one angry Negro."

McGrath raises his hands in submission. "Fair enough. But, Mr. Reynolds, there was a report of fleas being kept here, which is a public health issue. So before we go, we really do have to take a look around and make sure everything's all right."

Zeph glances behind him into the main room of the Cabinet. One of the dead men's intestines are leaking out onto the rug.

"Now," Spencer says, "I'm sure that's not necessary."

"I'm afraid it is, sir."

Spencer takes a step forward and looks McGrath straight in the eye. "The Dreamland Consortium pays your salary. Your commitment will be rewarded, I assure you. But for now? Take your men and go."

"Mr. Reynolds—"

"I'll say it once more. Take your men. And go."

McGrath blinks. "I…I gotta check with your father."

"Of course." Spencer smiles. "Tell him what I said about Pompeii. He'll like that."

The men shake hands with Spencer and depart. When they've gone, Spencer closes the door and slumps against it, rhythmically banging his head while the blood drains from his face. "For. The. Love. Of. Christ!"

Zeph laughs. "That was good, Reynolds. I gotta admit. That was damn good."

Spencer shakes his head. "I think I'm going to pass out."

"Go right ahead—*after* you get the bodies moved. You might have bought the Cabinet, but right now, you work for *me*."

Spencer smiles. "I consider it an honor. And once I get that done, I need to speak to Rosalind. I think I have an idea."

✦ ✦

23

MUMMIES

❦

KITTY WAKES IN A DARKNESS SO COMPLETE THAT SHE'S UNSURE WHETHER her eyes are open. She sits in the damp hull of the tugboat *Magpie*, crammed shoulder to shoulder with her fellow captives. Although it is too dark to see, she can feel their presence, hear their terrified breaths underneath the droning thunder of the boat's engine. Whispered voices and quiet crying, punctuated by phlegmy coughs.

P-Ray sleeps in Kitty's lap. The motion of the boat lulled him, despite their predicament. Kitty wishes she could sleep too—perhaps forget for a while that she's damp and cold and scared. She isn't sure how fast the boat is going or how far they've traveled. Far enough. Wherever this island is, there'll be no swimming back, that's for sure. There may be no coming back at all.

"Excuse me," a voice calls out into the void. "When will we get there?"

"Shut up," a gruff voice answers—presumably one of the sailors who met them at the pier and herded them down into the hold. "You'll get there when you get there. What, you in a hurry?"

Men's laughter. "Yeah, he's in a hurry," says another voice. "He's got a date!"

The first man guffaws at this. "Date with an oven, maybe. Relax, buddy. Swinburne crematorium ain't going no place."

The woman squeezed in against Kitty has a coughing fit and throws up on herself. Kitty's stomach flips over, and she shrinks away from the pool of vomit as best she can. But she's trapped in place, with P-Ray on her lap and captives all around. Kitty closes her eyes and tries to breathe through her mouth to avoid the smell.

The sick woman coughs more. "Thomas," she whispers between coughs. "Thomas, please forgive me." She lets out a little sigh, and her body relaxes completely, as though she fainted. But Kitty senses that a darker thing has claimed her. A moment ago, there had been a person sitting beside her; now, there isn't. Kitty imagines the woman's spirit floating away into the night. She hopes the spirit reaches heaven. She wonders if her mother is already there.

The dead woman's head lolls over onto Kitty's shoulder. Kitty gasps and pushes the head away. But as soon as Kitty lowers her hand, the head rolls back. Kitty's entire body tenses—every part of her begs to run. But the captives are packed into the hold like apples in a box. There is nowhere to go.

✦ ✦ ✦

Kitty, P-Ray, and Enzo join the rest of the captives on the *Magpie*'s tiny deck. Kitty tells the first sailor she sees that a woman next to her expired during the trip. Neither concerned nor especially surprised, he says, "I'll take care of it."

Kitty shudders. *It.* Just more landfill he needs to dispose of.

Is that how Mum was treated?

From the deck, Kitty can see that Hoffman comprises long, two-story dormitories laid out in neat rows. They surround an expansive hospital building with a central hall and multiple corridors stretching out like spokes. A second island across the way, which Kitty assumes must be Swinburne, seems to have only one major building—a large, brick structure with a tall chimney spewing smoke. The crematorium.

Like the sun coming out after a storm, a buzz of anticipation surges in Kitty's chest, breaking through the terror that had nearly consumed her on the trip over. Is Mum here? Could this be it? She imagines her mother's expression—first shocked, then relieved, then proud, so proud of her girl, her rescuer.

At last, it is Kitty and Enzo's turn off the tug. They each take one of P-Ray's hands and guide him onto the dock, joining the crowd standing outside the hospital building. A flock of nurses exit the hospital to manage the newcomers. They wear white uniforms, white gloves, white hats. White gauze is wrapped around their faces, leaving only their eyes exposed—the nurses look like a swarm of hastily created mummies.

High-ceilinged and airy, the hospital lobby was designed as a monument to turn-of-the century respectability—immaculate white walls, expansive bay windows, and a marble floor polished to a high shine. A mural depicting the Greek physician Galen dominates one wall; victims of another, ancient plague suffer theatrically at the good doctor's feet, and he reaches down to them like an angel.

But the tranquillity of this public space is overwhelmed by the sheer amount of public crammed into it. Every inch of space on every bench is taken; folding chairs and wooden crates have been brought in, and those are occupied as well. If there is a logic to the proceedings, Kitty can't find it. The nurses encourage men to remain on one side of the room, women and children on the other, but the crowds are too big and the staff too small to actually enforce this rule. And yet for all the overcrowding, the lobby is strangely quiet. Hacking coughs and moans of pain echo across the room, but no one cries out, no one protests. Instead, they whisper to one another in a variety of languages, in tones irritated, fearful, weary. Children complain to their mothers and are shushed.

Eventually, gauze-masked doctors arrive to make their inspections, for which the patients are grateful, if only because at least this is something new, a break in the tedium. The doctors make determinations about where patients should be placed—those who are not too badly off will be ushered to beds in the dormitories, while those deemed beyond salvation will be put on a boat for Swinburne, the most final of destinations.

Kitty threads her way through the crowded lobby, peering into every face. *Are you her? Are you?* No one is.

Enzo joins the men on one side of the room, while Kitty finds a spot for herself and P-Ray to stand at one of the broad windows. It's dawn, and the sun peeks timidly over the horizon, a reluctant witness. If she squints, she thinks she can see Coney Island in the distance. The gleaming Beacon Tower at Dreamland, the spectacular Ferris wheel at Steeplechase, the spires of Luna Park. Hotels and roller coasters and the gigantic Iron Pier. A dream city, miles away.

P-Ray rubs his sleepy eyes and follows Kitty's stare out toward Coney. He nudges closer, as though he'd disappear into her skirts if he could. Then he looks up, and although he doesn't speak, his face is easy to read. *I want to go home.*

✦ ✦ ✦

For the third time, the doctor feels Kitty's throat with his fingers. He holds her wrist and feels for her pulse. He puts his hand on her forehead to gauge her temperature. He shakes his head. "Is this a joke?"

The doctor's voice is dampened by his gauze mask; Kitty thinks she must have misunderstood. She stands before him in a paper dressing gown, exposed and shivering, as close to naked as she has ever been in front of a man. Joking is the furthest thing from her mind. "I'm sorry?"

"I need a break." He sighs and plunks down, exhausted, on his stool, the only place to sit in this stifling closet of an exam room. He reaches behind his head and loosens the mask, which falls off his face and onto his chest like a defeated cravat. "You are *not* sick; that much is clear." He removes his gloves and tosses them on the floor. He offers Kitty a cigarette, but she declines, so he lights his own. "I'm not supposed to be here either, to tell you the truth. When the Cough—which is the plague, by the way, it's the damn plague… Don't words mean anything anymore? When this plague got out of control, the city doubled the staff here at Hoffman. I used to deliver babies at City Hospital. Now I do this. Whatever *this* is."

The doctor takes a long drag on his cigarette and stares at the floor. Kitty isn't sure whether she is meant to fill the silence. She shifts uncomfortably on bare feet.

"We're moving hundreds and hundreds of patients through this facility. Some get better. Many don't. Nothing we do seems to make much difference either way. I asked a colleague of mine— an old friend from med school—to come out here and help. He was dead inside of seventy-two hours. So I've got *that* to answer for. Meanwhile, I get coughed on all day long and nothing. If we knew why... Is it biology? Diet? Is God a narcoleptic? Makes no difference, I suppose. The fact is, as busy as I am? As busy as all the Hoffman staff is? Another staff is busier."

He looks Kitty directly in the eyes, and a chill goes through her.

"Swinburne," she says quietly. "Swinburne is busier."

He nods and stands up. "In any case, you clearly don't need a doctor. I'm sorry we seem to have wasted each other's time."

"Please..." Kitty takes a deep breath. "You're right, I'm not sick. I'm looking for my mother, Jemma Hayward. I believe she has the Cal—the plague." Whether due to the cigarette smoke in her face or the words in her throat, Kitty's eyes well up. "Please. Have you seen her? Jemma Hayward? She would have been brought here some time ago."

"Don't know the name, sorry." He sighs again, stubs out his cigarette. "Now that you're here, of course, you've been exposed—so here you'll stay for the time being. I'll have a nurse bring you fresh clothes, and we'll find you and your friends some beds. The boy can stay with you, assuming he's healthy, but the Italian will have to stay in the gentlemen's dormitory." He moves to leave the tiny exam room.

"But might she be here?" Kitty asks desperately. "In one of the dormitories? Perhaps she survived. Perhaps she's one of the lucky ones?"

The doctor turns back and faces her. "Believe me when I say that the question of why some people survive while most don't is something that disturbs my sleep every single night. If Jemma Hayward were one of our mystery survivors, I would know of her. There is no Jemma Hayward on Hoffman."

"But—"

"I'm very busy, Miss Hayward. You need to face facts and turn your eyes to Swinburne."

He departs, leaving Kitty standing alone in her paper dressing gown, tears spilling down her face and onto the doctor's gloves abandoned at her feet.

24

GIVE MY
REGARDS...

❧

"Zeph sent some lunch for you." No answer. "Rosalind, please."

"Leave me alone." Rosalind's voice sounds strange. It's gone gray somehow.

"How long has it been since you've eaten?"

"Go away."

"I know you're upset. But I want to—"

"Nobody cares what *you* want, Reynolds."

"—talk to you, and I want you to listen. Please, just listen." Silence. Spencer sighs and puts the tray on the floor. "You win. I'm leaving your food here. But there's something I have to say. So I'll...I'll say it to your door, I guess, and you can listen, or not."

He takes a breath before continuing. Spencer has so little to offer, he wants to get it right.

"I'm sorry. It's my father's fault the Committee exists; it's Gibson's fault they took Enzo and P-Ray. I suppose you see it as my fault too, and I won't argue. And...I have no words. Which I suppose is fine, because words aren't what you want. But there's a Decoration Day party at the Oriental Hotel tonight. President Roosevelt will be there, and the governor. The mayor, the head of the public health department...*and my father*. I can talk to them, explain that there's been a mistake, that there are some folks on Hoffman we need to get back. They can fix this with the stroke of a pen, Rosalind, with one telephone call. And they'll all be at this party tonight. Hate me all you want, but the fact is, I'm the only person you know who can walk into—"

The door bursts open. "I'm going with you."

Rosalind stands in his dressing gown, hair unkempt, eyes red and wild. To Spencer, the thought of turning this creature loose on New York's elite class—his people—is frankly terrifying. But Spencer knows he'd have a better chance at turning back a hurricane than keeping Rosalind from the Oriental Hotel.

Well, Roosevelt, let's see how rough a rider you truly are.

✦ ✦ ✦

Zeph has finally swept up the last of the shattered glass and dead bugs. He climbs one of the cabinet ladders to inspect the damage. "Well… this exotic insect display is a goner. I'll have a look through the back room, see what else we got. Mary Surratt's noose, maybe…be patriotic for Decoration Day."

Spencer appears and leans against one of the cabinets. He wears a musty, out-of-fashion tuxedo.

"Look at you, Mr. Big Man."

"Rosalind has quite a costume collection. How do I look?"

"Like a maître d' at some joint where I don't wanna eat. That suit don't fit you even a little."

Spencer holds an arm out straight, and the cuff of the jacket pulls halfway to his elbow. "I'll have you know this is how all the Parisians wear it."

Zeph grins but then says, more seriously, "I hate this plan."

"I know."

"No, you don't. Before everything went crazy, I talked to this fella Joe. He's Black Flag. You know the Black Flag?"

"You mean anarchists?"

"I do mean. He said they'd killed the last president and Roosevelt was next. Tonight."

"You think Roosevelt's people aren't ready for that? My father's been in politics my whole life. Sad to say, there's always some kook threatening to—"

"Maybe. Joe would qualify. But that fella who killed McKinley seemed like just another kook too. Look, far as I'm concerned, whatever the Black Flag does to your kind, y'all earned it. Nothing personal—that's just how I see it. But Rosalind's been through enough. I don't want him getting blown up. And—"

"You're absolutely right. How about *you* go upstairs and tell Rosalind he can't go?"

Zeph raises an eyebrow at Spencer, and Spencer raises one right back. "All right, brother," Zeph says, shaking his head. "Guess it's gonna be how it's gonna be."

"Yep."

"Let me help out a little at least." Zeph climbs down from the cabinet and heads for the back room. Spencer follows. Zeph goes straight to the cabinet marked "Robonocchio, the Automatic Boy!" He pounds on the side. "Hey, Chio, wake up. I need a favor."

"What are you—"

Zeph puts up his hand. "Just wait. Listen, Chio, you remember Joe? He was at the last Race to Death? The anarchist? Spencer here might run into him tonight, and he needs to know what Joe looks like."

Spencer laughs. "You don't really expect—"

"Shush, you."

Chio's arm begins to move.

"This is the most ridiculous—"

Zeph looks at Spencer, genuinely confused. "How is it you've been making daily visits to Magruder's and ain't figured out that— oh, look." There are already papers sitting in the slot at the bottom of Chio's cabinet. Zeph takes the papers, looks through them, and laughs. He hands them to Spencer. "Looks like Chio has a crush."

"This is the silliest—oh." The first is a portrait of Nazan sitting in a chair, reading. The second is Nazan smiling at P-Ray, gesturing as though she's telling him a story. The third is Nazan riding the Steeplechase. Spencer looks up at Zeph, speechless.

Zeph grins. "Told ya."

Spencer peers at Chio's cabinet. "So the other day, when you implied that I didn't understand how this machine works…"

"'Cause you don't. But then, neither do I. Hell, the Doc built Robonocchio, and I ain't sure he completely understands either. You could maybe stop calling Chio a *machine*, though."

Ding! Another paper in the slot. Zeph grabs it and studies the image. "Yep. That's the son of a bitch right there." He hands the portrait to Spencer. A scrappy little man with black eyes, a nasty scar along one cheek, and one sleeve pinned at the shoulder.

"One arm short, I see," says Spencer.

"Blew it off making pipe bombs in Chicago."

"Wow. He's for real, then…"

"Depends what you mean. Joe ain't smart enough to get out of the way of his own bomb. But the folks he's in with? They're for real, like the Cough."

★ ★ ★

Hours later, the front entrance of the Oriental is in a state of high-society gridlock. The hotel is set at the end of a cul-de-sac, overlooking the ocean. A single narrow street runs alongside the enormous building, and it must be shared by both arriving and departing vehicles. The tiny road is so congested and the traffic pattern so confusing that no one can move either forward or back, and the air is thick with honking horns and whinnying horses. Some of New York's aristocracy arrived by horse and carriage, believing it makes them look traditional. Others arrived by automobile, believing it makes them look forward-thinking. To Rosalind and Spencer, who arrived by foot, all they look is ridiculous.

"Huh," Spencer says. "These idiots are my people."

Rosalind smiles a little. "Ready for your Black Flag tattoo?"

"Hardly. But speaking of that…see anybody familiar?"

"Joe?" Rosalind looks around. "No."

"Keep an eye out." Spencer takes Rosalind's hand and stares into his painted face. "Please listen to me. I understand how you feel about Enzo."

"Why? Because you pitched a little woo at that Nazan girl? I guarantee that you *do not* understand Enzo and me."

"All I'm saying is, if you make a scene, we won't—"

"Oh stop. I won't make a scene. I'm here so you don't get blasted on champagne and forget why you came in the first place."

"You think I'd do that?"

"I think it's fair to say that the jury is out on what you will or will not do."

"Thanks for your confidence." He turns and scans the crowd but can't see anyone who resembles the ghastly little villain of Chio's portrait. "Well!" He offers Rosalind his elbow. "Here we go."

★ ★ ★

Rosalind had spent much of the afternoon fretting that he and Spencer had no invitation to the event; he was convinced they'd be turned away as impostors. But just as Spencer promised, a few words with hotel security was all that was needed to get them into the Oriental's palatial ballroom. In fact, Spencer's presence caused the guard to stammer like a girl at the stage door of a Broadway theater. "Mr. Reynolds, what an honor!" And that was that.

He and Rosalind make their way through the crowded lobby, Spencer waving hello to the left and good evening to the right. The crowds part like he's Moses in an unfortunate tuxedo. Flutes of champagne appear in their hands as if by magic.

"Must be nice…" Rosalind murmurs.

The ballroom looks like the aftermath of a flag factory explosion. But despite the decor, the chamber quartet warbles Johannes Brahms, not George M. Cohan. Men with thick beards and vests straining against their bellies promenade around the room, displaying their wives, decked out in the latest gowns off the Champs-Élysée.

Rosalind grasps Spencer's arm a little tighter. "All these people…" he says breathily.

Spencer grins. "You aren't intimidated, are you, Rosalind?"

"*No... Maybe.*"

"You shouldn't be." Spencer raises his glass. "You're worth a dozen Dozens, easily."

Rosalind smiles. "That's very sweet. And perfectly true."

President Roosevelt and the First Lady greet guests from within a protected circle of security guards, while New York's governor and mayor hold court amid similar, if less-protected, circles of admirers. There are other recognizable faces, but Spencer can't yet find his father.

"Look," Spencer whispers. "You see that sour, pinched fellow over there? That's the newspaper man, William Randolph Hearst. And that's Henry Ford he's chatting with."

Ros cranes his neck. "Hearst and Ford? They're friendly? I would have thought they were in different political parties."

Spencer laughs. "It's all the same party—it's the Haves Party."

"Why, Master Reynolds! I'm starting to think you have more in common with Joe than you let on."

"No, I just grew up in the game, that's all."

"Doesn't feel much like a game where I'm standing."

Spencer frowns, his eyes serious. "You're right." He gently lays his hand on Rosalind's gloved elbow. "You know, for too long, I've been—"

"Spencer Reynolds, you old dog!"

Spencer turns to see a round man with white hair peeking from underneath a tall top hat. "Judge O'Gorman, how are you, sir?" He thrusts out his hand, and O'Gorman pumps it.

"Very well, son, very well! And who is this charming flower?"

Rosalind extends his hand daintily. "Rosalind Rosebush, of the Block Island Rosebushes."

Spencer shoots a look at his companion—*Rosebush?*—but he doesn't comment.

O'Gorman just laughs. "The Block Island Rosebushes, I never! Delighted. And, Spencer, it is delightful to see you. I wasn't sure I would. Apparently, your father isn't coming? That's what I heard anyway. Is he unwell? Or just unwilling to be bored to tears by one of these stuffy events?"

"Ah, he's…very busy." Spencer looks at Rosalind meaningfully. "He sends his regrets."

A waiter approaches with a tray of champagne flutes. "More champagne?"

"Always!" O'Gorman drains his glass and takes a full one, and Rosalind takes a deep breath and does the same. Spencer puts his half-full glass on the tray and stares at the floor.

"Young man," O'Gorman says to the waiter, "I can't help but notice your arm." One of the waiter's sleeves is pinned to his uniform.

Spencer looks up—the empty sleeve, the black eyes, the scar. *Shit.*

The waiter nods at the judge solemnly. "Yes, sir. Battle of Manila Bay."

"A veteran! Now you're serving drinks to useless old sods like myself? On Decoration Day, no less?"

"It's an honor to serve a great man like Roosevelt."

O'Gorman pats the waiter on the back, gently so as not to spill the champagne. "No, lad. It is you who honor us."

"Thank you, sir." The waiter moves on.

Spencer glances at Rosalind. The waiter gave no sign of recognizing Rosalind decked out in full femme, but Rosalind nods subtly at Spencer. *Yes, that's him.*

"Spencer," O'Gorman says. "I understand congratulations are in order. Graduated from Princeton this year, is that right? I'm a Dartmouth man myself, so naturally—"

"Yes… I'm sorry. I just remembered I have to…uh…"

Rosalind's eyes follow the waiter. "You have things to do. Go on. I'm sure Judge O'Gorman can keep me entertained."

"On with you, then. Don't embarrass your papa!" O'Gorman leers at Rosalind. "I am *dying* to hear all about those Block Island Rosebushes…"

Spencer jogs over to the waiter, who has approached another

group of partygoers to exchange their empty glasses. "Pardon me." He takes the waiter by his arm and steers him to an unoccupied spot by the ballroom's far wall. "Where is it?"

"I'm sorry, sir?"

"Don't play games, Joe. I'm a friend of Zeph's."

Joe's expression changes from servile to something darker. "I'm here making a living, just like any—"

"Tell me where the bomb is!" Spencer yanks on Joe's one arm, and champagne flutes shatter on the floor. The guests within earshot subtly adjust their positions, the better to listen in.

Realizing he has an audience, Joe slathers on the innocence. "Sir, I'm terribly sorry. I don't understand."

"You don't?" Spencer laughs. "Of course you don't. Because you've got nothing."

"I don't know what you mean," Joe says loudly. "Perhaps you've had a bit too much to—"

"Right." Unlike Joe, Spencer doesn't care who might be listening. "You make me laugh. You strut down Surf Avenue like you're commander of the Black Flag army, but when the big moment arrives, all you can do is serve cocktails and sneer. You think you're going to get famous, like that other fellow? What's his name—Czolgosz? You think we'll learn to pronounce *your* ridiculous name too? You're a joke."

Joe takes the bait. "Listen, I don't need a bomb to do what needs doing."

"I take it back. You're not a joke; you're less than a joke. You've got nothing. You are nothing." Spencer turns to walk away.

"Hey!" Joe grabs the hem of Spencer's jacket and spins him around. "You think I'm a joke? Well, the joke's on you, because it's your buddy Zeph who showed me the way. Zeph and that freak with his fleas. That kid, he got me thinking. Bombs are expensive. Even bullets cost. But who needs a human army when we've got an army of fleas?"

"Where are they?"

"Yeah, I don't think so."

Spencer grabs Joe's collar and stares into his face. Joe laughs, but then Spencer screams "Security!" and three guards materialize. "This man is an anarchist," he tells them, "and he bears ill will toward the president."

Joe keeps laughing as the guards drag him out of the Oriental. "You just touched the Black Flag, boy. Better wash your hands!"

Partygoers timidly looking on suddenly discover their bravery, and they dash to congratulate Spencer. He shakes their hands politely, but his heart is racing, and Joe's words echo in his mind. *Wash my hands? Why say that? Was it a joke? It's not funny… What could he… Oh God.* "Where's the washroom?"

Spencer sprints through the crowd, ignoring friends who call out his name and apologizing to debutantes as he elbows them out of the way. He passes Rosalind, who has managed to get himself introduced to Henry Ford.

"How goes?" Rosalind asks as Spencer rushes by.

"It's…complicated" is all Spencer can manage.

Rosalind bats his lashes at Ford. "As I was saying, Henry, is there *really* no other color than black for your cars?"

Spencer keeps running and dodging. He reaches a hallway off the ballroom, which normally would be crowded with men finishing their cigars, arguing politics, generally enjoying a respite from female company. But the hallway is empty, save for four men in tuxedos who clap hands on Spencer when he tries to pass them. "Sorry, son," one says. "You'll have to wait. The president is in there."

"You don't understand—"

"I understand fine. Sometimes nature doesn't just call—it shouts. But you'll have to wait."

"No, I… You need to—"

President Roosevelt explodes into the hallway, barking at the aides and Secret Service agents trailing behind him. "I don't care if you did find an anarchist in the building; this is Brooklyn, for Chrissake—the town's crawling with them. I'm not sneaking out like a frightened schoolgirl. Now, which of you pantywaists has my speech?"

The president stalks past Spencer without acknowledging him. But his aide notes Spencer's stricken expression and stops to whisper, "Don't feel bad. You didn't want to shake that hand. He didn't wash it after...you know."

With Roosevelt gone, the security team releases Spencer. He sprints for the men's room—a well-appointed lounge, spotless marble sinks, nothing unusual. He spins around, looking to the attendant for help. Anemic and shifty, the attendant refuses to meet Spencer's eye. Instead, he stares at his shoes and says, "Towel, sir?"

"A towel? No, I don't want—wait, what?" Spencer snatches the towel and shakes it roughly over the sink. A dozen fleas fall out.

Spencer quickly turns on the hot water, flushing the fleas down the drain. He looks up to see the attendant's sneering face in the bathroom mirror. "You bastard!"

"Yeah, well, fuck you, because Roosevelt didn't take a towel anyway!"

Spencer whirls around and moves to slam the attendant against the wall, but he stops himself when he sees the black lump on the man's neck. Instead, he shouts "Security!" and Roosevelt's men burst into the men's room. "You need to close these lavatories. *Now.*"

❧

THE SECRET SERVICE DOES FAR MORE THAN CLOSE THE BATHROOMS. THE hotel is evacuated while the Committee on Public Safety arrives in their trademark head coverings to scrub down the lobby, ballroom, restrooms, and kitchens. The truly important are whisked off to safety, while the less important are left to make their way home as best they can. Many party guests loiter on the street, gossiping as they watch emergency vehicles come and go. Absent any official announcement, the rumors percolate. There was poison in the food. No, there was gas in the air vents. No, the cellist had a gun; did you see him? He looked pretty shady.

Spencer is congratulated by the cops but also asked to answer a few questions. Secret Service and NYPD alike are curious how someone of his position knew of the anarchists' plans. Spencer readily agrees, but Rosalind quickly yanks him aside.

"I want you to understand something—"

"Rosalind, I'll just be a minute."

"No, you need to hear this first. After Leon Czolgosz killed McKinley, they had him tried, convicted, and executed in a matter of weeks. And after they electrocuted him, they poured acid in his coffin so there would be nothing left of him at all. And Czolgosz was *white*. Do you understand me?"

"No. What on earth are you talking about?"

"Zeph, of course."

"Zeph has nothing to worry about! He didn't do anything!"

"Reynolds, we could rebuild the Brooklyn Bridge with the bodies of black men who didn't do anything. Don't you *dare* point them in the direction of the Cabinet. We have enough problems already."

Spencer knows Rosalind is right: the last thing Zeph needs is the Secret Service taking an interest in the bodies decomposing in Magruder's backyard. And so the young prince of the city lies and lies and lies again. *You see, Officer, I just happened to be in Prospect Park a week ago, and...* His nausea grows with every falsehood. It's one thing to lie to Chief McGrath; he's essentially on the Reynolds payroll. Lying to the NYPD, on the other hand...and to the Secret Service, as well?

But Zeph is—unlikely as this may be—a friend. Spencer doesn't mention Magruder's once.

During the interview, a gaggle of hooded officers comes crashing out of the hotel. In their midst are five men, manacled together: Joe, the bathroom attendant, another waiter, and two janitors. They are pale, pockmarked, and coughing. Joe shouts, "I protest being chained to these men! I protest! These men are contagious! This is a violation of my—" Suddenly, the bathroom attendant stumbles, pulling Joe and the others down, one atop the other. They career down the steps as a unit and land in a heap on the sidewalk.

Spencer's interviewer pauses midquestion, and they all watch as the Committeemen hoist the anarchists up like so much soiled laundry and squeeze them into a waiting Black Maria.

"You think they'll even make it to trial?" one of the officers muses.

"Not with coughs like that," another scoffs. "*Anarchists*. Can't get outta their own way, those guys."

After every question has been asked and answered, some policemen offer to drive Spencer and Rosalind home. Afraid of giving Magruder's away, Spencer declines. The cops look Rosalind up and down and nod knowingly. "Best check each other for flea bites," one says with a wink.

Just then, Judge O'Gorman waddles over, an expression of sheer panic spread across his wide, white face. "Spencer, my boy! Are you all right?"

Spencer forces a smile. "I'm fine, sir."

"I shudder to think what would have happened had those bastards succeeded. Two presidential assassinations in three years. Can you imagine? I'll tell you, I hope our party has learned its lesson about holding major political events in a low place like Coney Island. Hardly a carnival of purity, am I right? It's a relief, in a way, to proceed with the quarantine. After all, if—"

Rosalind puts his hand on O'Gorman's arm. "Pardon me, could you repeat that? A quarantine?"

O'Gorman leans over conspiratorially. "The Committee had it as a backup plan, in case mere policing of the infected wasn't enough. Which"—he gestures around the street, swarming with police officers and firefighters and Secret Service—"you can see, it was not. There will be consequences, obviously—cutting off the oxygen for all these hotels and restaurants. But it's akin to lopping off a diseased limb—painful but necessary."

"A diseased limb," Rosalind repeats coldly. He doesn't take his eyes off Spencer.

"Well, now." O'Gorman chuckles. "We have to think broadly, Miss Rosebush. The president has to face the electorate in just a few months. It's vital that he respond to this catastrophe with alacrity and force; otherwise, he'll never win reelection! Just imagine the consequences if the Democrats take the White House in November."

"But, Judge." Rosalind struggles to keep his voice steady. "What about the consequences for the limb?"

"You are a clever thing! What an excellent question. Economic solvency of the tourist sector is a priority of the Grand Old Party, of course. But revenue lost can always be replaced. I'm sure the federal government can make it right with the hotels somehow. There's many—"

"No, sir. I mean the people. The people who live and work here."

"The *circus folk*?" he says with a laugh. "Why, the circus folk

will be fine, as circus folk always are. Don't worry yourself, Miss
Rosebush—a quarantine worked beautifully in San Francisco. They
threw a rope around Chinatown, and the whole mess was resolved
in a matter of months. In any case, I'm sure your young man here
can explain things in a far more felicitous manner than I. After all"—
the judge pats Spencer on the back—"I'm not telling you anything
Master Reynolds doesn't already know."

✦ ✦ ✦

Rosalind and Spencer walk back down Surf Avenue in defeated
silence. Rosalind has taken off his heels and walks barefoot down
the street. Electric lights turn out one by one as they pass. The moon
gazes down at them, a perfect crescent.

Spencer says, "Is that moon waxing or waning? I can never
remember which way the—"

"Who gives a shit?" Rosalind's voice is cold. "You knew the
quarantine was coming."

"I hoped it wasn't."

"*You. Knew.* And you didn't warn us."

"What difference would it have made?" Spencer stops walking.
The moonlight glistens on the bloodred roof of the Sea Beach Palace
Hotel. "What do you want from me? Christ, what do any of you
people want?"

"'*You people*'? Unusuals, you mean? I'd like P-Ray and Enzo
back, if you're offering."

"Rosalind, that's what I was trying to—"

"So where the devil was your father?"

"*I don't know!* He and Charlie could both be dead for all I know!"

"Don't be dramatic. Someone would have said something.
Anyway, your kind are perfectly safe—you always are."

"That so? Because it looks to me like we almost lost another
president."

"Yeah, well, the hero of San Juan Hill slumbers in safety tonight,
thanks to his own filthy toilet habits."

"But, Rosalind, how many *other* people used those washrooms tonight? Don't you see? This Cough doesn't—"

"Why should I care?" Rosalind's voice splits open. "Why in the ever-loving fuck should I care about *any of you*?" He puts a hand to his mouth, but he can't prevent the sobs from coming.

Spencer looks at Rosalind and sees him—truly sees him—for the first time. He looks past the gown, past the jewelry and makeup. He sees a human being, completely on his own. His beloved family gone, possibly for good. Just another person, not so different from Spencer himself.

Rosalind cries and hugs himself. "I want to go home," he says, and he starts walking down the avenue.

"Miss Rosalind! Stop." Spencer catches up and wraps his arms around him. "Please. Stop."

Rosalind struggles against Spencer's embrace at first, then gives in and sobs into his shoulder. "They took my beautiful boys. I broke it off with Enzo, but I never meant... I never thought it would really be good-bye, not like this. Now I'm all alone in the whole world."

"No," Spencer whispers. "No, I promise you aren't."

26

THE GHOST

☙

I T WAS TWO OR THREE YEARS AGO WHEN ZEPH BEGAN TO SUSPECT THE Cabinet was haunted. Unexplainable thumps in the night. Displays rearranged for no reason. Items going missing and then reappearing elsewhere. At Magruder's, with its clocks that chime when they like and automatons that draw what they will, a ghost seemed more or less the natural order of things. And so, Zeph accepted the presence as a matter of course. He even took to telling it "good morning" at the start of the day and "good night" at the end. This was before Rosalind moved in, before the Cabinet had a tavern. Back then, it was just Zeph and Timur all on their lonesome, and lonesome it was. Even spectral company can be preferable to none.

Then one morning, Zeph saw a bread crumb in a corner he'd just swept the evening before. Another just a few feet away. And another after that.

"Huh," he'd mused. "Hungry ghost."

He'd followed the trail of crumbs to Daisy and Maisy's cabinet. One of the museum's oldest exhibits, the conjoined skeletons held pride of place in the center of Magruder's maze. And there, curled up like a cat at the girls' bony feet, was a sleeping little boy, no more than five or six years old.

Rather than startle him awake, Zeph had created his own trail—but of cookies this time—that led from Daisy and Maisy to Zeph's stool at the front entrance. Eventually, the child woke up and followed the treats to find Zeph waiting. Instead of fearing Zeph's long braids and absent legs, the boy just smiled. Perhaps he was lonely too. Maybe he liked the fact that he and Zeph were roughly the same height. It could have been the cookies.

As the day wore on, Zeph shared everything he could think of—curiosities from the Cabinet and leftovers from the icebox and that one coin trick he'd learned. But no matter what he tried, Zeph couldn't get a single sound out of the boy. Not one word, not a giggle, nothing. *Amazing*, Zeph thought. *Actual ghosts make more noise than this kid.*

Until, that is, he pulled out a dusty, miniature circus that was once used by performing fleas. The boy's face lit up like he was seeing his first snowfall. "*Pire!*" he shouted suddenly. "*Pire!*"

"And what in heck does *that* mean?"

"*Pire!*" the boy said again. Then he laughed, and the sound of the boy's laugh was the first music the Cabinet had heard since who knew when.

"Okay, little man." Zeph smiled. "P-Ray it is."

✦ ★ ✦

As an angry-orange dawn streaks the sky, Zeph slips into the tavern. He hasn't been downstairs since the Committee took P-Ray the other night. He hasn't been avoiding the tavern, exactly—he's just busy. Very busy these days. But this morning, he has a mind to check the supplies in the pantry and the cash in the register. Something tells him Magruder's won't see more of either for some time.

The tavern is deserted, the aroma of better days hanging in the air. Drinks left half-finished when the Committee arrived sit on the bar collecting flies. Chairs overturned during hasty exits are scattered about. Somebody left a coat. A hairpin. Even a shoe. Zeph sees a napkin on the floor with "OCean-29" written in lipstick—just a couple of digits short of a full telephone number. "Aww," he says. "*So close.*"

He can see the precise spot where Rosalind went to war to get

P-Ray back. Sequins and sparkly bits ripped off his dress now lie on the floor, twinkling in the morning sun. Looking up at the door, Zeph can almost see Enzo, shouting and fighting, struggling against the four Committeemen it took to drag him out. Two years ago, a ghost in the Cabinet had turned out to be a real boy. Now, the ghost is all that's left.

Okay, yeah. He's been avoiding the tavern.

Zeph goes to the icebox and plugs in wires, looking for company. There's no music to listen to at this hour—at least, not what most people would call music. In the early mornings, instead of waltzes and ragtime, the receiver picks up the sounds of janitors and mops. The chatter of cooks and waiters as they drag themselves to work. Of busboys and clinking plates as tables are laid out for the new day. And at the whorehouse, muttered gossip of the ladies as they shrug off the night before. The symphony of the service class.

Zeph plugs in channel one, hoping to hear the tuneless whistling of Monty the electrician, who prides himself on always being the first to report to work at Henderson's Vaudeville Theater. But the receiver picks up only silence. No Monty. No anybody.

Zeph moves on: channel two, channel three. Stillness. A little static here and there. Silence.

Channel four, five. Nothing.

Channel six, the whorehouse. A woman weeps, her heart in pieces. "Please, Jesus," she begs. "Please don't take my little boy. Take me, please. I had my life already. Take me instead. Please don't take my—"

Zeph yanks the cord from channel six. Impulsively, he yanks out another cord, and another. And then every cord he can, as fast as he can. A few seconds of fury, and the entire panel is disassembled in pieces on the floor.

He looks at the mess he's made. At the mess the Committee left behind. Zeph closes his eyes, leaning his head against the cool wood of his silent box of sound.

"Jesus, if you ain't too busy, please look after my little man."

✦ 27 ✦

WHAT NOW?

∞

Dear Diary: My mother died of the plague.

The hobby of diary keeping, such the rage among her friends in London, never held much appeal for Kitty. But now, sitting on a metal-frame bed in the Hoffman Island ladies' and children's dormitory, Kitty wishes she'd kept a diary after all. She has no one else to talk to.

Dear Diary: My mother died of the plague. Horrible men made her disappear before I could even say good-bye.

Kitty was a difficult daughter but a dutiful one, and she would have done anything to help her mother. She would have stayed by her mother's side until the end. But the end of whom—her mother, or them both?

Dear Diary: My mother died of the plague. Horrible men made her disappear before I could even say good-bye. In doing so, they might have saved my life.

The truth. The truth shall set you free? Kitty isn't so sure.

The ladies' and children's dormitory, floor two, room C, consists of two long rows of beds separated by a narrow aisle. Light streams through the large windows lining the outside wall. Uniformed nurses patrol the perfectly spaced beds with brisk efficiency. Everything about the space suggests competence, organization, modernity. The beds are crisply made: white sheets, white blankets. With white patients to match. Hoffman's dormitories are strictly segregated by race, and P-Ray's less-than-alabaster skin tone raised eyebrows among their fellow patients.

But if the ladies of the ladies' and children's dormitory are troubled by P-Ray, the children are not. Within minutes, P-Ray has joined a group of children in a complex chasing game only those under age twelve can understand. P-Ray's muteness, so disturbing to adults, is a nonissue among children. He can chase, he can be chased; he fits right in, running and laughing like any other kid. The ability to find joy in a plague quarantine fills Kitty with wonder—and a little envy.

Nate would have joined them, she realizes. Crowned himself king of the ten-year-olds. With all her worry over Mum, Kitty hasn't had time to miss Nate properly. The pent-up grief swells in her and threatens to swallow her whole. An older lady mistakes Kitty's tears for worry about their confinement, and she comes to sit beside her.

"Our husbands are building a boat."

"Sorry, a what?"

"A boat, so we can escape this wretched place. My husband and her husband," she says, indicating another woman. "The men take walks outside, they say for fresh air. But it's not air they're after; it's materials. To build a boat, to take us home."

"Home," Kitty says, and despite herself, she starts to cry again. Whatever the men are building, it will never be big enough to take Kitty home.

Kitty's tears inspire an outpouring of sympathy from the women. They circle around, offering her handkerchiefs and cookies stashed away in their handbags. This much maternal attention only makes Kitty feel worse. She's relieved when the screaming starts.

The women shift their concern from the weepy British teenager to the source of the screaming on the far side of the dormitory.

"That's Edna!" one lady gasps, and the women move toward their friend, skirts rustling like a fretful wind.

Kitty looks around for P-Ray; it's been a while since she's seen him race by. She searches along the rows of beds. "P-Ray?"

Suddenly, the once-friendly lady with cookies in her purse barges up and grabs Kitty roughly by the elbow. "*You!*" Her bony fingers press into Kitty's arm. "You and your little darkie have some nerve! We should toss you both into the tide!"

"Oh no." Kitty sighs. "What now?"

✦ ✦

28

CAPTAIN
COURAGEOUS

⬲

SPENCER SEES A STILL-WEEPY ROSALIND SAFELY HOME TO MAGRUDER'S.
A gentleman, he waits outside, staring up at the building until a
light goes on in the bedroom window to show him Rosalind is
safe. Then he races back to Surf Avenue, begging for a taxi to take him
back to his family's brownstone off Prospect Park. Back to Charlie.

In the cab, all Spencer can think about is the frame. The Bradford
frame, they called it, as though tacking on a friendly surname somehow
rendered it less of a torture device. It was just pipes soldered together
and attached to a hard, unforgiving board, with a collection of rough
canvas ties to hold its patient captive, arms and legs immobilized. For
months on end, the Bradford frame was Charlie's home, his bed, his
substitute spine.

Spencer remembers the day they attached Charlie to the frame,
how his little brother raged and wept. Spencer wept along with him,
begging the doctor, "No, please, this is terrible. Please don't do this,
it's too unfair."

The doctor said, "Don't worry. This is how we help him. This is
how he gets better."

It sure didn't look like help. And Charlie didn't get better.

Spencer stayed with his brother every day that summer, ignoring
their mother's entreaties to *get some fresh air—just a few minutes—please,
Spencer, for me*. Instead, he'd sat beside that nasty Bradford frame, day
after day. Together, the brothers made plans for the future—where

they would go, what they would do, who they would become. They whispered criticisms of their father. *We won't turn out like him… Let's promise we won't…* And they read. The Bradford frame made the act of holding a book impossible, so Spencer read to Charlie, every single day for hours. Stephen Crane and Bram Stoker and H. G. Wells…and Rudyard Kipling. Him in particular. Spencer read Kipling aloud until his voice cracked and his throat went dry.

Charlie's gentle brilliance survived the polio, but his body withered. For three years, he only left his bedroom on special occasions like Christmas, and then only because their mother asked so sweetly. But then influenza came to the brownstone and took Mother with it. For the past two years, Charlie hasn't left his room at all.

Now the Cough lurks around every corner. Is it waiting for Charlie? After all he's been through, what defense can Charlie possibly have left?

Spencer knows the answer. *Me.*

✶ ★ ✶

Spencer creeps through the dim brownstone, making his way to Charlie's room. "Charlie…" he whispers, easing open the bedroom door. "Chaz, wake up. We need to talk."

Inside, Spencer navigates around multiple piles of books spilling from the bookshelves along each wall. Books beside the bed, under the bed, and stacked at the foot. As he picks his way across the floor, Spencer thinks—not for the first time—that if an earthquake hits Brooklyn, his brother will perish happily in an avalanche of printed pages.

"Charlie! Wake up. It's important!" Spencer grabs his brother's blanket and yanks it back.

Books. Just more books, carefully arranged into the general shape of his brother. Spencer frowns. Either Charlie finally found a genie willing to turn his broken body into literature, or…

He stalks off to find their father.

✳ ★ ✳

At an hour poised between far too late and far too early, the lights
in William Reynolds's study burn on. Approaching the closed door,
Spencer feels a familiar flutter of nerves—he has felt it every time
he's passed this door for as long as he can remember. But this night,
he ignores their warnings. This night, there will be no more fear, no
more deference. He takes a deep breath and turns the knob. This
night, he'll stand up to the old man and finally say—

"Gibson?"

Spencer's old school chum, Gibson Tilden Jr., sits at Father's
massive black walnut desk. He looks startled and slightly guilty
behind his waxed mustache. He papers over his guilt with accusa-
tion. "Spencer! Where in hell have you been?"

"Where's my father? What's he done with Charlie?"

"I asked you first."

"Yeah, and you're going to *answer* first. Where are they?"

"Really, there's no need for—"

Spencer takes a threatening step forward, and Gibson flinches, his
arm nearly knocking over a glass of whiskey beside him on the desk.
"Newport! They've gone to your mansion in Newport."

"That's a damn lie."

"Why on earth would—"

"His books are still here! Charlie never goes to Newport without
his books."

"Yes," Gibson admits, "he was none too happy about it. But your
father said there was neither time to pack books nor room to carry
them, and that was that."

"But those books are the only thing he cares about; they're all he—"

"You know, if you're so particular about the care and feeding
of your brother, perhaps you might stop by from time to time?
As it is, I've been left with all the paperwork, the time sheets
for the security guards, the bills for Dreamland food stalls, and
those"—he gestures at the overstuffed leather satchel on a chair

opposite the desk—"weekend receipts to deposit when the bank opens in the morning."

"Yeah." Spencer nods at the half-finished glass of whiskey. "Your suffering absolutely radiates."

"The point is, I could use some help around here."

Spencer turns his back to Gibson and sits on the edge of the desk, the sadness of this very long day settling on his shoulders all at once. "I don't understand. Why leave in such a hurry?"

"Hmm, couldn't be the epidemic, could it? Maybe if you spent a little more time at home, you might—"

"Shu-u-u-t up, you *bloviating* fool."

"A fool, am I? This fool was just put in charge of Dreamland."

Spencer whirls around. "What did you say?"

Gibson tilts his head in mock confusion. "Wait, you *want* me to talk now? I'm sorry. It's hard to keep up with—"

"*That park is mine.* My father doesn't even care about Dreamland, not really. He wanted to call it the Hippodrome, for Chrissake! I'm the one who loves it. *I'm* the one who—"

"Given your absence, your father had to make a decision." Leaning back in the old leather chair, Gibson takes a satisfied sip of his whiskey. "I'm sure he regrets it terribly."

Spencer stares at this clown he once called *friend*, sitting at Father's desk, swilling Father's liquor, lecturing him about how to behave. He opens his mouth to let his anger flow out…but then closes it. Going ten rounds of "Dreamland is mine!" "No, Dreamland is *mine!*" with this jackass would be a waste of Spencer's waning energy. No point in arguing.

A far better plan: he'll go to Newport and work it out with Father directly. Sure, the old man will be angry—*You let the family down*; *You disappeared in a time of crisis*; etc., etc.—but he'll get over it.

Won't he?

Of course he will. Father and son will sort it all out over a few rounds of golf. Eighteen holes, and it'll be like this scoundrel Gibson never existed.

Spencer goes to the sideboard to pour himself a drink, because why not? This is still *his* house, no matter what Gibson tells himself. He knocks the satchel of Dreamland cash off the chair and sits. He leans back and puts his feet on the desk, making a point of taking up as much space in the room as possible.

The two sit in silence for a time, lost in thought. Two boys finding themselves abruptly transformed into men.

After a while, Spencer sighs. "At least now I know why you did it."

"Did what?"

"Turned in that little boy, with the fleas. I've been trying to figure it out—why you'd bother. Now I know."

Gibson shrugs. "Fleas are a health hazard. I had a responsibility to—"

"Stop. You wanted to impress my father." Spencer raises his glass. "Kudos, I guess."

Gibson smiles, raising his glass in return. "You know, if you'd been thoughtful enough to have a sister, I could have just married her. But since Charlie isn't my type, I had to improvise. Of course, I didn't expect you'd make it so easy, wandering off in a moment of crisis like you did."

"No matter," Spencer says. "If a man's meant to rise, he'll rise one way or the other." He holds back a smile, thinking, *And if he's not meant to rise, even a plague won't save him.* Spencer swishes the whiskey around in his glass and downs it in one swallow. "After all, what's it matter if you kick a few orphans on the way up?"

Gibson's smile vanishes. "Tell me, old friend: Did that tender heart of yours come with the trust fund, or did you purchase it separately?"

"You can go straight to hell." Spencer stands, and Gibson defensively leaps up too. "This isn't over."

"I guess we'll see, won't we?"

Spencer bends down and picks up the satchel of Dreamland money. "I'll tell you what. Let me take care of this bank deposit for you."

"Now, now. Given your mood, I should probably handle that personally."

"You just said you needed help. Let me help. Unless," he says with a hard smile, "you'd prefer that I go back to Newport and explain to Father how you were *strangely insistent* on handling all the cash. How I offered to help but you just *had* to hold the money yourself. Father wouldn't find that odd. Would he?"

"He'll never believe you."

"I'm still the son, Tilden. Prodigal though I may be."

Gibson grimaces. "All right, fine. The deposit slip is filled out. It's in the front pocket of the satchel. And I do have a copy, so I *will* know whether it all gets—"

"Don't be a fool. You think a Reynolds needs to steal?" He wags his finger. "Low-class remarks like that will give your game away every time." Spencer slings the satchel over one shoulder and heads for the door.

"Enjoy your exile," Gibson calls after him.

"Enjoy your ascent," Spencer replies. "Just don't look down."

★ ★ ✦

On his way out, Spencer stops by Charlie's bedroom. He reckons the least he can do is grab a few books to bring him in Newport. Just something to tide Charlie over while they wait out the plague madness in safety. *That'll be nice, actually*, he thinks. *A little sea air, a little golf, maybe a lobster or three.*

Fumbling around in the near dark, Spencer's eyes fall on the book body Charlie assembled in his bed. Spencer realizes—slowly and not very happily—that these aren't just any books. Every title is one the brothers read together during that grim, Bradford-framed summer. *Dracula, The Red Badge of Courage, The Time Machine.* And nestled on the pillow, right where Charlie's head should have laid, is the book they read the most: a dog-eared *Captains Courageous,* Rudyard Kipling's classic tale of a spoiled rich boy who learns to stop being such a jackass.

"See?" Charlie had joked at the time. "There's hope for you yet, Spence!"

"You're not funny, Chaz," he'd said back then. He tells the empty bed the same thing tonight. But this time, his voice catches in his throat.

★ ★ ✦

As dawn arrives, Spencer stands before the locked front doors of the Gravesend branch of the People's Bank of Brooklyn. The bank won't open for several hours, which gives him time to think. Too much time. He walks away from the bank, then walks back, then away again. Finally, he crosses the street and sits under a tree in the middle of the traffic median. The grassy area divides northbound traffic on Ocean Parkway from south. It's not a common place for a Brooklyn prince to sit, and vehicles slow to peep at Spencer as they pass. He ignores them. If he were paying attention, he'd notice that the heavy traffic is heading north, away from Coney. But Spencer has other concerns.

The leather satchel sits by his feet, and he eyes it resentfully. He removes the deposit slip from the front pocket and glares at it awhile. Then he shoves it back in the pocket and gives the satchel a sharp kick.

"Give him his books, *Dad*," he says. "Why couldn't you let him have his damn books?"

Spencer replays his visit to the brownstone in his head, over and over, but he reaches the same conclusion every time. He's the only person who'd go looking for Charlie, the only person who'd bother overturning those bedclothes…and Charlie knew it. Which means, unavoidably, that the book body with its Kipling brain was a message from little brother to big. And that message sure as hell wasn't *Come hide in Newport*. It wasn't *Honor our father* either. Charlie left the books as a reminder of the long talks they'd had that summer. Of everything they'd wanted to do and be that Charlie now could not.

There's hope for you yet, Spence.

Spencer reaches into the pocket of the satchel and removes the deposit slip again. He holds it up to the sun. "'*Captains Courageous*,'" he recites, "'*whom Death could not daunt*.'"

He rips the paper in half. Then he puts the pieces together and rips them in half again. And again, and again, into smaller and smaller pieces.

Spencer opens his hands and lets the breeze carry the deposit confetti into the air over Ocean Parkway.

PRETTY GIRL

❧

AN OVERRIPE TOMATO SPLATS AGAINST THE SIDE OF THE TAXICAB, AND Nazan nearly jumps out of her skin. As the tomato's guts ooze down the window, she curses herself for being so easily rattled. Maybe Mother was right—she's just a girl, and she should stay home, keep well away from all the madness and misery on the streets. *No*, she thinks. *No.* That morning, Nazan had packed a bag, refusing to tell her mother why, and counted out her meager pocket money. She'd splurged on one of the city's red-and-green-paneled taxis because she knew time was running out.

"Sorry, miss," says the cabbie. "Town of Gravesend ain't usually so disrespectable. Dunno why the natives are so restless today."

Enraged citizens crowd the sidewalk, a phalanx of policemen on horseback only barely keeping them from spilling into the street. Nazan's stomach flip-flops. "I know why. It's the quarantine."

"Sorry, miss, the what? Did you say—"

An old woman skirts past the police line and dives in front of the cab.

"Whoa! Jaysus, Mary, and Joseph!" The cabbie stomps the brakes, stopping so quickly that Nazan nearly slides off the seat.

She sits back, brushing herself off in time to see the old woman shake her fist at the cab, her apple-doll face twisted in rage.

"You maggots!" she screams. "Who do you maggots think you—"

A police baton smashes the woman's head, and she drops to the street like laundry falling off a line. From atop his horse, the policeman waves the carriage on.

"You all right back there, miss? Terrible sorry about the quick stop—I didn't muss your pretty dress, did I?"

"I'm fine," Nazan asserts. Perhaps if she says this enough, it will become true.

Before long, the cabbie has to stop the horse at the end of a line of horse-drawn wagons, panel trucks, and black Ford Models A through R. Men in khaki uniforms approach each vehicle in turn, leaning in the windows to converse with the drivers. One by one, the vehicles are allowed to pass or, more often, directed to turn around and head back into Brooklyn.

"What's all this, then?" the cabbie wonders.

Nazan knows. "The quarantine is starting."

"Why would—oh, the Cough?"

She nods. "They're cutting off traffic onto Coney Island."

"But ain't the Cough all around the town nowadays? What use is it to man or beast to tie off one hand from the other?"

Nazan shrugs. "You didn't hear? Someone tried to give the Cough to Roosevelt. They say it was anarchists."

The cabbie turns around to face the backseat. "Jaysus, not our Teddy! They didn't do Teddy like they done McKinley?"

His distress is so genuine that Nazan reaches out to pat the cabbie on the arm. "He's fine. But the paper said that some of his aides took ill last night. As has Philander Knox, the attorney general. And Assemblyman Butler, a few others I forget. Probably more by now."

"God almighty, just last night this was?"

Nazan nods. "The papers are blaming Coney—Sodom by the Sea and so on."

"Jaysus and all the saints…"

"Did you really not hear?"

The cabbie shakes his head. "I'm a workin' man, miss. No time for papers. But why is a pretty thing such as yourself going toward such a place?"

"You sound like my mother. I have friends there—new friends, but still. And after today, you'll be on one side or the other, and that will be it. Everyone has to choose."

Her own choice had been easy. She wasn't going to sit around in her parents' tearoom, getting older every day—not while there was so much going on in the real world. *So very much to learn*, Rosalind had told her. Nazan knows it's high time she finds out what that might be.

✷ ✷ ✷

While the city seethes and rages, Archie enjoys a leisurely lunch under the chandeliers at Gage & Tollner, an extravagant restaurant in downtown Brooklyn. He holds court with an assortment of much younger swindlers and thieves. Archie has seen so many come and go, he no longer bothers to learn their names. All he needs to know is that *someone* is picking up the check, and it isn't him. He amiably stuffs himself with Lobster Newburg while they explain their plan to make the most of the quarantine.

Theirs is a black-market scheme, running food and sundries to the soon-to-be-locked-down population of Coney Island. *It's an all-right plan*, Archie thinks. *It's just so damn tedious.*

"And you see, Mr. Archibald," one of them says, "we understand that you're in a position to travel back and forth across the quarantine easily. Is that...accurate?"

"I may have some friends in inappropriate places."

"So what do you think? We'll cut you in. Say, 20 percent." Someone else at the table coughs pointedly. "Maybe 17.5?"

Archie wipes his mouth with another man's napkin and tosses it on the table. "Let me see if I follow you boys. Your big idea is to sneak tins of beans and tubes of toothpaste over the quarantine line? Glorified grocery shopping? Is that really a job for grown men?"

The man shrugs. "People need toothpaste."

"What you boys need is ambition."

"Oh really?" one of the younger men challenges. "What's *your* big idea then?"

"What is this, confidence-scheme kindergarten?" But he leans back in his chair, relishing the attention despite himself. "Okay, fine. Maybe lobster makes me expansive. Here's lesson one: never have one big idea—have multiple ideas. You never know what'll fall apart and what'll take off. Next, you're thinking too small. *People need toothpaste.* Sure, but nobody *cares* about toothpaste. They can get toothpaste from anybody. What do they really care about?"

None of the younger men has the answer.

"People are dying, boys. They're dropping like fleas out there. People are afraid. What they want, therefore, is to *not be dying.* Otherwise known as living. *Truly* living, in the moment, for right now. Living like you do when the world is ending."

"But," one of the men says, "you can't sell that."

"You're kidding, right?" Archie sighs. "It's the only thing worth selling."

He checks the time on his pocket watch and stands up. "I appreciate the offer—really, I do. But you can keep your 17.5 percent of the toothpaste market. Me, I have to see a man about a lion."

✶ ★ ✶

There's a crisp knock on the side of the taxi. A man with a bushy black mustache and a crisp khaki uniform leans in. He wears a wide-brimmed hat and a badge marked Pinkerton National Detective Agency. "What's your reason to cross?"

"'Tis me employ and calling to do so," the cabbie replies.

"Best rethink it," the man says. "Unless you intend to live under the Ferris wheel for the foreseeable future."

Nazan leans forward. "Sir, I've hired this gentleman to take me across—he needs only drop me off, and he'll return immediately."

The man shakes his head. "Sorry, miss. We're letting about a minute's worth of vehicles through, and then it's over."

"But, sir, I have to—"

The man has already stopped listening. "No hot dogs today, little girl. Off you go." He smacks the cab door and points. "Turn around over there."

The cabbie turns around. "Miss," he says, not unkindly. "You've had yourself a nice adventure, but it's time to go home."

"No, you don't—"

"Coney Island's too rough a place for you on a good day, never mind with all this going on. You're a just pretty young thing. You should be—"

Nazan's eyes flash. "Yes, call me pretty *one more time*."

A white vehicle behind them gives out an impatient *ah-ooh-gah*, insisting the hansom cab get out of the way. Men in khaki wave grumpily at the cabbie that he should pull forward.

"I'm sorry, darlin'." The cabbie turns back around. "But I have a family too. I can't be risking getting caught on the wrong side, *especially* not with some pretty little—"

Nazan snaps. "I don't care what you think, you cowardly old Mick! I am not going anywhere!"

In moments, Nazan has been deposited on the corner, and the cab takes off in a huff. "Sorry…" she calls. "Oh well."

She looks around. At what is now literally the end of the street, a platform has been hastily erected. Half a dozen burly men stand on the platform, gazing blankly at the crowd like resentful Unusuals in a freak show. Unusuals don't wear Pinkerton uniforms, though, and they don't have rifles slung over their shoulders. A hostile audience of Gravesenders stands on the street below them, staring up at this most unwelcome of performances.

One Pinkerton man, smaller and more officious than the goons surrounding him, stands in the center of the platform. He lifts a bullhorn to address the crowd. "CONEY ISLAND IS UNDER QUARANTINE," he announces. "PUBLIC GATHERINGS ARE UNSAFE. RETURN TO YOUR HOMES. CONEY ISLAND IS UNDER QUARANTINE…"

All around, people fume and mutter to one another, complaints
swirling like an angry summer wind. Some fear being closed off from
the fishing boats that work the waters of Long Island Sound. *How
shall we eat?* Many have jobs on the Coney side, which they'll now
not be able to reach. *How shall we live?*

A sad-eyed old man standing near Nazan shakes his head. "This no
America," he says to no one in particular. "This no America mine."

✦ ★ ✦

Archie takes a trolley from downtown to Gravesend but finds he
can ride no farther. The quarantine is on, all the streets are blocked,
and Coney is sealed off from Brooklyn. Unless, of course, you are in
possession of some rather colorful information about one of the city
contractors who maintains the Brooklyn sewer lines—a memorable
tale involving the contractor, three belly dancers, and a bishop. In
which case, Coney is perhaps not *entirely* sealed off.

Making his way through the festering near-riot that surrounds the
blockade, Archie spots a young woman who looks familiar. He can't
quite place her—really, twenty-year-olds all look alike these days—
but he knows that he knows her. With her small piece of luggage,
she looks like she's going on a weekend holiday, but her expression
suggests she's forgotten where exactly. She looks lost, like she needs
a savior. Or a partner.

Archie sizes her up. She's pretty if you're not too picky. She'd
most likely get prettier if somebody convincingly told her she could
be. The Mediterranean features are a bit of a problem; the Brit was
better—every door opens to a face like hers. But still. He supposes he
can spin her complexion as "exotic." Worked all right with Yeshi,
all those years ago.

"Pardon me, miss," he says to her. Archie turns on his Southern
affectation full blast. "Do you and I know each other?"

The young lady turns, first startled then relieved. "You're Archie!
We met at Magruder's a few days ago. I was with Rosalind when
Bernard…you know."

Archie smiles too widely. "Oh, of course! You're Spencer Reynolds's little friend."

She offers her hand, but she frowns. Not her favorite description ever. "Nazan Celik."

"Of course, forgive me for not recalling. So what brings you here to the end of the world, Miss Celik?"

"Trying to get to Magruder's to…see everyone, I guess. To see if I can help? But I can't seem to get past the quarantine."

Archie scoffs. "The quarantine is not a problem. Did you ever hear the one about the contractor, the belly dancers, and the bishop? Trust me, I can get you past the quarantine." He takes the carnation out of his lapel and hands it to her. "Question is, what can you do for me?"

EAT, DRINK,
AND BE MERRY

ROSALIND GROANS AND ROLLS OUT OF BED. BETWEEN THE DISTURBING visions of Enzo's captivity haunting his dreams and the violent sawing and hammering sounds drifting down from Timur's lab, more sleep is not an option. He goes to the water closet to draw a bath. As he passes the stairs to the lab, he shouts up, "Keep it down! It's barely dawn!"

"Bah!" is the only reply. And more hammering.

Rosalind grunts. At least Timur's experiments in chemistry and electricity, while smelly and life-threatening, had been largely silent.

After a bath that should have been relaxing but was somehow not at all so, Rosalind pulls on his silk robe and heads down to the Cabinet, his hair still wet. There's something that needs to be done, and unpleasant as it is, Rosalind knows it simply can't be put off any longer.

He fishes around in a drawer underneath the flea circus display. "Where are you?" he mutters.

When Zeph rounds the corner in his cart, Rosalind turns around guiltily, hands behind his back.

"Good morning, Zeph."

"Morning, Ros. It's okay. I fed 'em earlier."

Rosalind holds up the jar he'd been hiding. P-Ray's fleas. "You *fed* them?"

"'Course I did." Zeph scratches his left hand, polka-dotted with bites. "Ain't an altogether enjoyable experience."

"I was going to drown them in the sink!"

"What would ya do that for?"

"They're fleas! The Committee wouldn't have come here if it weren't for them. The Cough *itself* wouldn't even... Zeph, how can you *feed* them?"

"Now, Ros..." Zeph moves his cart forward so that he can pat Rosalind's arm. "I think you're getting yourself a little worked up here. Little man's been keeping those fleas long before this all started. You're right—there's bugs in this town that owe us one hell of an apology. But it ain't these little guys' fault."

"It's *all* their fault."

"No, no. Now, put 'em back in the drawer."

"Zeph—"

"I won't have our boy come home to find his pets all got murdered. Come on, now."

"But, *Zeph*..." Rosalind meets his eyes. Zeph isn't kidding. Rosalind sighs. He tosses the jar back in the drawer and slams it shut. "It's madness is what it is."

"Yeah, little man can always get himself more fleas. Still—"

"No," Rosalind says sharply. "It's madness to pretend they're ever coming home."

"Aw, hey. We'll figure something out. As we speak, Timur's upstairs working on something."

"I know. I can barely hear myself think because of it. But what could he possibly build? They're in a hospital. An *island hospital* you can't leave...a prison?" Rosalind laughs a little crazily and then starts to cry. "A pris-pital."

"They aren't sick, Ros," Zeph says gently. "They're fine."

"Correction: they weren't sick the last time we saw them. By now? Who knows?"

"Aw, please don't cry."

"You don't understand!"

"Ros—"

"We split! Enzo and I. We argued—about my outfit! How foolish is that? And I told him…I told him I didn't want to see him. That was the last thing I said to him, Zeph." He sobs. "The very last thing…"

"I'm sure he knows you didn't mean it. Please, *please* don't cry. Listen, have you eaten anything since…you know, have you eaten?"

Rosalind wipes his eyes. "I had some champagne at the assassination last night."

"Go upstairs and dress. I'll fix you something, okay? Meet me down in the tavern."

Rosalind looks away. "Enzo made lovely dinners for me."

"Yeah, I don't really—"

The tears start again. "*Zuppa di pesce, melanzane alla parmigiana…*"

"How about grits?"

Rosalind glares at Zeph. "Enzo is a brilliant cook. You're a terrible cook."

"I'm the cook you got, darlin'." A knock at the door. "Who is it now? Look, Ros, will you just get dressed, please? And stop snufflin'. I can't take it."

He wheels himself through the black curtain and opens the door. Archie stands there with Nazan at his elbow. "Zeph! Look who I found on the Gravesend side."

"Miss Nazan," Zeph says, grinning. "What are you doing here?"

She grins back. "I just thought I should check on you? Is this a bad time?"

"No, no, of course not. It's just…well, I'm sure happy to see you."

"And I you, Mr. Zeph."

"You look lovely. I mean—" He flushes.

The two smile at each other awkwardly. Archie rolls his eyes. "Bless your hearts, isn't this precious?"

"Yeah. Uh, hello, Archie," Zeph says. "You want something?"

He nods. "We need to talk."

✦ ✦ ✦

Down in the tavern, Zeph hauls a cast-iron pot over to the table and hoists it up. "There we go, just like mama used to make." He climbs on a chair, handing out plates to Rosalind, Nazan, and Archie. Zeph pulls off his gloves and places them neatly by his own plate. Over grits and the few lobster tails left in the icebox, he fills Nazan in on the past few days of lunacy at the Cabinet.

"Oh no, poor little P-Ray! And Miss Kitty—imagine going through all that when her mother isn't even on the island." Nazan looks over at Rosalind, who is forlornly pushing food around on his plate. "And Mr. Enzo too. Zeph and Doctor Timur will get him back somehow, I know it."

Rosalind just looks away.

Archie grows bored of all the tea and sympathy. "*Any*how... Zeph, the quarantine presents us with a number of interesting opportunities..."

"How fortunate for you." Rosalind's voice is ice. "To have so many interesting opportunities."

"Yeah, yeah, you call me *vile*, I call you a *fruit*, you storm out, et cetera and so on. Can we skip that part today? Look, Frank Bostock has a menagerie full of exotic animals that nobody wants to see. And if nobody wants to see them, there's no income coming in. They're too expensive to care for and too expensive to move. So Bostock is looking to...divest himself...some other way."

Zeph laughs as he wipes his plate clean with a piece of bread. "You're going into the wild animal business, Archie? Good luck to ya."

"Good luck to the animals." Rosalind slowly, deliberately, stabs a bit of lobster with his fork. "Perhaps one of them will eat you."

"You almost got it," Archie says with his mouth full. "Except it's not the *animals* who are going to eat *me*..." He looks at them expectantly.

Nazan gasps. "What? That's horrible! We don't eat lions and tigers!"

"Come on now, Archie," Zeph says. "She's right. Folks don't do that."

"It's the plague, Zeph. People are scared. *You could be dead tomorrow. Why not have a one-of-a-kind meal today?* That's the pitch. The way I see it, the richer people are, the higher off the hog they'll want to live. Can't live any higher off the hog than eating the king of beasts. Bostock will put the animals down; we'll butcher 'em up and sell to the highest bidder."

"Archie," Rosalind says, "if you're so bored of me describing you as *vile*, you should consider—"

"Let's be clear," he interrupts. "Bostock is putting those animals down either way. He can dump them in Coney Island Creek, or we can make a profit."

"We?" Zeph groans. "How did *we* get mixed up in this?"

"You have the space, and Timur has the equipment. I have the contacts, but I can't do it alone."

"You sure are doing it alone," Zeph replies, "and you sure as *hell* aren't doing it here."

"If we sell the steaks on Central Park West and the organs in Chinatown, we should do nicely. I figure you two"—he gestures at Nazan and Zeph—"can pitch in by making little speeches about how people eat lions and tigers all the time where you come from."

Nazan frowns. "I come from Tenth Avenue."

"All right, Miss Wisenheimer, you know what I—"

"And I will never help you."

Archie stands up. "I think you will."

"Pardon me?"

"I said I'd bring you to Magruder's, and I did. Which means you owe me."

Nazan's eyes widen. "But I—Zeph, I never told him I'd—"

Zeph shakes his head. "Don't worry. You ain't going anywhere."

Archie takes Nazan's arm and pulls her out of her chair. "Actually, you—"

Rosalind leaps up, sending the plates clanking against each other. "You take your hands off her!"

"Surely you understand quid pro—"

"And surely *you* understand that if you aren't out of my sight in ten seconds, I'm going to pluck your eyes out and toss them in these grits."

"Don't be ridic—"

"Try me. The taste can only be an improvement."

"Hey now…" Zeph protests.

"I'll do it," Rosalind warns. "You leave Nazan alone, or I will hurt you."

Archie scoffs. "You're a little boy wearing his mother's clothes!"

"Look at me." Rosalind speaks very quietly. "Look at the way I choose to live. Ask yourself just how tough a person has to be to live like this."

Archie meets Rosalind's eyes but quickly looks away. "Fine, forget it. I've got plenty of other irons in the fire. Lots of other plans, don't you worry about me."

"I'll do my best," Rosalind replies coldly.

Archie gazes down at Nazan with distaste. "There are a million girls just like you, you know. Greater New York is crawling with them." He glares defiantly at Rosalind. "She's your problem now."

✦ ★ ✦

Nazan washes the dishes while Rosalind dries. They don't talk about the confrontation with Archie, but every time Nazan hands Rosalind a dish, she mentally inscribes it with *thank you*. Meanwhile, Zeph putters around the tavern's tiny pantry, fretting over the dwindling supplies.

"What are we gonna eat with a quarantine on? Not lions, that's for sure."

"We'll figure something out," Nazan reassures him.

Zeph laughs at her confidence. "When'd you get so bold, Miss Nazan? Running off on your mama like that?"

"My mother would complain that I've always been bold," she says with a smile. "Maybe you're just getting to know me. Besides, it seems to me Rosalind was the truly bold one."

Rosalind puts some dry plates away. "I hate bullies," he says. "And I didn't care to lose anyone else."

Zeph sighs at the sight of yet another empty shelf. "Of course, this quarantine lasts too long, we may need his eyeballs." He climbs up on the counter beside the sink. "But say what you want about that ol' vulture: Archie did bring you across, didn't he? A *good* person woulda behaved himself and obeyed the quarantine."

"True," Nazan agrees. "Huzzah for misbehavior."

Zeph smiles at Nazan shyly. "Exactly."

Rosalind watches the two of them: glancing at one another, looking away, blushing. He's suddenly overwhelmed with jealousy—of their youth, of their obvious rapport, of the way the world looks when you're at the beginning of something. He tosses the dish towel to Zeph. "I'm going to lie down. Fetch me if you hear from Reynolds. He promised he'd find his father and speak to him about Enzo and P-Ray."

"Sure, you go rest. We'll handle things."

Nazan gives Zeph a plate to dry. "Poor Rosalind. He's bereft."

"Yep, Ros and Enzo, they're…ah…they're a little different."

"Different is okay. I like different."

Zeph and Nazan clean in silence, both painfully aware, all of a sudden, that they've been left alone.

"I have a question," Nazan says after a moment. "If Mrs. Hayward isn't on Hoffman Island, then where is she?"

"How about this: bellboy says they've got her at the Manhattan Beach Hotel, down the other end of Coney."

"What do you mean?"

He shrugs. "That's what he says. Bunch of kids took her. Kidnapped her? Or rescued her? Both, I guess. Before the authorities could take her away."

"And she's still there? Is she alive?"

"Don't know about that. But that's what he told us."

Nazan drops her dishrag in the soapy water. "What are we waiting for?"

Zeph shakes his head, uncomprehending. "I'm not—"

"We should go find her! Shouldn't we?"

"What, you and me?"

"Why not, Zeph? We can't reach Kitty, but we can surely reach a hotel up the street."

He looks at her. "Even if we find her, what'll we do?"

"I don't know—depends on what we find, I guess. But we can try, can't we?" Nazan grins. "Bold, right? Time to be bold."

31

HALFWAY DOWN
THE STAIRS

HOVED IN A CORNER IN THE HOSPITAL, KITTY AND P-RAY ARE BESIEGED BY A seething mass of women, all in the same beige, hospital-provided clothes. They glare and mutter. "How dare they?" "This is why his kind should be kept separate!"

Kitty bends down to make sure P-Ray is all right. She brushes some dirt off his beige outfit—likely the nicest clothes he's ever owned—and tries to keep her mood light. "What's happened, sweetie?"

The boy shrugs sadly. "P-Ray."

"Yes, that's your name! But might you break your vow of silence and tell me why these women want to toss us in the sea?"

He nods. "P-Ray."

Kitty sighs. "Well," she says to the women. "You lot have a great deal to say. Perhaps you might—"

"Show her!" The cookie lady elbows the woman beside her, who nudges her twelve-year-old daughter. When she steps forward, P-Ray shrinks. The girl stretches out her arm. In her hand is a small vial with a cork stopper. Half a dozen black specks dance inside.

Aghast, Kitty turns to her young companion. He shrugs again. "P-Ray."

For all its flaws, the awareness campaign of the Committee on Public Safety has had at least one clear victory: awareness of the deadly flea has never been higher. When the head nurse arrives in room C, she snatches away P-Ray's vial, tosses it into a bag, and sends the bag to the incinerator.

P-Ray sobs and tugs at Kitty—*do something, do something*—but she can only wrap her arms around him as he cries. "They can't be saved," she whispers. "I'm sorry, sweetie, but they can't be saved. I'm not even sure about us."

✦ ★ ✦

Kitty and P-Ray are dragged to the head nurse's office for a scolding. The nurse points to two metal chairs on one side of her desk, and she hefts herself onto a chair opposite. "What," she demands, "is your son doing with a vial full of fleas?"

"Actually, he isn't—" Then she stops herself. Things will go badly for the foreign-looking flea smuggler; the foreign-looking flea-smuggling *orphan* has no chance at all. "Actually, he isn't a naughty boy," she says instead. "He keeps them as pets."

"That is revolting and unsanitary."

Kitty looks the nurse up and down, taking her measure the way Archie once measured Kitty. *Archie wouldn't just sit here and welcome his punishment. He'd find an angle.*

Kitty leans forward, meeting the nurse's angry eyes full-on. "Ma'am, this is *such* an unfortunate understanding. My name is Katherine Hayward. Of the Cornwall Haywards. My father is in railroads, back in England. I presume you've heard of—"

"You are a patient in my ward," the nurse interrupts. "That's all I need to know."

Hmm. Wrong angle.

On the desk, among the stacks of patient folders, time sheets, and requisition forms, sits a framed photograph: a freckle-faced boy in a bathing costume, grinning from ear to ear. Kitty smiles. *Aha.*

"What a handsome young man! Your son, I take it?" The nurse's face does not soften, but Kitty barrels on regardless. "So you *must* know how children are—so charming and reckless and full of life. It was wrong to keep the fleas, but…" She gestures to P-Ray, who stares at the nurse blankly. "Look at that sweet face! Boys will be boys! Right? Surely you can imagine your son doing something similar?" Kitty smiles prettily. "Can't you?"

"I don't imagine my son doing anything. He died of the Cough a week ago."

Kitty closes her eyes in defeat. "I'm so sorry."

The nurse stands up. "You and your half-breed get out of my ward."

✶ ✶ ✶

Kitty and P-Ray are sentenced to the observation suite on the far side of the island—*far* to whatever extent anything on Hoffman's twelve miles can be considered *far* from anything else. But then, language on Hoffman is eerily flexible. There's little about the tiny shack, surrounded by a chain-link fence on three sides and open to the ocean on the fourth, that's suite-like.

"The Oriental Hotel has suites," Kitty mutters, stomping on a cockroach. "This is the pokey." Here, in this quarantine-within-a-quarantine, Kitty and P-Ray are sentenced for fourteen days to see if they develop any symptoms. If they do, "It's Swinburne for the both of you," the head nurse told them. "If it were up to me, you'd be there already."

✶ ✶ ✶

Kitty sits halfway down a staircase to the sea.

The observation suite has one charm only: a small, fenced-in backyard that opens onto the larger backyard of Lower New York Bay and, beyond that, the largest backyard of all—the Atlantic Ocean. Nestled into the giant chunks of shale that comprise the seawall, there is a narrow, metal-frame staircase, which probably once led down to a little beach. Hoffman's designers must have imagined a charming scene—patients picnicking by the water, soaking up the healing powers of sea air. But whatever beach once clung to the island's edge is gone now, washed away by the tides. The metal staircase is all that remains, and waves slosh ambitiously up the steps.

Kitty sits at the stairs' midpoint, staring out at a small ship flying a yellow flag—yellow for quarantine. The wind whistles in her ears, and the spray soaks her uniform. The dampness reminds her of the days spent sitting on that park bench—before Archie, before Zeph and Rosalind and Enzo and P-Ray. Funny, now, to think how irritated she was by the wet air; a short time in Coney Island, and the dampness feels entirely natural.

Another wave crashes on the steps, but this time, it leaves a small crab behind. The crab stumbles around on the step, dazed to find itself on solid ground. He waves his little claws in the air, and Kitty smiles. "Hello, little one. Washed up on Hoffman, have you? I know how you feel."

Kitty eases herself down the steps to catch it. Perhaps some company will cheer P-Ray a bit. She reaches out to grab the little fellow when another wave hits the steps. When the water pulls back, the crab is gone.

She glares out at the ocean. "So that's how it is? You just take whatever you like, whenever, however, whomever you please?" Kitty stands and brushes the sand off her skirt. "We shall see about that."

CHAPTER

32

ELIXIR SALUTIS

◈

L ADIES AND GENTLEMEN, WE LIVE IN DARK TIMES. ANARCHISTS SLITHER across the cobblestones, while death-dealing pestilence stalks us, even into our own homes. It kills with swiftness but without mercy. It's *the Cough*, or so the newspapers say, as though it were nothing but a slight chill, a mere bagatelle to be sent packing with a few aspirin."

A screechy voice in the crowd. "Them damn papers lie!"

"I'm afraid they do, ma'am. And now, a reckoning is at hand. This morning, we learn that traitorous miscreants have attempted to use the Cough as a weapon. This plague no longer threatens us as individuals. The Cough threatens the very body of our great nation. What shall we do? How shall we restore our own health and the health of the *corps d'état*? Is there indeed no balm in Gilead? My friends, I am no preacher, but I will tell you this: balm in Gilead there may not be, but rest assured, there is balm in Coney. May I humbly present for your edification and transformation Dr. Theophilus Magruder's Elixir Salutis!

"Ladies and gentlemen, I believe you to be not merely good people but wise. You know charlatans prowl these troubled streets, hawking spurious patent medicines of their own devising. You dare not trust the blackguards and thieves clogging Surf Avenue with empty promises. But my good people, I am one of you. A family man, a religious man, a good man."

Archie smiles. "You can trust me."

* ★ *

Spencer skirts around Archie's gaggle of customers. The crowd has a hungry look, like they'd tear each other apart at the slightest provocation. Spencer discreetly holds the satchel of money behind his back. The last thing he needs is someone from the crowd developing an interest in its contents.

Ducking his head and praying not to be recognized, Spencer yanks open the unmarked front door and bounds down the stairs to the tavern. Rosalind is there, sitting alone at a table, trying and failing to concentrate on the novel he's reading: *The Way of All Flesh.*

"Good afternoon. How are you feeling today?"

"Hello, Spencer." Rosalind sighs. "I'm the same. Very much the same."

But Spencer can see he has perked up at least slightly—the wig, gown, and makeup have returned at least. "You look lovely. So, where's Zeph gotten to?"

"No idea. I went to lie down, and when I came back, he and Nazan were gone."

"What? Miss Nazan is here? But why? How did she get across? Is she all right?"

"Ah, yes, she's your lady friend, isn't she? Archie helped sneak her across, and now she's off somewhere with Zeph." Reflecting on the many bashful smiles exchanged over the dishes, Rosalind arches an eyebrow. "It may be quite interesting when they return."

Spencer frowns. "I don't know what that means."

"Oh, you will. So, I don't suppose you were able to speak to your father on our behalf?"

"Rosalind, I'm sorry." He sits down, placing the satchel on the floor. "He's gone."

"Who is?"

"My father. He packed up my brother and took him to our summer place in Newport."

"Should have predicted that, I guess. *And then,*" Rosalind says

theatrically, "*across the land cameth the time of the Great Abandoning,
when all the rich shall bugger off to their summer homes*... I suppose you'll
be joining them?"

Spencer runs a hand through his hair. "No. I probably should—
Charlie needs me. But I don't think he wants me there. After all,
I did more or less purchase Magruder's." He looks pointedly at
Rosalind. "And I've made some promises. Which I no longer know
how to keep, it's true. But no. I'm staying."

Rosalind suppresses a smile. "What about your father's business
interests? Won't he want his right-hand man by his side?"

"Coney Island *is* a Reynolds business interest. And as far as my
father's right hand goes, Gib Tilden can have the right hand and the
rest of him too. I'm coming around to the notion that Gibson and
my father might deserve each other." He leans back in his chair.
"Nah. What in the hell would I do in Newport anyway?"

"Well, well. Good of you to join us in the real world."

"Actually, speaking of which..." He nudges the satchel with his
shoe. "Could you help me stow this away someplace safe?"

Rosalind frowns and stares down at the overstuffed bag. "Is it a
head in there?"

"What? No, certainly not. Goodness. It's just...insurance."

Rosalind eyes Spencer. "I suppose I can find a safe place for it in
the back room."

"Not somewhere obvious, now. Not somewhere anyone would
just happen into it."

"Somewhere in the back, I just said."

"Thank you."

They sit quietly, listening to Archie's muffled sales pitch continuing on outside. "Quite a business the old thief's got going out there,"
Rosalind notes.

"Yes, I saw the crowd on my way in. What is he up to, anyway?"

"Getting rich quick, he hopes. Patent medicine for the
Calcutta Cough."

"You're joking. What's in it? No rat poison, I hope."

"Rosewater, quinine, something else I forget now, and—here's the kicker—Zeph's homebrewed whiskey. He better sell it all. If he not only stole the whiskey, but *wasted* it too? Zeph will pitch a fit."

"Doesn't sound like selling it will be a problem," Spencer says. "Selling out is what's going to be dicey."

"That's Archie. Could sell ice to Eskimos. Isn't that the expression?"

Spencer nods. "But this is more like selling ice in the Sahara."

Archie's voice gets louder, seeping through the window. "Which of you will be first to purchase Doctor Theophilus Magruder's Elixir Salutis?"

A cloud passes over Spencer's face. "He's using the Magruder name? This phony medicine, it says Magruder's on the front?"

Rosalind shrugs. "What difference does that make?"

"What happens when those lummoxes go home, give the children a few doses of Magruder's elixir, and their babies all die anyway? Who will they blame?"

"Oh no. There's enough people wanting to torch this place as it is."

Spencer stands. "This ends now."

Out on the sidewalk, Archie can't collect cash fast enough. When he sees Spencer, his shark smile goes even wider. "Mr. Reynolds! Look, everyone, it's none other than Spencer Reynolds, one of the finest princes of this fair city! Young Master Reynolds, sir! I can only assume you've come for your family's portion of elixir?"

"I've come to shut your damned mouth."

Archie laughs uncomfortably. "I'm sorry, young sir?" He turns so his prey can't see the daggers he's shooting at Spencer with his eyes. "I'm sure you can't mean it."

"Give the money back, Archie."

"Ah, what?"

"You heard me, old man. Every dime."

"Hey!" screeches the woman. "What's all this about?"

Spencer pulls Archie down from the apple box and holds him roughly by the shoulders. "Sorry, folks. You see, this is…" He looks at Archie, a bit disgusted by what he has to say next. "This is my grandfather."

Archie gasps, appalled. "I most certainly am not—"

"My grandmother passed away from the Cough, and I'm afraid the old man has gone a bit...soft. Mentally. He's not himself."

"This is nonsense!" Archie wriggles but can't break Spencer's grip.

"It's the grief, you see. I'm very sorry he got your hopes up. If it's medicine you need, I beg you, please, go see a doctor. A real doctor. And I promise, if you all line up patiently, I'll make sure you're repaid." Spencer digs his fingers into Archie's shoulder. "Now, say you're sorry, Granddad."

"Fuck you," Archie spits.

Spencer shrugs at the shocked crowd. "I told you he was crazy."

CHAPTER

33

THERE'S NO
BUSINESS...

~◦~

H OW ARE YOU?
Such a common question with so little meaning. It's a question
that doesn't even desire an answer. *How are you? Good afternoon.*
Nice weather we're having. Words of ritual rather than significance.

But that's changed in Coney Island now. *How are you?* means *Are*
you dying? How is your family? Have they died? Will they die soon?

How are you? A once-empty query, now crowded with intention.

Meanwhile, the once-crowded streets of Coney Island sit largely
bereft. Zeph and Nazan walk along a Surf Avenue that looks like a
stage set after the play is long over. The shrieking roller coasters have
gone silent. The Ferris wheels are still, carriages swaying in the breeze
like loose teeth in a mouth. Zeph's leather gloves make a gentle scraping sound as they brush the sand-covered streets. The sound would be
pleasant if it didn't merely highlight the utter silence everywhere else.

From time to time, they pass an Unusual, or a waiter, or a cook.
If Zeph knows them—being a bartender, he often does—they stop
awhile and check in with one another.

How are you?

"See," Zeph notes when he and Nazan continue on their way. "*She*
don't have it." Or "Did ya hear that—*his* people are all doing good.
Not everybody gets it, Miss Nazan. Some people get it, but not everybody gets it." He's not sure which one of them he's trying to reassure.

"No," Nazan readily agrees. "Not everybody."

"We're gonna be fine. It's all gonna be fine."

But then a crumpled hot-dog wrapper skitters down the street like a tumbleweed, landing at Zeph's hip. And something about that dejected little wrapper nearly breaks Zeph's heart in two.

"Must be what it's like here in the winter," Nazan offers.

"It's quiet in the winter, but this is…" He doesn't bother to finish the sentence. They walk together in silence for a while, listening to the calls of dejected seagulls.

"I still can't believe Spencer knew this was coming and didn't say anything." Nazan shakes her head. "I should become a nun. Clearly, I have no instincts for suitors."

"Well, now…" He looks up at her. She's smiling at her little joke—smiling despite the eerie misery all around. Her eyes crinkle, and her unruly curls dance in the breeze, and something goes *ping* in Zeph's chest. Fortunately, he knows exactly what he ought to say: *Yeah, Reynolds, that no-account, good-for-nothing, rich boy. You're best rid of him, Miss Nazan, and that's the truth.* As well as he knows his own name, Zeph knows that's precisely what he should say.

But instead, he says, "Spencer could have let the Committee arrest me. Could've let me take the fall for those dead fellas in the yard. Instead, he lied to keep me outta trouble, and now he's an accomplice in two murders." Zeph sighs, disgusted with himself. "Reynolds ain't all bad."

Nazan nods. "That's big of you to say, considering how he acted toward you when his friend Tilden was around."

"I am a mighty big man, as you can surely see."

They laugh. "He's just so confusing to me," she says. "Do you remember, at the Cabinet that first day, when he saw the boxing kangaroo? And how delighted he was? *That's* the Spencer I met initially. That's the one I…" She blushes. "*You* know. But five minutes later, it's 'my father this' and 'my family that,' and his *friends*! My goodness, his friends are absolutely gruesome. Does he really think those nincompoops are going to be *my* friends too?" Nazan sighs. "I *am* fond of him. I just… I don't know."

"No rush," Zeph points out. "You got time to figure it out."

The entrance to Luna Park is barred with a long, heavy chain, and a lone figure leans on the chain, smoking a cigarette. As they approach, Nazan sees that the man's face is tattooed with an illustration of a collapsing castle. With one hand, he pets a rat, its tiny head peeking out of his jacket pocket.

"Afternoon, Zeph," he sneers. "Look at you—taking the air, enjoying the apocalypse."

"Pete," Zeph replies. He has to maneuver carefully so as not to put a hand down on one of Pete's many cigarette butts that litter the ground. "How are you?" Pete just shrugs. "What are you doing out here?"

"Nothing much. Just waiting on some friends."

"*Friends?* Hope you have a lot of tobacco if you're gonna wait that long."

"Ha. Now, look at this sweet thing you've got with you. Further evidence the Cough is the best thing ever happened to people like us. Think you'd ever land a piece like that a few weeks ago?" He tips his bowler at Nazan. "Welcome to the good days, baby."

Nazan looks shocked, but Zeph just shakes his head. "Don't bother."

"So," Crumbly Pete says, "you two headed over to the doctor's?"

"Never mind where we're—"

But Nazan says, "There's a doctor in Coney seeing patients?"

Pete chuckles. "*Seeing* patients? Ain't exactly seeing 'em."

"I don't under—"

"There's this building on Twelfth, all these people lined up? What you do is, you stand in this line, and when it's your turn, you shout up a description of whatever poor son of a bitch got himself sick. You know: *male, five foot eleven, one eighty.* And the doc lowers down medicine in this basket. You put every damn nickel you got in the basket, or some goons stomp the snot out of you. Good racket." Pete takes a contemplative drag on his cigarette. "Thinkin' about getting into it myself."

"Yeah." Zeph snorts. "You're quite the humanitarian." He nods to Nazan. "We should go. See ya, Pete."

They continue down Surf Avenue as Pete calls after them. "They say this Cough turned the city upside down, Zeph! You know what that means? Means the last shall be first, my brother!" Pete kisses his rat on the nose. "Last shall be first."

✸ ✸ ✸

The eerie quiet on Surf Avenue weighs on Zeph. "It's strange," he muses. "Usually I long for everyone to leave, because it's the only time I can go out."

"Honestly?"

"Come on, look at me. You walk on your hands, you're gonna get stared at. People gonna talk—that's just how it is. I don't care what they say, but…well, gets to the point I don't feel like going out. Just ain't worth the trouble. But now—here I go down the street, easy as you please. And suddenly I'd give anything to have somebody shout 'freak' at me." He chuckles. "Some people are never happy, I guess."

On their way to the Manhattan Beach Hotel, they pass bathhouses and tchotchke shops, boarded up and bereft. The silence develops a physical mass; Nazan can feel it on her shoulders like a heavy weight. To break it, she says, "Zeph, if you don't mind my asking, how did you lose your legs?"

"Oh, you know," he says. "Left 'em in a bar."

"Very careless!"

"Heh. No, it was… My people are down in Tennessee. After the war, my grandparents got…well, no forty acres, that's for damn sure. But they got themselves a little land to work, and that became our life down there. As for me, it's the old story. Boy fights tractor; boy loses."

"A *tractor*? Mr. Zeph, I'm so sorry."

He shrugs it off. "I spent a few months in bed, not doing much. Taught myself to read—that's something at least. Kept waiting to die, but after a while…just got bored, I guess. Finally, one day, I started trying to figure things out. How can I do that, how can I do this?"

"And what brought you up north?"

"Well, food's always scarce, of course, and feeding somebody who ain't contributing...that's tough on everybody. So one day, the circus comes to town, fella spots me up in the stands, climbing around on the bleachers like I learned. Next day, he shows up, sniffing around all sympathetic-like. Mama makes him a pot of tea, he takes his wallet out... Before you know it, I'm in show business."

"So she just..." Nazan bites her lip. "I don't know what to say."

"Aw, now. He paid enough to fix the tractor, so... And I saw the country. I've been to Syracuse, Columbus, Pittsburgh. Got all the way out to Cedar City one time. I've been a Wild Man of Borneo, a Caterpillar Man. I've been a Missing Link." Nazan gazes at him, horrified. "Aww, it wasn't so bad..."

But she continues to stare, and he wilts under her big, brown, empathic eyes. "*Okay*, you got me. It was horrible. Traveling in some penny-ante sideshow, acting the fool while a bunch of hayseeds gawk and throw rocks. Lucky you, Miss Nazan, because now you know what all my nightmares look like—me, in a cage, with some inbred toddler laughing at me till he wets himself. But I'm all done with that now. I got my friends, I got the Cabinet to look after, and there's no point in—oh, look," he says with relief. "We're here."

34

THE HOUND

KITTY SITS ON THE STAIRCASE TO THE SEA, TRYING NOT TO THINK ABOUT THE double funeral she'll need to arrange for her mother and brother, but thinking about it regardless. Should it be a proper service in London? But how will she get there, and with what money would she organize such a thing? In New York, then? But what would be the point when no one knows them here?

Surely Mum would want to be laid to rest beside Father. Good luck, given that Kitty can't even find her body. What a useless girl she's turned out to be. What did Shakespeare say? How sharper than a serpent's tooth to have a child *lose your corpse*?

She hates that she's so practical. Making jokes, even when she has no one to tell them to. She should cry more, shouldn't she? *Keen* or something? Isn't that what a good daughter would do? She'd shed a few tears in front of the doctor, but they'd soon dried up. Now she can't stop her brain from making and remaking funeral arrangements. *What's wrong with me?*

A few steps down, at the water's edge, P-Ray stands with his makeshift fishing pole—a stick with a long piece of string and a hook fashioned from a small piece of metal he'd found in the yard. He casts his line, over and over. Kitty hasn't bothered to tell him it's pointless. Even pointless fishing gives P-Ray so much happiness, and it's not as though the observation suite has much else to offer for entertainment.

But suddenly, a miracle. P-Ray hoots in delight and scuttles up the steps to show off his prize—a long, brown fish flops in his hands. "Look at you!" Kitty says. "That's brilliant! Well done, sweetie, well done indeed!" The boy squeals and jumps up and down with such enthusiasm that Kitty has to grab him so he doesn't tumble into the water.

"I am returned, signorina!" Enzo stands on the far side of the chain-link fence and begins to climb.

"I am glad, signore!" Kitty goes to the fence to greet him. For the past couple of days, Enzo has been sneaking out of the men's dormitory anytime no one is looking. Each visit, he brings a gift—a washcloth smuggled from the lavatory, a bag of cookies liberated from the kitchen. Tiny gestures, but exquisite kindnesses also. His visits keep Kitty from going completely mad with loneliness.

He drops down to her side of the fence and pulls a book from inside his coat. "For you."

She grins and snatches her gift, the title, *A Study in Scarlet*, in lurid print on the cover. "Oh, lovely, Sherlock Holmes! This is the one where the cab driver did it."

Enzo grimaces. "You already read…"

"Yes, but… Oh, Mr. Enzo, I'm sorry. It's a cracking good story. I don't mind, truly. I shouldn't have said anything."

P-Ray squeals and runs to them, holding up the fish to show Enzo. "What is it you have? *Un pesce*? *È fantastico*! Aha, a mummi-chog, you catch. *Molto bene*! You see these blue spots? This means he is…ah…" Enzo looks to Kitty to help him find the term. "He is… how you say, ah, looking for girlfriend?"

Kitty grins. "Spawning."

"*Sì, sì*. Spawning. So we must let go." P-Ray whinnies his disap-pointment, but Enzo eases the hook out of the fish's mouth and hands it to the boy. "Now, we no stop *amore*."

P-Ray returns sadly to the stairs. He pets the mummichog and whispers a mournful good-bye, while Kitty and Enzo confer by the fence.

"How goes the boy?"

"Fine. Bored. And hungry—the food they bring us is rather dire. I found a hairpin in my macaroni earlier."

Enzo nods. "Is no better in the big house, believe me. And? How is the young lady?"

"Me? I'm all right." Unconvinced, Enzo arches the eyebrow on the unscarred side of his face, and Kitty smiles. "Better for your visits, sir. Any progress with the boat?"

He groans. "Ach, these men, they work in the offices. I have to show which end of the hammer to use."

"Lucky they have you, then!"

Enzo looks out at the bay and shudders. He confesses, "I, ah…I no like the water so well."

Kitty frowns. "You don't swim?"

Enzo shakes his head.

"There's nothing to it! I'll teach you sometime."

He eyes her skeptically. "A *lady* swimmer?"

She gasps in mock horror. "How dare you, sir! This lady swims brilliantly!" She grins at him, and Enzo grins back. "In any case, you aren't alone—loads of sailors can't swim a stroke. If we sink in New York Bay, a few swimming lessons probably won't save you, anyhow."

"Is comforting, *grazie*. But we have nothing to…*come si dice*, control the boat. These tides…this is no lake, *sì*? We cannot just, ah"—he makes a flowing motion with his hand—"float along."

"Well, a sail, I suppose? You could steal some bedsheets?"

"Signorina, none of us know the sailing. Tides like this? We no careful, we end up in Cuba!"

"The food has to be better, right? Look, I don't know terribly much about it, but Nate used to sail. Perhaps I could—oh, pardon me. P-Ray! Do be careful. You're far too close to the water, and it's rather slippery! Apologies, Mr. Enzo. So, as I was saying, I could try to help with the sailing, perhaps?"

Enzo shrugs. "Is nice offer, but our problems, they are bigger."

"How can they possibly be so?"

"You see, these men… They say when boat is finished, they take me. They take you. But they no take the boy."

Kitty frowns. "Why ever not?"

He strokes his own cheek by way of answer. "Too dark. They no want."

"What! But that's horrible!"

"*Sì, sì.* So, I think, okay, I no help them. But boat is only option. I no know what else." He shakes his head sadly. "Miss Kitty, I no know what to do."

"I know precisely what to do! You finish that boat, Enzo. You solve the navigation problem, you sail off with them—and once you're far enough from shore, you clop their fat heads with an oar and toss them in the sea!"

Enzo laughs, shocked. "Miss Kitty! You no serious!"

"I'm utterly serious, Enzo. To leave a young boy like that, because of his race? It's unacceptable!" She stamps her foot in frustration. "Bastards!"

"You…" Enzo shakes his head. "You are…something I no know the English for."

"Well, I shan't have it."

"Okay, okay." He sighs. "I must get back, before they see I not there. I return soon." He calls to P-Ray. "*Addio, ragazzino!*" He climbs the fence and heads toward the hospital buildings.

"Mr. Enzo," Kitty calls after him. "See if you can find *The Hound of the Baskervilles* for me. A lot of mayhem in that one—quite suits my mood."

He shakes his head and laughs. "She is the troublemaker, this one."

Kitty returns to the staircase, where P-Ray stands, watching sadly as his mummichog swims away to freedom. She puts her arm around his shoulder. "Don't fret, sweetie. We'll swim off too. Together. I promise."

P-Ray looks up at her and nods. Then he coughs.

"Oh, sweetie." Kitty kneels down and wraps him in her arms. "No. Please, no."

Kitty ushers the boy back into the cabin as he coughs again.

35

THE GOOD THING

NAZAN AND ZEPH GAZE WIDE-EYED AT THE LAVISH GROUNDS OF THE Manhattan Beach Hotel sprawling before them.

"Would ya look at that?" Zeph says. "Two hundred suites in there. Archie told me about when it opened, 'bout thirty years ago? Ulysses S. Grant stood right there on those steps and made a speech. The man was *right there*! And now…" Weeds and patches of brown infect the once-perfect green lawn. Traveling along a path that leads to the hotel's main entrance, they can see the telltale divots and ridges poking through the grass: the moles have arrived to reclaim their kingdom.

Then Zeph does something he never thought he'd do if he lived a thousand years. He strolls across the veranda of one of the most exclusive hotels in New York City with a pretty lady at his side. On his own two hands.

★ ★ ★

The doors are locked.

"*Shit*," Zeph says. He looks up at Nazan. "Sorry for the language. It's just…" He sucks his teeth. "So close."

"There must be another way in. Maybe if we go around to the—"

Just then, one of the front doors pops open. A frantic-looking young man emerges, still in his waiter's uniform, knapsack slung across one shoulder.

"Miss Nazan!" Zeph says. "Quick, get the door."

Nazan leaps for the door just before it slams.

Zeph addresses the waiter. "Hey! Hey, mister. Got a question for ya."

The waiter starts down the steps without looking back. "Sorry, busy."

"Where's the Englishwoman?"

He stops short and turns. "What did you say?"

Zeph nods. "Uh-huh. Where they keeping her?"

The waiter opens his mouth, then thinks better of it. "I have no idea what you are talking about."

"Sure you do. The bellhops been keeping some British lady hidden in the hotel."

"That's absurd. Anyway, I'm a waiter. I don't associate with *bellhops*."

"Come on, you telling me the staff don't know there's some Limey squirreled away someplace? *Gotta* be gossip item number one."

The waiter looks pointedly at his pocket watch. "I'm late. I'm the last one out of the building, and if I have any chance of catching a ferry, I have to—"

"Don't worry," Zeph says reassuringly. "We ain't cops."

The waiter arches an eyebrow, gazing from Zeph to Nazan and back again. "Really. The olive girl and the brown midget aren't cops. What a relief."

Nazan frowns. "Hey, he's not a—"

But Zeph raises his hand—he's heard far worse. "Easy mistake. Listen, please. We're with the lady's family. We're not here to make any trouble. We just want her back, okay? In whatever…condition…she might be."

"Please, sir," Nazan says from the door, suddenly sporting the single worst British accent Zeph has ever heard. "Please, it's me mummy. I just wanna find 'er, take 'er 'ome. Can't ye 'elp me, please?" She bats her eyelashes and pushes out her bottom lip slightly.

The waiter sighs. "Fine. They *were* keeping her down in the laundry. I don't know if she's still there. I stay well clear of all that."

Nazan smiles. "Thanks ever so much, guv'nor! Now if you could tell me 'ow to find the laundry, I'd be proper grateful, I would."

"I'll direct you to the laundry," he says, "if you promise to stop speaking like that."

✦ ★ ✦

Nazan and Zeph make their way carefully through the empty lobby while their eyes get used to the darkness. Completely shut down, the hotel is lit only by a few emergency lights.

But despite the gloom, Zeph is giggling. "Oy, guv'nor! Spare a shilling, eh, guv'nor?"

Nazan rolls her eyes. "All right, all right."

"Best stay outta show business."

"I convinced him to help us, didn't I?"

"Tortured him into it."

They creep slowly along the wall, feeling their way to a side door the waiter said would lead to the basement. "I didn't notice you having any better—ah, here we go. These must be the stairs." She opens the door to complete darkness. Gripping the door frame, she takes a deep breath. "It's like stepping into my own grave."

"Nah," Zeph says. From his back pocket, he pulls a fistful of Enzo's handmade sparklers. He hands one to her and lights it. "We're okay, Miss Nazan. We're okay."

✦ ★ ✦

The Manhattan Beach Hotel basement is a maze of corridors, and both Zeph and Nazan pray silently that their directions were accurate. One wrong turn, and they may not find the laundry before Zeph's sparkler supply runs out.

But just as the waiter promised, around the next corner, they find the double-doored entrance to the hotel kitchens; he said the laundry should be just past there. Nazan holds up a sparkler so she can read the sign posted on the kitchen doors: CLOSED BY ORDER OF THE COMMITTEE FOR PUBLIC SAFETY. AUTHORIZED PERSONNEL ONLY.

"Hand me the light, would ya please?" Zeph says. "I want to see what they're hiding in here."

"Zeph, it says *authorized personnel only...*"

"Miss Nazan, this whole visit is unauthorized. Come on, let's take a peek." He leans his shoulder against the kitchen door and nudges it open. The smell thumps him immediately—rotting and sweet, like those two dead Committee boys in Magruder's backyard, multiplied by a hundred. In the sparkler's light, he can see a cabinet door left partway open. A gray, lifeless hand sticks out.

"Okay." Zeph lets the kitchen door swing closed again. "Seen enough."

✻ ★ ✦

At last, the laundry. They pause in front of the swinging doors. "This, um..." Zeph trails off. "This might not be..."

Nazan nods. "I'll be all right."

"You hold the light, and I'm going to push open the door. You ready?"

"Yes. No, wait." She closes her eyes and takes a deep breath. "Zeph? Next time I announce I want to be bold..."

"I'll tell you to hush up."

"Thank you. Okay, go ahead."

The laundry is a high-ceilinged room lined with pipes to usher clean water in and dirty water out. A huge copper boiler sits in one corner, flanked by washing and rinsing tubs almost big enough to swim in. Like the kitchen, the smell is overwhelming. The stench of death, but other things too: urine mixing with starch, rotten food with bleach. The only sound is the industrious hum of hundreds of flies. Just before Nazan's sparkler hisses out, she sees shadows cast by bodies lying in the tubs.

Hands shaking, she lights another sparkler.

Boys. Young boys, fourteen, maybe fifteen years old. They'd converted one of the tubs into a giant bed, and at least a dozen bodies are curled up among the sheets, wrapped around one another like kittens in a basket. And in the center, surrounded by fallen children still in their bellhop uniforms, lies an older woman, her eyes closed, her hair long escaped from what was once a proper British bun. In her arms, she cradles a boy with bright-red hair, his freckles unmistakable beneath the bruise-like spots covering his face. His mouth hangs open, and flies march in and out.

"Hello," Zeph says gently. "Hello, is anyone…is anyone still here?"

In the buzzy silence that follows, Nazan starts to cry. Zeph reaches up and takes her hand. "We did a good thing," he whispers. "It doesn't feel so good now, but it is. This way, Miss Kitty will know. She won't be left wondering forever."

Nazan nods and tries to speak, but a sob chokes out instead. "I know. It's just…" They stand together for a few minutes as the sparkler burns down and goes out. This time, she doesn't light another. She squeezes Zeph's hand as hard as she can. "They *stayed*. They stayed with her."

"I know, and ain't that a kindness, Miss Nazan? That she wasn't alone?"

"Zeph, I want to go."

"Okay, let's go. It's okay. I'll see you out of here safe, don't you worry." He guides her toward the double doors.

In the darkness, a woman's voice, weak and lost. "Kitty, is that you?"

TRUST ME

T HAT PEA-BRAINED, MOLLYCODDLED SON OF A WHORE!" INSIDE MAGRUDER'S,
Archie has been ranting at Rosalind for twenty minutes and
shows no sign of tiring. "That imbecilic stinkard!"

After issuing refunds to Archie's customers, Spencer comes back
inside with an apple box full of bottles. "You repugnant little shit,"
Archie says. "Give me my product back."

Spencer grins. "Nah, I think I'll keep these. Can't have you
selling those people false hope."

"False hope is the only kind there is, you *boob*." Archie scratches
at his scarred palm. "Who are you to interfere?"

Spencer twists open the cap and sniffs the bottle's contents. "Hmm,
quite a bouquet. Who am I? I'm the new owner of Magruder's is
who I am, and if you want to sell people a bunch of claptrap, you can
use your own damn name. Although I wouldn't advise it, because
I'm going to be keeping my eye on you."

Archie stalks up to Spencer. "Oh, you do that. You keep an eye
on me. That way, you'll be sure to see me laughing while your whole
world burns down." Archie turns and stalks out of the museum.

Rosalind grins. "That's our Archibald. Question is, what do we
do with this elixir now?"

Spencer takes a swig. "Hmm, not bad. Zeph can serve it at
the bar."

"Like a martini," Rosalind suggests. "A plague-tini."

Suddenly, a familiar voice drifts in from the street. "Hey! Hey, y'all home in there?"

"Zeph!" Rosalind rushes to the door with Spencer following close behind. Out on the street, they find not only Zeph, but also Nazan, who is pushing a large, wheeled laundry cart. The side of the cart is emblazoned with the logo of the Manhattan Beach Hotel.

Spencer goes to her. "Miss Nazan, are you quite all right?"

She smiles. "Hello, Spencer. Yes, I'm fine. A bit tired—this cart is very heavy!"

Rosalind shakes his head in dismay. "Is looting a hotel truly a good use of your—"

Zeph rolls his eyes. "Show them, Miss Nazan."

She pulls back one of the sheets to reveal an older woman, unconscious, her skin nearly as gray as her hair.

Rosalind and Spencer exchange glances. "Asleep or dead?" Rosalind asks.

"Somewhere in between," Zeph says. "It's Mrs. Hayward! Come on, you two. Help us get her inside. Poor Nazan's been doing all the work—she got herself stuck with a partner who can't walk and push at the same time."

She smiles at him reassuringly. "You did well, Zeph."

Spencer frowns. "*Partners* now, is it?"

"Spencer," Nazan says, "please don't…"

Zeph says, "Come on. Y'all can argue about this inside."

Rosalind stops him. "Wait, wait, wait. This woman has the plague, Zeph. The *plague*. You can call it 'the Cough' all you want, but we all know this is—"

"This is Kitty's mama, Ros."

"This is an infected person! You're risking us all by bringing her here."

"Rosalind does have a point," Spencer says carefully.

"And what do y'all suggest? Leave her on the street? We gotta look after her."

"How?" Rosalind says. "We can barely look after ourselves these days."

"We talked about this, actually," Nazan explains. "A man told us that there is a doctor, over on Twelfth Street, who is selling medicine. Spencer, perhaps you could go?"

"She's too far gone for any medicine, Nazan. Just look at her."

She rounds on him. "And how would *you* know? Are you a doctor suddenly?"

"Nazan, please…"

"Look," Zeph says. "Y'all don't have to cuddle her—we just gotta keep her safe till Miss Kitty gets back."

"Yes," Rosalind says, his anger rising. "And what *about* that? Have you all forgotten about Enzo and P-Ray? Suddenly, all you care about is this half-dead—"

Zeph's jaw drops at the insult. "Damn it, Ros, nobody's forgotten nobody! My heart hurts *every second* thinking about our boys. You know it does! But we gotta be able to care about a couple of things at the same—forget it, I'm through arguing. Let's get her inside."

"I want *no* part of this." Rosalind turns on his heel and stalks back into the Cabinet and up to his room.

Spencer is inclined to agree with Rosalind, but after a stern look from Nazan, he sighs and takes hold of the cart, maneuvering it into the Cabinet while Nazan holds the door. But just past the doorway, he loses his grip on the cart, and it rolls away, smacking into the wall inside. The jostling awakens Mrs. Hayward, and she sits up, panicked. "Kitty! Kitty, where are you?"

Nazan goes to her. "It's all right, ma'am. Kitty isn't here just now, but we are her friends. We're going to look after you until she—"

"You ungrateful girl!" Mrs. Hayward shrieks, wide-eyed and hysterical. "You wretched, ungrateful little girl! How dare you abandon me like this? Your brother would never treat me so! I never wanted a daughter like you!" She weeps, great heaving sobs. "You wretched girl…" Exhausted, she closes her eyes and falls back into unconsciousness.

"What is this shouting?" An angry thumping comes down the stairs. Timur appears, even grumpier than usual. "How can man think with this caterwauling?"

"Sorry, Doc," Zeph says. "We just... We found this woman. She's real sick, and we just need to get down to Twelfth Street and buy her some medicine is all. Sorry for the noise."

"Medicine! What for?"

Even Zeph, accustomed to Timur's strange ways, is caught off guard by this question. "What for? We got ourselves this little epidemic in town? You remember, them boys come to burn down the building on account of—"

"So? You have sickness, you make real medicine, not some rubbish from Twelfth Street."

"Well, but—"

"I'm sorry," Nazan says. "Doctor Timur, pardon me. Do you know about medicine too?"

Timur swats at the air with his hand, as though Nazan's question were a mosquito he'd sorely love to kill. "You electrify silver in a solution, you get medicine. Is nothing." He turns back to Zeph. "I need message delivered to telegraph office. Is important. You go now."

Spencer says, "Hold on, hold on. Silver? That would never work, would it?"

"And exactly what do you know, idiot? It worked for Romans, and they ruled world for a thousand years. Which is more than inbreds like you can say."

Nazan looks at Zeph. "Do you think?"

He shrugs. "I seen this man do stranger things."

Spencer frowns skeptically. "If you want medicine, Miss Nazan, you see a doctor—not some attic-bound lunatic. I will go to Twelfth Street for you."

"Telegram!" Timur barks.

"Yes, and I shall take care of your telegram."

"You don't mind?" Zeph asks.

"It's no trouble. Miss Nazan?" Spencer offers his elbow. "Care for a stroll?"

She shakes her head. "I should stay here and look after her."

Spencer glances from Nazan to Zeph and back. "Yes, of course." He approaches Timur, his hand extended to take the telegram.

Zeph eyes his boss carefully. "Okay with you, Doc, if Spencer takes it?"

Timur's lip curls a bit, but he swats the air again and thrusts a coffee-stained piece of paper at Spencer. "Here is message. Make sure you tell that the delivery boy must wait at address for reply." He turns to head upstairs.

"Ah, sir?" Spencer asks. "You probably meant to give me the money to pay for this?"

Timur doesn't even turn around. "Your father is burning the goddamned city. *You* pay for telegram." The old doctor stomps back up to the attic.

Spencer smiles. "He's really warming up to me. All right, I'll be off. But, Nazan, do you mind?" He gestures toward the door. "Could we speak outside for just one moment before I go?"

"I should probably stay and help—" Nazan looks at Zeph.

"Go on," Zeph says. "We'll get her upstairs when you're done."

Nazan nods, and she and Spencer step out into the hazy afternoon sun. "What is it, Spencer?"

He takes a deep breath. "I want to say… I'm not even sure how to put this… All right, here goes: if there had been a vote—there *wasn't*—but if there had been a vote about whether the Committee should take Mrs. Hayward, I would have voted no. If there had been a vote about hiding information about the Cough, or about the quarantine, or…all of it. I would have voted no."

"I know that."

"Do you? Do you truly? Because you act as though I'm—"

"Zeph told me how you stuck up for him. And how you tried to help Rosalind."

Relieved, Spencer takes her hand in his. "So you understand."

"I wouldn't go that far. You're a very confusing person." But she smiles. "I need to go help Zeph with Mrs. Hayward. But I'll see you when you get back. We'll talk then?"

He kisses her hand. "Until then."

★ ★ ★

A young woman with a handkerchief tied around her face exits an office building on Surf Avenue. In her arms is a large box packed with file folders, and she struggles a bit to get herself and the box out of the door before it closes behind her. To her rescue comes an older gentleman with a cravat and a shark's smile.

"Here, let me help you," he says, and he holds the door open for her.

"Thank you, sir," she says, her voice muted by the handkerchief.

"Pray, is this building home to the Dreamland Consortium?"

"Yes," she says, "but there's no one in."

"Oh no?"

"They just sent me over here to get some files."

"Is that so?"

She nods. "I didn't want to come out here, with the Cough and all. But I'm low on the totem pole, so…"

"Tsk tsk," says the old man sympathetically. "What a terrible thing to do to you."

"Yes! Yes, I agree." She giggles. "Don't tell my boss I said so."

He grins. "I wouldn't dream of it. Although I do, as it happens, have business with your boss. Senator Reynolds? Any thoughts on how I might reach him?"

"Humph. He's packed up and left for Newport. Decided to spend the summer there, away from the Cough. Nice life, huh?"

"Indeed. Left you with the cleanup, has he?"

"I don't even get to go! I have to take these files over to Dreamland."

"My dear, how fortuitous. Allow me to hail us a taxi, and I'll see you there."

"Ah, I don't know… I'm supposed to just—"

"I won't hear of it. You shouldn't be alone; it's too dangerous. Besides, I have information I know will be of great interest to the senator. I've no doubt he'll be very pleased with you for having brought me to him."

The young lady laughs. "You'll have to excuse me, sir, but there's very little that pleases the senator these days. I can't imagine how—"

"My information relates to the whereabouts of his son."

Her eyes go wide. "Spencer?"

"The very same."

"Well, but—"

"Did the young man not go missing the night of the quarantine?"

"Yes, but—"

"Would his father not be pleased to have information as to his whereabouts?"

"Well, I—"

"Come along now. Let's get that taxi." Archie pulls the carnation from his lapel and presents it to her. "You can trust me."

37

THE MONSTER

KITTY PACES IN A CIRCLE IN FRONT OF THE DOOR TO THE OBSERVATION SUITE while seagulls squawk and fight just offshore. Her hospital-issued skirt makes a quiet swishing sound as she stomps back and forth in the sand, flattening the beach grass over and over again.

P-Ray's cough spiraled quickly into full-blown illness—his little body wracked with fever, his neck sprouting black lumps. She'd gone to the fence and shouted to anyone and no one that they needed a doctor, please, right now, please. But the hours crept by with no response.

The head nurse's words thundered in her ears. *It'll be Swinburne for both of you. If it were up to me, you'd be there already.*

Kitty raced down to the water to wet a washcloth and soothe P-Ray's feverish head, but it didn't seem to matter. The boy lay curled on the cot, sweating and shivering and weeping. She tried to read to him, but she couldn't focus on the words. She tried to sing to him, but her voice cracked. She couldn't even hold him—the slightest touch seemed to send waves of pain across his body. There was nothing Kitty could do but watch. When she couldn't bear that any longer, she'd gone outside to pace in circles.

If it were up to me, you'd be there already. Both *of you.*

Enzo calls out from the other side of the fence. "Signorina! I am here! Signorina, come closer."

Kitty does not stop pacing. She does not even look up. "Climb the fence if you want to be closer."

"I cannot. They are watching." He gestures at a guard standing not fifty yards away, his eyes locked on Enzo. There will be no more casual, fence-jumping visits, not now that plague has come to the observation suite.

Kitty keeps pacing. "So? What did they say?"

"Please come closer, so I no holler."

"I'm not leaving him. What did they say?"

Enzo frowns at having to not merely deliver bad news but shout it. "The doctor, he is not coming."

"Why?"

"Why ask what you already know? They say they cannot help him."

"*Won't*. Won't help him."

"There are many other children sick, signorina."

She stamps her foot. "I bloody well know that, don't I? One of them gave it to him!"

Enzo sighs and says, "*Sì.*" But he does not sound so sure.

"He *did not* give it to them, Enzo. They gave it to him! He was *fine* until we got here. And now *those* children—those light-skinned children, English-speaking children—*they* get to see the doctors, don't they? Don't they?" Enzo looks away, but his silence only feeds her fury. "Of course they do. Of course! They get doctors and medicine, but what does P-Ray get? A mildew-covered blanket. A rag and some seawater to cool his fever. And a waiting oven when he's yielded up the ghost. And you! You stand there staring at me like a beaten dog. Are you up there fighting for him? Are you arguing against this slow execution? No! No, with you it's '*sì*, signorina,' 'no, signorina.' Won't even climb the fence now, because you're afraid of some guard!"

"I climb this fence, I no allowed back in the main building."

"And what a shame *that* would be—losing your comfortable bed in the dormitory."

He slams on the fence with both hands. "No dormitory, no boat!" He glances back to see if the guard might have overheard, but the guard looks distracted by the seagulls. "I try to finish boat, get us away from here! And *sì*, I argue for him! I love *il ragazzo* like a son. How dare you say this? I try everything I can think. But they no listen! Can you no see? To *their* eyes, I am monster too!"

Kitty stares at Enzo, the left half of his face purple and leathery, drooping just slightly lower than the right. Of course. She takes a few contrite steps toward the fence. "I'm sorry, Mr. Enzo. I don't even see your scars anymore, now that we're friends. I guess I wasn't thinking."

He sighs. "You are upset, I know. But remember not everyone glide across the world so easy like you."

Kitty goes the rest of the way to the fence. Her eyes are wet. "Does this look easy?" She gestures at her hospital uniform, the observation suite, everything.

He smiles a little. "No. But I do think…I think some of the people, like you, they…walk a path with fewer rocks. They expect differently."

"Should I just accept this from the doctors? Should I just… what, shrug?"

"No," he replies. "You rage. You rage, signorina. Just maybe you no rage at me, okay?"

She nods. "I promise." She hugs herself and looks down at her boots. "I'm just so frightened. The past few days have been difficult but…it's been me and him. Together. Do you know what I mean? But now…anytime I step back in that cabin, I might discover I'm alone."

"Aww, *il scugnizzo*, he's tough one. You also are tough one, I think. And like they say, I am monster. So."

Kitty reaches out, linking fingers with him through the fence. "Noble monster. Please finish our boat."

CHAPTER

38

BELLS

❧

FIRST, SPENCER TAKES CARE OF TIMUR'S URGENT, NONSENSICAL TELEGRAM. His steps are lighter due to his brief conversation with Nazan. Things were looking precarious for a bit, but now… Spencer smiles. Everything is going to work out after all.

That the telegraph office is open at all is a surprise. Nothing else seems to be. Storefronts have been repurposed for other, more pressing needs. The sign for Ira's Incredible Ice Cream is covered with a piece of cardboard announcing *XTIAN Baptism, 7:00 p.m. Saved & Sinners All Welcome.* What had been the Coney Island Souvenir Emporium advertises *Spiritual Cures and Prayers, His Holy Shree Harjeet Sundaravadhanam. The Mystic Is In.*

He stops short in front of another sign—an ornately painted human palm floating in a starry night sky, the constellations drawn to resemble the zodiac. *Tibetan Priestess Yeshi Rinpoche,* says the flowery script. *Palm Readings and Spiritual Consultation.* And then underneath, in fresh, wet paint: *Traditional Tibetan Burial Services.*

"Tibetan burial services!" Spencer scoffs. "Nothing but rocky slopes in Tibet—they can't even dig holes there." He shakes his head. "The con men in this town need to read a book once in a while."

As he walks on, Spencer can hear the ocean. He shudders.

The sea is normally drowned out by the carousels and roller coasters and general pandemonium. The crashing waves, so comforting when lying on the beach with a good book or a pretty girl, seem ominous now. A hungry tide creeping up to swallow the world.

A woman's sobs drift down from an open apartment window. Her voice is hoarse. She's wept as much as she can but not enough. He thinks of his brother, of his friends from school. Did they get out in time? Or are they gone forever?

Along the street comes the clip-clop of distraction. Spencer recognizes the tinkling bells of Children's Delight—a portable four-seater carousel pulled along by a fine white horse. The Children's Delight was such a part of his childhood; he and Charlie used to search for it on every family visit to Coney. What a relief that some things never change.

And yet.

A young girl with pigtails, no more than ten years old, sits atop the cart. It is packed with corpses. Bodies stacked four and five deep, from the base of the cart to the saddles of the ponies, mouths gaping, arms and legs flopping off the edges of the wagon. Flies hover over dead eyes searching the sky.

Spencer approaches. "Excuse me, are you… What is… Good God, child, what are you doing?"

She holds up her hand. "Don't get close. I got it."

"You have what?"

"The Cough, stupid. You got a body?"

"What?"

"Tell me the address, I'll go 'round the back, and you can put it on."

"No, I… You're a little girl! Why are you doing this?"

"This here is Daddy's cart, but he died yesterday. This morning, Mama died too. I got a baby brother at home. I didn't want him playin' around no bodies, so I put Mama and Daddy on the cart. They're down at the bottom of the pile—you can't see, but they's there. I was drivin' Bess—she's my horse here, this is Bess. You say hi to Bess now." Spencer just stares, which annoys the girl. "I says, say hi, dammit!"

"Uh…hi, Bessie."

"It's Bess. Bessie's a cow's name, stupid."

"Sorry."

"Anyway, so I was taking Mama and Daddy down to the beach. Figured I'd bury 'em in the sand? Me and my brother, we bury all kinda stuff in the sand. So I thought I'd take Mama and Daddy there. But this old lady stops me, see? She says, you got bodies—you collecting bodies? Whole family next door to her—mother, father, granny, two kids. All of 'em gone. Boy, they smell something fierce. But she gives me some rock candy, so I take 'em. Farther I go, more bodies I get. Don't care what people give me, you know—I got candy, few nickels, cinnamon bun. But…" She gazes at her cargo regretfully. "Sure a lotta diggin' to do."

Suddenly she's overcome by a violent cough that nearly knocks her off her perch. But she steadies herself, spits blood at the sidewalk, and squints at Spencer. "Mister, you wanna help me dig?"

"I'm sorry…I can't. I'm going to the doctor's. Hey, why don't you come with me? We can get you some medicine. My treat. What do you say?"

"Aww, I don't know. Mama always tellin' me don't go nowhere with strangers."

"Of course, yes, that's wise. But… Look, my name is Spencer." He gives an awkward little bow. "Now we aren't strangers. Right? Come with me to the doctor."

"Nah, I gotta go. Got a lotta diggin'." She thwacks Bess with the reins. "See ya, mister."

The Children's Delight clip-clops away toward the sea. Spencer can only watch her go.

★ ★ ★

Outside Luna Park, there's a line of Unusuals, patiently waiting for… something. In the middle of the line, Spencer sees Whitey Lovett with other residents of Lilliputia. "Afternoon, Chief," Spencer says. "Ladies, gents…" The little people ignore him, but Spencer pauses beside them anyway. "Whitey, what's the line for?"

"Na-Na Xiou. She's a healer."

"Whitey, not you too."

Whitey suppresses a cough. "Let's just say I've felt better."

The tiny woman beside him pats Whitey's arm. "You'll be all right. Na-Na will fix you up."

"Look," Spencer says, "why don't you come with me to an actual doctor? Don't worry about the cost. I'll take care of it."

Whitey frowns. "Na-Na Xiou *is* an actual doctor. Just because Chinese medicine didn't come from Harvard doesn't mean—"

"All right, I'm sure it's wonderful. But, Whitey, this is Surf Avenue! Last week, we were selling penny postcards. Now it's plague cures?"

"What do you know?" sneers Whitey's companion. "What have you Dozens ever done for us? Fleeing off to your summer houses and leaving us to die."

"Miss, as you can see, I haven't—"

She stomps her tiny boot in rage. "I don't care, I don't care! Go away. You aren't wanted."

"Whitey, come on…" But Whitey looks away.

Spencer sighs. "I can't force you. But if you change your mind, you can find me at Magruder's. In fact…" Spencer takes a step backward and raises his voice to address the entire line. "I'm on my way to a doctor right now. Come with me. Money is not an issue. Please, let me help."

The Unusuals stare balefully at the Brooklyn prince, reduced to pleading in the street. They can't help but enjoy saying no to someone who's enjoyed such a glittering lifetime of yes.

Spencer notices the sparkle of triumph in their eyes. He's wasting his time. "All right. Offer stands. You know who I am, all of you. I'm stopping at Magruder's, and I will help if you ask."

As he walks away, he hears Whitey's girlfriend mutter "jackass." No one argues.

✦ ✦ ✦

The gathering outside the doctor's apartment is even more chaotic than Spencer expected. People in the line, such as it is—it's more like a festering clot of affliction—have boils and hacking coughs. They wring their hands and moan and weep. They poke one another with gangrenous fingers. They mutter angrily to themselves and scream obscenities at the air. A man collapses, and the people behind step over him, happy to be that much closer to the front.

My God. It's like the dinner bell rang at the madhouse.

Spencer takes a position behind an elderly woman wrapped in a moth-eaten blanket. She's sweating and shaking and ranting at no one in particular. "Go up, thou bald head," she cries. "Go up, bald head! Go up, goddamn it!"

Spencer lowers his chin and tries to cover his mouth with the collar of his shirt but discreetly, so as not to cause offense. Then he thinks, *Offense? To whom, exactly?* So he takes his handkerchief from his pocket and ties it around his face.

A basket is lowered by rope from the window. The gaggle of deranged diseased all reach up to the sky, even though there's only one miracle per customer, and this one isn't theirs.

Before the lucky patient can retrieve his medicine, a lunatic war cry echoes among the buildings. A pack of young men comes screaming along the street, whooping and roaring, gripping glass bottles full of fire. They rush the building, throwing their bottles in high arcs toward the windows of the doctor's apartment. Some of the bottles smash onto the crowd, who shriek in terror at the shower of flames. But some hit their target, bursting through the windows and setting the doctor's curtains on fire. Seconds later, one of the bottles connects with the apartment's gas line. Windows blow out like a horizontal fireworks show, and the building is ablaze.

"Come out, come out, Medicine Man," taunts the pack. On the street, the sick, the mad, and the confused run every which way in panic. A thin man bumps into a fat one, the fat one screams, and the thin one vomits at the fat man's feet. The little old lady in her blanket cackles delightedly and points at the building. "Behold," she shouts, "the smoke goes up forever and ever!" She grabs Spencer with rotting hands. "Blessed is the one who stays awake! Hallelujah!"

Startled, Spencer pushes her away, and the weakened old woman goes sprawling. Muttering an apology, he reaches down to help her up, but she has already rolled away. Spencer takes a step to follow, but a child sobs, and instinctively, he moves toward the sound when a shriek makes him turn back toward the burning building, just in time to see some poor soul leap out a window and land with a smack on the sidewalk. He rushes over and asks, "Are you all right?" but the pile of bones makes no reply, and Spencer notes something unnatural about the way its neck is tilted. He looks around and spots the young men who threw the bottles—a murder of raggedy crows, robbing their way through the hysterical crowd. A necklace from her, a wallet from him, a handbag over here, perhaps a brooch. No pickpocket's subtlety required—stride up to a demented sack of pestilence and snatch whatever trinket is available, and if someone has the presence of mind to object, just punch them in the face, easy peasy. But most don't object; they don't see, and how could they? Spencer glances at the doctor's building, belching smoke from numerous windows on different floors, and his only thought is, *No. No, it does not end like this.*

He runs toward the front door, one fish swimming against the current, and a mad thought strikes him. *Actually, this is perfect; this is just the break I needed. I'll drag that goddamned doctor from his burning apartment, bring him back to Magruder's, and he'll toil day and night to bring Mrs. Hayward back to life. Nazan will be thrilled, I'll be a hero, and she'll forget all about Zeph.*

Spencer shoves his way toward the door, dodging thieves and vomit. He worries he'll have trouble finding the doctor—he has no idea what he looks like.

But somebody does.

Spencer reaches the stoop and looks up to see two figures emerge. First out is a small, gray-haired man wearing spectacles and a white coat. He looks terrified, and who wouldn't—there is a muscled arm wrapped around his neck. The arm connects to a brick wall of a man who follows right behind, a powerful, beefy slab of a human, but something is wrong, Spencer realizes; something is wrong with this man, and then he sees. The slab is rotting. Fingers black and skin mottled and nose missing and... *Nose missing?* Spencer blinks hard and looks again—perhaps the smoke is playing tricks—but sure enough, there's just a dark stain where his nose should be. Does he have the Cough? Can the Cough even do that? As the two men stumble a bit down the steps, Spencer gets a good look at the telltale obsidian eggs sprouting from either side of his neck. He has it. The noseless man has it, and now he has the doctor too.

"No! Leave him alone! You can't do that! You can't take him! It isn't fair!" Spencer knows he sounds ridiculous, like a child. But he can't watch his only chance get dragged away by some hunk of festering, noseless flesh. The man and his captive brush past Spencer on their way out of the building, and Spencer grabs the old man's white coat. "No, you can't do this. You mustn't—"

Something cold and heavy connects with the back of Spencer's head, and he goes down, his smooth-shaven face scraping across the sandy pavement as his own nose goes crunch. The whole world is suddenly a carousel, and Spencer grabs the sidewalk as it spins. He rolls onto his back and sees he's lying at the foot of an enormous castle.

No, not a castle. A man. A man who looks like a castle.

The Castle Man's green eyes gleam, and his yellow teeth glisten, and he holds a length of heavy pipe in his hand like a prize. A rat sits on the Castle Man's shoulder, and the rat is laughing.

No, the man is laughing. Maybe they both are laughing. It hardly matters, Spencer; you need to focus. There's laughing and spinning and blood everywhere—blood from his nose and his eyes and the back of his head. Bloody fire pours from the building, and Spencer's head is full of smoke, and it's too much, too damn much, and Spencer vomits, which makes the rat laugh even harder. *Bessie's a cow's name, stupid.*

Spencer rests his broken head on the sidewalk, and it hurts in a way that feels like it's happening to someone else. The pipe clanks down against the sidewalk beside his head, echoing in his ear like a bell.

"Hey, Goo-Goo," the Castle Man says. "C'mere and look at

this." He leans down and yanks the vomit-soaked kerchief down from Spencer's face. "You're that Reynolds kid. I recognize you from the papers."

No Nose stalks over, dragging the doctor along with him.

"Look," the Castle Man says to him. "A Reynolds! I caught us a goddamn prince of the city right here."

From his position on the sidewalk, Spencer sees two heads appear in a swimmy, confusing sky. They squint down at him angrily.

"So what are you gonna do with your prince now?" No Nose growls. "Keep him as a pet?"

The Castle Man frowns. "Nah, let's just take his wallet."

"Good thinking, dummy. Leave him here so he can describe us to the cops. You started this, Pete—you finish it."

"*What* cops? Haven't you noticed—everybody's gone! Besides, his head's gonna hurt so bad tomorrow, he won't even remember where he was."

"I said finish him off, Pete."

"Just leave it alone, for Chrissake."

"What are you, some little girl all of a sudden? Some pretty girl with pretty pictures painted all over her pretty face? I said *do it*." No Nose picks up the pipe and shoves it at his partner.

The Castle Man takes the pipe but shakes his head. "You lost your mind. I ain't killing this kid."

"Somebody fucking is."

"Well, I'm fucking not." The Castle Man holds the pipe out and opens his hand, letting it clatter to the street.

"You're useless." No Nose shoves the doctor at Castle to hold, and he picks up the pipe.

"Please," Spencer tries to say. "What are you doing?" But little red bubbles dribble from his lips instead of words. He tries to raise his arms to protect himself. "No…please…please don't." He gazes up at the gathering dusk, flecks of fire drifting across the sky like runaway stars, and he thinks, *Pretty*. Then the pipe comes down, and the sky goes out forever.

HOUSEGUESTS

Z EPH SIGHS AND CLOSES THE CHEMISTRY BOOK. "SORRY, MRS. H... WE'RE gonna have to wait for Reynolds. Maybe he can figure this bunkum out, 'cause I sure can't."

He looks over at Nazan, sitting beside Kitty's mother and holding her hand. "You sure you should be so close to her? Touching her and all? Is that safe?"

Nazan shrugs. "What do you suggest? Shall I watch her die from across the room? I'm sorry, but I won't allow a bunch of fourteen-year-old bellhops to be braver than me."

"I'm sorry too, but I'd like you to be *alive-r* than those bellhops are right now. That's all I'm saying."

"I'm not moving."

Zeph sighs, rolling his eyes in surrender. "She looks peaceful at least." Nazan nods in agreement. "Bit too peaceful. She looks like she's gone to a nice place and don't feel like coming back." Nazan, sadly, agrees with this observation too.

Zeph glances around the room helplessly. While Nazan made up a bed for Mrs. Hayward, he'd been up in the lab with Timur, trying to wheedle a practical explanation of this electrified silver business. All he got for his trouble was a stream of insults and a beaten-up chemistry book hurled at his head. He'd taken the book and come to sit with Mrs. Hayward, hoping the sight of her—okay, of her *and* Nazan—would inspire him. And it did, no doubt. But good intentions don't explain milliamps.

Spencer's been gone fetching medicine for the better part of the day. What could be taking so damn long? From the look of her, Mrs. H. doesn't have much time to spare. He opens the book again. "So, a milliamp. A milliamp is…" He sighs again.

"Milliamp?" Nazan asks mildly.

"Yeah, it's…well, damned if I know. Something I gotta figure out to make this silver solution Doc was talking about."

Nazan picks up a damp cloth and daubs at Mrs. Hayward's forehead. "A milliamp is a measurement of electrical current. One milliamp equals one thousandth of an *ampere*, which describes the amount of electrical current that can pass through a particular point in a circuit within a particular amount of time."

Zeph's jaw drops open. "Why…but…Miss Nazan, you been sittin' there *watching* me struggle! When were you gonna tell me you knew this stuff?"

She smiles mischievously. "I was just curious to see how long it was going to take you to figure out that a girl might have read a science textbook."

"You!" He laughs and shakes his index finger. "You are… You are a beauty is what you are, and I'm taking you up to the lab."

"I don't know… Doctor Timur sounds a bit formidable."

"Reckon you can handle him. Bold, remember?"

Nazan shudders. "We agreed I was through being bold."

"The world may think differently."

A knock at the front door.

"Thank the Lord. Prince Charming returns to the castle," Zeph says. He climbs off the bed. "I'm getting Reynolds. Hopefully, he's got a dose of that medicine. *Then* I'm introducing you to the Doc."

Nazan wipes Mrs. Hayward's forehead again. "You hold on, ma'am. Please hold on."

✦ ✦ ✦

But the visitor is not Spencer after all.

"*Bonjour?*" a feminine voice sings out. "Is anyone at home?"

Vivi Leveque waits fretfully in the blackness of the museum's entrance. She wears a primrose-yellow suit with a floor-length skirt and a wide hat with fluffy egret feathers.

Zeph maneuvers his cart past the heavy black curtains. "Hello there, Miss Vivi. What can I do for you? You need something?"

"Ah. *Oui*." She hesitates. "There is a question. But I admit, it may be…*difficile*."

"Well now. This sounds interesting."

"It is the leopards. You know, they are to me like children. We sometimes do strange things for children."

Zeph scratches his flea-bitten hand. "You got that right."

"Monsieur Bostock tells me that with quarantine and parks closed, we cannot keep the animals. He says he will *sell* my babies to some stranger!" Viv starts to cry. "I think they intend to eat them! I have to get them away from these terrible men!" She removes a handkerchief from her clutch and daubs her eyes like a silent film star. "Monsieur Zeph, I do not know what to do!"

Zeph shakes his head, thinking, *Goddammit, Archie, what have you gotten me into?* He sighs. "Look, Miss Vivi, you can keep your babies here. We'll protect 'em from Bostock and…whoever else."

"*C'est vrai*? It is this I want to ask, but…"

"Yeah, go ahead. Our yard's all fenced off in the back; they ain't goin' nowhere. Leopards aren't jumpers, are they?"

Vivi frowns. "But of course! However, they have the cages, so…"

"There you go. Magruder's is now in the big cat business."

"Oh, Monsieur Zeph!" Vivi hugs him impulsively, nearly toppling him off the cart. She smells of jasmine. "Thank you! *Merci*! *Merci beaucoup*!"

"Sure, I just got some old stuff I gotta move out of—oh." Zeph remembers what else is in the backyard: the two Committeemen, or whatever is left of them after a few days in the Coney Island sun. "Say, Vivi," he says, as casually as can. "What do leopards eat, anyways?"

"Meat, of course. Normally I give them chickens, because they love to chase. Of course, with this quarantine, I don't know precisely—"

"Right, right. But do they ever eat, you know...dead things? Maybe, say, dead folks?"

"Folks? *Qu'est-ce que c'est*? You mean, people?"

Zeph nods.

"Leopards kill what they eat, Monsieur Zeph. They are not scavengers."

"Right, of course. Just a question."

"A terrible question."

"Sorry."

Vivi wipes her eyes again and pats Zeph on the shoulder. "Thank you. I will have the cages delivered. Of course"—she bats her eyelashes—"I should stay also. To look after them."

"Yeah, yeah, sure. What with the quarantine, we gotta stick together anyway, right? We've got Ros, we've got Miss Nazan, now you... Timur will love the company."

Zeph says this, but he thinks, *Uh-oh*.

IMPORTANT MEN

❧

ARCHIE STOMPS BACK DOWN SURF AVENUE, RESENTING EVERY STEP. HE should be riding home in style, perhaps escorted by the Reynolds' family chauffeur. Instead, he's hoofing it down the street in his old, worn-out shoes.

He'd talked his way into the Committee for Public Safety's headquarters in Dreamland. He intended to rat out Spencer to his father, tell him all about how the kid was claiming to own Magruder's now. Magruder's! Some disreputable shit hole that should have been burned down by the Committee anyway. Was that *truly* the type of property the Reynolds family should be managing? Imagine the scandal in town…

Archie wanted so much to humiliate that smug bastard, see him disinherited, crush him under his boot like a bug. But instead of the great senator, the only person at Dreamland headquarters was some pompous strut-noddy called Gibson Tilden Jr.

Regardless, there was a time when he'd have had a nitwit like Tilden eating out of his hand. Instead? The kid had barely even listened to Archie's litany of complaints about the Reynolds boy. He rolled his eyes and sent Archie on his way. *Dammit*, Archie thinks. *At the very least, I should have gotten enough reward money for a taxi!*

Archie's poor performance at the Dreamland office fills him with self-reproach. "This," he says to the empty avenue, "this is the exquisite glory that age brings. Bah."

He knows he would have done better with that child Kitty by his side—she's got the makings of a proper confidence man, that one. Reminds Archie of himself at that age. He feels a pang of worry about what's become of her, but self-pity pushes it aside. She thinks *she's* got problems!

Archie's knows he's lucky to have naive optimists like Zeph to fall back on. No matter how many times he burns that kid, no matter how many times Zeph says, "That's it, we're through," Archie can always talk the lad into one more chat, one more drink, one more ride around the...

Jesus H. Christ.

Tilden hadn't been interested in Archie's complaints. He clearly didn't give a damn about whether Spencer was alive or dead. But he had, just for a moment, shown a flicker of interest in Magruder's. "Magruder's should have been torched days ago," he'd said. "We'll need to rectify that."

Archie abruptly stops walking. "Oh. What have I done?"

✦ ✦ ✦

Gibson Tilden Jr. sits in the gilded lobby of the Dreamland ballroom. Under the quarantine, the building has been taken over by the Committee for Public Safety. Where once ladies and gents waltzed the night away, now there dwells an unromantic landscape of file cabinets, desks, and bureaucrats who study maps from morning till night.

The Committee on Public Safety loves its maps. Street maps. Topographical maps. Epidemiological maps most of all, draft upon draft, all projecting different "what if" scenarios. If the Cough strikes here, it will then travel there, but if it strikes there, it will then go here. These projections are invariably wrong. But—make no mistake—they are loved.

However, these maps all have a flaw, a blemish marring their beauty like a cold sore.

Magruder's Curiosity Cabinet.

It had been Gibson's idea to burn it. He'd made the case—and

Senator Reynolds had agreed—that a seedy little sewer like Magruder's, with its profane exhibits and uppity caretaker, had no place in the glittering future envisioned by investors. Gibson's discovery of fleas in the museum provided a convenient excuse to eliminate what had long been a pockmark on the island. And now that old clown Archibald Deschamps claims that Spencer, of all people, has appointed himself Magruder's protector? Spencer, who abandoned his family in a time of crisis and left Gibson to take up the slack? And that damn bag of cash never did show up in the Reynolds' account, just as Gib had feared.

When the senator had packed up for Newport and realized that Spencer was nowhere to be found, he'd flown into a rage. He'd announced he was done with the obstreperous boy—that he'd lost one son to polio and been abandoned by the other. That he no longer had any heirs at all.

Hmm, Gib had thought at the time, *is a position open?*

If so, Gibson Tilden Jr. was just the man to fill it. Magruder's was clearly the key—it was, in Gibson's view, the very wellspring of Spencer's betrayal. But so far, he hasn't had any luck in convincing the Committeemen to go anywhere near the actual building, much less burn it down.

In fact, Gibson has spent most of his time skulking around Dreamland, trying to get someone to pay attention to him. He'd arrived grandly, blustering his way through the quarantine checkpoint and announcing himself as Senator William Reynolds's aide-de-camp…a phrase that departed Gibson's mouth tasting of honey and reached the Committeemen's ears stinking of shit. Gibson's position as aide-de-camp was of utmost importance to him, but it appeared to be of absolutely zero importance to anyone else. Which strikes Gibson as not merely offensive, but also odd—the senator founded the park, so how is it that the Reynolds name carries no weight in Dreamland?

But this afternoon, finally—a break in the weather.

"All right, Mr. De Camp," the secretary mutters. "Chief McGrath will see you."

41

THE TELEGRAM

LIKE A STREAM FLOWING OVER ROCKS, THE ROUTINE OF DAILY LIFE HAS A way of smoothing out even the sharpest of edges. Even someone as determinedly strange as Timur can become predictable if you live with him long enough, and over time, Zeph had become acclimated to Timur's quirks. The doctor's inscrutable but urgent errands, his obsessive secrecy and intense dislike of fellow humans, his near-magical command of the principles of engineering… Over time, it all came to seem utterly normal. However odd Timur might be, Zeph believed there was nothing the doctor could do to surprise him.

Then Timur met Nazan.

That evening, Zeph had prepared dinner for her, Rosalind, and Vivi.

"Hoecakes they call these?" Nazan asks, reaching for a second helping. "These are *wonderful*."

"You aren't even slightly curious what the meat is?" Rosalind asks, eyebrow raised.

Nazan turns to Zeph, worried. "This isn't—"

"A lion? No, no, don't worry." He shrugs. "It's, ah, you know… pork?"

Rosalind holds up his fork and displays a crunchy strip of something fried. "And which part of the pig would *this* be, Zeph?"

He frowns. "Ya know, Ros, I'm not sure that's really—"

"I think Miss Nazan would love to know… Feet? My guess is feet."

Nazan puts her fork down. "Pardon me?"

"Feet?" Zeph asks, mock-scandalized. "I would never, *never* serve hoecakes with pigs' feet." He smiles mischievously. "The feet you pickle. These are snouts."

During the meal, Timur emerges from his attic lab, demanding an update on the whereabouts of his expected telegram. Pausing to shovel an entire hoecake into his mouth, he overhears Zeph and Nazan chatting. As Nazan explains to Zeph for the second time what exactly a "damn milliamp" is—what it measures; how it might transform a lump of silver into a cure—Timur draws closer. Suddenly, he interrupts their conversation to interrogate Nazan about something called Faraday's paradox. He fires off a series of gruff questions that Nazan, although startled, apparently answers correctly. There's a quick round of "Doc, meet Nazan Celik" and "Nazan Celik, meet Doc." And that's that.

Timur helps himself to a glass of whiskey and elbows Zeph out of the seat beside Nazan. To the amazement of the rest, they discuss hydraulic canals beneath Niagara Falls and high-voltage power lines in Montreal and a dozen other topics that not one other soul in the tavern can comprehend. Nazan even musters her courage to ask him about Mrs. Hayward and the silver colloid that Timur seems so sure will be her salvation. When the hour grows late and Nazan's eyelids heavy, Timur stands. "You sleep. I must work. Tomorrow, you come to attic, see laboratory. We talk colloid. Also, Theobold will be interested about you."

Zeph cocks his head at the Doc. "Theobold? Who's Theobold?"

"Bah." Ignoring the question, Timur turns to waggle a finger at Nazan. "Celik, do not sleep late. I no like."

Zeph gives Nazan a wink. "Welcome to the circus, my friend."

✦ ★ ✦

The next morning, Zeph goes to wake Nazan, but he needn't have bothered. She's awake and waiting, sitting by Mrs. Hayward's bed and wiping her brow.

"She any better?" Zeph asks.

Nazan shakes her head. "Worse, if anything. I think her breathing is slowing."

"Okay," Zeph says, "let's you and me go visit the big man, see what he can do."

As she and Zeph climb the stairs, Nazan can see a pale, peach-colored glow emanating from the attic.

Entering the lab, Nazan doesn't see the worktables with gas jets sprouting like metallic bouquets. She doesn't see the rows of metal shelving, packed with glass bottles of every size and style. She doesn't see the library of technology journals in a variety of languages, or the metalworking table with piles of brass watch works in various states of assembly. Nazan doesn't see any of it, because she can't take her eyes off the dozens of large, rubber balloons, floating and bumping against the attic ceiling. They glow a soft, orangey pink, like tinted moonlight.

Timur bats one of the balloons out of his way. "Much to show, Celik. In corner, that is induction coil, generating electrostatic field, and—"

Zeph waves at Timur to slow down. "Give her a minute, Doc."

Nazan boggles at the pink balloons, riding air currents like glowing jellyfish on the tide. "I… It's just…" She looks at Timur. "You said last night that you had wireless power up here. I heard you say it. But I didn't imagine…" She stares some more, shaking her head. "I didn't imagine."

Zeph climbs up on the worktable beside her. The table is covered with sawdust, which surprises him. Doc's not the carpentry type normally. Then again, who knows what he gets up to up here? Zeph reaches out and taps one of the balloon lights, sending it careening into another, and that one into another. The balloons ripple and bounce, some drifting up toward the ceiling and some down toward the floor. "Neat, huh? Hate to say it, but I kinda got used to them. Forgot how pretty they are."

Timur grunts. "Yes, you forget. I know this because so many are leaking helium since someone *forget* to refill."

Zeph sighs. "I'll get to it, Doc. Been a little busy."

"Bah." Timur smacks another balloon in annoyance. "Argon, I tell you. Argon better than helium."

Zeph disagrees. "Do you know what I'd have to go through to get this much argon? Helium we got in Coney in spades, but argon? Plus, you said argon glows blue, which ain't as good a light source as—"

"*Color* of light is not relevant to—"

"Argon won't float," Nazan interjects. She gazes at the glowing balls as they dance. "The floating is important."

"Ugh," Timur says. "Another romantic. Just what I need."

From downstairs, a voice calls out, "Hello? Anyone there? I'm from Western Union. I have a telegram for Mr....Teemoore?"

"Ahh!" Timur does a little dance, like a young boy who needs to pee. "Am coming," he calls. "Celik, you make the colloid. I busy." He dashes downstairs. "Am coming!"

Nazan watches in amazement as Zeph flutters around the lab, climbing up and down shelves, gathering the equipment. Zeph navigates the room as though his lack of legs is no bother at all—indeed, as though having legs would only slow him down. "So, *Celik*," he says, gently mocking Timur's rather impolite nickname. "How'd you learn all this science anyway?"

"I read too much." She reaches up and brushes one of the balloon lights with the tips of her fingers; it pirouettes away flirtatiously. "As it happens, my father is the purveyor of an extremely unpopular tearoom."

Zeph laughs, climbing another shelf to grab some more supplies. "Too bad for him, I guess?"

"Yes," Nazan agrees. "Bad for him, but very good for me. After I finished secondary school, I wanted to go to college, but—no, that's not the truth. I *begged* to go. Pleaded. Threw tantrums. Everything. But my father said I'd already had more education than was healthy. College is not what good girls do, you see. Good girls work for no pay in their fathers' failing tearooms until such time as they throw their lives away in arranged marriages to odd-smelling strangers from the old country."

Zeph whistles. "You really gave up a lot coming to Magruder's, huh?"

She laughs. "Definitely. At least the shop's extreme unpopularity left me with time to read. But I'm just an amateur—I love the *idea* of chemistry, but I've never actually… For pity's sake, this is the first actual lab I've ever been in. I wouldn't get my hopes up, if I were you."

Zeph climbs down with the supplies and spreads them out on the worktable in front of Nazan. "Well now, my *amateur* lady scientist, don't you be so hard on yourself. Let's see here: we got ourselves some test tubes and batteries and silver wire. We got a buncha other mess I don't hardly know what it is. Let's you and me save Mrs. Hayward, yeah?"

She smiles.

✦ ★ ✦

Hours fly by as they work on the medicine. The first batch turns to an ugly black sludge, but Nazan deems the second attempt a success. "We should give this to her right now."

Zeph nods, tucking the vial of silver colloid into his pocket. "Why don't you start another batch, and I'll give this to Mrs. Hayward?"

"Yes, of course. But, Zeph, I'm concerned about Spencer. I thought he'd be back last night, or surely by this morning. Do you think someone should go look for him? I don't know how much sense that even makes, but…I just…"

"Don't worry," Zeph says. "I'll see to it. Rosalind won't admit it, but he's worried too."

✦ ★ ✦

Zeph heads for the spare room where Mrs. Hayward lies unconscious. He looks around for a handkerchief to tie around his face before getting too close. Then he stops. "To hell with it." He climbs up on the bed, tilts her head back, and pours the medicine down her throat. She coughs, sounding like she might choke, but the liquid goes down. "Come on, Mrs. H. You stay with us, you hear?"

He goes downstairs and finds Rosalind gazing out the open Cabinet door.

"Hey, Ros, you think you could take a walk, see if you can find Spencer anywhere? Nazan's getting nervous, and frankly, I'm—"

"I'll go," Rosalind agrees. "But we have another problem." He points outside.

"Oh, what is it now?" Zeph joins Rosalind at the door and gasps. Walking down the middle of the street is Vivi. In one hand, she grasps two leashes, with two leopards tied to each leash. In her other hand is a long-handled whip, which she flicks at the cats whenever they start to wander.

"What the devil, Vivi?" Zeph calls. "You promised me cages!"

"*Bonjour*, Monsieur Zeph. *Oui*, I am so sorry. Monsieur Bostock say he own the cages, and I may not take them. I did not know what to do!" She reaches the stoop with her cats in tow. She mutters to them in some hybrid of French, English, and meowing, and they curl up around her feet. But the smallest of the four glares up at Zeph, a hungry glint in its yellow eyes.

"Vivi, I…" Zeph chuckles uncomfortably. "I don't know…"

"Please, Monsieur Zeph. Bostock will kill them."

He sighs. "Okay… Just for now, though, just till we figure something out. Take them out back and… I dunno… There's an old crabapple tree. Tie 'em to that, I guess."

Rosalind's eyes go wide. "Zeph! Are you out of your—"

"We can't leave 'em in the street, can we?"

"No, but—"

"Ros, it'll be fine. They're… Look at 'em. They look well behaved." The leopards flick their tails against the hot sidewalk. "Ain't they well behaved, Vivi?"

"But of course!"

"Show Vivi through to the backyard." Rosalind glares at Zeph. "*Rosalind*, we're keeping these leopards safe for a while."

"These are dangerous creatures, Zeph. You don't just—"

"It'll cut Archie something fierce, Ros, us keeping 'em when he wants to"—he waggles his eyes in Vivi's direction, not wanting to say it in front of her—"*you* know. Wouldn't that be worth it, just to see his face?"

"All right, all right." Rosalind storms back into the museum with Vivi and the leopards following. Zeph is pretty sure he sees the little one lick its chops on the way in.

"Ros, wait," Zeph calls. "You seen the Doc?"

"Tavern," Rosalind shouts back.

"Right."

Zeph hustles downstairs to find Timur at the bar, curled over his telegram. He's reading and rereading it, making notes and sketches on the envelope it came in. He mutters to himself. "Yes...no, what? No, no, this no right. Why does the fool think—oh, but maybe like this..." He scribbles some more.

"Doc," Zeph says, "sorry to interrupt, but we got a little situation up at the—"

Timur leaps up. "Zeph! Good. We go up to lab." He stalks out, not waiting for Zeph to follow.

"Wait, we—" Zeph scuttles after him, crashing right into the knees of Archie, just arrived at Magruder's.

"Zeph, thank goodness," Archie says. "I need to speak with you. The Committee on Public Safety is—"

But Zeph doesn't even stop moving. "Not now, Archie. I got half a dozen things in the fire more important than you."

Archie follows. "But this is very—"

"Not now!"

Upstairs in the museum, Rosalind has sent Vivi to the yard with her cats and is giving Timur a piece of his mind. "Doctor Timur, I've had about enough of—"

Timur ignores him. "You, to attic. I have pieces built, must be carried to roof for assembly."

"What are you talking about?" Rosalind sees Zeph enter with

Archie following. "Zeph, what is he talking about? There are dangerous animals with—"

"They wait," Timur says. "We take pieces to roof. Assemble."

"Actually," Archie interjects, "I believe my news trumps all of—"

Timur points at Archie. "You too. Attic."

Rosalind combusts, tears of rage spilling down. "I have had as much of you as I can take. There's a plague! We've had thugs wanting to burn down the museum at the front door, and now we've got man-eating beasts at the back. Spencer's missing, and a little boy has been kidnapped, *our* little boy! All you can talk about are the gadgets in—"

"I do this for him!" Timur shouts. "Since that night, when the men come, I no sleep, no eat—I work. For the boy, to bring him back to us."

"How is some ridiculous contraption going to bring P-Ray back?"

Timur shakes his telegram. "Orville promise this work."

42

DIGBY

◈

UP THE NARROW STEPS CONNECTING MAGRUDER'S ATTIC TO THE ROOF, Rosalind and Archie each carry one end of one section of Timur's mysterious contraption. Two long, thin rails are connected by a series of struts and covered with an expanse of canvas. A cyclops is painted on the canvas, and its one eye glares angrily into space as Rosalind steps on his skirt, stumbles, and loses his grip. The wood-and-canvas construction falls, pinning Archie underneath.

"Christ on a bike!" He shoves the canvas aside and stands, brushing himself off indignantly. "Enough with the charade. Go change into something sensible."

Rosalind gestures at his full-length walking skirt. "This is perfectly sensible."

"Look, dress however you want on your own time. You can play the goddamned Queen of Sheba, I don't care…"

Nazan and Zeph are coming up behind them, dragging a smaller part of Timur's project.

"…but when manual labor is required, it is beyond ridiculous for you to carry on like—"

"Mr. Archibald," Nazan interjects. "I must insist that you not speak to Rosalind that way! What difference does it possibly make what he wears?"

Archie glares at Nazan for a second, then bursts out laughing.

Rosalind elbows his way past Archie. He stops beside Nazan and

strokes her cheek. "You are an angel, Miss Celik." Rosalind straightens his skirt. "I will fetch some help, *actual* help, to assemble Timur's
contraption, whatever it is. And I will find Mr. Reynolds. I will do
these things, even for individuals in this stairwell who do not deserve
them." He lifts his chin high and goes downstairs.

✦ ★ ✦

Out on the street, Rosalind quickly regrets having made such bold
claims about all the things he'd accomplish. He'd known things were
bad, but he didn't expect Surf Avenue to be quite this desolate.
Seagulls swoop overhead, cawing in annoyance—no abandoned
hot dogs or dropped ice cream cones to snatch. A crumpled food
wrapper dances down the street, caught in a breeze. Carriages dangle
lifelessly from the Ferris wheel at Steeplechase Park. Coney Island is
reduced to a box of broken toys.

A cat in heat howls painfully from an alley. "Sorry, kitty,"
Rosalind says. "The whole town is lonesome today."

Finally, Rosalind discovers a small group of men loitering around
the Rough Riders coaster with their hands in their pockets. One of
them is familiar. "Digby," he shouts. "So very glad to see you!"

The strongman grins, opening his arms to embrace Rosalind.

"How are you holding up, Digby? I haven't seen you since
Bernard's funeral."

Digby shrugs sadly. "I miss my friend."

"I know, love," Rosalind says. "We all do."

Digby introduces Rosalind to the other men—an electrician from
Dreamland, a waiter from Feltman's, a bartender from the Oriental,
and a carousel repairman on loan from the World's Fair. "How are
you lads?"

The repairman shrugs. "We ain't sick, so that's something. But
there's no work."

"As it happens, there's work over at Magruder's. Timur the
inventor has a machine that needs building. He could use all of you,
I'm certain."

"Any pay?" asks the waiter.

"Ah, I'm not sure…but if the machine works as designed, you'll drink free at the tavern for the rest of your days."

The men eyeball one another, hesitant.

Rosalind bats his eyelashes. "Tell me true, boys…did you get any better offers today?"

Digby agrees. "I'm in. Got a new job, but I don't much like it."

"Really?" Rosalind asks. "You've found a job already? What is it?"

"You don't wanna know."

"I do! I'm very curious about employment opportunities on post-quarantine Coney."

"Well," Digby says, "I'm what's called a body breaker. Basically, I—"

Rosalind raises his hand. "On second thought…"

Digby nods. "Like I said. Pay or no pay, anything's better than that."

Rosalind sends them off to Magruder's. Then he walks down a side street toward the doctor's office. Turning the corner, he gasps. The doctor's building is completely destroyed—nothing left but the charred frame and piles of burned, broken furniture. A bitter smell hovers over the smoldering remains—objects were melted that shouldn't be made to melt. The buildings on either side are also charred, but at least they're standing.

A woman sits on the stoop, weeping. Rosalind approaches. "My dear, what happened?" But the woman shrugs off Rosalind's comforts.

On the ground is a dark, sticky puddle. Leading away from the puddle, a long smear points in the direction of the alley.

Don't, warns a voice in Rosalind's head. *Don't follow it.*

But he does.

At the back of the alley, in a heap, is a body. Spencer. A pair of seagulls sit on his chest, pecking away at his face. He's no ice cream cone, but he'll do.

Rosalind chases the gulls away in a rage. "Go away, you winged rats, go away! Poor prince," he says, his eyes filling up. "Oh, you poor prince…"

He tries to wipe the blood from Spencer's handsome face, clean off those cheekbones. But the skull is too broken, too far gone to restore.

Rosalind looks around helplessly. "I can't... I don't... What do I..." He covers his mouth with both hands as the tears come.

✷ ★ ✦

Zeph takes a break from the frenzy of construction on the roof and goes down to the museum. He feels for the first time in weeks like the world is finally coming back into focus, and he sings to himself. *"My little Coney Isle, dear little Coney Isle..."*

He opens the drawer under P-Ray's flea circus and takes out the pickle jar, home to the boy's few surviving pets. He carefully unscrews the lid and flips the jar over, covering the opening with the palm of his hand. *"Folks say the Bowery*—eww, how does he do this every day?—*is not very flowery, but that is the place for me...* Wow, y'all hungry today, huh? Well, don't you worry yourselves, 'cause we gonna get your boss man back for you any time now. You should see what the Doc's got going on up on the roof—your tiny flea brains wouldn't never believe it. And apparently Doc thinks I'm gonna steer the damn thing, which..." He laughs, frightened by the idea and delighted by it equally. "We shall see, little fleas. We shall see."

Rosalind steps around the black curtain. He stands there, stricken, his beautifully painted face now a soggy, raccoon-like mess.

"Hey, it's our hero! Thank the Lord you thought of sending Digby and his boys down here, Ros. Timur's contraption is coming together so quick! Digby, he tosses around these big ol' boards like they're toothpicks. Gonna be finished any minute." Zeph shakes the fleas off his hand. "Okay, that's my donation for the day. Don't get greedy, now. So, where's Reynolds?"

Rosalind opens his mouth. Closes his mouth. Shakes his head.

"Couldn't find him, huh? Well, goddamn. Where'd that boy get himself to? Wait, I know! Did you look over at the—"

"I did find him." Rosalind hugs himself, looks at the floor, the ceiling, anywhere but at Zeph. "I did find him."

"Fantastic! Did you tell him Nazan is working on some—"

"Zeph." Rosalind stares at him.

"Ros?" Zeph stares back.

Silence.

"Now, Ros, what are you even…"

Rosalind drifts over to one of the cabinets. He leans on it, resting his head against the cool glass front.

"Come on, don't… You don't mean… Jesus, no." Zeph climbs up the rungs alongside the cabinet so he's face-to-face with Rosalind. "What happened?"

"I went to the doctor's office. It's gone."

"What do you—"

"Burned down, blown up, I don't know! There's nothing left. Piles of ash, still smoking. I keep smelling it—even now, I still smell it."

Zeph reaches over and strokes Rosalind's face. "Oh, darlin'… I bet he wasn't in there. He's a smart boy; he coulda gotten out. Maybe he's—"

"He never got in! I found him on the street; he wasn't burned. He never got in before they…" He chokes off a sob. "Sorry, I'm trying not to…" He takes a few deep breaths.

"But that don't make sense. Who would do that?"

"*I don't know!* He's dead, that's all."

Zeph feels his grip on the rungs start to loosen. He eases himself down and sits on the floor. "Jesus."

Rosalind dabs his eyes with a handkerchief. "Someone has to go get him. I couldn't carry him alone, so I had to leave him there. Maybe Digby can do it. But we—"

"But why, though? Why attack the doctor?"

"Who knows?" Rosalind says. He sniffles and wipes his nose. "Who knows why any of us does anything? Unusuals make anarchists look organized."

Zeph rubs his eyes, picturing the scene. "Reynolds must have got in their way somehow. Tried to stop 'em."

"Maybe. Hardly matters *why*, anyway."

"Uh, Ros? It's gonna matter a lot to Miss Nazan."

"Oh no. Miss Nazan. I hadn't even... That poor little thing."

"I'll do it," Zeph says. "Don't worry—it's bad enough you had to be the one to find him. I'll do this next part."

Rosalind straightens his spine, wipes his nose. "We'll tell her together."

THE DRAGON

P-Ray isn't better. Kitty tries to focus on the fact that he isn't worse. As she contemplates the fine line between *not better* and *much worse*, an odd humming noise drifts into the cabin. Not an ocean sound—not a natural sound at all. Mechanical? But what? She squeezes P-Ray's hand one more time and steps outside to find the source of the humming.

A strange beast hangs in the sky over New York Bay like a toy that God forgot to put away.

Back in England, Nate had often bent Kitty's ear about the wonders of heavier-than-air flight, boring her with the adventures of American madman Gustave Whitehead, who flew a glider into a three-story building, or the martyr Percy Pilcher—the British Icarus, Nate said—who died in a glider crash just days before his invention's public debut. But this beast over the Bay…this is something else. To Kitty, it looks like an overgrown dragonfly, its double wings carrying a tiny body straight at them. This beast is no mere glider; it has power and will. It means business, and its determined drone fills the air.

"Signorina!" Enzo comes running down from the main building, pointing at the sky. "Our taxi is here."

Kitty joins him at the fence. "What makes you think that thing is coming for us?"

He turns to her, the tiniest smile playing on his face. "A machine of wood and metal has taken to the air. Who *you* think build it?"

The beast is closer now. She can hear the propellers, like giant moths caught in a fan. Their guard hears it too; he ogles the sky for a moment and then abruptly turns and runs toward the main building, yelling, "Hey, you gotta c'mere and see this!"

"What is that pattern?" Kitty asks. The wings and body of the contraption are covered with ornate designs in blue, white, and gold. "Do you recognize it?"

Enzo squints, then snorts with laughter. "Homer's Carousel! Instead of horses, she had cyclops and sea monsters and cannibal giants. Steeplechase get rid of her because the children are too afraid to ride. I always wonder what become of the pieces, but, of course, Timur have them. Who else?"

Kitty gazes up at the flying machine, beautiful in its own strange way, with two sets of enormous wings, one atop the other, connected by gold struts. It's fitting that the glider was built from the bones of monsters, as it looks like one—a gas-powered dragon about to swoop down on them. But the flying machine is belching oily, black smoke. "My goodness! Do you see that?"

"*Sì*. She going down."

The dragon looks a little drunk, listing left and right and drawing a woozy smoke trail in the air.

"What shall we do? Should we…"

The drone of the engine turns to a splutter, an ellipsis of sound. Then it stalls entirely. The flying monster drops from the sky like a nickel in a slot machine, splashing into the surf and skidding across the water before flopping down, exhausted.

Enzo gazes at Kitty regretfully through the fence. "You get him, lady swimmer?"

"Get whom?"

"What, you think *il Dottore* fly his own glider? No, he give to someone else the dirty work. You swim, *sì*?"

"Yes, but I don't—"

A panicked shout emerges from the wreck. "God*damn* it, y'all!"

Kitty gasps. "Zeph!"

"*Sì*, and he no swim so good."

Kitty jogs toward the jagged pieces of shale. At the top of her stairway to the sea, she pauses. Then she shrugs and sits down to unlace her shoes.

As the belly of the glider starts to sink beneath the waves, the pilot lifts himself up. He climbs atop the highest wing and balances there, dark-skinned and damp.

Kitty yells, "Mr. Zeph! Are you all right?"

Zeph shoves some wet locks of hair out of his face and grins at them. He stretches out his arms like a conqueror. "Lady and gentleman! Fear not! I've come to rescue—*whoa*!" A wave hits the side of the glider and sends Zeph skidding across the wing. He pulls himself back up, laughing a giddy survivor's laugh. "It ain't gone exactly according to plan!"

"Do hang on. I'm on my way out to you!" She tugs off her skirt and tosses it aside.

Enzo runs down to the water's edge on his side of the fence; from the water, he gazes at his old friend perched atop a miracle. "Hey, *stupido*! You hang on!"

"Nice to see you too, Enzo!"

Clad in her sleeveless chemise top and knee-length drawers, Kitty races partway down the stairs and dives into the bay. The cold water takes her breath away, but she swims efficiently to the side of the glider. Zeph climbs down and eases himself in, howling at the temperature. Kitty turns her back to him, and he wraps his arms around her shoulders and holds on. The two of them half swim, half drown their way back to the staircase.

Still in the water, Zeph gingerly lets go of Kitty and grabs hold of the staircase railing. Kitty climbs up with him following behind.

"Thank you kindly, Miss Kitty!" They both collapse on the grass, panting and laughing. "That's for sure the most scandalous thing you ever gonna do, right?"

Kitty reaches over and pulls a piece of seaweed from Zeph's damp locks. "Oh, I hope *not*!" She looks out at the wreckage, bobbing in the current. "I don't understand what I just saw. My brother was fascinated by aeronautics, but those were gliders. But this…this is not a glider, is it?"

Grinning widely, Zeph pulls himself upright. "Nope, it ain't."

"That's an actual *flying machine*."

"Yup, it is."

"But that's impossible. Magruder's is miles away. It's…it's impossible is all."

"It's Timur. What'd Mr. Lewis Carroll say? Six impossible things before breakfast? Hate to brag, but I reckon Doc could beat that if he set his mind to it." Enzo waves at them delightedly from the far side of the fence, and Zeph waves back. "Signore! Hey, why is Enzo on one side of the fence and you on the other?"

"We're in quarantine."

"Oh no! You ain't sick, I hope?"

"P-Ray."

"Dammit! How is he?"

She sighs, wringing out her braid. "Feverish, sleepy, with the lumps on his neck. He cries when he wakes; it seems like everything hurts. I've begged for a doctor, but no one comes."

"No! Oh no, no, no… Oh, my poor little man. He in that shack there? I'm going to go see him, okay?" She nods. "But wait, I got news for you first. We found your mother."

"I… You… What?" Kitty shakes her head; she must have seawater in her ears. "You mean her *body*. You found her body?"

"Yeah, we found her body, but she's still using it! She's alive, English! About the same as P-Ray, sounds like—sleeping mostly, but breathing."

Kitty herself can barely breathe. "Zeph…"

"What'd I tell ya?" He pats her on the shoulder. "That's two impossible things, and I ain't been here five minutes."

"I don't know how to thank you."

"Don't, 'cause it was mainly Miss Nazan's doing."

"Is that so?"

"Yep. She's even working on some kind of cure up in Timur's lab. Turns out we got another mad scientist on our hands."

"But how did you even manage to—"

"Zeph!" Enzo bellows an interruption before Kitty can get her question out. "Why you approach from the west? Coney, she east of here."

Zeph laughs and gives Kitty a little "be right back" gesture as he moves toward the fence. "Yeah? Let's see *you* steer that bastard. Timur said it would be easy, but I missed the whole island on the first pass! You shoulda seen me. I had to"—he gestures in a circle—"kinda ease myself around and—"

Enzo interrupts again. "What sort of engine is this?"

"How should I know? Timur bought it off some fisherman. Fella said what with the quarantine, he wasn't doing no more fishing anyway, so…I *told* Doc it was too heavy, but you know how the old man can—"

"Boat engine! I knew it. I want this boat engine."

"Nah. See that smoke? Engine's a goner. I think a seagull flew in it. I heard a hell of a squawking, and then—"

"Is no matter. I fix. But how is engine connected? What, bolts? Bolts, *sì*?"

"I s'pose? Rosalind was on wrench detail."

Enzo stops short. "Oh, *cara mia*…" He lets out a half sigh before noticing Zeph's raised eyebrow. "How is? Okay?"

"Well, he's a wreck worrying about y'all, but—"

Enzo nods. "He feel better soon. You stay here. Signorina!" Enzo gestures that Kitty should approach the fence, and she hurries over. "Signorina," Enzo whispers urgently, "that is boat engine."

"That's… Oh! That's interesting."

Enzo nods. "In the morning, be ready. Five a.m. is window."

Kitty shakes her head in confusion. "Window?"

"No guards. Window between night shift and day. I come in boat, remove engine, and we are off."

"But what about P-Ray? And Zeph now too? If they don't want P-Ray, they certainly won't let us bring—"

He shrugs. "Engine problem, I fix. That problem, *you* fix."

"How on earth do I—"

But Enzo is already jogging away. He passes two guards, who are thoroughly distracted by an argument about the glider.

"I'm telling ya, it was up in the air!" says the guard who saw it.

"It's just a boat wreck. They wash up all the time," scoffs the other, who did not. "You're losing your marbles."

"Miss Kitty," Zeph asks, "what's Enzo talking about?"

"Come, let's go inside—I'll explain while you visit with P-Ray. I want to hear about my mother. I want to hear everything. Then you and I have a magic trick to sort out."

"Magic trick?"

"Yes. How do we make some bigots disappear?"

Zeph laughs. "Wow, that'll be a good trick! I only know this one thing with a coin…"

CHAPTER

★ ★

44

HA, HA, HA

❧

IN FITFUL SLEEP, NAZAN REMEMBERS.

She's sitting on a bench in Tompkins Square Park, across from the Carnegie library. She'd checked out too many books on her last visit and hadn't had time to finish one. But she hates the thought of renewing the book and dragging it all the way home just to read the last few chapters—there were so many unread books clamoring for that precious space in her satchel. It is an usually warm April day, so she sits in the sun to read the ending. She is dimly aware of people walking by, shaking their heads at the sight of a young woman sitting alone with her nose in a book. She ignores them, diving headlong into the story in her hands.

A shadow falls across the page. She looks up to see a young man standing over her, grinning. "She ends up with Darcy," he says. "Not to ruin it for you."

"Is that so? Are you an admirer of Austen?"

He plunks down beside her on the bench. Extremely presumptuous—but then, a boy with those cheekbones can get away with a lot. "Austen's all right, I guess. That Darcy is a bit full of himself."

Nazan shrugs. "What do you expect from a boy named Fitzwilliam—he was doomed from birth, really. Besides, Elizabeth is rather full of *her*self. I suppose they're made for each other."

"Suppose so."

"Sir, I don't mean to be rude, but…" She gestures at her not-quite-finished book.

"I see. Of course." He stands up, brushes off his trousers, and jogs across the street into the library.

A half hour later, *Pride and Prejudice* finished, Nazan enters the library as well. There he is again, lingering by the entrance. He smiles when he sees her and holds out a book.

"Try this. Much more exciting."

She inspects the cover. "*The War of the Worlds*. Sounds unpleasant."

"No, great fun. My brother got me started on it. He says H. G. Wells is writing the best stuff out there. And trust me, he'd know— he reads *everything*. That's why I'm here, actually. I have this shopping list of books he wants. If Charlie says something is good? It's good. Give it a try."

She shrugs agreement. "Why not?"

"But first have lunch with me."

"What? Why, I don't even… Goodness, you're forward, aren't you?"

He matches her shrug with a sly one of his own. "Why not?"

Something gently shakes Nazan awake. "My dove, wake up." She realizes she's no longer drifting. She's lying in a bed at Magruder's, very far from the Carnegie library.

Nazan opens her wet eyes, wiping them with a clenched fist. Dawn peeks through the blinds.

"I'm sorry," Rosalind says. "It's time."

✦ ★ ✦

Archie sits alone in the tavern, smoking his pipe. He takes another swig from a bottle of Magruder's Elixir Salutis. Not a bad concoction, if he does say so himself. At least his customers would have died happy. That's more than Reynolds can say.

He scratches idly at his scarred palm. Reynolds. It's not his fault. *He* didn't tell the kid to go down to the doctor's office.

Archie had accompanied Digby to collect the body. Digby was grateful for the company, until he realized Archie's primary interest was not Spencer but Spencer's wallet. Archie figured the kid owed him after the elixir incident, and anyway, Reynolds certainly didn't need the money anymore. But when Archie and Digby found the body in the alley, the wallet was gone.

Archie sighed. "Looks like somebody had a good day." Kneeling beside Spencer's stiffening corpse, Digby shot Archie a disgusted look. "Well, not *Reynolds*, clearly."

In the tavern, he takes another sip from the bottle. There's no question the kid had money—an apparently endless supply stashed away somewhere. But where was he hiding it? Wherever it was, that's probably what got him killed.

Not my fault.

The situation with Papa Reynolds and his Committee, on the other hand... But then, the Committee hasn't come. Papa Reynolds left that oily little twat in charge... What was his name, Gibson? Who knows if the kid will even follow through? Another wet-behind-the-ears rich boy. Maybe he won't have the guts.

But Archie remembers the hungry look in Gibson's eyes—like a starving wolf with only one succulent baby left in the village—and his stomach turns sour. *Gibson is coming, and he won't come alone.*

None of that is his fault either. He'd tried to warn them. They should thank him, really. They won't, of course. No one ever, not once, has thanked the bearer of bad news. Which is all he is, when you think about it. *Not his fault.*

And now this: some sort of beach funeral for Reynolds—the most reckless, least deserving corpse in a city overflowing with them. Archie runs his finger along a cigarette burn in the wooden bar. Well, "funeral." A traditional Tibetan funeral, supposedly, as conducted by that paragon of authenticity, Yeshi Lowenstein. It would be funny if it weren't so pathetic.

Yeshi had wandered off the boat a few years ago, not knowing uptown from down. She didn't know two and two was four until Archie taught her. He'd shared everything with that ungrateful little scallop. Find the Lady. Pig in a Poke. Pigeon Drop. He taught that girl everything. Then her brother arrives in New York, jabbering about Tibetan independence, and suddenly Yeshi's too good for Archie. She has *real* things to do. *A calling.* Now Archie is expected to stand at this funeral, listening respectfully to Yeshi Rinpoche without laughing his socks off.

Rosalind pokes his head around the door to find Archie draining the bottle of elixir. "A little early, isn't it?"

"It's cocktail hour in Tibet, my dear."

"Ha-ha. We're leaving, so come if you're coming."

✷ ★ ✷

As the sun rises over Dreamland, three bodies lie exposed on the beach, ready for burial. But not any burial. A sky burial.

Spencer is placed in the middle, with one rotting Committeeman on either side. Rosalind objects to the two bodies from Magruder's backyard being dispatched along with their friend. "We don't even know those men, beyond the fact they tried to burn us down. They're criminals as far as I'm concerned. Spencer ought to be... This should be just for him."

But Nazan disagrees. "Spencer wouldn't want that. No. If there's three, then that's how many there are." She looks at Rosalind and tries to smile. "It's fine."

So off they go. Rosalind wears a striking but respectful gray pin-striped suit and a platinum-blond wig piled high. Nazan grips his elbow, Timur walks beside them, and Archie skulks along behind. They go to the small public park and down toward the water.

Digby walks up to greet them, an enormous mallet in his meaty fist. Grasping Nazan's hand, he says, "I'm sorry, Miss Celik. I surely am."

The mourners stand at a safe distance, while Her Holiness Yeshi Rinpoche/Lowenstein arranges ornate silver pots in a circle. She walks around the circle, reciting a prayer as she drops a lit match into each pot. A wispy, gray smoke rises in the air—juniper incense, to summon the Dakini. "The Dakini are sky walkers. My people say—"

"You can tell whatever fairy stories you like, Lowenstein," Archie interrupts. "That doesn't make those things not vultures."

Yeshi rolls her eyes and ignores him.

The juniper incense does its job, and before long, the sky is crowded with large black birds with bloodred, featherless faces. They ride the wind silently, the early morning sun glinting against their dark feathers. They soar in ever-narrowing circles, like a slowly gathering tornado. Yeshi stretches out her arms and prays to them.

Rosalind puts his hand on Nazan's shoulder, and she reaches up and grabs it tightly. "It's not too late to change your mind. We can fetch the police, or we can find an undertaker, or we—"

But then the vultures move in, perching on the bodies and squawking as they jockey for position. They shove long, pointy beaks into soft bellies. One rips off a long ribbon of flesh from Spencer's arm and chokes it down in toothless gulps. Two vultures perch on either side of his face and hiss, arguing over who gets to eat his eyes.

Nazan puts her hands to her mouth, trying not to sob. "Oh…" An ambitious black crow joins the pack, pecking at the flesh along Spencer's thighs.

Rosalind gasps. "This is barbaric."

Yeshi comes over to stand beside Nazan and takes her hand. "Listen to me. No, don't look there; look at me. I see you now, and I see a young woman, maybe not so strong. But is that the total of what you are? Is this body all you are?"

Blinking back tears, Nazan shakes her head no.

"No, you are not. You are not this body. And neither is he. Nazan, my people believe that the body is a vessel. An imperfect, short-lived vessel—that's all. Spencer's vessel is now empty, and so we release it to the sky."

Nazan nods. She bites her lip, and tears spill down her cheeks.

"Don't think I do not understand. My brother, Tenzin, succumbed to the Cough ten days ago. That's how I came to perform this ritual—I wanted it for him, and then I realized I could honor his memory by sharing our custom with others. It is terrible to lose the ones we love. We miss them, their physical presence. We ache for those vessels, feeble as they are. But my brother, your friend, they are free. And for this, we rejoice. Now they can soar, and the Dakini will carry their empty shells to a holy place."

Archie nods. "A holy place. They'll shit him out over Hoboken."

"Oh, you wretched man." Rosalind groans. "Why did we bring you anyway?"

Nazan forces herself to watch the vultures feast on Spencer. "Empty vessel," she says quietly. "Empty vessel released to the sky." She feels like throwing up.

It takes time for the buzzards to consume their meal. The process is agonizingly slow and yet somehow far too brief. *Is that it? Can a man really be erased so quickly?*

When the birds have had their fill, when there is little left but skeletons in the sand, Yeshi nods at Digby. "It is time."

Digby sighs and takes up his mallet. He takes a step toward the bodies but turns back to address Nazan. "Miss Celik, I want to explain—"

"It's all right, Mr. Digby. I understand your role."

"No, it's just…" He leans in. "Yeshi says I have to laugh."

"What? I don't under—"

"Because these are vessels? It's no different from breaking stones, she says. So to emphasize this, I am supposed to laugh, like…I'm happy in my work. But I want you to know…"

She smiles a little. "Thank you, Mr. Digby. You are very kind. But you should do as Yeshi says. I'll be all right."

Digby nods and picks up his mallet. The tide roars in and out, but not loudly enough to cover the cracking of bone and the thud of Digby's mallet against the sand as he brings it down again and again, slowly reducing the bones to a powder. Yeshi stands by with a saddle-bag full of barley flour, which she will mix with the shards to attract more birds. The seagulls have developed a taste for bone meal.

"Ha," Digby says cheerlessly. "Ha, ha, ha."

Nazan covers her face with her hands. "Empty vessel, empty vessel…" But with every whack of Digby's mallet, another sob threatens to break free. "Talk to me," she says suddenly. "*Someone* talk to me about something."

Rosalind shakes his head. "I'm not sure what you—"

"I won't leave until this is finished, but…someone has to talk to me. You!" She catches Archie scratching his palm yet again. "Why do you do that? Scratch that scar so much? What is that scar?"

"The scar on my hand," Archie says, "is none of your business."

"I want to hear the story."

Archie rolls his eyes. "Little girl, now is as good a time as any for you to learn one does not always get—"

"Tell goddamn story," Timur growls suddenly. "Celik want to hear."

"Agreed," Rosalind says, and he arches an eyebrow for emphasis. "Don't test us."

Archie sighs. "For crying out loud. All right. My family was quite prominent in New Orleans. My father, *his* father, et cetera. We were in the import business."

Nazan considers this. "Sugar, coffee, that sort of—"

"People. We imported people. And sold them. At a fine price, I might add."

"Unbelievable," Rosalind says. "Just when I think you can't get any more unlikable."

"Do you want to hear this or not? So, as a young man, I did as young men do, taking advantage of what amusements my town had to offer—cards, rum, women. One night, after an evening out, I took a walk by the river. I came upon a young couple. Negroes. And there was…oh, who can remember? Some gibber jabber about her being with child, him about to be sold…a slave Romeo and Juliet, let's say. They'd stolen a boat, but it was full of holes. They entreated me to help them. I'd have none of it, of course. We stood there, them begging and me trying to extract myself, and along comes a group of men with their slobbering canine. Hunting the Negroes, you see. They loosed the dog, and it went for us, teeth bared. So I did what anyone in that situation would—I pulled my pistol from my boot and shot the mangy bastard. That's it. That's the story. Happy?"

Digby finishes with Spencer's remains and moves on, smashing the other two skeletons. "Ha. Ha-ha."

"But," Nazan says, "what happened to the couple?"

"*I don't know.* It was half a century ago." He gazes out at the sea and sighs. "I suppose in all the confusion, they may have gotten away."

Nazan nods. "Good story."

"It's a *terrible* story. They got away, and I got *this*." He holds up his hand, the letters *SS* seared into his palm. "Branded. Slave stealer. Tossed in jail, excommunicated from my family. I was a man of position! I lost my inheritance, and I've wasted my life scamming rubes out of five and ten dollars apiece. And for what? Some dead dog." He eyes Nazan contemptuously. "There's a lesson for you, Lady Celik, if you care to learn."

"There *is* a lesson," Rosalind agrees. "But I don't think Nazan is the one who needs it."

CHAPTER

✦ ✦

45

HMM...

∞

KITTY STANDS AT HER STAIRCASE TO THE SEA, WAITING IMPATIENTLY FOR Enzo to arrive with the boat. She and Zeph have hashed things out, made a plan. A mad plan, but a plan nonetheless.

This must work, she thinks. There will be no second chance, and even if there were, P-Ray won't live long enough to see it. Miss Celik's medicine is his only hope.

She thinks back to that first "little favor" she had to do for Archie. Walking into Pearson's art gallery, looking like a sunburned Dickensian nightmare, but still convincing Pearson she was an heiress. How terrified she was. *But I did it*, she reminds herself. *I can do this.*

"Any good confidence game is based on what people want and what they fear," Archie had told her. The question is, has Kitty guessed correctly this time?

This must *work. Just one more impossible thing today.*

✦ ★ ✦

Aboard their rickety boat, Enzo shares rowing duties with fellow escapee Max Teufel. Together, they steer their handmade rowboat around the perimeter of Hoffman Island. They try to keep the boat as close to the man-made shore as possible, but the tide seems determined to suck them out into the bay. This forces Enzo and Max to devote most of their energies to rowing against the current rather than moving forward. It's slow going. Max's wife, Ruth, and her sister, Janet, pass the time by whispering commentary back and forth: about the quality of the men's rowing (or lack thereof), their rate of travel (any slower and they'd be going backward), the temperature (far too cold), the sea spray (sure to give them all influenza), and the state of their bellies (empty, as the hospital-provided food is an absolute scandal). Their sotto voce cascade of complaints has Enzo reflecting a bit more fondly on Kitty's initial suggestion that he simply murder them all.

The rowboat's other passenger, Seward Miller, sits quietly, staring off into space. The plan to build a boat and escape Hoffman had been hatched by Seward's teenage daughter; it was she who suggested that Seward scour the shoreline for cast-off lumber. But then she took ill, and her mother soon followed. Timur's engine dropped from the sky too late: Seward's wife and daughter both died this morning, their bodies already on the pile at Swinburne.

Enzo can see the dark outline of the observation suite in the near distance. Just a bit farther now. He can't imagine how Kitty is going to talk the Teufels into allowing P-Ray and Zeph to escape along with them. But she's a fast talker, that Kitty—quick-witted. And she has the accent. Enzo muses, not for the first time, that her accent sounds like the opening of a door, while his sounds like a door slamming shut. Kitty will figure out the problem somehow. He takes a deep breath and keeps rowing.

As if she can read his thoughts, Ruth Teufel pauses and turns to Enzo with a direct question. "Are you sure your wife will leave without her little monkey?"

The question has so many errors, Enzo doesn't know where to begin. He glares at her instead. "She come."

Ruth nudges her sister. "'She come,' he says. *Immigrants, honestly…*"

Seward Miller's mind returns from his lost family, refocusing on the present. "There's room enough now," he says. "There just wasn't room before. Now there's plenty of room."

"Not for him," Ruth snaps. "Believe me, Mr. Miller, a boy like that…you know, *undesirable*. He's better off here. We're doing him a favor."

Enzo keeps rowing.

They finally reach Kitty's stairway, and Enzo tosses a line of rope around the railing to tie off the rowboat. He points to the wrecked plane, the upper wings just peeking out above the incoming tide. "Engine is there."

Seward carefully stands up. "Give me the wrench. I'll swim over, unfasten it, and float it back to you."

"You sure?" Enzo asks gratefully. "Water is terrible cold."

Seward nods and eases himself into the frigid water. He can't feel a thing.

Meanwhile, Max helps his wife and sister-in-law off the rowboat and up the stairs.

"Miss Hayward!" Ruth calls. "Miss Hayward, it's time to go."

Kitty dashes out of the cabin, a panicked look on her face. She runs up to them at the stairs. "Shh! Please, you must be quiet. There are guards everywhere!"

Ruth looks appalled. "What? But your husband told us—Max! Do you hear this? There weren't supposed to be any guards! Do something!"

Max, leaning on the railing, looks down at Enzo in the boat. "You told us no guards?"

Enzo shakes his head. "Is no possible."

Kitty whispers urgently to them. "I swear to you, I saw them all night. One came by just moments ago."

"We believe you, dear," Janet says reassuringly.

"Of course we do," Ruth agrees. "It isn't the first time an *Italian* got something wrong."

"But…" Enzo peers up at Kitty.

"You were wrong." She shakes her head and turns away. But Enzo thinks he sees something flit across Kitty's face. Was that a wink? To the Teufels, Kitty says, "I suggest we all wait in the cabin while the gentlemen fix the engine. Much safer that way, in case a guard happens by."

Max nods, but Ruth recoils. "Isn't the boy ill?" she asks.

"That's what we heard," Janet confirms.

"He's…ah, a bit fluish… I'm sure that's all it is."

"*Sure*," Ruth says darkly. "But I think we'll stay out here just the same. Besides, my dear, it's much wiser for us to slip off quietly while he's sleeping, don't you think?"

"He'll be better off," Janet says.

Kitty nods. "Certainly."

Down in the water, Seward has unbolted the engine from the wreck. He balances it on top of a broken-off plank and nudges it carefully toward the rowboat. Enzo reaches out and grabs the engine, pulling it into the boat and crouching over it to try to figure out, as best he can in the darkness, what went wrong with it. Seward lifts himself gingerly into the boat to sit beside him.

"How are you coping?" Ruth coos at Kitty obsequiously. "You poor dear. Imagine, Janet, taking a holiday to America and getting caught up in all of this!"

"Such a shame," Janet agrees.

"It will all be over soon." Kitty pats Ruth's arm consolingly. "My family are rather prominent, you know. They will be so pleased that you've helped me escape."

"It's the least we can do," Ruth says. "Your family is *prominent*, you say?"

"Oh yes," Kitty assures her. "Father is in railroads."

Enzo peers at the belly of the engine, frowns, then reaches in and pulls something loose. He holds it up triumphantly. "Seagull! He was right."

"Who was right?" Seward asks.

"Uh." Enzo tosses the seagull carcass in the water. "I was right. English not so good. Pronouns…"

"Hmm," Seward says.

"Perhaps we should accompany you back to England," Ruth suggests. "Take a steamship, see you safely back to your family's arms. Wouldn't that be lovely, Max?"

Kitty says, "They'll be ever-so grateful."

A low, moaning sound reaches their ears. "Oh," a voice says. "Oh, please…"

Startled, the women and Max look to the source of the sound—down in the water, a few feet to the left of the stairs. A figure bobs in the tide, gripping onto a wooden plank.

"My goodness!" Kitty cries. "There's someone out there!"

"Please, somebody… Please help me…"

Ruth swats at her husband. "Max! Max, someone needs help."

Reluctantly, Max clambers over the shale and gazes down into the water. "Good God, man! Are you all right?" He reaches down, pulls a young man out of the water, and drags him onto the sand. The young man curls up on the ground, coughing up seawater in misery.

The women race over and squint down. "You poor soul," Ruth says. "Are you—oh!" Her voice changes. "It's a Negro."

Janet points at him and shrieks. "His legs! Where are his legs?"

Kitty shushes her. "Ma'am! Remember the guards." She kneels beside the nearly drowned young man, gently removing his wet braids from his face. "What happened to you, poor thing?"

He coughs again and looks up at Kitty miserably. He whispers, "Shark…"

The women gasp. Janet looks out at Lower New York Bay. "Sharks? Here? Max, what do we do?"

Zeph moans theatrically. "They were holding me in the Negro ward. I kept looking out at the shore, thinking, 'It ain't that far. I can swim back.' Got about halfway across when…"

Max frowns. "I've never heard of sharks in the bay."

"Oh, my legs, my poor legs…" Zeph gazes up at Kitty pitifully. "Am I gonna die, miss?"

She suppresses a smile. "Someday, certainly."

Ruth smacks her husband on the shoulder. "Max! Do something!"

He spreads his arms helplessly. "I'm an accountant!"

Kitty stands up. "Please, I must insist you be quiet. The guards…"

"I'm *not* going out there in some leaky rowboat with *sharks* in the water," Ruth declares.

"Me neither," Janet says.

"Darling," Max says, "we've already snuck out of the dormito-ries. We can't go back now."

"My legs…" Zeph sobs.

"I did not come this far to be eaten by sharks, Max!"

"But, Ruthie—"

"Please be quiet!" Kitty says fearfully. "Look, why don't we all go in the cabin and talk about it there." Ruth eyes her skeptically. "Please, ma'am. If you stay clear of the boy, you'll be fine. Just don't get to close to him, that's all. Come along—"

Ruth flinches. "I will not enter a tiny cabin with some diseased little creature, and I am *certainly* not going out in the bay when there are sharks about!"

"Shh!" Kitty hisses. "*Please*. With all respect. If you keep up this noise, the guards will come and throw you back in the dormitory. *Everyone* there will witness your failure, but this time there will be no escape, because the guards will watch you *every single second*, and you will sit there in that ward until you *rot*." She takes a step toward Ruth, looking her squarely in the eyes. "Is that what you want?"

Ruth looks at her sister hesitantly. "Oh, all right," she finally says. She tilts her head toward the cabin. "Let's go." The Teufels allow Kitty to herd them toward the observation suite.

Down in the rowboat, Enzo has been listening to all this but keeps focused on the engine. "Almost finished," he mutters to Seward. "You go talk sense to the ladies."

"Hmm," Seward says. "I think I'm fine right here."

Enzo sneaks a glance at him but returns to the engine.

Kitty opens the door to the cabin and ushers the Teufels in. "Please come along. Quickly, now."

Ruth peers around the empty cabin. "But where is the boy?"

Kitty slams the door, grabs a piece of lumber she'd set aside earlier, and slides it through the handle, locking the Teufels in. She races around to the back of the cabin and lifts up an unconscious P-Ray, who'd been set to rest in the grass.

Zeph sits up, but then he realizes that Seward is still in the rowboat. He immediately flops back down. "Oh, my legs... I'm gonna die for sure..."

On the boat, Enzo and Seward eyeball one another. "Clever," Seward says.

"We no leave without."

Seward settles himself down in the rowboat. "You are under the mistaken impression that I give a damn."

"So," Enzo says, "we good?"

Seward shrugs.

Enzo calls out, "Okay, Zeph."

"Thank God for that." Zeph pulls himself over to the stairs, meeting up with Kitty and P-Ray. "I am never getting in that damn water again."

A muffled pounding comes from inside the cabin. "What is going on? Let us out! Let us out, damn you!"

Kitty carries P-Ray down the boat, kissing his slumbering head. "It's all right, little one. We're going home."

46

TO HELL WITH IT

❦

THE SKY BURIAL ENDED, THEY RETURN TO THE TAVERN: NAZAN, ROSALIND, Timur, Archie, and poor old Digby. A sad little parade. Archie heads straight for the apple box of Elixir Salutis and passes out bottles to anyone who's interested, which is everyone.

Digby sits beside Nazan and pulls a handkerchief from his pocket. "I did what you asked, but I can't figure what you want this for."

Wrapped inside, Nazan finds a tiny finger bone and a lock of Spencer's black hair. "Thank you, Mr. Digby. And don't worry, it's all right. I'm going to make something from them. To remember him by."

Digby grimaces.

"It's not strange. In the old days, people used to make jewelry or…" She takes in Digby's appalled expression. "It's not strange."

"Dead's dead enough." He sighs. "Don't know why folks gotta get creative." He wanders away to the window, lost in thought.

Nazan looks around at the group. "Well, that…that was horrible. A bit beautiful. But mostly horrible."

Rosalind reaches over and squeezes her hand. "I believe that's the best one can expect from a twenty-two-year-old's funeral, Tibetan or otherwise." He sighs. "Perhaps we should go check on Mrs. Hayward."

Nazan nods and downs her elixir in one swallow. "Agreed."

"This is all very touching," Archie mutters, "but you seem to have forgotten that the Committee for Public Safety has a bull's-eye painted on the roof of this building."

"Yes," Rosalind agrees. "And I'm left to wonder how that came to be."

Archie flaps his arms and shouts, "It's not my fault!"

Timur, Rosalind, Digby, and even Nazan from the depths of her sadness all stare at Archie.

"Archie," Nazan says slowly, "we didn't think it was."

"Of course," Rosalind says, "we do now."

Timur jumps up and shakes Archie by the shoulders. "What you do, nasty bastard?"

"I'm innocent," Archie declares guiltily.

Rosalind touches Timur's arm. "Forget him. What shall we do about the Committee?"

"Bah, I have gun."

"You can't shoot them all."

"Watch. They try take my home, you watch."

Archie stands. "And that is my cue. This is one tragic denouement that does not demand an audience."

He moves for the door, but Timur grabs him by the coat, spins him around, and plants him back on a stool. "You sit! You bring hell down on our heads, now you stay!"

"This. Is not. My fault! I am not the trigger-happy lunatic with the—"

"Uh, everybody?" At the window, Digby points. "Isn't that Zeph outside?"

Rosalind leaps up and dashes out the door, and Nazan follows. Timur stands to leave, but first he points at Archie. "You. No move." Then at Digby. "You. Put eye on him."

Digby nods. Archie shrugs and opens another bottle of elixir.

Outside, Enzo, Kitty, and Zeph are coming down the street. Enzo carries an unconscious P-Ray in his arms.

Zeph waves. "Hey, y'all!"

At the sight of them, Timur spreads his arms out wide. "You fly her! I know you can!"

Zeph laughs, scuttling across the sidewalk to Timur, then reaches up and pumps his hand. "Yeah, I flew her, then I crashed her!"

"Idiot! You owe to me one aeroplane." Timur nods hello to Kitty and Enzo but saves his face-cracking grin for P-Ray. "My stupid boy... What has happened?" He reaches out and snatches P-Ray from Enzo's arms. "What has happened to my boy?"

"I'm afraid he's taken ill," Kitty says. "I'm so sorry."

"Bah," Timur says, pulling the boy close. "We fix. Celik make the medicine." He turns without another word and carries the boy back to the Cabinet. On the way, he passes Rosalind, who stands by the stoop, gripping the railing.

Rosalind reaches out for P-Ray. "Oh no...little angel..."

"Bah," Timur says again, and he disappears with the boy into the building.

Enzo approaches shyly. "*Passerotta mia*...no. No. I'm sorry. *Passerotto mio.*" He smiles. "*Caro mio.*"

"So." Rosalind sniffs. "You finally came back. I wish I'd known to expect you..." His eyes are wet, and he touches his blond wig self-consciously. "I look a fright."

"No...no. *Così bello.*"

Rosalind reaches out and strokes Enzo's face, first the scarred half, then the other. He whispers, "I didn't mean the things I said..."

Enzo blushes a little. "I know this." He looks into Rosalind's eyes and then glances at the many people around them. "To hell with it." He puts his hands on Rosalind's face, pulls him close, and kisses him on the mouth.

Rosalind yanks himself away, shocked. "Not here!"

But Enzo doesn't let go. "Yes, here. Anywhere. Everywhere." He kisses him again, and this time, Rosalind does not pull away. They stand together in the street, all alone in the crowded world.

Zeph and Nazan gape at the couple and then look to one another, scandalized. When their eyes meet, they giggle. "Well," Zeph mutters, "*that*...was memorable."

Nazan blushes. "It's so good to see you, Mr. Zeph."

"And you, pretty lady. I'd give ya a hug, but…" He gestures at the difference in their heights.

Nazan smiles. "You know what, Enzo's right. To hell with it." Nazan drops to her knees on the sidewalk and squeezes Zeph as tightly as she can. "Thank you," she whispers into his ropes of hair. "Thank you for coming back."

"What? Ain't nothing…" He pulls back and sees Nazan is crying. "Aww, now, don't. C'mon, you have no idea how much I hate that."

"I'm just so relieved to see you! You're the only friend I have here, Mr. Zeph."

He wipes her tears away. "You're gonna find you got plenty of friends at Magruder's, Miss Nazan." She hugs him again, tighter still. He knows he ought to pull away—decorum and all. But, well… wouldn't be polite.

Amid all the hugging and kissing and crying, Kitty shifts awkwardly from foot to foot. She longs to ask where her mother is, but this doesn't seem to be the moment. She tries to use one fingernail to clean the others. She picks some seaweed out of her hair.

Zeph breaks away from Nazan to address the group. "So, y'all, what'd we miss?"

"Just a typical few days at Magruder's," Rosalind says. "Plague, death, imminent doom."

"Excellent." Zeph grins.

Enzo sighs. "*In bocca al lupo*…"

"What's that mean, darling?" Rosalind asks.

"Is, ah, 'into mouth of the wolf.' But means more 'good luck.' Is like actors say 'break a leg,' you know this? And your response is '*Crepi il lupo*.'"

"*Crepi il lupo*," Rosalind repeats. "And this means?"

"May the wolf die."

CHAPTER

47

POLITICS

❧

"MAGRUDER'S IS A PRIORITY," GIBSON ANNOUNCES. HE SITS AT MCGRATH'S desk, which sits upon what used to be the Dreamland ballroom's orchestra platform. Gibson leans back and starts to put his feet up on the desk, but a death-dealing stare from McGrath changes his mind. Instead, he leans forward and tries to sound authoritative. "Magruder's is a priority of the Dreamland Consortium."

McGrath pointedly puts his feet up on his own desk. "It isn't a priority of mine."

"The Consortium pays your salary."

"Not anymore. Funny thing about attempts on the president's life—they attract attention. The boys in Washington have been watching things play out here in Coney, and an opinion has taken hold that local powers like Reynolds and those Tammany weasels may not be up to the job. So the Committee on Public Safety has been federalized."

"But…I hadn't heard this!"

"Why would you? Who the Sam Hill are you?"

"I represent the senator," Gibson says huffily. "Who I'm quite sure doesn't know about this either."

"During his city's time of need, the Great and Powerful Reynolds bravely fucked off to Newport. Instead of coming down here himself, he sends some little fart catcher to try to push me around? Go tell your boss that if he doesn't like how I'm running things, he can take it up with the attorney general. Assuming he has the balls to come back to Brooklyn."

Gibson starts to reply but is interrupted by a series of frenzied shrieks and high-pitched whoop-whoop sounds. "Chief, what is that noise? I've been hearing it all over Dreamland, but I can't quite—"

"It's the monkeys. Goddamn Wormwood's Monkey Theater. Employees are all F/D, and now the monkeys are loose."

"F/D?"

"Fled or dead. Don't know which. But whether they went to the next life or just New Jersey, the result's the same—a beach full of monkeys flinging shit and playing with themselves."

"That's...troubling."

McGrath grunts. "That's nothing. A lot of animals got out. My boys put down the dangerous ones, the big cats and so on, but the nuisance animals...well." McGrath narrows his eyes at Gibson. "I've got more than my share of nuisances, let's put it that way."

"But Magruder's is a question of public health!"

McGrath frowns. "You know, kid, it occurs to me that the person who fingered Magruder's as a problem, the only person who seems to care about some dusty warehouse full of shrunken heads, is you. What's your problem with that place, boyo? Lemme guess: Your girl decide she preferred that legless Negro to you?"

Around the lobby, checklists and maps flutter as the Committeemen try not to giggle.

"What! Most certainly not!"

"Are ya sure, 'cause I was over there a few days ago, and...he's not *my* type, but he's one damned attractive little man."

More fluttering of paper, like an amusing wind sweeping across the ballroom floor.

"Listen..." Gibson senses a great fortune slipping through his fingers. "Magruder's is bigger than the Cough."

"What's bigger than the Cough?"

"Politics."

McGrath laughs. "That's the first honest thing out of your mouth in two days. So, how about I be honest with you: I tried with that place, I really did. I got two men still missing, remember? So I go out there, figure I'll check it out myself. The Reynolds kid says no, this building is ours. I don't like it, but I do as I'm told. Why? Politics. Now here you are, telling me never mind, go torch the place as planned. And why? Politics."

"Yes, but Senator Reynolds—"

"Reynolds is just another escaped monkey to me, you follow?"

"McGrath, the senator gave me strict instructions to have Magruder's destroyed. And I promise you, I'm not going anywhere." Gibson shrugs. "Truth is, I've got nowhere to go."

McGrath leans back in his chair and rubs his eyes. All that shrieking is making his head pound. "Kid, I never liked Magruder's—I hate all that creepy stuff, to tell you the truth. But you know what I like even less than Magruder's?"

Gibson rolls his eyes. "I get it. Politics."

"No," McGrath says. "*You*. I don't like you. But you're one nuisance animal I *can* get rid of. So, all right, I'll send a team. I'll even go with you. And if I see something I don't like, maybe we'll torch it. Then you scuttle out to Newport and let me get on with my job. Understood?"

"Yes, sir!" Gibson smiles. He can almost feel Newport's exclusive ocean breezes whistling in his ears. The next map they draw of Coney Island is going to have his name on it.

48

KNOCK KNOCK
KNOCK

∽◯∼

AZAN AND ZEPH LEAD KITTY TO THE ROOM WHERE HER MOTHER LIES
unconscious. Kitty gasps when she sees her—the black poison that
started in her mother's neck has crept through her veins, giving
her whole face a dark, spidery appearance. She looks a thousand years
old, and her breath comes out in long, slow hisses. Kitty sits beside
her, trying not to cry.

"Kitty," Nazan says miserably. "The medicine… I don't know.
It doesn't seem to work like we hoped. I just don't know what to
say. I'm so sorry."

"No!" Kitty turns her fierce eyes on Nazan. "You *mustn't* say
you're sorry. You mustn't. You've done so much for us. You've
tried so hard—both of you. No, you mustn't ever be sorry. No one
could ask more." She wipes her eyes and turns back to her mother,
reaching out to move a strand of hair from her face. "Has she spoken
at all? Anything?"

"Um." Zeph glances at Nazan, remembering all too well Mrs.
Hayward's one moment of consciousness, in which she hysterically
cursed her daughter for abandoning her. "You see, English—"

"She said she loves you," Nazan interrupts. Zeph opens his
mouth but closes it when he sees Nazan's you-shut-up glare. "She
only woke up once, and she thought I was you, and she said how
much she loves me and how relieved she was to see me. Meaning
you. She said she always knew you'd come."

Kitty nods. "Thank you."

Nazan touches Zeph's shoulder. "Let's leave them be. Kitty, let us know if you need anything."

In the hall, Zeph whispers, "That for sure *ain't* what she said."

Nazan nods. "It's what she meant."

By the bed, Kitty swallows hard. There have been many things Kitty has been wanting to tell her mother, so much she wanted to say and thought she'd never get the chance. But now, sitting in this strange bedroom on the third floor of the strangest place she's ever been, Kitty can't remember a single thing.

✦ ✦ ✦

Inside the tavern, chatter is split between the past—*Where have you been? What has happened?*—and the future—*When will the Committee arrive? What will we do?* Enzo collapses, exhausted, into a chair, and Rosalind perches on his knee, whispering secrets in his ear. Timur has joined Archie and Digby at the bar, but he turns when Zeph and Nazan come in.

"I put the boy in the lab," he announces. "I give the medicine, but he need more. Celik, you get to work."

Nazan sighs, frustrated. "Dr. Timur, I just don't think the colloid is working the way you want. Mrs. Hayward just keeps looking worse, and I—"

Timur waves a hand in front of his face, dismissing this notion. "The old woman is sick too long, is too late. P-Ray, you save. Go. Work." He turns back around.

As she heads up the stairs, Zeph announces his total disinterest in anything beyond the contents of the icebox in the tavern's back storeroom.

"Nothing in it," Rosalind says. "I've had no luck at all finding supplies under the quarantine."

Zeph scoffs. "What do you mean, no luck at all? I ain't been gone forty-eight hours! How'd you let this place go to pot so fast?"

"I've been a little busy with a certain funeral, Zeph!"

"Funerals are supposed to have food, Ros! Don't you know anything? Let me go look. There must be something." Zeph makes his way toward the back room, but his path is blocked by a fashion-forward floor-length skirt. Vivi.

"Monsieur Zeph," she says breathily, "I am so happy to see you!"

Archie recognizes Vivi immediately. "What is Mademoiselle Leopard Lady doing here?"

Zeph can't help but grin. "We got her cats in the back, Archie. They're under Magruder's protection."

She kneels down to Zeph's height and bats her eyelashes. "My cats, they are so hungry! I am sure you can help us, *non*?"

"You know," Zeph says, "the humans are pretty hungry too. So you'll forgive me if—"

Archie raises his glass. "Leopard steaks are excellent."

Vivi gasps. "*Mon Dieu*! How dare you! *Vil mécréant*! *Accapareur de merde d'abeille*!"

"Stupid boy!" Timur snaps at Zeph. "Get your woman under control."

"*His* woman?" exclaims Vivi, and "Oh, good Lord," groans Zeph, and then Archie offers his opinion, and the room is a swirl of dissension and then *knock knock knock* at the door.

Silence.

Knock knock knock.

"I told you," Archie mutters.

Panic shoots across the room like an Edison experiment gone awry. Timur stands. "I get gun."

Zeph hustles over. "No. No, Doc, that won't get us anywhere. Let me...I dunno, let me talk to them."

From his perch, Archie hoots. "*Talk* to them? About what, exactly?"

"I don't know, Archie! Maybe I'll tell them to shoot the useless jackass at the bar, how about that?"

"I tried to warn you! Would you listen? No! You'd all rather snuffle over the corpse of some blue-blooded microphallus than attend to the—"

"You watch your mouth," Rosalind snarls.

"Yeah," Digby agrees. "Shut up about whatever that was."

Knock knock knock.

"All right," Zeph says. "*Someone* is gonna have to answer that. I'm open to suggestions."

A whispered debate. The most socially useful person to answer the door—Timur, Magruder's white male owner—is also the least likely to respond to inquiries in an appropriate manner. But the most skilled at politic responses—Zeph, Magruder's Negro half man—is the least influential face for the Committeemen to see. Digby is too easily confused, and Rosalind too confusing. Nazan is deemed too honest, while Archie can't be trusted any farther than he can be thrown.

Knock knock knock.

In desperation, Rosalind suggests they split the difference between most appropriate and most able—Timur can open the door, while Zeph lurks behind, ready to tell the doctor what to say. Timur retorts that he does not care to be told what to say.

The knock comes again, this time accompanied by a voice saying, "Open up in there!" The voice of a man who means business, a strong man who will enter this establishment no matter what. Archie whispers to Digby that he should peek out the window to see how large a contingent is waiting outside. Digby nods and sidles over.

With a sigh, Timur agrees to let Zeph tell him what to say and goes to the door. He pauses, rolls up his sleeves, puts his hand on the doorknob…then changes his mind and rolls the sleeves back down.

Knock knock knock.

Finally, he throws open the door, just as Digby says, "My God, look at 'em all."

At the door, Timur stands speechless. Zeph prompts from his hiding place, "Can I help you?" But Timur doesn't speak. "Doc! Can I help you?" No response, so Zeph repeats the question, a bit louder this time. "Can I help you?" Still no response. In frustration, Zeph pokes his head around the door. "I said, can I—oh."

The street is lined with carnies, all in various stages of illness. There's a cigar vendor and a magician and a three-legged man. A single giantess, a trio of electricians, and the entire Razzle Dazzle Spasm Band. All of them sweaty and sickly and sad. An ice-cream truck is parked on the sidewalk, its back doors propped open, and the bodies of plague-ridden Chinese acrobats spill out. Beside the ambulance is an elephant, half a dozen clowns sprawled across the carriage on its back. An ornately embroidered blanket underneath the carriage declares *Steeplechase, the Funny Place*.

An underfed pony drags a miniature fire engine. Whitey Lovett is slumped unconscious in the front seat. His fellow firemen hang solemnly onto the sides of the engine, sad eyes clamped on their dying chief.

"No," Zeph says. "Whitey, no." He approaches the pony slowly, so as not to frighten it, and hoists himself up the side of the fire engine.

Whitey has the telltale buboes—the thick, black lumps on his neck that declare the end may be near. The blackness has spread—his face is stained like a tattooed man. Zeph puts his arm around his old friend's shoulder, and Whitey's head lolls over onto him.

"Zeph… Hello, Zeph." Whitey's voice is raspy and weak, as if broadcast by wireless from a distant shore.

"Don't do this, brother," Zeph whispers in his ear. "You can't be Jewish *and* a dwarf *and* have the plague. That's the trifecta, remember?"

Whitey laugh-coughs. "Yeah."

From atop the fire engine, Zeph can see janitors and Siamese twins, snake charmers and security guards, tightrope walkers and waitresses. Rotting limbs and aching groins and coughing and tears. All on his doorstep, all looking at him, all wanting…something.

"Whitey, what is going on?"

"Spencer Reynolds said come. He said, 'You want real medicine, find me at Magruder's.' Word gets around…"

"Seems like. All right. Nazan!" Zeph shouts up at the attic window. "Poke your head out here. We need you! Nazan!"

After a moment, the black cloth covering the attic window falls away, the window opens, and Nazan leans out. "What on earth?"

"Spencer told these folks to come to Magruder's for help."

She gazes out at a sea of plague-ridden faces. "Zeph," she calls down, "is there enough silver in the lab to cure all these people?"

"Sister," he shouts back, "I don't know if there's enough silver in the world, but you best get busy." Zeph squeezes Whitey in a sideways hug. "Half men gotta do what half men gotta do."

✦ ★ ✦

Gibson stalks across the bridge straddling Dreamland's brackish lake while monkeys shriek in the distance. He clutches a requisition form signed by McGrath. Cans of fuel, drip torches, fire brooms. Leather boots, goggles. Cotton mattress covers.

"Mattress covers?" Gibson had asked McGrath's secretary. "Why are—"

"For the bodies," she replied.

"Bodies?"

"After the fire, of course. Did you think this was a school picnic, Mr. De Camp?"

Bodies. Well, it's not his business how these things are done. His job is to make sure the thing is done at all, and at this, he has been a rousing success.

Gibson congratulates himself again and tries not to remember the last time he visited Coney Island—strolling Surf Avenue, holding hands with Chastity, the afternoon sun glinting off her long, blond hair. Back at the beginning of summer, before the sickness. Before Spencer basically mugged him in his father's office. Before Chastity caught the Cough, her porcelain skin going black, her blue eyes filling with pus. Back before everything went wrong.

The once-refreshing lake is a sickly green color. Dreamland's landscaping staff is, in McGrath's terms, F/D, and the lake sits dormant, covered with a film of algae, pockmarked with seaweed and rotting fish. It smells even worse than it looks. A flock of underfed flamingos pick their fussy way across the muck, cheeping at each other about the poor accommodations.

When Dreamland is mine, Gibson thinks, *I'll make sure things never sink this low. I'll have a full-time employee who does nothing but hunt and destroy algae, someone who lives to clean and won't be put off by a little Cough. My personal Algae Man.*

Yes, one day. When Dreamland is mine.

LITTLE GIRL

TUPID BOYS!" TIMUR BLOCKS THE TAVERN DOORWAY. "WHAT DO YOU THINK you are doing?"

Digby stands at the door with Whitey flung over his shoulder. Zeph climbs up the side of the door so he can face Timur directly. "It's pretty simple, Doc. These folks are sick, and Spencer promised 'em medicine. We have medicine."

"Spencer is dead! Any minute, Committee is coming, burn our home to the ground."

"If we ain't careful, nobody'll be able to reach our home 'cause of all the dead bodies in the street. We can't just let them—"

"We have no time for play hospital."

"He's right," Archie calls, lurking in the back.

"*Silenzio!*" Enzo approaches the door, and Rosalind follows. "The people need help; we help the people."

"Darling," Rosalind says. "The people have the Cough. We don't."

Zeph nods. "Ros has a point. We should all take doses of Nazan's cure, every one of us, just to be safe."

Kitty has heard the commotion from upstairs and comes down to see what's going on. "Is everything all right?"

"Kitty," Rosalind says as gently as he can. "How is your mother?"

"Much the same, I'm afraid. Why?"

"Don't you see, Zeph? That cure, as you call it, has yet to work on even *one* person. We have no way of knowing if—"

Zeph replies, "Only one way to find out. Besides, if Magruder's is a plague hospital, maybe they won't be so quick to set it on fire."

"Don't bet on it," Rosalind counters. "We don't have time for—"

"Actually," Digby interrupts, "he's the one who doesn't have time."

Whitey writhes in pain, murmuring, "Zeph... Where's Zeph?"

Zeph reaches over with one hand and squeezes Whitey's leg. "It's all right, brother. You just hang on."

"Zeph, darling," Rosalind says, "I know he's your friend. But what's the point of bringing him inside so he can die in a fire?"

"Fire?" Whitey whispers. "What fire? I'm the fire chief. Where's the fire?"

Zeph says, "Shh, don't worry yourself, Whitey."

"Oh, we got fires," he says, dazed. "Beautiful fires. We burn at 10:30, 12:00, 1:30, 3:00, 4:30, and 6:00. Special show Saturdays at 8:00, with extra victims..."

"Shh, now, Whitey. This ain't that kinda fire. This is a real fire."

"Wait," Kitty says slowly. "What if it wasn't? What if it wasn't a *real* fire at all?"

Everyone at the door frowns in confusion. Zeph shakes his head. "What are you even—?"

But Archie nods. "I *knew* she had potential."

✦ ✦ ✦

Gibson tries to direct the Committeemen loading the big, white vehicle. But wherever they need to be is invariably the exact place he happens to be standing. He gets pushed and shoved so many times, he starts to wonder if they are doing it on purpose. He walks farther away and leans against a tall, wooden fence that marks the outer limits of the park.

Never mind them, he tells himself. *Just this one errand, and I'm off to Newport to deliver the good news*. Perhaps there will be a ball going on, incense drifting down from chandeliers as big as automobiles, all the heiresses decked out in ermine and silk. And the senator will greet him with open arms, embracing him, whispering in his ear, *I wish I had a son like you.*

Laughter. He glares at the Committeemen, but they all seem occupied with the vehicle—if they are laughing at Gibson, it's on the inside. But this is explosive, unrestrained laughter, right behind him.

Behind me? Gibson turns to the fence. A pack of hyenas shoves their snouts between the slats, slobbering, chortling, staring up at Gib with dead, black eyes. He jumps away, cringing.

Spotting the hyenas, the men reach for their pistols, firing *pow pow pow* at the slobbering beasts. The men climb the fence to give chase, while the hyenas hit by gunfire curl up on the ground, bleeding and whimpering.

"No!" Gibson shouts, suddenly brave. He turns to the one Committee officer who stayed behind. "We're going to Magruder's!"

"Sure," the officer replies, "but they gotta take care of that first. Hyenas are nasty. We can't let 'em run around free."

"But…they're just dogs!"

"Dogs built by Satan, maybe. There ain't many animals I'd *less* wanna run into than a pack of starving hyenas." The officer chuckles, tossing another pile of mattress covers into the vehicle. "Of course, they really seem to like you."

Gibson grunts and wipes some sweat from his eyes. "I'm going to wait inside. Let me know when the hunt is over."

✦ ★ ✦

Kitty quickly assembles a crew of the least-ill Unusuals, and together they race around Magruder's, gathering blankets and pillows and yanking tarps off windows. They set up beds on tables, on the floor, on a few chairs set side by side. No sooner is a bed created than some desperate soul collapses into it.

"Rosalind," she says, "could you show some of these people up to your room? I bet we could fit several in your bed if we try."

Rosalind shudders. "Oh, now, I don't think—"

"We can't leave them on the street, surely!"

"I'm certainly not putting them in—"

Enzo coughs at Rosalind meaningfully.

Rosalind sighs. "All right, all right. Honestly. Those are my best sheets too."

★ ★ ★

Zeph, Kitty, and Archie quiz Whitey on the workings of Lilliputia's fire show, and between coughing fits, Whitey tries his best to explain. But his description makes less and less sense as he gets closer and closer to passing out.

"Never mind." Archie groans. "Somebody find the midget a bed, will you? We'll figure it out ourselves. Half of Dreamland is here at the Cabinet. There has to be somebody who—"

A young woman with long, dark hair steps forward. "Excuse me, perhaps I can help? I'm in the tenement fire show. I fall out that window about thirty times a week. I can tell you how it works."

Kitty grabs her hands. "Brilliant! There's gas, is that it? In the windows?"

"Right, there are holes drilled in the sills for the pipes and fuses. Light the gas, and it looks like fire shooting out of the windows."

Kitty looks at Zeph. "Have we any gas?"

"Sure," he replies. "Timur's lab has gas piped in, and we got a big tank of the stuff out back."

"This will be easy enough." Kitty grins.

"Not really," Archie says. "Unless we have enough pipe to run from a centrally located tank to every window in this building *and* the time to solder it all together."

Zeph shrugs. "I'm thinking no and no."

"Hmm." Kitty frowns. "What about smaller tanks? One per room, maybe? Far less pipe that way, less soldering."

Zeph nods. "This we can do. If you check in back of the tavern, there's a storeroom with a pile of empty ten-gallon canisters. I was supposed to fill 'em with helium for Timur's lights, but I never got around to it."

"Pardon?" Archie says. "Helium for lights?"

"Long story. Just grab the tanks and fill 'em up out at… Oh. Damn."

"*Oh damn* what?"

"Gas tank's buried in the backyard." He shrugs apologetically. "Where the leopards are."

Archie sighs. "I love this plan more and more."

"Oh, Vivi?" Kitty calls. "Mademoiselle Vivi, we need you."

Satisfied that Kitty has the situation in hand, Zeph gives her a nod and heads up the stairs to join Nazan in the lab. He stops suddenly, leaning over the railing. "Hey, English! Make sure you grab the empty tanks and not the one full of naphtha. Powers my cart something beautiful, but naphtha ain't an especially polite little gas—I don't think we want it shooting out the windows."

"Got it," Kitty calls back. "All right, everyone. Who'd like to assist me in the storeroom?"

✦ ★ ✦

Compared to the chaos in the rest of the building, Timur's attic lab is an oasis of quiet. Nazan studies P-Ray as he sleeps. Is his color better? Maybe? Or is she kidding herself?

Zeph arrives and hunts through Timur's equipment for the largest flask he can find.

Nazan joins him at one of the worktables. "I don't know about this plan, Zeph. A day ago, I'd never been in a lab before—now, I'm in mass production? I'm not even educated, not really. I just read a lot is all. When you come right down to it, I'm just a—"

"Nuh-uh." Zeph stops organizing instruments and looks at her intently. "You gotta let those thoughts go. Timur believes in you. I believe in you."

"I appreciate that, but—"

"No, listen. You want to do something to honor Spencer? This here—with the colloid—this is how we do it. 'Cause if Reynolds were here? He'd tell you to get it done. You know he would. We can't afford to have your head on anything else. Otherwise, all those folks outside are dead, like him. You hear?"

✦ ★ ✦

Timur stands guard atop the stoop, keeping an eye out for the Committee. He shouts at the crowd gathered on the street. "You be patient. Boys make the medicine. You must wait. And you there! Get your elephant away from building! No, no, not there. *Away* from building. There will be fire, you hear me? This is no-clown zone." He glances back at the frenzy in his home. "Too many clowns already."

As the Unusuals back reluctantly away, two men terrify their way to the front. Crumbly Pete limps through the crowd, half carrying and half dragging Goo-Goo Knox, a sickly mess of a man with no nose. "Out of our way," Pete mutters through gritted teeth.

They head straight up Magruder's front steps, paying no mind to Timur until the old man puts his hand out to stop Pete from opening the door.

"No," Timur says. "You wait outside."

But the young thugs barge past. Goo-Goo jams an elbow into Timur's chest, sending him stumbling down the stairs.

Timur shouts. "Stop, *kutok bosh!*"

Kitty passes on her way upstairs to visit her mother. She gasps at Goo-Goo's advanced affliction. "Poor man! Come in, come in. We'll make room for you."

"Stop, no!" Timur says. "These boys no good!"

But the decision is made. Kitty takes Pete by the arm and pulls the two men farther into Magruder's. "He can have a lie down in the back room; we've extra space there. Come with me. This way..."

Timur leans on the heavy oak door, catching his breath. "Little girl...little girl, no..."

50

WHEN IT'S OVER

A FESTERING BUBO ERUPTS.

Black liquid sprays across the sheets and dribbles down Goo-Goo's neck.

Crumbly Pete retches. He stands up. "I'm out."

Goo-Goo moans. "Don't you move, boy. I ain't too sick to snap your little neck."

Sighing, Pete sits back down. One way or the other, it will be over soon.

★ ★ ★

An arc of flame shoots from a second-floor window. Its orange tendrils stretch out into the street. A clown screams.

Kitty's head pops up in the window. "What do you think?" she calls down to Timur. "Too much?"

The mad scientist applauds. "When this is over, I hire you."

★ ★ ★

Faceless men sit on piles of mattress covers.

McGrath leans on the vehicle door. "Now, listen up. I'm going to drive by this place real slow, see what I can see. If I decide we should burn the place, I'll pull over and let you boys out. And if we do have a burn, I want a nice, controlled one. We want to take down one building, not the whole neighborhood." He glances over at Gibson. "And that's *if* we have to."

Gibson locks eyes with McGrath. "You have to."

McGrath shakes his head and sighs. "All right, let's get this over with."

★ ★ ★

Porcelain nails on a young man's fingers.

Enzo squints out the window, watching Vivi try in vain to coax the disobedient leopard from his perch in a nearby tree. "*Caro mio*," he says to Rosalind. "I must help Leopard Lady. This may go badly."

Spooning him from behind, Rosalind rests his head on Enzo's shoulder. He'd changed from his female dress into trousers so that he could be more nimble helping Kitty organize Magruder's. But he couldn't bear to remove his favorite porcelain nails, and he runs them through Enzo's hair. "Let the others handle it," Rosalind whispers. "I almost lost you once already."

"*Caro…*"

"I won't hear it." He turns Enzo to face him. "You know, darling, I've been thinking… When this is over, we should go somewhere. Someplace no one knows us. We can take P-Ray, live as a family. I don't know, maybe out west somewhere. Maybe Nebraska."

Enzo laughs. "Nebraska!"

"I can pass, Enzo! You think I can't? Let me tell you, I can pass anytime I—"

He puts a finger to Rosalind's lips. "Of course you pass. It is I who no pass." He takes Rosalind's hand and puts it on the scarred half of his head. "This face, this is a Dozen's face? Is this to you a Nebraska face?"

"I love your face. I'm glad there *aren't* dozens of you."

Enzo kisses Rosalind on the forehead. "I go help Leopard Lady." He heads down the stairs, chuckling to himself. "Nebraska…"

★ ★ ★

Hydrogen bubbles rise from silver ingot at the bottom of a flask.

"Nearly done over here," Nazan says.

"Good," Zeph replies. "How about you distribute that to some of our guests downstairs? Meanwhile, I'll get some more water from the storeroom, and I'll meet you back up here to start making more."

"Sounds fine. How much colloid do we need, do you think?"

Zeph pulls another flask from the shelf. "How much sand is on the beach, know what I mean? This won't be over any time soon."

✹ ✹ ✹

A British rose withers away.

As Kitty races up and down the stairs of Magruder's, organizing the gas canisters, overseeing the soldering, instructing the troops, a voice in the back of her head continuously nags that she's been away from her mother too long. When she finally pauses on the third floor to peek into her sickroom, Kitty knows the voice was right.

Too long, and far too late.

"Mum, are you all right?"

Her mother's mouth is open and slack. One arm hangs off the side of the bed.

Kitty goes to her; the hand is cold. "Oh, Mummy, no." Kitty puts her hand to her mouth to stifle a sob.

She hears voices out in the hall, confused and worried, looking for direction. "Has anyone seen Miss Hayward?" one asks. "Miss Hayward, how does this valve work?" asks another. "Kitty, where are you?"

Kitty wipes her tears and gently tucks her mother's hand back into the sheets. "I'm sorry, Mum. I can't stay with you now—I have to go make myself useful. I know you understand." She squeezes her mother's hand, then pulls the blanket over her mother's face and leaves the room.

When Zeph passes Kitty on the stairs, he sees something is wrong. "Hey, English, everything okay?"

She bites her lip and says simply, "It's over."

✹ ✹ ✹

A wavy metal dagger with an ivory handle.

Archie reaches into the cabinet, removes the Indonesian *kris* blade, and slides it into his coat. For the past hour, he's been floating mock-innocently around Magruder's, squirreling away whatever treasures he can into the pockets of his coat. But in the back room, Archie discovers the very opposite of treasure: Crumbly Pete and a half-dead Goo-Goo Knox. "What are you cretins doing here?"

Pete leaps up, ready for a fight. "That girl said we could be here! Goo-Goo needs the treatment, and—"

"All right, don't get yourself in a twist." On a shelf, he spies a blue-and-white teacup. Ming Dynasty. He slides it into his coat pocket. "Reynolds should have let you all die, but nobody ever listens to me."

"The Reynolds kid is—" Pete catches himself. "I heard Reynolds is dead. That's what I heard someplace."

Archie chuckles. "True. But as it turns out, Reynolds's lady friend fancies herself quite the chemist. And it's *her* medicine that may save your pointless lives. Funny old world, eh?" Archie glides out of the room to find someplace he can loot uninterrupted.

Pete bends down to Goo-Goo. "That's it, we gotta go."

Goo-Goo moans. "Don't be a baby. They don't know you killed him."

"What do you mean *I* killed him? *You* killed him."

"I fixed a problem you made."

"Well, we got a new problem now. And we wouldn't even be in this situation if you'd let the doctor treat you. Jesus, we go to all that trouble to snatch him, and then you lose your temper and wring his fucking—"

Goo-Goo grabs Pete by the shirt and pulls him close, and Pete grimaces at the stench. "The doctor annoyed me. Kinda how you're starting to. You want this over so badly, go find that skirt and get my medicine."

✦ ★ ✦

A cup of silver colloid raised to a little man's lips.

"You're good at this, you know," Whitey says weakly. "This nursing business."

Nazan smiles. "Let's hope for your sake that I'm as good a scientist as I am a nurse."

She stands to leave, but Whitey takes her hand. "Sorry about Reynolds. Personally, I always hated the guy, but...I heard about you and him and...about what happened. Terrible."

"Thank you."

"When this is over, you want to get a drink sometime?"

"Oh, Mr. Lovett." She smiles, shaking her head. "I've heard about you too."

✶ ✶ ✶

A gentle knock on an old pine door.

"Come on in," Rosalind says. Kitty peers around the door to find Rosalind sorting through a bag of fabric. "Kitty, how's your mother doing?"

"Oh, she's...um." She swallows hard. *Neither the time, nor the place.* "She's the same. I was hoping I might borrow a pair of trousers? I've lost count of how many times I've run up and down these stairs, and I thought trousers might—"

Rosalind smiles. "Say no more. Let me see what I have that might fit." He puts the bag of fabric down and sets to hunting through his wardrobe.

While she waits, Kitty idly picks up the fabric. "What's all this?"

"Nothing really. It's just, everyone else has jobs. Enzo's out in the back with Vivi. People are drilling and soldering. I'm not sure what to do with myself. But I remembered that I have all this fabric left over from my dressmaking and—wait, what about these? Will they fit? No, I think I have better somewhere... Anyway, I thought I could wet this fabric down, and we could dampen the window sills with it. Might help keep the wood from catching fire... Aha! Here we go. If we roll these up a bit, they'll do nicely." Rosalind brings the trousers over and helps Kitty out of her skirts.

"I wouldn't bother," Kitty says. "The fire is powered by gas. A little moisture won't make a difference."

"I suppose, but I just thought any little thing could——"

"Really. There's *no point*. You'll just get in people's way."

"Surely a damp sill is preferable to a——"

"Rosalind! Am I in charge or not? Why am I even bothering if no one will *bloody well* listen to me? Do you think there's *nothing* else I'd rather be doing right now?"

Rosalind rears back a little in surprise. "There's no need for you to——" He stops himself. "This isn't like you. What's happened?"

"Nothing happened! I simply don't understand why you all can't——"

Rosalind puts his hand tenderly on Kitty's arm. "Kitty. Stop. What happened?"

Kitty's eyes well up. She bites her bottom lip, then the top, then the bottom again. She clamps her hands over her face—perhaps there is some magic switch near her eyes that will stop the tears. Finally, she says, "She's gone. Mum's gone."

"Poor little bird." Rosalind wraps his arms around her, and they sit together on the bed while Kitty cries. "You poor thing, I'm so sorry."

"It was too late. *Everything* was too late. I was so stupid to leave Mum alone at that hotel in the first place. I *never* should have agreed to it. And even more stupid to go to that island. All that trouble you went through, and the airplane, and it was all for nothing, and I should have been *here* the whole time! I've done absolutely everything wrong."

"Angel." Rosalind takes a piece of his scrap fabric and uses it to wipe Kitty's face. "Listen to me. You acted on the information you had. And P-Ray was being taken to Hoffman no matter what— that wasn't your fault. Enzo, Zeph, and me, we'd knock the Earth off Atlas's shoulders to get that boy back. So not one word about troubling us. And hey, usually Timur's inventions have no purpose whatsoever, so really, you did him a favor. C'mere." He wraps Kitty into another hug.

"I let her down," she says into Rosalind's neck. "I let them take her."

"No. No, no, no. Stop that. What happened to you and your mother was a crime. What happened to P-Ray and Enzo was a crime. All over the city, it's not right. And think about this. Most of the people being treated this way, they have no voice. They're dead by now, or they're poor, or they look like Enzo, and no Dozen would ever believe them. But you. You have your fine education, you have your accent, you have this pretty face—or it would be," he says kindly, "if you'd stop snuffling. You can be their champion, Kitty. You can stand up and say, *This is what's happening, and I know because it happened to me.*"

Kitty peers at him. "You think?"

"Someone's going to have to. Who better?"

Kitty laughs sadly. "Lots of people would be better, I'm sure. But I think Mum would like that, if I...took the lead a bit."

"There you go." Rosalind nods. "But, darling, could you help us save the Cabinet first?"

"Yes." Kitty wipes her eyes and pulls on the trousers. "We'll fight the next battle when this one is over."

✦ ★ ✦

A machine in the corner goes *ding!*

Ding!

Ding!

Ding!

"What in hell is that noise?" Goo-Goo mutters.

Pete sighs. "I don't know, just something in the corner."

Ding! Ding!

"Make it stop. It's giving me a headache."

"Goo-Goo, it's just—"

"I said make it stop!"

Zeph enters. "Sorry to interrupt, boys. I just need a jug of water from back here."

Pete stands. "Hey, since you're here. One of them machines started making this—"

Ding! Ding! Ding!

"See, there it goes again. It's bothering Goo-Goo."

"My stars, I'd hate for our guests to be uncomfortable."

"Watch your mouth, Stumpy," Goo-Goo growls.

Ding! Ding! Ding! Ding!

As Zeph approaches, the dinging intensifies. There's a new picture in the slot. "Chio, what is your—" Zeph takes the picture and examines it. He looks up at Pete and Goo-Goo, then back at the picture. "Oh my God." His eyes widen for a split second, then he crumples the picture and shoves it in his shirt. "Machine was malfunctioning. It's over now."

"Fucking better be," Goo-Goo says.

✶ ★ ✶

Heavy wheels crunch along sandy, unswept streets.

Gibson sits in the passenger seat, his dread increasing. He checks his pocket watch. Will this be over in time for him to make the last train to Newport?

Up in the sky, large black birds ride the wind.

✶ ★ ✶

A big cat sprawls across the limb of a tree.

His fellow leopards stalk the backyard in circles, chuffing as they test and retest the strength of their leashes.

The alpha cat sees their mistress enter the yard. "*Venez ici, mes bébés. Venez ici.*" She's calling them to join her on one side of the yard. But no matter what she says, the alpha will not come.

The time for obedience is over.

✶ ★ ✶

A clown runs across a roof.

"They're coming," he shrieks. "I see them! They're coming!"

Nodding, Timur dashes inside. "English! They come!"

"No!" Kitty panics. "No, we aren't ready!" The alpha leopard in the yard had so far declined to eat Enzo and Vivi, but his presence had slowed down the whole operation. "We don't have nearly enough tanks filled!"

"Will be enough."

"It won't!"

Timur gives Kitty an awkward pat on the head. "Must be."

Magruder's is in a frenzy. Kitty pushes the image of her mother's body out of her mind and rouses the Unusuals from their sickbeds, barking out orders, assigning one to this window, another to that.

Nazan passes by on her nursing mission. "Kitty," she says, "can I do anything?"

"No, no," Kitty replies distractedly. "You keep on. We're all right."

"Okay. I have one more dose to give out, to that poor man in the back. So if you need any help after that, let me know." She turns to go but quickly turns back. "Kitty…"

"What?"

"Good luck." Nazan hugs her. "You're my hero, you know."

"Don't be ridiculous," Kitty demurs. Nazan grins and heads for the back room, and Kitty returns to business.

"Mr. Archie! You take charge of the windows in front of the tavern. When you see flames from windows above, you light yours. And stay away from the Elixir for five minutes, would you? We get only once chance at this."

Archie bows carefully, so his loot doesn't tumble out of his pockets. "Lady General, I obey. But I must ask…*what* are you wearing?"

She smiles self-consciously and smooths the linen trousers with both hands. "I borrowed these from Rosalind. I had to roll them up a bit, but they're beautiful, don't you think?"

Archie rolls his eyes. "Not even slightly."

Kitty smiles. "They are practical, and practical is beautiful." She darts upstairs, issuing more instructions as she goes.

✦ ★ ✦

Enzo dashes to the second floor with the last gas canister. He spots Kitty and goes to her. "Miss Kitty, *mi dispiace tanto*! I am so sorry…"

"It's fine—"

"No, is no fine! We try to fill the tanks, but Vivi must watch the leopard while I fill the tank. It just take too long."

"Enzo, please. We have what we have, and we will make do with it. *Sì*?"

He nods, heartbroken. "*Sì, sì*. I no want to lose Magruder's because of me."

Kitty smiles. "Silly man. I wouldn't even be here if not for you. You must stop being sad and be useful instead. Take that canister upstairs for me, all right?"

"*Sì*, I do this," Enzo calls after her. "Maybe I look around the building? Maybe Zeph forget something!"

"Sure," she says, dashing off. "Can't hurt to look around."

✦ ★ ✦

Archie feels a tug at his pant leg and looks down. "Master Zephaniah! Don't tell me you've escaped an assignment from our young Napoleon-ette!"

Zeph thrusts a piece of paper up at Archie. "Shut up and look at this, and keep your damned voice down."

With a grunt, Archie goes down on one knee to study the paper. "I have no idea what—"

"Look, dammit! See the castle tattoo on that one? And the big fella with no nose?"

"But who are these two on the ground? What's on that fellow's coat? Is that a staff with snakes?"

Zeph nods. "It's the doctor, the one whose building blew up. And look at the hair on the other one. That's Spencer!"

"But they have Xs for eyes, for crying out—" He stops. "Zeph, what are you saying?"

"I'm saying nothing. Chio is saying. Pete and Goo-Goo killed Spencer and the doctor."

Archie shakes his head like there's water in his ears. "How could a machine know—"

"Keep up, brother! Chio's not just any machine. He drew this picture for me to tell me *this*. Boys were probably whispering about it, right in front of him. Pete never could keep his mouth shut."

"So Nazan's medicine is saving the life of Spencer's killer? That's quite the irony!"

"No, it ain't, because that is not a thing that's gonna happen."

"That thing is already happening, friend. She just went back there with Goo-Goo's dose."

"Dammit! No. No." Zeph scrambles after her.

Wistfully, Archie picks a wax grasshopper off a shelf and puts it in his coat. "I'm going to miss this place."

✶ ★ ✶

Enzo runs downstairs to the tavern storeroom. He knows Zeph to be a pack rat, even saving piles of empty gas canisters of no conceivable use. Maybe there's something else there too.

He tears through the shelves in a furor, knocking useless junk to the floor, giving angry kicks to the empty gas canisters he had no time to fill. Most of the canisters roll away apologetically, but one stands firm when he kicks it. He picks it up. It's heavy.

"A full one!" Enzo laughs, delighted. "I get one more!"

✶ ★ ✶

When Zeph reaches the back room, Nazan is hovering over Goo-Goo, measuring out the medicine.

"Stop!"

"Zeph? What's wrong?"

Goo-Goo moans. "Give me the goddamned medicine. I'm dying here!"

Zeph scuttles across the floor, climbs the bed, and dives between Goo-Goo and Nazan. "No! It's...um...it's a bad batch, okay? It ain't good."

"It's the same batch I've given everyone, Zeph. What are you even—"

"I'm telling you, Nazan, stop!" He smacks her hand, and the medicine bottle smashes on the floor.

"Zeph!"

"You goddamned freak!" Goo-Goo grabs Zeph.

Nazan tries to intervene, so Pete leaps up and pulls Nazan away. But he says, "Goo-Goo, cut it out! Relax, would you?"

Goo-Goo flips over, pinning Zeph on the bed, choking him. "I'll kill you, you useless little—!"

"I won't be the first!" Zeph squeaks.

Goo-Goo loosens his grip slightly. "What was that?"

✦ ✦ ✦

The armored vehicle makes the turn onto Magruder's street and lumbers up to the building. As it approaches, orange fire explodes from the third floor. Soon, more flames emerge—from a second-floor window, another from the third floor, and after a moment, two flames from the windows at ground level.

On the street, the crowd of Unusuals all seem to lose their minds at once. People wave their arms and shout theatrically. "Fire! Fire!" "Somebody call the fire department!" "Oh, Lord help us!"

McGrath puts the engine in neutral but keeps it running. "Well now, would you look at that?"

Gibson peers out in disbelief. "What? No. What is that?"

"That, young man, is what's called a best-case scenario. You wanted a fire? Fire. Go tell Big Daddy that Magruder's is on fire." He makes to pull the vehicle forward, but Gibson grabs his arm.

"No, no. Look at those flames. That's fake, transparently fake."

"You're saying they're *pretending* to set themselves on fire? Are you listening to yourself?"

"But…look! Just look! The pattern doesn't even make any sense—flames up there, flames down there. What fire does that, and all at once? *Look!*"

"I am looking, Gibson, and that building is—"

"No, it's not! It looks just like that show, that stupid Dreamland show! It's a bunch of carnies over there. Obviously, they know how to—"

McGrath grabs Gibson by the lapels. "Listen—"

"Don't you touch me!"

"This city is in crisis, do you hear me? *Real* problems, *real* people dying everywhere! I said I would indulge you, and I did. You wanted a goddamned fire, you got one. *We're done.*"

Gibson wrenches himself away. "We are certainly not done! I demand that we investigate this blatant fraud!"

"You *demand*, do ya? Kid, you want to investigate? Knock yourself out."

"But—"

"Get out! Me and my men have actual work to do."

Gibson is left standing on the curb as the Committeemen pull away. He screams at the departing vehicle. "The senator will hear about this! Make no mistake, the senator will hear!"

✦ ✦ ✦

Kitty runs up to the lab to get a better view of the street. She'd considered returning to her mother's room to watch from there, but no. One crisis at a time.

Entering the lab, she pauses to marvel at the helium lights but gasps at the sight of P-Ray curled up in the corner. Fearing the worst, she runs to him and grabs his hand tightly. He's warm. He murmurs softly and opens his eyes.

"You're awake!" she cries. He smiles at her, and she hugs him. "It worked! I can barely believe it worked!"

"P-Ray," he says quietly, but then he squawks at Kitty's too-tight embrace.

"Sorry," she says, laughing and crying at once. "It's just...the medicine didn't help Mum, so I thought...I thought it was *all* pointless, all of it. But it was just too late for her, I guess. Perhaps she'd been sick too long. But you!" She grabs his little face with both hands. "You are a tough little thing, just like Enzo said. Mum would have loved you so, *so* much."

Suddenly, they hear the squeal of brakes on the street. Wiping her eyes, Kitty goes to the window and yanks down the tarp, just in time to see a young man in old man's clothes ejected from the Committee vehicle. The vehicle drives away, which pleases her, but the young man remains, which is troubling. Supposedly, there is a sucker born every minute, but judging by the skeptical look on the young old man's face, Kitty fears they may be one sucker short.

She gathers P-Ray up in her arms, and together they perch at the window, waiting to see what the young old man will do next.

✶ ✭ ✶

"Enzo, my darling, where are—"

He holds up his prize to show Rosalind. "One more canister I find! I take to your bedroom. It has no fire."

"I beg your pardon!"

Enzo laughs as he dashes up the stairs. "*Passerotto mio*, you know this I mean!"

"You are incorrigible!"

"I get one more! We light this bastard!"

✶ ✭ ✶

The Unusuals continue to go berserk over the pretend fire. Gibson surveys the scene bitterly. He can't decide if they are overly commit-ted actors, complete idiots, or a mix of both. But regardless, the chance of him making his way through this mad crowd and up to the front door of Magruder's seems virtually nil.

He considers surrender but then thinks, *Newport. Incense. Heiresses.* Surely, there is a back way in. *I could go down the alley, maybe climb the fence into the backyard?*

Capital idea.

✦ ★ ✦

Down in the tavern, Archie looks up from his elixir when he hears the Committee vehicle depart. He shuts off his gas jets and goes to congratulate Kitty. She pulled off quite a con today. He needs to chat with that young lady about her future.

On his way up the stairs, he pauses to scratch the scar on his hand. He thinks of Zeph, dashing off to confront Pete and that other one. Goo-Goo Knox. Goo-Goo, the goose who lost his beak. Bane of Brooklyn cops and gangsters alike. Nasty piece of work. Far too nasty for Zeph to handle on his own.

Not my problem.

But that old scar keeps on itching.

"Oh…*fine.*" He slouches off to see about Zeph.

✦ ★ ✦

Kitty is still cuddling P-Ray at the window when they hear the screaming. She sets P-Ray down and races to the back of the building, peering out a window that overlooks the backyard.

There he is, the young man in old man clothes. He dangles from the fence, howling as the leopards swipe at him with their sharp claws. Up in his tree, the alpha leopard observes the scene with interest. Vivi is there too, shrieking at the cats to stop and swatting impotently with her little whip. She may as well be invisible.

The young man tries desperately to swing his legs back over the fence. But as soon as he gets one foot free, the leopards grab the other, his shredded pant legs turning dark crimson. He begs for mercy, but there is none.

The alpha leopard leaps from the tree, its open jaw glinting just briefly in the sunshine before it lands on the young man's back, sinking its four sharp canines deep into his neck. Man and cat tumble off the fence.

Vivi's screams don't mask the sounds of tearing flesh and breaking bone. The leopards yowl and hiss at one another, squaring off over who gets which part of the body.

"Well, well," Kitty says coolly. "*Someone* ate today at least."

✦ ★ ✦

Archie rounds the corner into the back room to find Goo-Goo on the bed, choking the life out of Zeph, while Pete holds Nazan. "Best you stay out of this," he tells her. She struggles against him and shouts, while Pete yells over her, "Calm the hell down, Goo!"

Archie pulls the *kris* blade from his jacket and holds it out. "Stop! Whatever you children are doing, stop right now!"

"Go away, old man," Goo-Goo snarls without looking up.

"Let's be reasonable." Archie moves slowly toward the bed. "Is it money you want? Just look at this museum. It's like Aladdin's cave around here. This blade in my hand is worth more than you could steal in a year. And look." He reaches into his coat. "This teacup? Ming Dynasty, which is code for mind-bogglingly valuable. Take whatever you want. Live out your lives as rich men."

Pete nods. "Goo, listen to him."

But plague madness has taken Goo-Goo away. He leans harder on Zeph's neck. Zeph goes limp.

Archie moves toward the bed. "Okay, kill Zeph if you want. You're halfway there already, from the look of it. But this building is swarming with Unusuals. You want to tangle with Digby the Strongman and all the rest? Go now, and we won't stop you. But continue with this nonsense, and may God help you."

Goo-Goo whirls around, eyes blazing. "You think I'm afraid of you freaks? *I'll kill you all and your fucking God too.*"

"So be it." Archie jams the blade into Goo-Goo's eye.

He rears back, shrieking. Nazan screams. Pete slams her head against the wall and tosses her on the floor, springing to Goo-Goo's aid. As she falls, Nazan grabs for Pete's thigh and yanks as hard as she can. He loses his balance and goes down, slamming his head on the metal bed frame. Goo-Goo wrenches the blade from his eye and slashes blindly at Archie, ripping open the old man's cravat with the first pass and his jugular with the second. Goo-Goo collapses on top of Archie, and they fall together on the bed.

On the floor, Nazan weeps.

★ ★ ★

In Rosalind's room, Enzo hurriedly attaches the tank to the pipe.

One of the Unusuals in Rosalind's bed says weakly, "Mr. Enzo, they're gone. I don't think you need to—"

"No, no, no, better to have one more window." Triumphantly, he pushes the button that lights the fuse.

Naphtha hits oxygen, spark hits naphtha, and Enzo realizes too late that he's just set off the biggest firework of his life.

DING!

☙

THE ENTIRE BUILDING SHAKES WITH THE BLAST. KITTY RACES DOWNSTAIRS, a stream of invective racing through her head. This was her worst fear, an explosion just like this. It's not like she didn't think of it, but she'd been so sure she could pull this off, so bloody cocksure of herself, and now look, everything in ashes. *You bloody idiot! Did you not know this would happen, you stupid, stupid, stupid, useless girl?*

"Out!" she screams. "Everybody out! Get out! Get out now!" Running down the stairs, she meets a hysterical Rosalind running up. "Get out, Rosalind!"

"Enzo is upstairs! He's up there. I have to go. I have to—"

Kitty grabs Rosalind and drags him back down the stairs with her. "Rosalind, you can't help him. You must get out of here, now!"

On the first floor, they run into Timur, demanding, "Where is Zeph?"

"I don't know," Kitty says. "I'm sorry, I don't know. I'm so sorry."

"What about the boy? Where is the boy?"

Kitty cries out. "I left him in the attic!"

✦ ★ ✦

P-Ray gazes out the small attic window, thoroughly enjoying the drama of the Unusuals on the street. He wonders idly if Kitty will be his *anne* now. His mother.

By way of reply, the universe blows up the building.

P-Ray grabs the windowsill just as the fire swallows the floor under him.

✦ ★ ✦

Nazan pulls herself up. "Zeph…" She climbs on the gore-splattered bed and shakes him, tears falling onto his face. "Zeph, please… Please wake up… Zeph?"

His body shudders suddenly, and his eyes open. "Sweet Jesus," he croaks. "Nazan?"

"Zeph, thank goodness! You're all right! Are you all right?"

He coughs wretchedly and strokes his aching neck. "Not exactly… Am I bleeding?"

"No, they are."

He sees the two bodies sprawled at the foot of the bed. "What the—no, not Archie."

"He saved you, Zeph."

"*Archie* did?"

Nazan nods. "He made a speech, threatened them, gave them a teacup, and when nothing worked, he just stabbed the big one in the eye."

"Sister, you are making this up. Archie *gave* somebody something?"

"Zeph, we have to go. I think the building's burning for real now. Can you move?"

He coughs some more. "God, I don't know… Yeah, yeah, let's go." Then he stops. "Chio! I can't leave Chio here."

"We can't carry him, Zeph!"

"No, of course. Chio, listen. I won't forget about you. Don't be scared. We'll get you out."

✦ ★ ✦

P-Ray hangs on to the side of the dormer, his legs dangling. Flames tickle the gas pipes in Timur's worktables. As the smoke intensifies, he clenches a fist and punches out a windowpane. It hurts, but the blood mainly just reminds him he's still alive.

He watches the glowing lights ride the wild air currents; some melt, but nothing explodes. Pretty.

"P-Ray!" Across the lake of fire, he sees Timur standing at the door. "Boy, you listen! I can no reach you. But hang on. We no leave you." Timur then disappears as mysteriously as he arrived.

The heat increases, and the flames creep ever closer to the gas lines.

✶ ★ ✦

Out on the sidewalk, Zeph says, "I'm going after him."

"Oh no, you are not," Rosalind says.

"Oh yes, I am."

"Oh yes, he is," Kitty agrees. "I'll help."

"No way, English," Zeph says. "You stay here and look after everybody. Look after Nazan. She's real upset."

"I left him up there, Zeph. I'm going with you."

"*None* of you should go," Rosalind argues. "The fire trucks are coming."

"Yeah? Will they come before the gas in Timur's lab explodes?" Zeph reaches up and squeezes Rosalind's hand. "I can do this."

Rosalind grips Zeph's hand as hard as he can. "I won't let you. I've lost too much today."

"What did Enzo say earlier, Ros? *The people need help; we help the people.*"

"Get going!" Timur says.

✶ ★ ✦

Crumbly Pete opens his eyes, touches the tender spot on his forehead. "Ugh, that little bitch." He stands. "Goo-Goo? Hey, Goo-Goo. Archie? Anybody?"

No response from the seeping corpses on the bed.

"Yeah, well."

He looks up. Heat drifts down from the ceiling something fierce. He should leave. Business first, though.

Using a pillowcase to protect his hand, Pete gingerly rolls the bodies over. He releases the *kris* blade from Goo-Goo's death grip, then the teacup from Archie's. He shrugs, not unhappily. "Last shall be first."

✦ ✦ ✦

Moments after the explosion, the Lilliputia fire truck sprang into action. Plague or no plague, Whitey Lovett is fire chief, period, and he takes command. The pumper is too small to force water all the way up to the third floor, but Whitey puts it to work wetting down the lower levels in hopes of sparing at least part of the building.

Rosalind dashes to the fire truck. "Whitey, do you have a ladder?"

"Not that high, I don't! This one's all up to Zeph."

"We have to do something!" Rosalind turns to the crowd. "Who has a tarp? Or a blanket, a big one?" His questions are met with a round of helpless shrugging, and Rosalind can feel tears prickling his eyes as he scans the crowd. "There must be something we—"

Halfway down the street, he sees the elephant standing patiently at attention, the howdah on its back now empty, the intricate embroidery of its blanket seeming to twinkle at Rosalind like a present on Christmas morning. He claps his hands. "There!"

✦ ✦ ✦

Zeph, Kitty, and Timur reach the roof of the building next door. While Zeph wraps himself in a length of rope, Timur paces impatiently. "Go get our boy."

"Make sure you tie that line real tight, yeah? If I slip, it's the only safety I've got."

Timur rolls his eyes. "Yes, yes, I tie. You go." He turns away to secure the rope but then pauses. "You go, Zeph, and then you come back. Understand?"

Zeph smiles. "Yes, sir."

"You no come back, I am annoyed."

"Got it." *All right*, Zeph thinks, *let the heroism commence!* But as he gingerly climbs across onto Magruder's roof, he realizes just how high off the street he actually is. Meanwhile, the heat from the fire is already softening the tar. *Dear Lord, please let this not be a mistake.*

✶ ★ ✶

Nazan helps Rosalind organize some Unusuals to hold the elephant blanket beneath Magruder's flaming windows. Heat and smoke roll off the building in waves, but Rosalind will brook no hesitation. "Let's get it closer to the building. Hold on tightly—no, not like that, like this. Tighter, Hector! Well, get someone else to do it if you can't!" A snake charmer has a coughing fit, vomits, and faints on the sidewalk. "Oh, *not now*," Rosalind admonishes. "Die on your own time! You, over there—yes, you! Roll her out of the way and take her place! We need to hold this very tightly if we're going to catch them!"

The crowd holds its breath as Zeph clings onto the side of the dormer and pulls P-Ray out the window. The boy dangles perilously from Zeph's shoulders, his legs flopping.

"Funny," Zeph mutters. "I recall you being lighter."

Then it happens. The flames finally eat their way through the metal pipes in Timur's worktables. The attic detonates, sending Zeph and P-Ray flying out over the street, battered by chunks of wall and sliced by shattering glass. Zeph stays tethered to Timur's rope, but he loses his grip on P-Ray, and the boy falls, limbs waving helplessly in the air. He plummets like a sack of dirty clothes into the blanket's waiting embrace. Zeph is slammed into the side of the building next door. His arms are in searing pain, his face is scraped and bleeding, but he has only one thought. "Did you catch him?" he screams. "Did y'all catch him?"

Rosalind waves up at him. "We caught him, darling! Now get your ass down here!"

The crowd gently lowers the elephant blanket, and Rosalind scrambles across it, kissing P-Ray's head. "You're okay, baby," he says, crying. "You're okay."

Zeph looks up and sees Timur and Kitty peering over the roof. Gripping the rope, Timur looks more panicked than Zeph has ever imagined the old man could be. "I'm all right, Doc!" Then he looks down and sees Nazan peering fretfully up at him, her dark, curly hair dancing in the wind. He shouts down to her. "You sure look beautiful today, miss!"

She laughs. "So do you, sir!"

He pulls himself up the rope, hand over hand, but pauses to watch the helium lights spill out of the burning attic. The balloons shimmy across the street and drift up into the smoky sky.

✴ ★ ✴

At last, the local fire department arrives to take over for the Lilliputians. But if the professionals think they will be allowed to take charge of the operation, they're sorely mistaken. Now that Nazan's medicine has kicked in, Whitey is back at his post, cursing out the professional firefighters for everything they do wrong, which, in Whitey's opinion, is everything.

But with the fire under control and P-Ray and Zeph returned safely to earth, Rosalind has run out of distractions. He stands as close to the building as the others will let him, waiting for Enzo to come out. Eyes glued to Magruder's front door, he hugs himself and rocks back and forth, distractedly biting off each porcelain fingernail in turn and spitting them out absentmindedly. They hit the sidewalk with sad, little tinkling noises. Tears run down Rosalind's face, seemingly of their own accord. He doesn't wipe the tears away. He doesn't respond to friends who call out to him. He doesn't even blink. He watches the door.

One by one, the Unusuals who'd been too ill to evacuate on their own are brought out of the building by firemen. The ones from Rosalind's bed are also carried out, charred almost beyond recognition.

"Are they all right?" Rosalind cries out. "Was there anyone else in the room?"

The firemen glance over but only shrug in reply.

Rosalind howls, and Nazan dashes over to hold him up. "It's okay," she repeats. "It's okay, it's okay, it's okay."

✳ ★ ✦

Timur and Zeph loiter across the street from Magruder's, watching helplessly. Zeph knows he should be by Rosalind's side, but he can't make himself go over there. Rosalind's agony is too much: it shimmers like the summer sun beating down on the pavement. Zeph doesn't know how Nazan can do it—be so close to so much pain. Run toward it, even.

"Enzo," he says quietly.

Timur nods. "Enzo."

"How many wonders we got left in that building, Doc? We got any more?"

Timur doesn't answer.

Kitty approaches them carefully and only when she thinks she can have this conversation without falling apart. But despite herself, the words "I'm sorry" come out trembling and weepy.

Zeph shakes his head. "None of that, English. You did everything you could."

Timur keeps his eyes locked on Magruder's, but he agrees. "No crying girls. We no like."

In the building, the third-floor joists moan, sigh, and surrender, sending furniture careening down to the floor below.

"Bye-bye to bedrooms," Timur says.

Zeph reaches up and pats Timur on the small of his back. Uncharacteristically, the old Uzbek doesn't move away. "You think they'll save the first floor, Doc?"

"Does it matter?" Another interior wall groans and collapses. "No laboratory, no home. No money even for telegram to Theobold."

"Theobold again!" Zeph looks up at Timur. "Enough mystery. Who's Theobold?"

Timur huffs. "Theobold Gruber, obviously."

Zeph and Kitty exchange glances. "And Theobold Gruber is…"

"Bah. Theophilus Magruder."

Zeph is gobsmacked. "You're saying, all this time, there actually is a Theophilus Magruder?"

"No, half-wit! There is Theobold Gruber only. He invent this stupid name. He want something less Prussian."

"Okay, but—"

"Theobold goes…you know…he…" Timur gestures vaguely, searching for the English word. "He *circumnavigates*. Buying, trading, stealing. For the Cabinet. Where do you think our treasures come from? You think conjoined twins sell two-for-one at Sears Roebuck?"

Suddenly, Magruder's oak door opens again and out comes Digby with a large bundle wrapped in a blanket and slung awkwardly across his shoulders. Sticking out of the blanket are a pair of legs, shod in a fine pair of Italian men's shoes.

"Yes, Zeph," Timur says. "I think one wonder more."

✷ ✷ ✷

Rosalind perches on the back of Whitey's fire truck, cradling Enzo's head in his lap. Kitty, Zeph, and Timur race across the street to join them.

Enzo mutters incoherently as Rosalind strokes his hair. "*Amore mio… Mi dispiace…ma tanto…è tutta colpa mia…ho rovinato tutto…*"

Zeph looks at Rosalind. "You get any of that?"

Enzo murmurs again. "*Amore mio…*"

"Just enough," Rosalind says, crying. "I understand just enough."

Whitey nods to one of his fellow firemen. "Take them to Reception Hospital, quick as you can."

"No," Kitty interrupts. "I'm sorry, but Reception can*not* handle injuries this serious."

Whitey rolls his eyes. "Lady, we don't have time for your Limey bullsh—"

"It's certainly not—"

"—and Enzo *definitely* doesn't have—"

But Rosalind's anguished voice cuts through the debate. "She's right. Reception won't help him. Forget Reception—everyone dies there."

"What do you suggest?" Whitey asks. "I'd like to see him in Brooklyn Hospital too, but we're under a goddamned quarantine."

Nazan steps forward. "I think I can get across." Everyone turns to look at her, mystified as to what this Dozen could possibly know that they don't. "But someone should come with me. Miss Hayward, if you don't mind. I do think you're better at this sort of thing than I."

"Anything for Enzo, but I don't understand. What do I do?"

"We'll need to tell someone a convincing story. Perhaps I can explain on the way? It involves three belly dancers and a bishop."

✦ ✦ ✦

As dusk arrives, Whitey grants Zeph permission to reenter the museum. At the entrance, he roots around the shelves until he finds P-Ray's dog-eared copy of *The Wizard of Oz*. He slides the book into the back of his trousers.

The museum is pitch-black and eerily quiet. Many of the cabinets have toppled over—whether from the force of the explosions or from the pumper trucks, Zeph can't say. As he picks his way through the soggy debris and ruined artifacts, Zeph takes a quick inventory in his head. The two-faced baby pig is smashed on the floor, its yellow liquid oozing. The saber-toothed tiger jaw is broken, the shrunken head shattered, the peacock boots melted, but the Tibetan thigh trumpet lost only a few of its jewels. The boxing kangaroo kinetoscope is knocked over on its side but is probably fixable. Maisy and Daisy, the skeleton Siamese twins, stand unscathed. Zeph nods, proud of the girls for making it through. *Still*, he thinks, *Whatshisname Gruber's gonna have his work cut out for certain.*

In the back room, he climbs on the bed and looks at Goo-Goo, his poked-out eye a perfect complement to his missing nose. "Got what you deserved, didn't you?"

Beside Goo-Goo is Archie, now cold and gray, his silk cravat torn and soggy with blood. "And you." Zeph shakes his head. "Gonna miss you stealing from me, you old bastard."

Ding!

The sound startles Zeph, but of course it shouldn't. Chio.

"Hey, brother, told you I'd be back." Zeph hustles over to check Chio's clockwork. "Let's see here. Smoke didn't do you too bad, huh? Let me give your insides a look-see, though. Some of them gears are a little fussy." He opens the door on the bottom of Chio's cabinet, and a leather satchel falls out, spilling its contents on the floor. Thousands of dollars in cash, wrapped in thick rubber bands printed with one word: Dreamland.

Zeph looks up at Chio, down at the money. He laughs. "Well now, what do you say to that, Herr Gruber?"

Ding!

EPILOGUE

As the sun drops low, Zeph, Kitty, Nazan, Rosalind, P-Ray, and Timur walk a few steps into the tide. Zeph hands each of them a carnation. "Anybody wanna say something?"

Kitty says, "Thank you, Archie. For everything you taught me. For everything you gave me by bringing me to Magruder's. I suppose you saw something of yourself in me." She smiles sadly. "Only time will tell if that's good news or no."

"Good-bye, Archie," Zeph says quietly.

"Good-bye, you terrible man," Rosalind says. "You were a bastard, but no one could insult me quite like you did."

"Yes." Timur nods. "Safe travels, old criminal."

One by one, they toss their flowers into the tide. Then they sit together on the sand, staring out at the sea, thinking of the past. Of Maggie and Bernard. Spencer. Mrs. Hayward. Archie. And of course, of beloved Enzo, now ensconced in a private room in Brooklyn Hospital, thanks to Spencer's money and Archie's skill at blackmail.

Kitty gives P-Ray a kiss on the head and walks up the beach to greet her old enemy, the bench. Nazan sees her sitting there, looking so very young and alone. She goes to the bench and joins her.

"Miss Hayward—"

"Kitty. Please, I'm Kitty."

"Kitty. I just… I'm so sorry I couldn't save your mother. I can't even say how sorry I am. I used to think I knew a lot of words, but I don't know those."

"Didn't we discuss this already? No apologies from you, please. Not after all you've done." She sighs. "I was just sitting here thinking. Mum would want to be sent back to England, put to rest next to Father. And my brother's body is still out there somewhere. I'll have to…I don't know exactly. Speak to the city? Find the *Arundale*? Someone must know something."

"And then? Will you go home too?"

Kitty looks out at the water, watching the little birds as they *flap-flap-flap-drop* their way across the surf. "You know, when Archie found me, I'd been sitting on this bench for days, just watching those birds. They make no sense at all. They do everything the hard way. But they keep on going, no matter what." She smiles at her new friend. "Will I go home? Do *you* intend to go home?"

Nazan looks over at their little group. At Zeph. She smiles back at Kitty. "I'm pretty sure I already am home."

"Well, there you are." Kitty takes her hand and squeezes it. "There's your answer."

❧ AUTHOR'S NOTE ❧

Every sideshow talker assures his audience that the marvels lurking just behind that tent are *absolutely, completely, 101 percent gen-u-ine and for real*...and I'm no different.

Every sideshow talker is a big ol' liar...and I'm no different there either.

Still, I want to say something about aspects of this book that really are 101 percent gen-u-ine, and I should start by hat-tipping my source material. My favorite resources for all matters Coney were the primary ones. For example, the Brooklyn Public Library has a fantastic site called Brooklyn Newsstand (http://bklyn.newspapers .com), which makes papers like the *Brooklyn Daily Eagle* searchable online, with articles dating well back into the nineteenth century. I also leaned heavily on the 1905 publication *Souvenir Guide to Coney Island* by W. J. Ennisson. Ennisson's descriptions of Coney's many spectacles are spectacular in their own right. Significantly, the foldout map indicated a spot for me to place Kitty's park. This was a great gift because so much of the shoreline was held privately in this era—specifically, owned by businesses that might not have appreciated a Tibetan-style funeral on their property.

Among secondary sources, I have to mention the indispensable *Coney Island: Lost and Found* by historian Charles Denson. Denson runs the Coney Island History Project and hosts walking tours throughout the summer season. (If you are interested enough in Coney Island to pick up this book, you will thoroughly enjoy touring the real place.)

The extensive website of Jeffrey Staunton (http://www.westland .net/coneyisland/) was another vital resource. So was the book *Secrets of the Sideshows* by Joe Nickell and back issues of the journal *Shocked and Amazed! On and Off the Midway*, which is helmed by the inimitable James Taylor.

Now a quick trip into the real/not real…

✴ ✴ ✴

I'm not aware of any major outbreaks of plague on the East Coast. However, Honolulu and San Francisco both had quite dramatic experiences with the disease in the early 1900s. This was part of the "third pandemic" of the plague, which impacted parts of China, India, central Africa, and Australia.

At this point in history, knowledge of plague transmission was a bit sketchy. The idea that plague was caused by bacteria was not unheard of at the time—in fact, the guilty party, *Yersinia pestis*, had been discovered in 1894. But the discovery was controversial; many doctors had yet to be convinced that *Yersinia pestis* was to blame.

Consequently, plague-fighting efforts in the 1900s were a mixed bag. Some steps were taken that still seem logical—a greater emphasis on hygiene, for example—and some seem like madness now, like burning an apartment building to the ground because one resident died of the plague. (I'm sure the fact that many of these buildings were taking up valuable shorefront property never entered into the minds of city planners.) Fumigation with sulfur was used occasionally too; it was an old-school, yellow-fever-fighting technique in New Orleans, as described by Archie.

As for the symptoms and course of the illness, I based my version of the plague mainly on texts like Giovanni Boccaccio's *The Decameron* (1351) and Daniel Defoe's *A Journal of the Plague Year* (1722). Those works and others portray a disease horrorscape in which healthy, young Europeans enjoyed breakfast in the sunshine only to die in agony before dinner. Modern scientists would say that although pneumonic plague *is* highly contagious, the actual course of the illness is probably not quite as swift as I've suggested here. It may be that people back then were in poorer health generally, which perhaps allowed the disease to work its terrible magic more quickly. Or maybe that strain was more virulent than the one existing today. Or maybe Boccaccio and Defoe were big ol' fibbers. In any case, I hope readers will forgive my adoption of the more romantic (if more dire!) scenario outlined by writers who came before me.

✶ ★ ✶

Historically, half-and-half performers like Rosalind Butler tended to sell themselves as hermaphrodites. As with most sideshow advertisements, this was largely untrue. That being said, Josephine Joseph, who appeared in the classic film *Freaks*, strongly insisted on the identity of hermaphrodite, even when arrested for fraud after a performance in Blackpool, England. In any case, whatever *else* the half-and-half performance might have been, it certainly was an embodied threat to the binary gender system.

With Rosalind, I tried to imagine a character who is not merely a threat to that system but is consciously at war with it. The character was inspired by real historical figures like the Chevalier d'Éon de Beaumont, a French spy who switched gender presentations multiple times throughout life until being forced to choose and stick with one by Louis XVI. I was also thinking about Civil War surgeon Dr. Mary Edwards Walker. The first (and so far only) cis-female Congressional Medal of Honor winner, Dr. Walker nonetheless suffered multiple arrests and indignities for her lifelong insistence on dressing "like a man."

In contrast to Walker's time, recent years have seen a welcome—if slow and stuttering—movement toward acceptance of people with nontraditional gender presentations. While I have never considered the character to be transgender, I'm certain that *gender fluid* is a term Rosalind would have adored and embraced. Given the period setting of this story, however, I didn't feel like it was plausible for me to use here.

✶ ★ ✶

Zeph's Race to Death show is a fictional Frankenstein monster assembled from real parts. The road race did indeed occur in 1903, with events unspooling *kinda sorta* as Zeph describes. In turning a real-life tragedy into a spectacle, Zeph is making his own contribution to a type of performance that was very much in vogue at the time. Reenactments of disasters such as the Galveston Flood and the Boer War drew huge audiences. Meanwhile, both Luna Park *and* Dreamland had their own versions of the tenement fire show witnessed by Kitty and Archie.

Another precursor of Zeph's show is, of course, the flea circus, and to that, I've added the tradition of *pulgas vestidas*, or "dressed fleas." The folk art of creating teeny-tiny costumes for fleas was practiced in Mexico a hundred or so years ago. The Phoebe A. Hearst Museum of Anthropology has some examples in their collection, should you care to get out your magnifying glass.

✦ ★ ✦

Despite her mystical claims, the character of Yeshi Lowenstein is more truth-based than one might expect. The Tibetan practice of sky burials still continues to this day, more or less as described in the book. A lot of that scene is based on descriptions in the online *Travel China Guide* and in Pamela Logan's "Witness to a Tibetan Sky-Burial: A Field Report for the China Exploration and Research Society." Logan's essay is available online, as are many photographs of the sky burials—they are not for the faint of heart.

As for Yeshi's other "miracle," levitation… Well, it wouldn't be proper of me to ruin that. But if you are a truth-seeker with an Internet connection, just plug "levitation" into YouTube, and all will be revealed. Be warned—the truth, once known, can't be unknown.

✦ ★ ✦

Speaking of YouTube, Robonocchio was inspired by a real automaton created by Henri Maillardet in the eighteenth century, and you can see it in action online. Even better would be to visit Philadelphia's Franklin Institute, where the automaton resides. Maillardet's machine can draw only four pictures, but it made me think, *Wouldn't it be great if...* And Chio was born.

If Maillardet's robot were the father of Chio, then his mother would surely be the fortune-telling machine called Grandma's Predictions, which dates back to the 1920s. Grandma is still in working order, and you can seek her counsel anytime at Deno's Wonder Wheel Amusement Park in Coney Island. Grandma also tweets (@ConeyIslGrandma), because of course she does.

✦ ★ ✦

William Reynolds was a real person who served a single term as a New York state senator but found more success in real estate. He and his consortium shepherded Dreamland into existence, and Reynolds was also involved in developing the Chrysler Building. According to Charles Denson, Reynolds was a "slightly shady, larger-than-life character." In *Coney Island: Lost and Found*, Charles Denson alludes to a story about Reynolds being "'accidentally' shot in the groin by New York mayor John Mitchell." A story published in the *Brooklyn Daily Eagle* in 1909 mentions Reynolds returning from a sojourn in Europe "accompanied by his friend W. J. Urchs and his Negro mandolin quartet." Sure, why not?

All that being said, I have no knowledge of his children—Spencer and Charlie are entirely fictional.

✦ ★ ✦

Finally, no historical evidence supports the idea that Teddy Roosevelt was a poor hand washer. I'd like to extend my sincere apologies to all surviving Roosevelts for any insult to their ancestor's personal hygiene.

—H. P. Wood

P.S. A bibliography and more information about these topics and much more can be found on my website: hpwood.net.

READING
GROUP GUIDE

1. *Magruder's* takes inspiration from plague outbreaks that occurred in San Francisco and Honolulu in the early 1900s. If there were a case of the plague in your neighborhood, how do you think you would react? How about in your local school? Did the plot remind you of more recent events, such as the Ebola outbreak? Or did this seem entirely different? Why?

2. Kitty starts the novel alone on a bench, thinking about drowning herself. She ends as the leader of a fairly big con to save Magruder's. How does she get from point A to point B? What motivates her to change and grow? Does she fail at any point?

3. Some of the characters are "unusual" because of their physical bodies, while others are "unusual" because of their lifestyles. How does the question of choice impact the characters? Does a character like Rosalind have more choice than a character like Zeph? Or not?

4. What attracts certain "normal" characters like Nazan and Spencer to the Magruder's world? And on the other hand, why do you think some characters find the world threatening?

5. Whitey the fireman warns Zeph to stay away from anarchists because of the "trifecta"—meaning that membership in three minority groups is too many. This idea is sometimes described as "intersectionality," which refers to being affected by multiple types of oppression (such as racism, sexism, classism, ablism, and homophobia). What other examples of intersectionality do you notice in *Magruder's*? How does intersectionality impact how characters understand the world and one another?

6. Books play a fairly large role in the story: *The Souls of Black Folk* and *The Wizard of Oz* both appear in the first chapter, Nazan and Spencer's first conversation involves Austen and Wells, and a copy of *Captains Courageous* changes Spencer's mind about what his next move should be. Why do you think authors reference other books in their own stories? What do you learn about a particular character based on what book he or she is reading?

7. What role does friendship play in the story? What are some of the key friendships that develop over the course of the book? How and when do characters such as Zeph and Spencer start to see each other as individuals rather than types?

8. At one point, Rosalind tells Seamus the bellhop, "Not one of us knows what we can do, until one fine day, we stand up and do it." What other instances did you notice where characters "stand up" and do something they didn't intend? How does it work out for them?

9. The story of *Magruder's* is told from a few different points of view. There are certain points—for example, the death of Bernard the Giant—where the reader knows more about what's happening than the characters do. Why do you think the author decided to tell the story this way? How do changes in point of

view affect the plot, the characters, and the reader? Was one character's point of view more compelling than another?

10. The conclusion of a novel can leave the reader satisfied or disappointed, happy that it's over or wanting more. How did *Magruder's* ending affect you? Why?

⁂ ACKNOWLEDGMENTS ⁂

Like a starlet on Oscar night, I've no way to know if I'll ever get up on this stage again. So with apologies to the orchestra conductor, I offer the following thanks while I can.

Thanks, Mom, for being my first teacher and greatest supporter.

Thanks to the many other teachers who inspired and shaped (and occasionally terrified) me, including but not limited to Mrs. O'Brien, Mr. Sullivan, Steve Schieffelin, Tori Haring-Smith, Paula Vogel, and also Anne Bogart and Eleanora Von Dehsen, who weren't technically my teachers but—let's be honest—pretty much were.

Thanks to my father, who said he liked this book when I really needed to hear it.

Thanks to my friends Kate and Charlene and Tom and Ronnie and Jessica and Tim and George, who read lousy drafts I wrote and helped me make them better. (Special thanks to my friend Kat: I guess it's okay if you read this now.)

Thanks to the entire team at Sourcebooks, and most especially my editors—Shana Drehs, Stephanie Bowen, and Grace Menary-Winefield. Their enthusiasm made this possible, and their wisdom challenged me to push harder and do better. Heather Hall and Sabrina Baskey made invaluable contributions as well, saving my hide a number of times—my thanks to them too.

Thanks and XXOOs to Courtney Miller-Callahan, for giving me a shot. This would not have happened without her.

Thanks to the entire sprawling Wood family—the kindest, most lovely circus I could ever have the great fortune to join.

Thanks to Valerie Tomaselli, my colleague, mentor, and friend, who believed in this project when I didn't.

And thanks most of all to Mark and Maia Rose, who believe in *me* when I don't. Without you, nothing.

All my love,

—H. P.

ABOUT THE AUTHOR

Credit: Nicole Friedler Photography

H. P. Wood is the granddaughter of a mad inventor and a sideshow magician. Instead of making things disappear, she makes books of all shapes and sizes. She has written or edited works on an array of topics, including the history of the Internet, the future of human rights, and the total awesomeness of playing with sticks. She lives in Connecticut with a charming and patient husband, a daughter from whom she steals all her best ideas, and more cats than is strictly logical.